"Satisfying, smart, startlingly funny, and always entertaining, Jeff Hess's wonderful debut novel is squarely in the tradition of the best of Robert Stone and Elmore Leonard. You will love the hero in this, but the villains are also tantalizingly human and engagingly complex. And the prose is, first to last, riveting and artful."

—Fred Leebron, author of
Welcome to Christiania and *Out West*

"Jeffery Hess' *Beachhead* comes to ground as Navy prison parolee, Scotland Ross, puts his life on hold, along with his path to an honest life, to lend help to his sister and her struggling family, only to find the hand of help may be more disastrous than no help at all. Hess moors together a compelling story of land grabbing, political aspiration, government graft, and adulterous jealousy that will leave you in reeling its wake."

—Ron Earl Phillips, editor of
Shotgun Honey and One Eye Press

"Jeffery Hess's *Beachhead* hearkens back to the work of brilliant 20th century crime writers like John D. McDonald, and his Scotland Ross is a Travis McGee for this millennium: gratifyingly unvarnished, physically tough, and just naive enough to involve himself in the troubles of other people. An admirable debut."

—Pinckney Benedict, author of *Dogs of God*,
Miracle Boy, and *The Wrecking Yard*

BEACHHEAD

ALSO BY JEFFERY HESS

Home of the Brave: Stories in Uniform (editor)
Home of the Brave: Somewhere in the Sand (editor)

JEFFERY HESS

BEACHHEAD

Down & Out Books
3959 Van Dyke Rd, Ste. 265
Lutz, FL 33558
www.DownAndOutBooks.com

Cover design by Eric Beetner

ISBN: 1-943402-18-3
ISBN-13: 978-1-943402-18-2

To those we've lost

CHAPTER ONE
Tampa, Florida, August 13, 1980

Scotland Ross heard a noise he didn't immediately recognize as the sound of a boot heel on the living room tile. He stood barefoot in boxer shorts; elbows propped on the pedestal sink in his bathroom, his index fingers strangled red by the tension of waxed, white dental floss. The better part of the day had been spent sautéing his brain in vodka, but he never missed a night, no matter how late he worked, or, since losing his job, how much he drank, or how tired he was, or how long it took. It was three o'clock in the morning. Since he'd been on parole, he no longer had to face the painful memories sober in that dead time before unconsciousness. The noise had made him lose track of where he left off. He paused the taut string in front of his open mouth—anticipated the next footstep, but heard only the hiss of florescent bulbs that attached yellowness to everything in the room.

He dug the floss in the tight space between his bottom front teeth, and tugged back and forth. Most likely it was Dana in the other room. She had a key and was the only reason he'd moved to St. Pete. Being his sister meant she could come and go as she pleased. No questions asked. Being a booze whore meant periodically she got too drunk to go home and in too bad of shape for any man with a roof over his head to take her in and do what he wanted. She'd crashed at Scotland's a few times in the year he'd been a free man and a civilian. She probably kept the lights off in an effort not to wake him this time.

"Hello?" he called, walking into the hall, untwining his index fingers, looking both ways.

1

It could be that red-head from the Publix on Gulf Boulevard desperate for another overnight trip to tingle town. Or it could be some coked-up loon out to score enough cash for more drugs or maybe some psychopath jonesing for the thrill of homicide. The only thing of value in the place was a few bucks stashed in a shoebox beneath the old Webley .32 he'd bought from a carny behind the Tilt-A-Whirl at the State Fair back in February.

Chilled air from the living room moved across his bare skin, while sweat beaded on his forehead. The bathroom light went dark behind him. His vision became orange and brown spots, like soup stains. "What the fuck?" he called into the darkness as he dropped his floss. He had no proof that the Webley shot straight, but even if he could get to it quick enough, he wouldn't know where to fire. He crouched and swung wide at the soup stains in front of him, trying to protect himself. The last time his heart raced this fast had been with a skinny kindergarten teacher with disco hair. His adrenaline spiked differently now—a fight of some sort was unavoidable. He felt it in his stiff fingers, which throbbed with his pulse. His eyes hadn't adjusted yet and he felt naked despite his boxer shorts. He groped his way back toward his bed hoping to get to his revolver and use the mattress as cover if shots were fired, but stumbled over the corner of the bed opposite the door and smacked his head on the nightstand. His fingers came back dry after he searched his skull for blood, but his ears rang with a high frequency hum that sounded like the flush of a public toilet. His breath cycled fast and shallow, filling just the top portion of his lungs. He needed to deepen his breathing, slow his heart rate, and calm his mind so he could think rationally—just as he'd learned in Leavenworth.

With the room lost in flashes of orange and brown, he focused on his breathing. He stood, shook his head to clear his vision, but failed. He reached and felt the rough-hewn paneling as he groped his way toward the door. With his other hand, he threw blind jabs. The rattle and hum of the wall unit air conditioner in the living room filled the quiet. Cold air carried the smell of cologne. Scotland never wore cologne. He jabbed and listened for footsteps.

Without a sound, someone grabbed Scotland's wrist in mid-air, twisted it behind him, and crimped his windpipe in a headlock, all in one fluid motion. As a bouncer, Scotland had earned a living using his muscle and practiced moves. Now he found himself the disgruntled drunk on the wrong end of a choke hold, his right arm pinned behind his back and his lungs demanding oxygen in a new way. He hoped the elastic in his boxers held.

Even with his breath shallow, Scotland got a nose-full of the cologne the guy wore. It was a strange thought to register in his brain, but he guessed dime-store Brut. It made him cough, and he took advantage of that moment to try and push back with his legs, but he was barefoot and his calloused heels provided no traction. He dug in on the balls of his feet but he was anchored. Locked in the choke hold. The arm twisted behind his back had somehow become part of the hold. Any struggling to break free only deepened the grip around his throat.

The guy with the death grip pushed against the back of Scotland's skull and kicked his bare ankles to get him moving. An awkward march forced him out of the bedroom into the area between the living room and the kitchen that was meant to hold a small dining table. Scotland never had what Floridians called a dinette, but rather a few square feet of open floor space where he did push-ups and sit-ups every morning, right on the Mexican tile.

Scotland's cinder block duplex sat in a line of eight rented units on each side of the street, all with matching lawns in need of mowing and driveways with oil stains. It was late. The neighbors worked during the day and would be asleep now, but maybe if gunshots woke them, they'd report them so he wouldn't fester on the floor for the critters and insects.

Beams of light shone from the bedroom and from the streetlight outside the kitchen window, casting the living area in shadows. The muted TV glowed white and gray with the snow of an off-air station. His vision adjusted, but he still couldn't get a full breath.

"What the fuck is going on?" he tried to say, but couldn't manage more than a gurgle.

He made out the shadows of three men, counting himself. They were all silent. The faucet leaked into the kitchen sink with patient drips while Scotland's heartbeat thundered. He pawed at the forearm around his throat. Swung back with his left fist, but hit nothing. The guy holding him had the speed to evade and the grip to hold onto all two hundred fifteen pounds of Scotland. He had to give the fucker credit, he'd never been this immobilized. Not even as a twelve-year-old, when the Casta brothers jumped him outside the Stop & Shop on their way home from school.

Between shallow breaths, he heard the same boot heel as earlier as it clicked across the kitchen floor. With the sound came the smell of cigars.

"You have no idea how disappointed I am."

The first syllable chilled through Scotland. He always had a talent for recognizing voices he'd heard even once. He could name the celebrity selling floor polish or dog food on the radio, or when facing away from the television.

"Kinsey?" he mumbled through a jaw locked by the other guy's grip.

"Don't act like this is a surprise, son," Kinsey said.

Scotland should never have gotten mixed up in that card game a couple weeks ago. The stakes got way over his head, but he couldn't leave a loser. In moments like that, he never thought about repercussions, only rewards. This is what it got him, this time. "Who's the asshole you brought with you?" he asked.

The guy who held him applied more pressure, doubling Scotland over until he felt pain sear his armpit and his ribs. It felt like muscle ripping off of bone. From his hunched over position, Scotland's face was roughly waist-high to the two guys. The one holding him down wore tan, bell-bottom polyester pants that crested over the tops of black platform shoes. Kinsey wore brown pants with starched creases down each leg that pointed to the toes of leather cowboy boots. They looked like burgundy mirrors, hand-shined and stitched with gold thread.

Scotland struggled for a little room under his chin, just long enough to take a clean breath. He tried to pry some slack around his neck, but the grip wouldn't budge. He tried to turn his head—he wanted to see how far he was from the kitchen counter, where he'd left a knife with a wood handle next to a block of sweating government cheddar before he'd collapsed in bed. He needed that knife, now. He mumbled, "This is bullshit, Kinsey."

Kinsey snapped his fingers and the guy released Scotland and backed away.

Scotland rested with his hands on his knees, sucking in good air. His throat felt like a garden hose kinked by a shovel, but he wouldn't show Kinsey and his thug that it bothered him.

His buddies would never believe this story, and they believed everything Scotland said. His closest friends were three guys he'd worked with at Sharky's, two line cooks and a waiter. They ate up every story Scotland told about his Navy days in Pusan, Subic Bay, and Hong Kong with laughter, "Hell yeah!" and "Tell another one!" but they'd never believe this.

As he stood, Scotland moved his head side-to-side and stretched his jaw. He rolled his shoulders forward and back and flexed his major muscles as a way of taking inventory. His sight had adjusted enough to see the other guy stood a head taller than Kinsey, but still a good couple inches shorter than Scotland. He guessed the guy topped out at one hundred sixty pounds. No more imposing than any other swinging dick you'd see in line at the bank, except for the ridiculously blond hair hanging down to his neck.

Kinsey looked exactly as he had the night Scotland had met him at the card game. Waves of dark hair covered his ears, the front slung low diagonally. His beard was the same dark shade as his hair. Scotland had guessed mid-thirties that night at the card game. Like then, Kinsey wore a short-sleeved white dress shirt with the collar open, as if he'd just taken off his tie. All business despite the Purina Feed & Grain ball cap he wore.

"If it's all the same to you," Kinsey said, hands on his hips, "I'd rather dispense with the small talk and get right to business this fine evening. Okay there, son?" He moved assuredly, his posture perfect, but not stiff. Scotland imagined a young Kinsey training with his mother by walking with a book on his head. The only posture training Scotland got was at boot camp, where his Company Commander barked, "Stand up straight, you big, dumb redneck." Yelling never bothered Scotland, but the "dumb redneck" stuff had raised anger in his veins. Despite that, he'd kept secret his three years of college.

This conversation with Kinsey felt like the same thing. Scotland crossed his arms over his bare chest. Hugged his forearm to his heart. Pretended to scratch his shoulder. "Look," he said. His mouth ran dry before he finished the word. He didn't know what to say next, but figured it better be something this asshole wanted to hear if there was any chance of keeping things friendly. "I got laid off. I'm none too happy about it myself."

"You must've played football in high school," Kinsey said.

The comment washed over Scotland like cool air from the wall unit AC. Instead of sports, Scotland had started bagging groceries when he was fourteen. He mowed lawns for five dollars apiece before that. Did both all through high school. During his time at college he augmented his student loans by tutoring algebra. "Nope."

"What a waste," Kinsey said. "You'd've made a hell of a linebacker, son."

"If I had a dime for every time I heard that…" Scotland shrugged. "I wouldn't owe you any money."

Kinsey reached up and grabbed Scotland's hand, pulled his arm straight, stared at Scotland's forearm. The tattoo had the distinct shape of a football with a triangle at the end near his wrist. He'd gotten the tattoo in the time between being released from The Castle and getting the fuck away from the Navy and Kansas for good. The tattoo had taken less than an hour and only cost him sixty bucks, but he forever had a reminder to be a better man.

"I bet there's a fascinating story behind this tattoo."

Scotland pulled his arm free. He didn't like to talk about it. It was not meant to be a conversation starter.

Kinsey toed one of the empty vodka bottles on the tiled floor and it rolled in a trail of glass-on-glass noise.

Scotland never drank at home before he lost his job.

Kinsey's boot heels clicked to the kitchen, where he fingered a full-page ad for Daytona that Scotland had tacked on the fridge with a magnet shaped like an alligator. In the ad was the most perfect beach-front cottage Scotland had ever seen. He imagined cooling off in the blue pool as muscle cars drove on the beach, pictured himself behind the wheel of a '67 'Cuda and becoming the guy in his bathing suit standing with his gorgeous wife by the pool surrounded by a white picket fence. Atop the scene was DAYTONA in yellow script. At the bottom, blue text read "Sun, Surf, and Muscle Cars." Scotland wanted to live in that place. Wanted that life. His classmates from college used to brag of spring breaks there, about the parties and the bikinis. Nothing had worked out for him in Tampa like he thought it would.

"You didn't bust into my place to hear a sob story," Scotland said. "You want your money. I don't have it."

"The fishing ban cost you your job, if I recall correctly." Kinsey said.

Scotland may have mentioned this the night they met. He could have talked about it now. Could have told him about getting the job almost a year ago and how happy his parole officer had been about the steady employment. Could have showed him the scars and improperly healed knuckles from keeping the peace at Sharky's most nights. None of that was Kinsey's business. Instead, Scotland offered the briefest summary he could think of. "Yeah."

Kinsey's features contracted with a flash of recognition followed by a smile. "You don't say?" He looked over to the other guy, who also smiled.

Scotland stood on the balls of his feet, ready to spring if provoked.

"Relax, son," Kinsey said. "If I was so inclined, you'd be dead as a doorknob by now."

Scotland shook his head and felt the kink in his throat slowly returning to normal. In a different situation, like when they'd played cards, the way that guy butchered the English language made him laugh. Instead, he ignored the malapropism because this twisted bastard insinuated death like it was nothing more than discussing the weather.

"Isn't that right, Platinum?" Kinsey asked his buddy.

The guy nodded and clapped his hands twice. "Yes, sir, Mr. K."

Scotland turned his head to see the man standing with his arms crossed over his chest, his fists leveraged to make his biceps look bigger. It made Scotland laugh. "Platinum?" He turned back to Kinsey. "Is he some kind a rump ranger?"

Platinum grunted and took a step with his arms still crossed. "Did that feel like a hug to you, smartass?" he said.

"All right," Scotland said, trying to slow things down as he did anytime he found himself outnumbered. "This will be easier for all of us if we remain friends."

That line had often kept things from getting physical at Sharky's. Sometimes, those same words only escalated the violence. He still hadn't figured out any pattern when he'd lost the job.

"That's a fine idea, son. I am happy to receive your long-overdue offer of friendship."

"Well then, Kinsey," Scotland said as he worked his jaw up and to the left to stretch out the remaining stiffness, "between friends, I gotta tell you, your poker game was rigged. Way I figure it, I don't owe you shit. So let's wrap up this little visit so I can get some sleep."

Kinsey looked at Platinum and then to Scotland. "Rigged?"

"Marked cards. Inside dealer." Scotland should never have played on house credit, but every time he wanted out he'd win a hand, and a pile of chips. Bet bigger. Lose bigger.

"Ah." Kinsey took a few steps in his direction. "We have no way to prove it was or it wasn't. So that is a mute point, son."

Scotland ignored Kinsey's mispronunciation again.

Kinsey patted the back of his hat before continuing. "But let's be perfectly honest with one another, son. You would've gladly taken my money if you'd've won." He paced a bit then came to rest with an elbow propped on the back of the stool near the counter.

Scotland stood tall, his shoulders wide, arms out. "Ten grand is pocket change to a heavy hitter like you." Scotland wasn't sure if he'd been able to hide the contempt in his voice long enough to sell the false compliment.

Kinsey slapped his hand on the counter. "The value of my

pocket change is greater than any man's life if he's on my shit list, son."

Scotland shook his head. "I don't have shit for money, so I guess you're going to have to kill me. Or die trying."

"Killing you," Kinsey continued, "doesn't solve our best interests. I mean, you've got no way to pay me back and you're too proud to come tell me so." Smugness filled every inch of the rock he called a face. "I can only imagine what it must be like to be in your position. I do, however, know for a bona fide fact that I wouldn't enjoy it. No sir. But let me tell you, son, necessity is the brother of invention, and I've invented a solution."

Scotland looked at the darkened ceiling. "Mother," he said, to no effect.

Kinsey walked into the kitchen and leaned on the counter near the sink. "Don't play possum with a country boy, Scottish."

Scottish. Scotland had been called every variation of his name in high school, during his time in college, the Navy, and Leavenworth, but never this. And he hated the way Kinsey said it.

Kinsey picked up the knife and pushed the orange block of cheese away with the blade. "Now see here," he said. "The deal I'm offering you is to take it out in trade."

"Trade?" Scotland grunted a laugh. "Give me a fucking break."

Kinsey charged Scotland, who dropped into a fighting stance, fists chest high, feet spread front and back. Kinsey stopped and nodded to his buddy, who grabbed Scotland by the throat in a grip that felt like a gator jaw closing on his windpipe. More pressure applied than before. Scotland hadn't seen the move coming. He couldn't believe it went down so fast, but there he was being choked and bent over in pain, again.

Kinsey yanked Scotland's head back by his hair. Stared

him dead in the eye as he pressed the tip of the cheese knife into the narrow exposure of throat between Scotland's chin and Platinum's forearm. Kinsey got down low, in Scotland's face. "I could slit your damn throat right here." His teeth were clenched and spit formed in the corners of his mouth. "I could slit it and bleed you like a buck in the woods."

Scotland thought about driving his weight backward with his legs to try and catch Platinum off balance enough to break his hold or maybe grab the knife. He tested the maneuver with a push of his left leg, but there was no movement. Pinned as he was, Scotland felt certain he'd pass out from lack of oxygen, perhaps die as a result before Kinsey broke his skin. He clung to consciousness. Listened to the AC's hum and that steady drip in the kitchen sink.

Kinsey lowered the knife.

Scotland didn't have clearance enough at his throat to attempt an exhale of relief.

Kinsey reared back and punched him in the left eye. The bastard's fist was like a cue ball driving straight into the socket. Scotland's vision changed to a strobe effect before he even felt the pain. He strained to raise his hands to cover his face, to defend himself from another blow, but he still couldn't move. If he didn't lose the eye and lived to tell the tale to his buddies from Sharky's, he'd gladly sport the shiner as proof.

Kinsey smacked the other side of Scotland's face twice with an open palm. "Stay with me, son," Kinsey said, tugging on Scotland's chin. Kinsey let go and walked back to the kitchen. Let the knife clang into the stainless steel sink. "Now, by trade I mean in services that you'll render on my behalf. You follow me, son?"

Scotland grunted, more in frustration than acknowledgment. His vision was a swirl of reds with flashes of blinding white. He gasped twice before he realized he was no longer being choked. He took in short breaths and braced his hands on his knees. After a moment, he stood and took a few aimless steps, raising his hands. He grabbed the top of the refrigerator to keep himself upright. He stared at the Daytona Beach scene on the ad as he gasped in three more full breaths without consciously exhaling. Even if he could beat that bastard to the knife, Scotland wasn't sure he'd have enough in his tank to do anything with it. He swallowed. "What kind of services?"

Platinum stood by the window, his ass only inches from a potted cactus on the sill that Scotland hoped the guy would sit on.

Scotland looked out the window toward the palmetto scrub surrounding his small backyard. Caught his breath. Pulses in his left eye made everything look as if underwater. Exhaustion and his hangover added to the unpleasantness. If he'd been dressed, he'd have had his lighter in his pocket and he'd spin it around that portion of his thigh. But there were no pockets on boxer shorts.

"I'm not goin' to lie to you." Kinsey's face smoothed out and he smiled with teeth like a TV weatherman. "Some of the tasks you'll be assigned might encroach on the letter of the law. But we know you're on parole, which means you'll be extra careful."

That Kinsey knew this information surprised Scotland. "Is that right?"

Kinsey nodded and kept his smile. "You volunteered for military service. A decision that very well could have cost you your life in battle. That tells me you're brave."

Scotland gave his full attention.

Kinsey continued, leaning an elbow on the barstool again. "While on shore leave you were arrested for beating up your brother-in-law, which I can only assume was in the honor of your sister. That shows great loyalty. Doing so cost you two years in Navy prison—time you spent without a lick of trouble, which tells me you're good at taking orders. And your record this past year you've been on parole is whistle clean. That proves you've assimilated back into civilian life without a chip on your shoulder."

Scotland felt a flush in him at the same instant he smelled the cheese sitting on the counter. The scent distracted him from Kinsey. It had been a long time since anyone said anything nice about Scotland. The cheese smell made him hungry.

"And yet," Kinsey said, "you lost a son, which tells me you have a fire in you."

That last detail stopped Scotland cold. His ribs clenched and he felt a dry heave well up in him as the image of the infant's casket filled his mind. He felt his arms flung across two and a half feet of white ash, a wood chosen because baseball bats are made of it and that was the only way of sharing the game with his son.

Sadness and guilt gripped Scotland's chest. He ignored the pressure, stayed strong in front of these two bastards. "How the hell you know so much of me?"

Kinsey didn't smile, but his eyes betrayed a happiness Scotland resented. "I don't let just anyone into my life, Scottish."

Scotland turned to look at Platinum, who stood silent, shaking his head.

"Now, you do a few odds and ends for me and your debt goes down," Kinsey said. "Get us back to even and we stay friends. Once we're square, you can stay on and keep money you earn." He rested his hands on his belt buckle. "Mutual interests, mutual benefits."

"And if I say no?" Scotland asked, before he could control his curiosity.

Kinsey laughed. "You're not going to refuse, son." He looked around at the shabby furniture and the empty bottles. "You're already in the shits, but I can cripple you in more ways than one. But let's not talk about the nasty underbelly. It's simple, son. My deal's better."

13

Scotland watched Kinsey's mouth as he talked. It moved fast, like a salesman's, and Scotland had always hated salesmen. He shut his eyes to better see that beach scene in the ad for Daytona. Nothing good could come from getting mixed up with a guy like Kinsey, but he had no choice, other than telling the little bastard what he wanted to hear.

"Fine," Scotland said, tucking his forearm behind his back. "Where and when?"

CHAPTER TWO

The next night, Scotland laid low in his living room and waited. From his seat on a lumpy couch that might have been new during the Depression, he checked the clock above the stove: 9:58. His plan entailed hanging here until eleven p.m., when most people would be in bed, so he could slip out unseen, take off in his rusted Ford Pinto, eastbound on State Road 400 to Daytona, and put distance between him and Kinsey. Coast-to-coast in three hours if the car held up.

He sat upright as the thought of leaving *now* crossed his mind. He sank back down just as quickly. Changing plans midstream always brought trouble. Regardless, he killed the time with a cold glass of vodka pressed to his blackened eye, which was now swollen and purple as an eggplant—an ugly reminder of Kinsey's visit the night before. He repositioned the glass and leaned his head back. It did little to cool him down or stop his forehead and armpits from sweating. The windows of his duplex were open to the darkness on the other side, but there was no breeze. The August heat kept temperatures near ninety degrees at night. He could have turned on the air conditioner full blast, but he didn't want to stick the landlord with a huge electric bill when he skipped town.

He tapped his toe, his whole body pulsing with the energy of the fight-or-flight instinct he'd learned about in physiology, sophomore year of college. That knowledge, like the bulk of his education, had done him no good.

The noise of field crickets and tree frogs came through the open windows along with the damp air. The street lamp outside streaked into the room. Particles floated in the beams of light. Thirty years of dust and the previous tenant's cigarettes. There'd be nothing to miss when he left—including the stupid fucking cactus in a coffee can on the windowsill.

He raised his legs high enough to rest his boots on his packed seabag—original-issue, boot camp, San Diego. The green canvas frayed at the strap connections—the worn bottom was stretched thin. This faded military item might not have belonged in the polished civilian world, but it reminded Scotland that anything was possible and that he should pack lightly in case something came up. That was something he wanted to maintain as long as he lived. Just him and as much stuff as would fit in his seabag. There was no room for excess baggage if he carried everything on his back. And function outweighed fashion any day. He'd worn his black molder boots every day in The Castle and hadn't polished them once since he got out. The scuffed leather looked dry and the rubber soles had worn thin enough to split under the balls of his feet. Scotland couldn't remember when the opening around the ankle lost its elasticity, but it made slipping the boots on and off easier. He left them on now as he wore Navy-issue dungarees, and a sleeveless blue T-shirt with "Hang Ten" across the front because the car would get hot on the drive.

Keeping him company now was the drone and glow of a thirteen-inch black-and-white set that got sketchy reception with its tinfoil antennae. All three channels were broadcasting the Democratic National Convention. The crowd on television cheered in anticipation of Carter coming out to give a speech accepting his bid for re-election. "Calm down, maniacs," Scotland hollered at the television. He didn't care about politics but, in a very distant way, the President had once been his boss.

From his seat on the couch, Scotland looked over at the Daytona ad tacked on the refrigerator. He'd always wanted his nieces' drawings up there, but he never got any. Instead, he had an advertisement from the back page of *Auto Trader* from a few months ago.

His infatuation with Daytona involved more than just the Atlantic surf and sand. It was that, for sure, but it was also a fresh start in a place where nobody knew him or who he could become. He'd do it right this time. Maybe get a job renting jet skis to tourists. Maybe someday even own an auto body business, find a girl to marry, and set down roots. Make Kinsey nothing more than a bad memory.

He wanted to call his buddies to say goodbye, but the duplex didn't have a phone and he wasn't about to walk to the convenience store to do so. He'd miss those guys. They'd probably love to look at the shiner and hear why he had to leave.

He fidgeted in his seat, adjusted the cold glass over his eye. Wished he'd gotten a strong box or a bank account and socked money away instead of going out every night after work and running his air conditioner so cold. He'd already be in Daytona, if he had. Never would have crossed paths with that psycho Kinsey. Wouldn't have this black eye.

Knock. Knock. Knock. Knock. Knuckles rapped like a ball-peen hammer on his front door. Scotland flinched, the recoil in his wide shoulders splashed vodka from his glass. It was too late to shut off the lights and turn off the television; they had surely given him away.

He tightened his jaw, swallowed heat from his grinding teeth. His heart quickened and he reached for his seabag. Before he pulled out his revolver he realized if it was Kinsey or one of his knee-breakers, there wouldn't have been a knock.

He dropped the seabag, swiped at his cheeks and his sweaty biceps smeared the vodka on both sides of his face as he crept toward the front door.

The door was hardwood stained by a varnish of weather on the outside and history on the inside. Scuff-marks marred the bottom from being kicked closed over the decades by other renters, their hands full of groceries or a baby, perhaps.

Scotland dug his free hand into his pocket and found his silver Zippo. He spun the lighter around in his pocket as if it were rosary beads. The edges were warm from the heat of his leg. Before he reached for the knob, there were four more raps on the door. Scotland looked through the peephole.

His sister, Dana, and her ugly wig stood on the other side of the door. His heart didn't skip a beat, but it pounded stronger in his chest than normal. He couldn't open the door fast enough.

She wore a jean skirt and a red tanktop with "Spirit of '76" in blue cursive on the front. He'd bought her that shirt the summer he left for the Navy. As small as the shirt was, it had gotten baggy on her in the last four years.

"Scotland, thank God," she said. Her skirt was short enough to show the freckles all the way up her thighs. Part of him wanted to leave her on the other side of the doorway. Wanted to hide the hurt over being shut out of her family's life.

He grabbed her waving hand and tugged her into his place. "What's wrong?" he said, following her toward the kitchen.

They stood in the opening between the living room and kitchen—about a foot from where Kinsey had held a knife to Scotland's throat the night before.

Dana took the glass from his hand, smelled it, rattled the ice cubes, and downed the remaining vodka in one swallow. Her collar bone and bare shoulders revealed more freckles. If you stared long enough, a leopard pattern emerged. She still didn't answer. Her skin was dried out from too much gin and the sun. Since she'd been drinking, her face had thinned, but her legs were full. The creases around her mouth framed lips painted too red to tell where her lips ended and the lipstick began.

Concern bubbled like battery acid into his throat. He

coughed once into his hand before putting it in his pocket, where he spun his Zippo. "What's going on?" he asked.

"Your air conditioner broke?" she asked, fanning herself with her hand.

Scotland listened to the faucet drips hitting the kitchen sink. One-two-three, one-two-three. He wondered how long it would take her to comment on the swollen and black mess that used to be his left eye. "Something like that," he said.

Dana pointed toward the seabag. "You going somewhere?"

Scotland walked to the open window and pressed his face to the screen. Checked to see if anyone was in earshot. Mosquitoes buzzed and thunked into the screen. Through the darkness, he pictured the same wading pool he always envisioned for Dana's daughters off to the side and saw himself grilling hotdogs and trying to convince them to skip the ketchup in favor of mustard.

"Daytona," he said, still looking out the window. His view wasn't of a park or the water—only another 1950s duplex with the same lead-painted cinder block walls. In the beginning, he'd planned to stay until he met the right woman and settled down into a real home.

"Why Daytona?"

The question stunned him like a punch to the ear. He stretched his neck to stall for time. "It's not like I've got a reason to stay around here," he said.

Dana stopped chewing an ice cube long enough to ask, "What am I, a tree?"

He turned from the window and exhaled as deeply as his lungs allowed. "Just tell me what's going on."

She gestured toward the seabag, "You're just going to leave me?"

"It's the other side of the state, not the world. I never get to see you anyway. You wouldn't even be here if you didn't need something."

"I'm the only person in this world who knows you, Scotland. Why would you want to give that up after what we've been through?"

Her words tugged at the emotional side of his brain. He looked at his forearm, traced the edges of the Jesus fish image there with his thumb as he stared at Dana. "I don't get to see you or the girls, so I was going to go start my own life. Get a family of my own. Do it right this time."

"You can do that here," she said. "We need you."

Any other time, that was all Scotland would have to hear, but he had Kinsey to worry about.

Dana stared into the ice cubes in the glass. Her silence ran cold through him. She was never at a loss for words.

Scotland grasped her by the shoulders, hugged her to him. Her wig tickled his chin and he was surprised how close his fingers were to her bones. He pushed back, tried to look into her eyes. He stood a head taller, and easily three times her width at their widest. "You okay?"

She rattled the ice cubes around as if they'd produce more vodka and tipped the glass to her lips again. She licked at the ice cubes before lowering the glass. She pulled a cube from her mouth, sucked off any last traces of alcohol. "You should put some ice on that eye. It hurt?"

"It's almost gone." Scotland took an ice cube from the glass, handed it back.

"Job-related injury?" she asked, dropping her ice cube into the glass.

"Enough about me. What's the problem?"

She swiped strands of the wig she'd long quit brushing away from the side of her face. "Things are all fucked up right now." Stray hairs stuck in the corners of her mouth. The dark circles around her eyes could have been poorly applied mascara, lack of sleep, or pain. The hollowness there begged for something.

"How fucked up?"

"I'm okay," she said, gesturing with her arm wide enough to expose a yellowing bra through her shirt's arm hole. "You're on your way to Daytona. You don't need to hear my bullshit." She sat on the windowsill opposite the window with the cactus, legs crossed, one foot bouncing inches off of the floor. Her white sandals were scuffed and her toes were dusty from the crushed shells of the parking lot out front. She rattled the ice cubes some more.

"Tell me what's going on," he said.

She bit at a loose part of a fingernail cuticle. "Mark needs money to keep from getting his boat repo'd. We're desperate."

Scotland walked to the far window and picked up the cactus in the coffee can. The tin can was blue with "Maxwell House" painted on the side in white letters. It was the same brand his ex-wife used to make. The kind he'd missed when he was swilling down liquid tar aboard ship. The cactus had been there when he moved in, and it was the one item he thought about taking with him. "Now? You don't come see me for a year and you pick now to ask me for money to help your dumbass husband?"

"That's not fair, Scotland." She looked at her toes. "He's a good man."

Scotland slapped the counter. "I'm the one who forgave him."

Dana looked off. "We don't really need to get into all this again, do we?"

But he did want to go through it with her again. He always did. Because a part of him believed that she'd just never heard him explain it right. Like the more he got to say it, the better her odds of agreeing. "He's the one should be apologizing to me!"

"Fuck. All right. I get it." She flicked her tongue into the ice. Setting down the glass, she said, "You're not going to help us."

Dana had a history of getting to him. "I lost my job," he said, not wanting to admit it.

Her face crumbled as she broke into tears. She didn't cover or hide it, just let the tears stream openly.

The crowd on television roared, whipped into a frenzy. They sustained applause and added woots, whistles, and other unintelligible noises. Scotland ignored it and looked at Dana. If only he'd allowed himself to leave an hour earlier, he would've been halfway there.

He tore off a couple paper towels and handed them to her. "Don't be so emotional."

She looked six years old when she cried. Always had. When they were kids, he used to be able to make her stop crying by pretending to be a dog chasing his tail or another old standby, which he did for her now. He lifted his leg, pulled at his ass cheek and forced out a fart that squeaked like a rusty gate. The laugh he added for effect was of no use either. "Come on."

"Goddamn it, Scotland!" She stood and pointed at him. "You have any idea how difficult it is to ask my little brother for money?" Dana turned her back to him. "It reminds me too much of Daddy. You ever thought of that, ass face?" Her eyes softened around the edges. "I never thought about it before right now, but it's true. The only difference is that Mark's still around and he's been so bad to you."

Scotland could focus on the wrongs and make his point, like he always wanted. Maybe she was in a receptive enough mood to hear him, but she was also hurting over this and he just wanted to make her feel better. "Can't you borrow some money to get you by?"

She wiped at her face with the paper towel and smeared mascara out wide onto her temples. "Mark took a loan to buy the damn boat, put the house up for that and a line of credit. We didn't know a fishing ban was right around the corner. Now, banks won't give him another dime, or an inch of slack." She blew her nose on the paper towel. "We could lose the house."

"Jesus Christ," he said, looking at the cactus on the windowsill. The cactus itself stood half a foot tall, stuck in the dirt inside. Tampa, the entire Gulf Coast for that matter, was his coffee can—job market was as dry as the dirt. He didn't want to be the cactus anymore. "Can't you rent a place?" he said.

"Mark ain't much use to anybody on land." She tugged at the soggy paper towel. "Fishing's all he knows. How would we make rent?"

"Why don't you sell the boat?"

"How well you figure *fishing boats* sell during a *fishing ban*?" She chewed an ice cube, said, "Without the house, me and the girls would be left to live in our car or under a bridge."

From the television, President Carter emerged on stage and the crowd at Madison Square Garden erupted with louder applause, whistles, and woots. Carter smiled wide and tried to look humble despite the racket. Scotland walked to the television and turned down the volume.

He touched the raw skin beneath his eye. It wasn't numb from the cold glass earlier, but it was still a little wet.

"And you're just going to fucking leave me," Dana said, wiping at her nostrils with the soggy paper towel.

"I never thought you'd care so much."

Dana let the ice cubes fall to the bottom of the glass, raised her chin and sighed. "Why couldn't you just have finished college?"

Scotland found his fists clenched. "Don't start that," he said, and relaxed his hands. Of all the violence he had the potential for, none was more severe than the shit he beat himself up about. And he couldn't tolerate having it shoved in his face two days in a row. At least while he was awake.

"You were so close."

"Let it go, Dana."

"Babies die in their sleep, sometimes. Your studying had nothing to do with it."

"We're done talking about this." He turned his back to her and made fists again as he walked to the sink to fill a coffee cup with sulfur-tinged water. The image of his lifeless baby burned as bright in his mind as the nightly dream. He chugged the whole cup of water and set it in the sink, then exhaled and looked at his seabag. "You sure you don't just want money for booze?" he asked as he turned to look at her.

She uncrossed her legs. "Booze is cheap. What I make at the diner covers it. But that boat of Mark's is a different story."

Scotland sat on the vinyl stool by the kitchen counter and listened to a motorcycle's loud pipes revving at the stop sign on the corner. He couldn't see it, but he imagined it was a Harley. He wished it was him on that bike, with nothing but his seabag on his back as he rode down the wide-open road. But, damn. She was his sister. Blood and history. And his nieces, no matter how little he got to see them, were important to him. The Harley's husky purr faded. "What's Mark say about all this?"

She leaned her elbows on the windowsill, staring out the window. "Are you crazy? He doesn't know I'm here."

"Then what's he doing to save his boat?" Scotland picked up the vodka bottle, confirmed it was empty and set it back down.

"You know him," she said, as if he and Scotland went way back. She stood and fished out a partially crushed box of Marlboro Reds from the back pocket of her jean skirt and put a bent cigarette to her lips. "You got a light for me, Scotland?"

He reached into his pocket and retrieved the lighter, had the flame lit by the time his hand was hip high. He'd long ago kicked cigarettes, but he kept the lighter because it had been in his personal effects when he was released from Leavenworth. Standard chrome case, but on the front was a picture of the U.S.S. McCreight. She was a gorgeous ship, all sharp lines and radar arrays as she cut through the Pacific. Tall and proud. This was his only true memento from his Navy days. He cupped the flame and brought it to Dana's waiting cigarette. Watched the flame bounce, tried not to notice how the cigarette shook in her lips.

"Wow," she said. "Who are you? Doug Henning?" She puffed on the cigarette and exhaled smoke in his face.

"What's Mark been doing every day?" he asked, pocketing his lighter.

She exhaled long and slow, the smoke disappearing into the air above them. "Painting and cleaning, mostly. Says he ain't a man if he don't get his hands dirty."

"The house or the boat?"

She spun around and leaned on the windowsill again. "Both. Paint is the only thing we had a surplus of in the garage."

"Why don't he paint houses for money?"

"He is, but that don't pay much. Besides, this stretch of Gulf is all he knows."

Scotland crossed back to his stool. "Why don't you just get the government money?"

"Those kids don't deserve to see two parents destroyed."

On television, President Carter said, "And I've learned something else, something that I have come to see with extraordinary clarity: Above all, I must look ahead, because the President of the United States is the steward of the Nation's destiny. He must protect our children and the children they will have and the children of generations to follow. He must speak and act for them. That is his burden and his glory."

Scotland said, "A father has to provide. That's on him."

She hit her cigarette deep, and through her exhalation said,

"That boat is all he knows. It's his only way of providing. Them kids..." Smoke hovered around her shoulders and head in the hot, breezeless air. She faced his direction from her seat on the windowsill, but focused her stare on the cigarette. "Somebody in our family has got to be of some use to them."

Scotland worried she didn't have any mothering left for her own kids because she'd used it all up on him. "Maybe if I was a better brother, things would have gone differently," he said.

She hit the cigarette again fast and deep, then pushed the screen away and tossed the hot butt onto the ground outside. "This fishing ban has nothing to do with you, Scotland."

It was the way she hit the "L" in his name that made her pronunciation unique. She never abbreviated his name or called him by a nickname. Even when they were kids or in a hurry or she was sweet-talking him out of pocket change in high school. And for the first time in their lives, it seemed like a really big deal to him. He had heard her say his name more than any other person in the entire world. He'd never realized that before, and he took no comfort in knowing it now. Seeing her this way made him feel like shit. "I'm worried about you."

"Mark's boat is the only stick in my spokes," she said.

"You're sure?" He traced the sweaty edge of the tattoo on his forearm. The fluorescent light made the ink glisten green-black.

"I'm telling you," Dana said. "If we can get by until the ban is lifted, everything will be fine." As she spoke, he looked past the darkened circles and saw the expressive eyes from her youth. She was the same girl, deep down. The same girl who had watched him while their mother was "out"—a catch-all term they'd used to describe most evenings when she was either not home or unconscious. In the summers when he was a kid, Dana used to make bologna sandwiches for his lunch. She pressed them with a brick wrapped in tinfoil, saving him the effort of smashing the white bread together between fingers and thumbs until it was flat enough to fold. When he wrestled in high school, he'd had to subsist on plain tuna fish and water to make weight. She'd chop up jalapenos to mix into the tuna for flavor without calories.

He rocked on the stool, hands beneath his thighs, and swiveled to look at the front door. If only he'd left at ten, he could have avoided all this. He looked back to Dana, who was fluffing her wig in her reflection in the window. She was at once desperate, pathetic, and proud. Just like always. More so than usual. Scotland rubbed his arm and closed his eyes for a moment. It was only a three-hour drive. One hundred and seventy-two miles. The other coast. Dammit. He deserved to start over, clean. But there Dana sat—the echo of his name in the air between them.

"You're not going to help me. And that's okay." She walked over to him, placed a hand on his face beside the blackened eye. "Go to Daytona."

He made his way to the area in front of the couch and picked up his seabag. It felt full in his arms. He dug in and pulled out the sock with his emergency twenties. He held out three folded bills. "Take this. It'll get you started."

That left him with forty-seven dollars, which wasn't enough for gas and a couple nights at some rundown motel. Staying had its own dangers. Leaving now, though, would sever the last thread of family he had left in the world. He was so close to getting out clean, but she had a rope tied around his waist anchoring him there.

He tossed the seabag just inside his bedroom door and spun his lighter in his pocket. "I'll find a way to raise more cash."

CHAPTER THREE

Allan Kinsey sat in a leather desk chair in his office talking on the phone. The AC vent above his desk rattled from the force of the cold air blowing out. The sleeves of his white dress shirt were rolled up to his elbows, his tie loosened around his throat. He lifted his Purina Feed & Grain ball cap by the bill and reset it farther back on his head. The coiled phone cord dangled back and forth in arcs as he devoted his full attention to the little voice of his son on the other end. It was the kids' first week back to school. "My new teacher is so nice!" The excitement in his boy's voice kept him on for ten minutes. Kinsey talked to his kids for at least five minutes every night if he wouldn't make it home in time for their bedtime.

After saying, "Good night, no bite," his wife, Christine, got on the line. Kinsey sat upright, pulled out the bottom drawer of his desk. He flexed his fingers, made a fist a few times. His hand was still sore from punching Scotland Ross two nights ago. He propped his feet on the open drawer as he prepared for untold minutes of Christine discussing the minutiae of her day, ranging from repeating actual conversations she'd had with a priest at the kids' school, one of the other mothers, or even the supermarket butcher.

Kinsey faced the picture window behind his desk and stared out at the swimming pool downstairs as he tugged at the chin hairs of his beard. He was on the second floor of the Gulf Breeze apartment complex clubhouse—a space he'd made his personal office. The closest whiff of the Gulf of Mexico was thirty-five miles west, in Clearwater Beach, but he kept the name. Loved the name. Everyone called it "the

Gulf." Kinsey owned the entire property, including the thirty-two units occupied by tenants he charged little or no rent. They all worked for Kinsey in some capacity, but the pool outside his window was accessible by invitation only. Of the dozen such complexes that he owned, this was his favorite, nestled, as it was among fifty acres off the beaten path.

Kinsey hurried the conversation with his wife along with one-word answers and uh-huhs when required to acknowledge what she'd said. To wrap it up, he said, "Hey listen, my sweet missus, I hope you're able to remify all of that. But I'll be at the salt mine late tonight." This last part wasn't a lie so much as it was a withholding of specifics. He did plan to be in the office most of the night and into the early hours, but she didn't need to know he spent less time in his office at the Tampa Beef and Bird plant in favor of spending it there in his apartment complex office, because that was where he got his serious work done. He needed to keep Christine in the dark about this place only long enough to file the nomination paperwork with the state. Afterward, he could open legitimate election offices festooned with "Kinsey for Governor" banners, buttons, and bumper stickers. By then he will have raised enough money to leave all the shady practices behind, perhaps even turn this place back into a clubhouse for the people living in the apartments. He blew kisses into the phone and said, "I'll see you in the morning, honey."

"But I haven't told you about the dress," she said.

Kinsey stared at the pool. There was no one there now. Sometimes he'd watch his girlfriend Maria swim naked at night. He wished she were down there now to distract him with her tanned ass breaking the water as she swam laps. This evening though, the water was still, a mirror for the moon shining through a palm frond. He looked at the phone's rotary dial and imagined spinning Maria's number. He wished he could dial her, have her come up. Instead, he said "uh-huh" for the hundredth time as his wife continued on about the finer points of chenille and chiffon as if lives depended upon the information.

She looked fine in everything she put on. Everyone always thought so. She wasn't the kind of pretty that made men stop and notice, but she was attractive enough to make anyone she talked to smile. "Oh," she said, "be sure to work the room. Brag on the company. Make sure everyone knows about the record quarter we just had."

She said "we" as if she'd actually had a hand in the company's success. They were known to many in the Tampa area as "college sweethearts," but in reality, she had been a blind date who'd just never gone away. She was from a good family and belonged to the right sorority so he found no reason to push her away, and she had campaigned hard for the position of being Mrs. Allan Kinsey. A year after graduation they married on a ship sailing around Tampa Bay with two hundred of their closest friends. She played the role expertly. Except for these daily calls when she rambled. "Yes. Uh-huh," he said, again.

He never needed her for the business, but she was an integral part in his political ambitions. Being pretty enough to make people smile went a long way at fundraisers. She was all for it, loved the prospect of being Florida's First Lady.

Kinsey's lieutenant, Platinum, entered the office, the blond hair draping his forehead almost too light to look natural. He was thin and had rigid posture. He gestured to show he'd knocked, but Kinsey waved him in. Platinum walked to a guest chair, cutting through the room like scissors. He sat and kicked back, his arms on the rests, and stared at the pool behind Kinsey.

When Kinsey hung up, he shifted gears from husband and father into full-throttle boss. "Give me some good news, Platinum. Tell me we heard from Trafficante's people."

"I did. That's what I came to tell you, Mr. K. They said he isn't interested in talking to you unless you've got Wilson Whittacre in your corner."

Kinsey sprung up and raked his arms across his desk, sending his blotter, pen set, and the telephone scattering to the floor. "Son of a bitch," he yelled. Kinsey put his hands on his hips but the posture didn't suit him. He straightened his ball cap, which had shifted into his face with the outburst. He finished by tugging the sides of his beard for a moment. "Whittacre has been kicking up to Graham's camp for years. He's entrenched."

"We don't need Trafficante," Platinum said.

"That reeking degenerate can't light a candle next to me. And let me tell you, son. I'll make that bastard pay mightily if I have to go the long way around the barn and win this thing without him." Kinsey sat and leaned back in his chair, rocked a little to calm himself.

The two of them sat in silence long enough Kinsey began wondering if Platinum would speak up about something. Anything. The fluorescent lights hummed in the ceiling. Platinum's sideburns reflected white. He fidgeted his shoulders.

Finally, Platinum said, "This might not be the best time to tell you, but I also talked to our guy at the Fish Commission."

"That doesn't sound like good news, my friend."

Platinum leaned forward and kept his hands on his knees as he said, "Eddie Joyner's taking a lot of heat. Wants another ten grand a month to keep the fishing ban going."

"Ten?" Kinsey stood and walked to the map hanging above an oak credenza behind his desk. The map of the county was dotted with pins. "Was he asking or demanding?"

"He sounded more anxious than angry."

Kinsey studied the map. The pins represented land he owned. Blue pins for undeveloped property—green pins to show the tracts of land he owned that were currently being developed into residential communities. Both sets of pins were still too sparse for his liking. His goal was to grow those scattered pins into clusters greater in size and density north of Hillsborough and east of US 41. Just thinking about it straightened his posture, made him feel taller. Each green pin represented hundreds of thousands of dollars coming into his operating fund—his war chest—through the real estate operations.

The cash flow coming in each month through the spoils of the fishing ban was a bonus. It wasn't huge sums, but it was tax free and he reaped profits from the increased demand in beef and chicken. The fishing ban stretched from Tarpon Springs to Manatee County and a hundred and fifty miles out into the Gulf. There was no way for family-owned fishing boats to get out that far, and therefore no way for them to make a living. But the commercial fishermen could and did, and Kinsey was friends with the owner of such an outfit. Kinsey wasn't even Governor yet, and already he was granting exclusivity to a kindred spirit he'd met at a convention a few years ago, a guy named Herb who accepted Kinsey's first offer of nineteen percent. Kinsey liked odd numbers for their shock value. He assumed Herb was glad to get a discount of not being asked for a full twenty percent, though in reality, Kinsey really only wanted ten. Herb was from Texas, so sending his boats across the Gulf was quick and steady and efficient. Herb's fleet collected grouper and took it home to his Galveston processors, all the while keeping the entire Tampa-St. Pete area without the state's favorite fish. The restaurants didn't have it to serve their guests, and fewer tourists came because they could eat grouper in Panama City and Ft. Myers and go on deep sea fishing excursions to catch their own. Which was the way Kinsey planned it.

"Give Eddie Joyner five grand," Kinsey said, turning his attention to the window. "Tell him I was going to offer before he asked. Then tell him we'll add another five each month for months six through twelve."

"That's a hell of a deal."

"Yeah, for us," Kinsey said, staring at the pool below. He'd run for Governor on a platform of boosting tourism and then put an end to the ban. But all that hinged on Eddie Joyner. Kinsey turned to Platinum. "What else you got?"

"Donny Benes is outside."

"Pay Donny his usual amount and tell him there's a bonus if this Scotland Ross is half as valuable as I think he'll be."

A smile spread on Platinum's face, sudden and harsh like a dent in a melon. "A bonus?"

"Don't go putting the car before the whores there, son. I don't know if he'll ever be half as valuable as you, but we'll see what we'll see."

"I still don't see why we need to bring in a new guy." He glanced at Kinsey, like a yard dog waiting to be smacked.

"We need some dumb muscle. That's all."

Platinum laughed from deep within his stomach. The sound of it rolled out in waves. "Yeah?" Platinum said. "The bigger they are, the dumber they are."

Kinsey began to laugh. "He could be an absolute moron for all I know. But what I meant is the Kula brothers are smart muscle, despite your opinions of their size. They perform certain tasks, sure, but they know things about me. I trust them."

"What about me?" Platinum asked. He was raised off his seat back, upright, uptight. Like an anxious toddler waiting to be picked up.

Kinsey had to choose his words carefully. Platinum was known to lose himself to self-loathing if not stroked properly and Kinsey needed him sharp to wrangle the new guy. "Well..." Kinsey said. He searched for the right words, deciding there was no danger in being honest in this situation. "To be honest, I don't mind telling you I'm so pleased with your performance of late that I want to officially promote you to the position of my security chief."

"Security Chief?" Platinum still sat too straight for his seatback, but now he seemed to bounce. "I like that."

"Well, congratulations. Don't fucking let me down."

Platinum sat still and stared at Kinsey.

"Is there something else?"

Platinum rose, said, "Right. I'll get out of here now." As he reached for the door he turned and said, "Oh yeah. Donny Benes is here."

"I told you what to pay him already."

"He wants to see you."

"He does? Well then," Kinsey sat back, looked at his watch. "Make him wait twenty more minutes, then send him in."

Donny Benes sat in one of two folding chairs outside Kinsey's office. The chairs were positioned between the door and the stairs, where the Kula brothers perched on stools, arguing over the intricacies of a Rubik's Cube one of them held.

Platinum exited Kinsey's office and pulled the door closed behind him. He was a wiry bastard. Five, maybe ten years younger than Donny, but smug. "He'll be with you in a few minutes. I'll let you know when he's available," he said without breaking stride. He slapped the Kula brothers on their backs and disappeared down the stairs.

Donny didn't mind waiting, but he damn sure didn't like that white-haired sonofabitch acting like he was better than everybody. The last time Donny had wanted to punch somebody this bad was the Saturday night a few weeks ago Scotland Ross tried to sell him a broke-dick '73 Ford Pinto, sky blue under the Bondo. The car was only seven years old, but it had one hundred thirty thousand miles on it. And

Donny was convinced someone had turned back the odometer before Scotland bought it back in Kansas. The tires were mismatched and none of them had hubcaps. The body was dented like a face with acne scars, and rust had eaten away the rocker panels and most of the floor boards. When Scotland drove in the rain, he must have to avoid puddles or water would splash through. Nighttime driving was difficult because the headlight on the driver's side dangled by wires from the socket. He'd be lucky to get a hundred dollars for it.

"I won this faded beauty in a poker game." Scotland had said that night.

"That must have been a sucker's bet," Donny said. "You got stuck."

Scotland turned and faced the Pinto. "Laugh it up," he said, spreading his hands over the roof. "It's always gotten me from point A to point B."

"What'd you have at stake in that poker game?"

"A hundred bucks and this lighter." He held up his Zippo between his index finger and thumb.

"And now you want to sell this fart-knocking car to me?"

"I just need cash, Donny. You can keep the condescension."

"I didn't know big guys like us got so sensitive."

"It's that time of the month." Scotland patted the roof with a grin. "I'll let you have it for four hundred."

Donny loved cars, but wasn't a car guy. He was more of a car enthusiast than a car guy. He never worked on one in his life, didn't own a tool-box filled with wrenches and he never knew what spark plugs were filled with. He was a driver, not a shade tree mechanic, and as long as he drove a brand new car that was fine with him. He had no need for a Pinto, and zero interest. "That piece of shit isn't worth half that." Donny checked his teeth in his side mirror. "Besides, what's that going to get you? A month of rent, maybe? Hold onto your fucking car. It's worth more to you as transportation."

"I need cash."

"Shit," Donny said, wiping his hand across his large forehead. He didn't know what decisions Scotland had made along the way—why it was he got thrown in Navy prison—but he knew plenty of ex-cons and Scotland was about the most trustworthy despite his desperation. As far as Donny guessed, Scotland was the kind of guy who held open doors for people and picked up something if someone dropped it, and not just when there was a good looking woman involved. Just a good-hearted guy. Donny admired that about him and looked forward to profiting from it. If all went well, this would parlay into some respectable cash for them both. "Since you're such a poker master, I might could set you up with a high stakes game."

"Don't think a card game's going to help much even *if* I win." Scotland looked down, scooted a bottle top in a diamond pattern on the cement with his foot. "How high are the stakes?"

"I walked away with fifteen thousand from there before."

The number seemed to punch Scotland in the sternum. "Damn!" he said. "It would take me a year to make that much money."

"You got money to get you in?"

"I got enough to make some more."

That conversation had earned Donny a finder's fee, and he couldn't wait to collect from Kinsey.

CHAPTER FOUR

Scotland's second trip to Kinsey's apartment complex office had him on edge. The last time he'd driven there had been five weeks ago, when he went for the card game that landed him in Kinsey's crosshairs. He drove the same route he had that night.

The apartment complex was in Brandon, a bedroom community of Tampa where pine trees and palmetto scrub dotted cow pastures. It seemed hotter in the country than it did along the beaches or even in the city. The air blowing through the car's open windows kept the sweat away from his face, but his back was drenched in his seat. He passed the quiet time by squeezing his brain to come up with options. That's all he'd done since Dana left his place the other night, like a broken bird back into the wind. But as hard as he thought, he couldn't come up with a better way. He slapped the heel of his hand on the wheel and shouted, "Fuck!" and drove on.

Overconfidence in his card skills had proved costly, but Scotland's biggest mistake the night of the card game had been showing up drunk. The game started at seven, and in the days since losing his job he'd been downing at least a couple vodkas by the hour McDonald's stopped serving Egg McMuffins.

His plan that night had been to win a few hands and ding the room out of as much as he could, then fake some shit about having to get up early, and split. Playing aboard ship in his Navy days had meant concealing his tells if he wanted to win anything. He'd made some decent money most nights at sea. Gambling was forbidden at Leavenworth, and the only time he'd played since was when he'd won the Pinto—all because he remembered to conceal his confidence.

The free bourbon had fueled him that night with Kinsey. By the end of the night, he'd racked up ten thousand in debt and Kinsey cut him off. "That's it," he'd said.

But as he drove back this second time, he tried to wipe that from his mind. His stomach wouldn't unclench because he was sober this time. He stopped at a couple of stop lights on Highway 60, in that part of the unincorporated county that had little more than a McDonalds and a few convenience stores. The sun hung low and beat down on his Pinto, cooked his arm where it hung out the open window as he drove.

It was early enough in the day that his vision was sharp, but he drove slowly just to be safe. This time he didn't need the directions that Donny had written on a torn scrap of brown paper bag that had guided him last time. He found the sign down a ways which read "Gulf Breeze Apartment Homes" in bright white script set against a background of oak wood, shellacked shiny as a mirror. The place was set off the main road in an area surrounded by trees and the scrub of undeveloped land. The green grass was trimmed and there were purple and yellow plants and flowers. The yellow buildings reflected the sun. He hadn't noticed last time how quiet it was out there. Quiet, but not quite silent. Frogs and insects ground out a symphony in the rain soaked underbrush that surrounded the place. A playground with an institutional swing set, a merry-go-round, jungle gym, and a tennis court sprawled across the far side of the property. All the metal glistened in the glare. No one was playing, but the net looked new and the lines were painted whiter than the letters on the sign out front. Scotland rolled to a stop in front of the clubhouse and spotted a red T-bird just like the one Donny Benes drove. He loved that car, the long, sleek hood with all those badass horses beneath. The soft leather seats in the cockpit. Scotland could see himself driving a car like that someday.

On the porch, just to the right of the door, stood the largest Coke machine Scotland had ever seen. Its height and width covered one of the windows. The paint was red and white and it shined like a new car. Six large buttons offered the one product. He didn't remember seeing it there the night of the card game. He pulled a quarter from his pocket and got a Coke. The can was cold and he pressed it to his head before he opened it. The condensation dripped down his face and into his mouth. He blew the water from his lips and popped the top of the can, listened to the fizz before he tasted it. He hoped the sugar or the caffeine in the cola would at least sharpen his reflexes.

When he walked through the main clubhouse doors, a wall of Hawaiian print greeted him. It was the twins he'd seen there last time, both bigger than Scotland and perhaps from the islands where they got their shirts. Scotland assumed their shirt-tails were untucked so as to conceal pistols wedged into their belts.

This time they sat on stools atop the stairs. One of them struggled with a Rubik's Cube. The other twin leaned over him. "You're not doing it right," he said.

"Fuck off. I'll do it my way."

"Suit yourself."

Scotland spun his Zippo in figure-eight patterns in his pocket. He'd gotten so adept with it he could open and close it without making a sound, could strike the flint wheel with just enough force to ignite. The warmth of the flame between his hand and thigh only lasted a second or two. He always closed the lid. Nothing harmful. Nothing sexual, either. He didn't get off on it, but there was something calming about being able to do that at work or at the grocery store or in front of guys like this, without anyone noticing.

Scotland looked at the two massive guys, both with slicked

back hair and skin the color of leather. "Who are you?" the one with the Rubik's Cube asked.

"I'm here to see Kinsey."

"What for?"

"That's between me and him," Scotland said, spinning his lighter in his pocket.

"You're Ross, yeah?"

These guys never cracked a smile, and this unnerved Scotland. They didn't look pissed off enough to do anything stupid, but they didn't look pleased to be there. They didn't say anything about his eye.

"Yeah," Scotland said. "I am."

Neither guy spoke. Instead, they pointed, simultaneously to a couple chairs outside a closed door.

It brought back the memories of that awful night of the card game. He'd been drunk then; wished he were now.

As Scotland sat, he bent forward and adjusted the height on his socks so they didn't cut off circulation in his calves. Halfway through the second sock, Donny Benes walked out of Kinsey's office. He stood six feet tall, thick in the chest and torso, with an envelope in his hand. When he saw Scotland, Donny stuffed the envelope into his back pocket like a kid hiding a *Playboy* magazine. "Hey there, Scottie," he said. "Jesus, what happened to your eye?"

"Holy shit," Scotland said, shaking his head as he spoke. "You're on his payroll?"

"You kidding me?" Donny double-checked his back pocket. "I can't afford to live like I live on the money I make otherwise."

"You're under his fucking thumb, too?"

"Ain't we all?" Donny said, walking toward the stairs. "Take care of that eye."

* * *

Platinum used the occasion of Kinsey being tied up in meetings all evening to walk through the Gulf's parking lot to Maria's apartment. He could have strolled openly, but he was too anxious. He knocked rapid-fire on her door. The wait for her to answer was torture. His head was floating a foot off his neck and his blood felt radioactive. He doubled over to contain himself. While he waited, he imagined her having just risen from a nap. He imagined her padding to the door barefoot, wearing an oversized T-shirt, her hair mussed. His news of being named Security Chief would surely wake her up.

After another painful minute Maria opened the door, fully dressed in jeans and a blue oxford shirt tied at the waist. She wasn't trying to look sexy, but she would have failed if she'd tried to hide it. "Are you crazy?" she asked, her voice thick and accented with her native tongue. "He's here. In his office."

"He'll be in meetings for a while." Platinum wanted to pull her to him and brag about his promotion all at the same time. Instead, she leaned on the open door. She had a pin-cushion attached to her wrist and her hair was coiled up on the back of her head, held in place with a pencil. The only thing he'd imagined correctly moments before was her bare feet. "Don't look at me. I look terrible," she said, ducking behind the door as she let Platinum enter.

She looked better without makeup than most women did with it on. She was naturally tan, with thick lashes that fluttered when she blinked.

On the couch sat Maria's little lapdog. Small as a cat and with a disposition to match. Every dog Platinum had ever known was excited when someone entered the home. Not this dog. It continued to lie on the arm of the couch as if it were enthroned royalty surveying its dominion. The first time Platinum had been in Maria's apartment, he'd mistaken the dog for a stuffed animal until it sneezed. The unexpected noise startled Platinum enough to bite Maria's tongue. There'd been no blood and they were able to continue, but he'd never trusted the dog since. The dog raised his head enough to eye Platinum dismissively.

Her apartment was the same size and dimensions as his, which was in a different building on the other side of the property. The familiarity of layout always made him feel at home, except for the dress form that stood on the far side of the living room. Tonight it was draped in red fabric pinned halfway into a new dress Maria was making. It was like a socialite missing a head, as well as lacking all the important organs.

Big band music played on a boombox and an opened bottle of Chablis sat on the floor next to the couch. Sketches of dresses lay scattered in loose piles. She'd tacked one to the wall. While he and other people might have seen an artful illustration suitable for framing, she thought nothing more of it than a builder views a blueprint. Her talent and creativity appealed to him as much as her looks, but the size and shape of the wooden dress form always gave him gooseflesh. Standing so prominently, glowing in red fabric against the white wall, it was creepy the way mannequins are creepy.

Her dining room table served as her desk. Patches of green glass revealed themselves beneath sketches and fabric samples. Four antique chairs surrounded the table. Three were snugged up, while the fourth was askew. Receipts scattered on the surface faced that one chair.

"You're working," he said.

"I want to get this one ready." She walked to the sewing form and pulled the fabric down from the waist. "Do you think this looks nice?" Before he could answer, she tugged the fabric up and said, "Or is this better?"

Platinum swung his leg atop the back of the couch and leaned forward. If foreplay was going to be her talking about dresses, he might as well use the time to limber up. Time was a luxury they didn't have today with Kinsey in his office.

It wasn't his style to rush the woman he loved. He'd been raised by a woman who cleaned other people's homes in the expensive suburbs of Charlotte, North Carolina, and she taught him etiquette and how to treat a lady. She'd also taught him to draw and, as a way to teach him to defend himself, she'd bartered to enroll him in karate lessons at a strip plaza dojo around the corner from their trailer. While the other kids played Little League, he was barefoot in the strip plaza learning to kick, strike, and exhale. In high school he switched to Tae Kwon Do, and quickly earned a black belt there as well. After the Army, he competed on the pro circuit for a couple years, but the judging was political and he soon developed a reputation for inflicting too many injuries and was quick to be disqualified and fined. He ate two apples and an orange every day for breakfast, and could be seen at various points in his day stretching his hamstrings like a ballerina—even while wearing the tightest jeans. Like now.

Platinum walked up behind Maria and ground his pelvis into her.

"Letting you in," she said, removing a pin from the dress, "does not mean we will sleep together today."

"But you look so beautiful and I'm so excited."

She pinched fabric between her slender fingers and reinserted the pin. "I do not have time to talk about your day."

"I don't want to talk." He pulled her closer so she could feel his excitement.

"Not now." She turned and kissed him. "I'm supposed to be with Papi tonight."

Platinum let go and stepped back. "I've asked you not to call him that. It's creepy."

She faced him. "Whatever I call him, he wouldn't want you oozing between my legs."

"I'll make like a train and pull out on time."

"That is gross."

"I've always wanted to cum on your tits."

"You talk to me like a whore."

"You like that." He walked to her, brushed back hair that had escaped her coil. "You've always liked that."

She pushed. "Only when time is right."

He loved her Spanish accent. "Now is the right time." He pulled her back to him. Their height matched and he stared into eyes, at once brown and green. "And I am the right man. Not Kinsey. You know I love you."

"There is no time for love." She went to turn but Platinum had her surrounded. "We shouldn't even be together," she said.

"You and him? Or me and you?"

"Both. Neither." She turned and walked back to the dress form. "It's just so wrong."

Her bedroom door was open, the bed unmade. If he could just get her in there, he could make her forget Kinsey and maybe even this dress business for at least a little while.

A bookcase ran the width of the far, gray wall, waist-high with a round mirror above it. A lamp on either side. Shelves held her collection of eight-track tapes. The curtains were brown, as were the kitchen cabinets that showed through the cutaway wall. Her couch was blue Naugahyde and loaded with red pillows. An afghan her grandmother had knitted was draped over the back of a rocking chair.

He nodded toward the kitchen, "You have a Coke in the fridge?"

"There's 7UP in there."

Platinum couldn't stand 7UP. It tasted like carbonated piss to him. "What the fuck are we doing here, Maria? You don't love me, you don't love him, but you're fucking us both. What the fuck?"

Maria held up the loose edge of the fabric draping the dress form. "When I started, my dream was to have my dresses sold in stores alongside Gloria Vanderbilt." She looked at the dress as she spoke. "Now, with Papi on my side, I will become the Spanish Versace."

Platinum laughed. "How much wine have you been drinking today? That man doesn't know the first thing about the fashion industry."

She smoothed the fabric back into position and inserted another pin. "No, but he has money." Without looking up, she added, "And he knows people with money."

"Money is all it takes?"

"No. But without it, my talent go unseen. And I never say I no love you."

He wanted to shove the dress form through the window. Instead, he picked up one of her sketch pads and a pencil from her desk. He tore off the first page which had the beginnings of a new dress or raincoat, he couldn't tell which, and took a seat on the arm of the couch. He scratched the pencil around to make light marks that took form as a series of shapes. Maria was crouched to better see the hemline of the dress, so Platinum filled the page with a sketch of her face and hair and neck. He drew quickly, without looking at the paper. The light lines in various shapes filled the page and he began looking up at her and down at the page as he increased the line definition. He loved to draw her. She kept every sketch he made of her in the top drawer of her dresser. She'd told Platinum that Kinsey had asked about the artist once after he'd snooped in all her drawers. Maria had told him that they were self-portraits. Kinsey didn't have the eye to see the difference in perspective.

After Platinum drew in the values of her eyes, he held up the sketch for her to see.

"This is good. I want to. But not today. For sure, not now."

"You've got to be kidding. He probably banged his wife this morning."

Maria walked to the coffee table, picked up a book of matches and lit another stick of incense. She shook her head. "She is not sexy."

His breath hitched. The accusation surprised him. "Sure, she is." When she looked back at him, the smolder in her eyes made him admit, "Not like you. But I've seen her. She's plenty pretty."

"I see picture. She is plain."

"In comparison to you, everyone is plain." He returned his pencil to the sketch, focused on her lips, shaded the top darker than the bottom because that's what he saw as he looked at her.

"You are full of shit," she said, brushing hair from her cheek with her palm. "But you sound so sweet when you say it."

Platinum dropped the drawing on the couch and walked to her. He grabbed her hand and held it against his chest. "I mean it."

"And I meant what I said. You must go. I must work and keep myself clean for him today."

Platinum turned to leave, but hesitated. He threw a look back at the little dog that always blended with the furniture. Platinum had walked in feeling like an alpha dog, a pit bull, but now he was no better than the little lapdog.

An empty aquarium sat on a stand she kept in the little hallway leading to the door. It was a place where a family might have kept a bench for putting on and taking off shoes. The aquarium still had some gravel on the bottom, a miniature castle knocked over on its side. He turned to her and said, "He won't want you around when he's Governor. You know that?"

Maria stood beside the dress form, a pin held in her fingers. "By the time he's Governor, I don't need him no more. Yes?"

* * *

Scotland sat outside Kinsey's office trying to figure how he'd missed that Donny was working for Kinsey. He rolled the sour notion of it around his head and tried to decide if it mattered. Either way, it didn't sit right.

Ten minutes later, Kinsey swung open his door. The hinges groaned in that instant before the knob hit the wall behind with a *thunk*. Scotland didn't have to look to know the knob dented the wall.

Kinsey held one of his elbows in his hand and his chin in the other. "My dear Lord, Scottish. That eye looks downright horrendous."

Scotland squeezed his fists. He wanted to knock Kinsey out, make him wake up with a black eye of his own. Scotland stood. Shoved his hand in his pocket. Spun his lighter. "I don't know what kind of scam you're running, but I'm only here because I need money."

"That's the spirit, Scottish." Kinsey flicked through the underside of his beard with his thumbnail.

"How long will it take?"

"To pay me back? Well, that depends on many factors, son. Many factors."

"We talking days? Or longer?"

Kinsey scratched his beard with both hands as he laughed that thin laugh of his. "Why don't you come on in and we'll discuss the details."

Kinsey's office was bigger than Scotland's entire duplex. In addition to a desk the size of a garage door and a sitting area with couches, a television, and floor lamps, where there had been a casino-grade card table with cup holders the last time Scotland was here, now stood two leather, wingback chairs with a low, round table between them. It looked like an area more suited for high tea than a rigged card game.

The temperature inside was easily five degrees cooler than

in the hallway. Scotland's shirt still wasn't dry in the back and the sweat turned cold.

Kinsey's desktop sat cluttered beneath stacks of papers and files, two telephones, and a pen set with a thick marble base. On the front corner of the desk was a golden trophy, or maybe it was just a champagne bucket, but a photo behind the desk showed a guy on a motorcycle in the air as if he'd jumped a ramp, so it could be a trophy. The dirt bike was sideways, wheel turned, ass off the seat. Scotland couldn't help wondering if that was Kinsey on the bike and if that moment had won him the gold trophy bucket.

Scotland hadn't noticed the map on the wall the first time he'd been there. The map of Hillsborough County was something he recognized from a smaller map he'd seen in the phonebook. There were blue and green push pins in clusters on the map. The blue were near the bay, the green were inland.

Kinsey sat at his desk, his boots kicked up on the top, his white shirtsleeves rolled up to his elbows, collar unbuttoned, tie piled on the desk by the phone. Kinsey pointed over his shoulder. "That map signifies my real estate ventures. I can tell you're impressed."

"I thought you were in the meat business."

"Well, let's just say there's not much difference between potential homeowners and cattle. At least not as much as a young man might think." Standing from behind his desk, he tucked a pencil behind his ear and waved at the map. "This is just the beginning."

They both studied the map. Kinsey's eyes were glossed over, but steady on a clump of pushpins. After a moment, he turned and said, "Now what I need for you to do is go and pick up some papers for me." He handed Scotland a sheet of paper with "1205 30th Street" typed at the top. The rest of the page was blank.

"What's this?"

"It's directions to a real estate office. North of the university."

Scotland was sort of relieved about such a menial task as currier duty, but this bastard could have given him the address over the phone and saved him the trip here. "I'll stop by first thing in the morning."

Kinsey laughed. "If I wanted it done tomorrow, I'd have waited until tomorrow to give you the assignment."

"Is somebody still there?"

"I certainly hope not." Kinsey didn't smile, but he didn't frown either. Nor did he offer any explanation.

Scotland reached his forearm behind his back, as if the Jesus fish couldn't hear from back there. He said, "Look, Kinsey, I'll work, but you're going to split the value between what I owe you and cash directly to me. Is that understood?"

"You're in no position to set to conditions, Scottish."

"I'm telling you, it has to be like this or I'm gone."

Kinsey pulled at the center of his whiskers. "I have ways of making you stay."

The hair on Scotland's neck rose up at those words. He thought of Kinsey holding a cheese knife at his throat the other night, the way this bastard suggested murder so casually. "Then I'll have no choice but to work half as hard," he said.

Kinsey laughed. "That's very good, Scottish. You're quick with the wit." He walked around his desk. "I've got a tickle in my gizzards that tells me you have potential. So, I'm going to honor the half-and-half payment plan."

Scotland would be able to contribute to Dana's needs, but he had no good feelings about the implications of doing Kinsey's dirty work. Scotland's heartbeat quickened. He shoved his hand back into his pocket and spun his lighter. He still didn't know a better deal. "All right," he said. Bringing in cash was his only hope of helping Dana and the girls, but he also wanted to stash away a few bucks here and there to finance his trip to Daytona.

Kinsey clapped Scotland on the shoulder and pointed to the address on the page. "There's a back door," he smiled as he spoke. "Use a knife to jimmy it. Platinum can show you if you don't know how."

Just then, Scotland heard a splash in the pool below and looked in time to see Platinum breaking the surface, tossing his unmistakable blond hair away from his eyes.

Scotland had known how to gain entry to locked doors since he was five and his mother first locked herself in the bathroom, passed out, and Dana was worried she'd choke on her own vomit. "I'll be fine," Scotland said through gritted teeth. "But since this isn't legal, I'll assume we're talking about a big pay-day."

"Oh, Scottish, my boy." Kinsey laughed again. "We'll see about that."

"What's that supposed to mean?"

"It means that I could hire a couple boat-lifted Cubans to do this kind of thing for five dollars a day. Don't even think about being even. You've got any number of jobs to do for me before you earn back the thousands of dollars you owe me. Hell, the first couple jobs will barely cover the interest accruing as we speak."

"I'll need some sort of proof of employment to show my parole officer."

"Well, if a paystub is all it takes to keep you square with the man, you shall have it." Kinsey said. "I'll frame a copy of your W-2 if that'll make him happy."

"So what are these papers I'm getting for you?"

"All right!" Kinsey clapped his hands once and leaned in to speak low. "Contracts, mostly. They should be in a brown accordion folder with a rubber band holding it shut. Somewhere on the broker's desk."

"That's it?"

"That's it."

"You've got to have a guess about how much this folder will take off of the ten grand I owe and put in my pocket."

"That's impossible to know, son." Kinsey sat in his desk chair and swiveled toward the end with the sports page spread out. "And will be until I see the contracts and have my attorney go over the land use and zoning issues. It's a protracted affair. I'd hate to bore you with the details, but suffice it to say that it'll get the ball rolling and you'll have cash in hand."

"So just the one file folder?"

"And, most importantly, Scottish..."

"What's that?"

"Don't get caught."

CHAPTER FIVE

By the time Scotland arrived at the real estate office, it was past midnight. The standalone building sat dark in the night air, a patch of woods behind it. He parked a block away to minimize the chance any witnesses would associate his car with whatever might be reported missing the next day. He couldn't shake Kinsey's parting words: "Don't get caught." He hadn't gestured when he'd said it and his facial expression hadn't changed. Scotland didn't know if it was some sort of fatherly advice, or if Kinsey was taunting him. For all he knew, this could be a trap that Kinsey had in store for him. Or some bullshit initiation where Platinum and the other guys would rush him and whack him around like they did in the Navy to initiate new Shellbacks whenever a ship crossed into the southern hemisphere.

He pushed off the Pinto's headlights. To prevent his car door from squeaking, he climbed out the window holding a flashlight. He thought about taking the baseball bat, but it was in the backseat and he'd need to open the door to get it. Just as well—he didn't think a real estate office would resort to junkyard protection practices and he needed at least one hand free. He paused and listened for the hum of tires rolling on the street behind him. Hearing no such sound, he sprinted across the darkened parking lot to the back door and shined the flashlight on the doorknob. He wedged the light between his knees and unfolded the Case knife he kept under his driver's seat. He looked over his shoulder to check again for cars that might be passing by. No headlights headed his way.

Scotland worked the blade between the latch and strike plates. Of all the bullshit things he'd done in his life, he'd never been a thief. He hated the idea of taking something that wasn't his. Always had. He never forgot the scumbag aboard ship who'd been heavily suspected of stealing anything that wasn't nailed down or locked up in the berthing area. Scotland had an alarm clock and three *Playboys* stolen, so he and a couple of other guys who got ripped off threw the thief a towel party in his rack one night. Sanchez held his feet while Andersen clamped a towel over his face and pinned him down while Scotland whacked at his torso with a truncheon made of a soap bar inside a sock. Now, Scotland was to be made a thief. He tried to convince himself it was only paper he was taking, but he didn't know the real story written on those pages. He assumed they had to do with the map and pushpins behind Kinsey's desk, but he wasn't sure. He bore down on the knife handle and slid past the latch bolt and the door popped open.

The hinges croaked and sand grit scraped the threshold from the door's bottom sweeping open. He closed the door behind him and paused in that entrance to ensure he made no noise. He shined the flashlight on a refrigerator surrounded by filing cabinets. A folding table and four chairs occupied the middle of this makeshift break room, while a microwave oven sat on a table near the door he walked through to find the offices. He moved slowly so as not to make a sound or risk shining his flashlight through the window.

The smell of new carpet and polish on the wooden desks made him cough. He wiped his mouth on his sleeve and searched for the biggest office, which had the biggest desk, which had the accordion folder right in the center. He changed hands with the flashlight and reached out for the folder. The phone rang mid-reach. Scotland dropped the flashlight. It thudded on the floor and went dark. A little white light flashed on the phone to indicate line two.

The darkened flashlight rolled somewhere under the desk. It was impossible to see. He sank to his knees and felt around on the floor.

The phone stopped ringing, and in the quiet, Scotland heard muffled voices. Keys jingling.

Scotland's throat constricted from the adrenaline. He hunkered down to his knees and felt for the flashlight, wishing he'd brought the bat.

The front door opened and the voices grew louder. Scotland stayed low. There was laughter. A man and woman, but the woman's laughter was louder. Scotland tucked himself under the desk and found the darkened flashlight with his knee.

The man's voice said, "They always have at least one bottle of Champagne in the fridge. I'll just grab it and we can get our party started."

The woman laughed some more.

The area near the door filled with light. From under the desk, Scotland saw their loafers and pumps facing each other. Heard kissing noises. After a moment, he saw the refrigerator light flash on as the door opened. He heard a bottle rake across a metal grate inside. "Ah. Hello, Cold Duck. Nothing but the best."

The fridge door shut and there were more kissing sounds, and the woman's laughter as high-pitched and obvious as an alley cat in heat.

Scotland braced himself. Any guy familiar enough to help himself to company booze would surely notice the unlocked back door. Instead, Scotland heard their voices grow louder until the lights clicked off, and they disappeared behind the front door and the reassuring click of the lock.

He waited awhile. Heard their car fire up and back out. As he rose, he shook the flashlight a couple times until it shined a steady beam. He picked up the file folder and walked back the way he'd come, passing the refrigerator. He'd never drunk Cold Duck in his life.

Scotland sat in his car, shivering despite the heat. His breath had fogged the windows against the humidity kissing the glass from the outside. He rolled down his window. Tried to breathe in the night air. Wished the wet air could wash him clean. He felt dirty—the air in his lungs tasted like shit. The file folder lay in his lap. He tossed it onto the passenger seat. He didn't want to see it ever again. It had made him a thief.

He passed uncounted moments cursing Kinsey and the day they'd met. But he blamed himself for getting into this situation. Stealing shit for some type of lowlife mobster. He didn't want to do this again. He wasn't a thief. Couldn't take what wasn't his. But what would running away solve? Not just for him, but for Dana. He didn't know how long it might take to work off his bullshit debt, but he had no other prospects for the cash Dana needed.

He reached his foot to push in the clutch, but his leg felt weak. His whole body felt drained. He looked over at the file folder on the passenger seat as if it contained his soul lying there, lifeless, ready to be handed over to Kinsey. He started the car. Shifted into first gear. "You can shove this folder up your ass," he said out loud.

Scotland drove to Kinsey's office determined to throw the file folder in his face. He didn't want to thieve any more shit for that little motherfucker.

He skidded on the crushed shell as he parked next to Kinsey's Mercedes at the Gulf Breeze. Scotland's throat ran slick, he spat out the window into a planter with ferns, and wiped his mouth with the back of his hand. His breathing felt rapid and he tried to slow it. He tried to control the adrenaline, but still, the hinges on the driver's door groaned just before he slammed his car door and stormed up the steps to his office.

The Kula brothers weren't in position at the top of the stairs, and Scotland found Kinsey behind his desk, feet propped up on an opened drawer, a drink in his hands. "That didn't take you very long," Kinsey said.

From the doorway, Scotland said, "I almost got caught."

"Is that the folder?" Kinsey jutted his chin.

"What's it look like?"

"Hand it over."

Scotland wanted to throw it at his fucking head, but he slid the folder across the desk to Kinsey's waiting hand.

Kinsey stood the folder on his desk and threw off the rubber band. He pried the folder open and rifled through the papers. A smile that looked too severe for his face appeared. "This is good, Scottish. Very good."

"It better be," Scotland said. "I'm out of the paper stealing business."

"Scottish," Kinsey said, looking up from the papers. "Let me let you in on a little secret. Give you some perspective on what we're doing here." He stood, tugged up his pants by his belt. "You see, son, I discovered this loophole while one of my companies bought and developed land. If I stumbled into it, imagine what out of town marauders might do. My first goal as Governor will be to put into motion a Managed Growth mandate that minimizes the burden of current residents to readily absorb new residents so as not to be inundated."

Scotland sifted through the bullshit to follow along.

"Our infrastructure is burdened, our natural resources overwhelmed. We've got to manage the growth of this wonderful state or our grandchildren won't have any woods to hunt in and the bay, rivers, and lakes will be as crowded as the interstates."

Scotland didn't care much for the ecology debate, and he knew what side of the issue Kinsey was on, no matter what he said. "Spare me," he said. "The land you're buying and the houses you build will make that happen faster."

Kinsey crossed his arms over his chest. "Buying and building are necessary evils, Scottish." He dropped a hand and raised it to adjust his ball cap. "Like the barbers in the fifteenth century used to say, 'sometimes saving a baby requires a little bleeding.'"

"You can't stop people from moving down here. It's a free country."

"But it's not a state without laws. I'm going to win this election with my plan for a balanced approach of fees and laws that manage the influx. Some won't want to pay the fees and will not relocate here. Others will find the cost worth the price for all of Florida's beauty. With those fees we will be able to develop our infrastructure to ensure the growing needs are met while preserving all the natural resources that lure people down to this great state."

"That sounds like a stump speech."

Kinsey's face dropped into a grave seriousness Scotland had never seen before. "It's passion, Scottish. Pure passion, my boy." He slapped his thigh and his face lightened. "But I need to be Governor to make these things happen." He faced the map and said, "Look here, Scottish. You like a big breakfast, don't you?"

Scotland nodded. "What's that got to do with any of this shit?"

"Well, think of my run for Governor as a nice thick omelet and these little jobs as the eggs. You see? We've got to break some eggs to make an omelet. That's all it is, son."

Scotland shrugged off the hard sell. "Maybe so, but I'm still on parole for fuck's sake."

"But you're good at this, Scotland. Don't you see? You're more than just muscle. You're smart muscle and I will always need a guy like that near me. If you know what I mean."

Scotland turned to leave, but before he got to the door Kinsey cleared his throat. "Why don't you hang on a second?" he said, thumbing through more papers, pausing to pull out a sheet and reading it. "You've taken a tremendous chunk out of your debt here tonight." He set down the folder and reached into his pocket. "In fact," he said, "I think you've also earned this tonight." Kinsey retrieved a wad of bills from his pocket. He tossed it on the desk at the spot in front of where Scotland would be sitting if he'd taken a seat.

The cash landed with a smack and a bolt of electricity shot through him. Scotland didn't know how much cash was there, but anything was more than he'd earned in over a month. He wanted to reach out and grab the money. Somehow, he managed to restrain himself. "What's that?"

"A little walking around money. Consider it an advance. You deserve a little reward for this." Kinsey patted the file folder on his desk. "It's better than five hundred, I'm pretty sure."

Scotland spun the lighter in his pocket. Flipped back the lid, spun the wheel. Felt the familiar heat of the flame licking up his thigh. Scotland could give half that cash to his sister and live on the other half for another month or so. The idea of keeping a roof over his head, and helping to do the same for his sister and his nieces worked over his mind. It was paper. That's all. Nothing of value, just paper. The thought of being a thief worked the pit of his stomach like a speed bag. It was just paper, he kept saying to himself as he spun the lighter. Getting paid for getting that folder made him feel the same way he felt when he rousted drunks from the bar as a bouncer.

Kinsey thumbed through the papers, paused to read a page. "Is there anything else?" he said without looking up.

Scotland didn't know what to say. He took the money. Put it in his pocket with his lighter and walked down the stairs.

CHAPTER SIX

Scotland sat in the same chair he sat in every Tuesday during mandatory check-ins.

His parole officer, Dave Adams, sat bent to his task of finishing the paperwork on the previous ex-con who had sat in front of him. He was always trying to catch up.

On the corner of Dave's desk sat a copy of *Trouser Press* magazine from May of the previous year, with a picture of John Lennon on the cover wearing a floppy cap and sunglasses. The headline read, "Come Back, Johnny! Lennon In Limbo." Scotland had asked about it once. Dave had told him it was from his collection, but he kept it at the office because it made him happy. "You collect magazines?" Scotland had asked. "No," Dave had said. "John Lennon's on the cover. I collect anything with him or the other Beatles on it. I've even got a Yellow Submarine shower curtain." Scotland didn't particularly care, but he smiled and nodded through the explanation because Dave's eyes swelled with excitement and he smiled in a way Scotland didn't recognize on his sedate and monotone parole officer.

Dave was in his late thirties and the kind of tall that couldn't be disguised while sitting. In order for his tie to reach his belt, the thin end always landed a couple inches from the knot and today it stuck out to one side. "What happened to your eye?"

Scotland turned his face away from Dave. "It was an accident."

"You better not be fighting or fucking around in shit you shouldn't."

"It's not like that," Scotland lied.

Dave tugged his tie. "Find another job, yet?"

Scotland studied that thin end of Dave's tie pointing at him. It was sloppy. Such disregard for details would get you hollered at by the Master Chief aboard ship, or issued demerits in The Castle. It was the kind of thing that might've made Scotland lose respect for Dave, but in order to survive on the outside he had to overcome judgments like that. Plus, Dave always treated Scotland fairly. Gave him free coffee and a heads-up about the next random drug test, even though he didn't need it. Dave had a picture of his wife and daughter on his desk next to a jar of root beer hard candies shaped like barrels.

"As a matter of fact..." Scotland said. He reached out slowly and gripped the warm Styrofoam coffee cup into his hand before bringing it up to sip. The coffee didn't burn his lip, but the heat got his attention. He thought about Kinsey. The money he owed. The interest accumulating. The money in his pocket. Scotland didn't want to get into this with Dave. There was no way to rationalize breaking the law. As a way to make Dave happy, Scotland said, "I'm close to getting a new job. I sort of interviewed for it a couple times already."

It was such bullshit. Scotland didn't believe Kinsey was anywhere near level with him. He could have told Dave the whole story, but there were no brownie points for being honest and, in reality, that would just bring down a whole bunch of heat. Dave was cool when he wanted to be, but he was a lifer when it came to paperwork. Totally by the book. His bosses read the reports and they made decisions based on those.

"Be sure to bring me paperwork so I can file it," Dave said. "You're long overdue."

"It hasn't been that long."

"I know you've been clinging to hope you'd get back in at Sharky's," Dave said, "but you can't wait out this fishing ban." He took a pull from his coffee cup. "Your best bet is to jump out there and grab something, anything, for now."

Scotland sat back and looked out the window behind Dave's left shoulder. "I washed dishes for half a year to get where I am. Was." It was a sunny day out. The clouds and treetops belied the heat and humidity on the other side of the glass. The thought of the ten grand he owed Kinsey made his mouth pasty inside. "I'll figure out something," he said. Every dollar he owed was a dollar he couldn't give to Dana.

The coffee burned on the way down. It was impossible to know if the shock of it showed on his face, but Dave was shuffling papers on his desk and without looking up said, "Anything would be good. Don't hold your breath on this new development, either. You've got to at least go on more interviews, show me you're out there looking."

Scotland looked out the window, wishing he could escape this conversation.

"You've got fourteen months and you're done," Dave said, looking up from his paperwork. "You were on a good roll for the better part of a year, but we need to show movement along the right track on these reports or the people upstairs get nasty."

"It's not like I want to be out of work," Scotland said, breaking his stare out the window to look Dave in the eye.

"I never said you did, man." Dave picked up his coffee cup with a hand steady and devoid of adrenaline. "Go get something," he said before taking a sip. "Shit, dig a ditch or scrub a toilet, just get your boss to sign off, collect a few pay checks. Do your time out here the right way so you never have to go back to the other side. You know?"

Scotland looked to the framed picture on Dave's desk, his wife and daughter on the carousel at Busch Gardens. "How're your daughter's legs?"

"The braces will be off by Christmas." Dave patted his hands on the desktop, a smile wide across his mouth. "We're getting her a bike."

"Great news!" Scotland wondered if she'd be pedal-ready right away. He leaned forward and tossed his empty coffee cup into the trashcan and stood. "All right, then."

"You know, Ross? You're the only one of my fifty-three cases who shows any interest in my little girl. Maybe that's why I like you so much."

Scotland didn't know what to make of that, so he nodded as a way to agree.

"Hey," Dave said. "How's your sister?"

Scotland stiffened where he stood. "Why?"

"You haven't mentioned her in a while." He patted uselessly at the short end of his tie. "I was just curious."

Scotland tucked his forearm behind his back. "Fine, I guess."

Dave nodded at Scotland. "Okay, then. I'll see you next week."

CHAPTER SEVEN

Scotland aimed his Pinto away from Tampa and toward the beaches, his sister's place. The windows were down and the wind washed over his face. He still sported the reminder of the punch Kinsey had landed and sweat pooled where the black and purple began to fade to yellow along the edges. The sun was high in a pale blue sky which made him think of lunchtime which made him realize Dana would be at the diner serving fried shrimp and sandwiches to truckers, rail yard workers, and Tampa Electric pole men.

He veered onto the ramp to the Howard Franklin Bridge and hit a puddle from last week's rain, which splashed up through the rusted floorboards and soaked the sock on his right foot. He squished the accelerator and drove across the bridge.

The excitement of delivering money to Dana made him speed, and he allowed himself to wish for a moment that he'd get to see the girls. He continued his practice of sending his nieces, Rachel and Josie, postcards on their birthdays. Every May 6th and August 1st. Scotland had wanted to be a part of their lives, but he never held it against Dana or the kids that he wasn't. That was on Mark. Scotland had served his time and made his apologies, even stayed in town hoping Mark would come to accept him despite the old shit between them.

Scotland parked in front of the diner where Dana worked. The glare was too heavy on the glass to see inside and he couldn't tell if Dana was in there. Part of him didn't expect that she was. She'd looked ragged and desperate when she'd shown up at his place the other night, and he hadn't seen her since she left with nothing but a twinge of hope and the few bucks that he'd offered her. Scotland patted the envelope of Kinsey's cash in his pocket. He'd originally wrapped the money in a bandana, but stopped at a post office and spent a nickel on the envelope.

His car door creaked as he shut it. His shoe and sock were still wet from the puddle on the bridge that splashed through the floorboard which caused him to limp to the door over the cold, soggy sock.

Inside the diner, a pot-bellied guy in overalls slid a quarter in the jukebox and looked pleased with himself. On the short walk to his table, a George Jones song kicked on. Dana stood behind the counter holding a coffeepot. "Scotland," she said, raising the glass pot as if toasting him.

Scotland approached the counter slowly to minimize the squishing noise he made with every step. She looked better than last time. Not a hundred percent, but presentable in her waitress uniform with her shoulders covered. The hem of her dress reached her knees and she wore hose and white shoes. She put the coffee pot on the burner and wiped her hands on her apron as he made his way to a stool and slid onto it.

"What a nice surprise," she said, turning to face him with a smile. Dana looked around the diner and nodded to a round, bald man signaling for his check.

"Holy shit," Scotland said. "A normal person could get fat from the crumbs down his shirt and the shit stuck between his teeth."

"Scotland Ross," she slapped the counter beside his arm. "That's a person. You watch your attitude."

Scotland felt like a kid again. He moved his arm. "It's true though."

"Look," she said. "I can't sit and chat until after the lunch rush, but stay here and we'll talk after."

Most of the tables were occupied and other people were

still walking in the door. He'd love nothing more than to sit there for a couple hours and drink watery coffee, but his wet foot was cold and felt heavy, as if the pruning skin was already hanging off his foot. Besides, there was no telling what Kinsey might have cooking for him and he couldn't help being excited to go find out. "No," he said. "I can't stay. And this can't keep." He tugged the envelope out from his back pocket and slid it across the counter toward her.

She lifted the flap with her pencil. "There must be some mistake," she said, and tucked the pencil beside the order pad in her apron.

"This is the money we talked about, Dana. Almost three hundred dollars. And it's just the start. I'll be able to give you more as time goes by."

She pushed the envelope back toward him. "Don't you dare humiliate my husband in public like this," she said through clenched teeth. "I know these people." She waved her hand toward the diners at their tables.

Scotland said, "Take it easy. And take the fucking envelope. No one has to know what's in it. Just take it."

Dana stormed off and spoke to a table of truckers with beards and mesh hats.

"So this is the way it is?" Scotland called out.

Dana ignored him and continued on, removing plates from another table and walking toward the kitchen.

Scotland thought about following her through the double doors, but instead walked out the way he'd come and into the parking lot, not even thinking about his wet foot.

The next day, Scotland gambled and won by driving to his sister's house. Dana ran out of the house barefoot and into the driveway as Scotland drove up. Scotland checked for Mark's truck, and waved back at Dana when he didn't see it there.

"Jesus, Scotland," she said, her facial muscles tensed. The afternoon sun broke through the oak trees in front of her place and she raised a hand to shield her eyes. She wore tan pants with the elastic ankles pulled up around her knees and her old "Spirit of '76" tanktop. "What's wrong?"

Scotland sat behind the wheel, his window down. He was far enough he had to raise his voice. "Nothing's wrong." And in that moment, he'd meant it.

"What are you doing here?"

Scotland closed his door behind him and his boots clicked on the asphalt driveway. He walked up and held her hand in his. "I can't see you at the diner," he said, "so I thought I'd come here."

"I never said you couldn't come to the diner," Dana turned away and walked back to her front door. "But you can't be handing over envelopes full of cash in public."

He followed her.

She turned and hugged him briefly before letting go to hold open the door. "Get in here quick. Mark will be home before long."

The first thing Scotland saw when he walked in was their wedding picture, in a silver frame he'd gotten them as a wedding present, on the table next to the couch. Dana had met Mark in St. Pete at the Woolworth's lunch counter where she was working. She hadn't picked the place to continue her waitressing career once she moved down from Cleveland, but that's where her car broke down on her way to Key West the year Scotland started at the university. It was her friend Patty's car and by the time the car was fixed Dana had made other friends and discovered the beaches. The car repair took all of Patty's money and she had to return home. Dana had kissed her friend goodbye and waved as her taillights inched closer to Ohio. Mark was a fisherman, even then, but he talked of one day owning his own boat. Running his own crew. He studied for his captain's test every night for three years and worked extra hours cleaning or fixing the boat.

Scotland and Dana walked through the living room and into the kitchen. The wallpaper was mustard colored, with the texture of an orange rind. Brown ears of corn formed a pattern in vertical rows. The pale oak cabinets were pinched by rusty hinges with many doors missing knobs. For a handle on the cabinet under the sink, someone had rigged an old telephone cord with a knot in the back to support a loop as a handle. An open jar of peanut butter sat on the counter. A butter knife used to make a sandwich, perhaps, next to it.

He spun his lighter in his pocket—steady rotations in one direction as if it were a plate on a stick. With his other hand, he removed the envelope from his back pocket. "I expect I'll be able to give you similar amounts once in a while."

"What's going on?"

"It's nothing. I just got a new job."

Dana took the envelope and opened the flap, thumbed the stack. "What kind of job pays enough to have enough left over to give me this?"

"Don't concern yourself with the details," he said.

"Don't smart talk me," she said, staring up at him, her chin an inch from his chest. "You're not too old, Scotland Ross, that I can't take a strap to you." She'd done just that on occasion while growing up when he needed to be disciplined and she didn't want their mother to know. Scotland had taken his punishment humble as could be, because her heart was in the right place and because he knew right from wrong.

"It's nothing to worry about," he said. "I work for a guy who has dreams of being Governor."

"Governor?"

"Relax. It isn't that glamorous, and I don't know if he'll ever have a shot."

"Is this work illegal?"

"Some of it, I suppose."

"Goddamnit, Scotland," she said, her voice hushed low

like a busted steam pipe on a rusty furnace. She stared at him and gnawed on her lip until she reached over and laid her fingers on his forearm. "Well, do not get caught, Scotland. You'll do hard time up at Starke if you get caught."

Scotland leaned back and rubbed his forearm over his abdomen. "Don't worry, Dana. Everything is fine."

She nodded and exhaled. "That's what they all say."

"It'll be fine. Especially if you're getting money every week or so. Wouldn't that keep Mark happy? You meeting the bank note?"

She nodded.

She kept the kitchen much the way their mother did, except for a filthy fucking toaster oven. Fuzzy black grime was visible on the ceiling fan blades. Spaghetti sauce had splattered and dried down the front of the cabinets. The tile behind the sink held a half-moon stain from a hard water leak, and the grout was black enough to look green.

The base of their kitchen table was a wooden spool that Tampa Electric had left on the side of the road after they'd strung miles of power lines. For a table-top, Dana used the sheet metal remains of a Gulf Oil sign flipped upside down. The dull gray indentation of the G was partly visible underneath a bolt of black felt.

She picked up scissors next to a pin cushion. Her sewing machine sat on a folding table along the back wall where a china cabinet should have been.

"Since when are you Mary Poppins?"

Dana smiled.

He recognized a clarity in the whites of her eyes which told him she was neither drunk nor hungover. Her pupils, however, were dilated. She was on something. Her mouth slanted in a half smile, and it took her a full minute to raise her hand and scratch her nose. Scotland guessed pills.

"The girls start back to school. They grew this summer. Their pants legs didn't. I got to add some fabric," she said.

Dana held up a bolt of black felt and dropped it down again. The table recoiled, but did not cave in.

A garbage bag between the counter and the back door overflowed with empty beer and Chef Boyardee cans. A white clock on the wall read 2:15, though Scotland knew it was past three.

His chair was metal framed with a silver Naugahyde-covered cushion, which had a split just off center. The sharp edges of the split material dug into his low back where his jeans and T-shirt rode in opposite directions. As he shifted to get more comfortable, Dana's cat came out from the shadows in the hallway and made its way to lick tomato sauce from the inside of an empty Spaghetti O's can.

The refrigerator door was covered with the postcards he sent the girls every year on their birthdays. He was surprised to see them up there. He half-expected to hear the girls playing in their rooms or arguing or something the way siblings do. He heard nothing except the refrigerator compressor as it kicked on. "Where are the girls?"

"Staying with Mark's mom."

"They stay over there often?"

"Some."

On another day perhaps Scotland would have been worried, but she looked better now. Healthier. And no gin bottles fell out of that bag of trash. That had to be a good sign she was shaping up.

"I'm happy as hell to get the extra money, but you can't bring it to me at the diner. Them people know me. Some of them are cops. What will they think if an ex-con brings in a wad of stolen cash?"

"The money wasn't stolen. I earned it."

"Stealing."

Scotland laughed, nothing more than a couple low rolls of air. "It's not the kind of thing I'd be doing if you didn't need the money," he said. "But it's a good gig."

"You better not get your ass in any trouble."

Scotland sat back, felt the Naugahyde tear in the seat sear his skin again.

And for a minute all was right with the world, until Mark entered the kitchen with a sudden opening of the back door.

He wore painter's pants with blue paint splattered on one of the legs. No shoes or shirt. The outline of muscle and ribs was visible on his leathery skin. His wavy hair held onto its brown color and reflected the ring from a ball cap he'd worn earlier that day or the day before. His eyes were close together and set deep in his skull. His face was made darker by the full beard surrounding his features. All he needed to make him look mythical was a trident and net. He washed the paint from his hands at the sink and dried them on his pants legs before yanking open the refrigerator door. The bulb inside didn't kick on. He grabbed a beer without offering Scotland one.

Dana's face folded in on itself in that worried look of hers. The look that made Scotland feel guilty when he caught the flu that winter in ninth grade that kept him home from school and her by his bedside. The look that made him beat up Johnny Miller when he spread rumors about her during her senior year of high school. She slid Scotland's envelope inside the leg of Josie's altered slacks.

Mark leaned an elbow on the toaster oven. Its little door had been left open to reveal what Scotland guessed was cheese that had melted and dripped onto the heating element and coated the bottom. Empty and open, the burned out appliance looked stupid and useless, yet ready to come up to temperature when called upon. He couldn't imagine having or using one, but obviously Dana found it necessary in her life, like Mark himself.

After a thirsty gulp of beer, he said, "That must be your piece of shit car out front."

"I see you're still painting," Scotland said, leaning back in his chair, his hand in his pocket, spinning the lighter.

"Why is he here?"

"Family is always welcome here," Dana said, crushing out her cigarette. "Now let us talk."

"I know blood is thicker than water, but I want him gone before my girls get home. You hear?"

Scotland kept his mouth shut. He was curious if Dana would speak up in his defense, but that was her business.

"Why are you screwing around with that?" Mark asked, indicating the sewing project. "I told you I'll be back in the water before they need long pants."

"My girls aren't going to school in short pants every day. It's un-American."

"Fine," he said. "Whatever." He slammed the door, exiting the way he'd come in.

Scotland said, "He really doesn't know I'm trying to help, does he?"

"Maybe I did tell him, I don't recall. But it wouldn't matter if he wasn't in a mental state that would let him hear me."

"You sound just like Mom."

"Don't say that."

Scotland reached out and capped her shoulder with his hand. "You look squared away. More so than last time."

"You mean sober?" She laughed and lit a cigarette. "Yeah. I still have my days, don't get me wrong. I'm thirsty all the time." She got up and dragged her sandals across the linoleum toward the sink. She scooped instant coffee into mismatched juice glasses she must have gotten free with a tank of gas. She microwaved them and waited the three minutes to hear the ding.

"Whatever you're doing, just be careful," Scotland said.

She clanged a spoon around in one of the cups. "You're telling *me* to be careful?" She switched cups and stirred that one just as noisily.

"Hey, it's your business. If you like pills, great. There're some cool ones out there. Just be fucking careful."

"The girls like me better like this."

"I bet they do."

"What's that supposed to mean?"

"It means I'm sure the girls like you better like this. Shit."

"Okay. Okay." She waved her hand as if patting a child on the head. "There's no need to get excited." She looked toward the door and back to Scotland. "I get enough of that around here, thank you very much."

The refrigerator compressor kicked off with a rusty clanking which made the postcards on the front dance for a few seconds until the room was quiet again.

Dana threaded a needle with black thread and went to work on a pair of jeans, adding two inches of fabric with blue and white flowers.

Scotland wanted to laugh. Not just because she was being so domestic, but also because it was a treat to partake in this kind of mundane family life.

The refrigerator compressor kicked on again as Mark came back in. There was less sunlight in the doorway behind him. He wore his hat this time, a black mesh ball cap with a Jack Daniels patch on the front. He slammed the door. The trash bag caught a vibration or wind from the door and shifted, then crumbled as it spilled empty cans and paper plates onto the floor. Mark ignored the clanging behind him as he pointed a finger at Scotland. "Why the fuck are you still here?" Mark leaned a fist on the Gulf sign near the inverted F. He reeked of paint fumes and sweat, but he was like any of the irate drunks Scotland had dealt with at Sharky's. "Say your piece to your sister and get the fuck out. I have to disinfect your germs from this whole house before my daughters come home."

Heat shot up through Scotland's neck and he felt a vein on the side of his head swell. He jerked his legs in position to spring up, but saw Dana's wide eyes. They seemed to holler,

"Don't do anything." He felt the galvanized metal of the Gulf sign bend beneath his clenched fists. He had eighty pounds on Mark, but this was his place. Here, Mark was the bouncer and Scotland was the one causing trouble. Scotland released the table top and straightened his legs to a relaxed posture again. "I don't want no trouble."

"Don't yank my ass hairs, Scotty. You're bad news. Period. Get yourself gone, ASAP." He grabbed another beer from the fridge and slammed the door hard enough to rock a magnet loose. One of the postcards slid to the floor.

"We'll wrap this up before you're back for dinner," Dana said. She folded the jeans.

Mark stepped on the postcard and kicked aside the empty cans. He threw open the back door. As he walked out, he cracked the beer and flicked the pull top behind him to land on the mess he'd made.

Scotland stood. "He sure don't make it easy to be nice to him. I'd better go."

"Fuck that. At least for a few more minutes. He'll get over it."

Scotland didn't sit again. Instead, he walked his cup to the sink and washed the undiluted grounds into the drain, watched them swirl before the water went down. "It probably is best that he doesn't know where the money comes from."

"After today, he'll have a more accurate guess. He won't ask though. He doesn't want to know."

He dried his hands on a used Burger King napkin he found near the drain board and walked over to Dana, kissed her on the head. "I'll figure out a way to keep the money coming." As he made his way out through the living room, he noticed the windows were gray with the darkness of an oncoming rain. He called back to the kitchen's overhead lights, "Tell the girls I think their pants are pretty."

CHAPTER EIGHT

On a quiet October night, Kinsey sat on the buck-skin couch along the far wall of his office. He usually spent most of his time at his desk on the other side of the room, but today he focused on the television in front of him. Game six of the World Series was on.

Knuckles wrapped on his office door. Kinsey knew he wouldn't get through the whole game uninterrupted, but he looked at his watch and back to the door. If the world were perfect, Maria would be on the other side, with love on her mind. His neck tingled with the possibilities.

"Enter," he hollered.

Scotland Ross entered, wearing the same jeans and T-shirt as the last time Kinsey had seen him. The guy wasn't so new anymore, and had done great work for the past couple months, proving himself smart and capable, but he obviously didn't blow the money on clothes. Kinsey was left to believe it was booze, or steroids maybe.

"Ah, Scottish," Kinsey said, not bothering to hide his disappointment and looking, only briefly, in Scotland's direction. "You're early."

Scotland walked in and stood tall. "I've been driving around," he said. "Probably burned up five dollars in gas." The bulk of his upper arms forced his elbows out wide and his hands hung near his thighs. "I don't see the benefit of waiting around when I could get busy on your next assignment."

"Excellent." Kinsey waved him closer. "That shows ambition." Kinsey looked at Scotland and then at the television in front of him.

Scotland said, "That's a hell of a TV."

"You like that? It's brand new."

Scotland took a few steps closer. "The picture's so clear, and there's no antenna."

"Cable, my boy. It's the way of the future. I even have a channel on there that plays nothing but movies. All day and all night, if you can believe that."

The game was between innings. A commercial showed a brand new Lincoln Continental—white with a blood-red vinyl top. Kinsey pointed toward the love seat to his right, inviting Scotland to sit. Though the man had proven himself little more than a knee-breaker willing to follow instructions, Kinsey sensed that Scotland was capable of rising to the top of his ranks.

As Scotland walked around the couch, his face was clenched fist-tight.

"I sense something is on your mind," Kinsey said. "Or maybe something is wrong."

Scotland sat on the couch, his eyes on the television. "Don't concern yourself," he said.

Kinsey's blood surged and he felt his face flush, but he also smiled. In a way, he admired the boy's directness. But still, he slapped the arm of the couch. "I don't appreciate the tone there, son."

"Then don't concern yourself with my tone either." Scotland shrugged. "What can I tell you?"

Kinsey uncrossed his legs and raked his fingers through his beard a couple times. "If we're going to get along, Scottish, you might have to dig down and conjure up some courtesy. Do I make myself clear, son?"

"I ain't here to kiss your ass."

"Well, now." Kinsey stood and walked around the couch to his desk. "Daddy raised me well enough to know you're dealing with a fine fellow when you're dealing with a straight shooter." Scotland sat with no change in his face. "I think we're going to get along just fine," Kinsey said.

He wanted to pick up his trophy and bat Scotland around for no other reason than because the big bastard was lippy, and because he had wasted his size. If Kinsey had been that big, he could have pitched his way through high school and college, maybe well enough to have played Triple-A ball. That was what he'd always wanted. The one thing he never could have.

"Who are you rooting for?" Scotland asked, pointing toward the game.

The Phillies wore their home whites and the crowd roared as Pete Rose stepped to the plate.

Kinsey looked to the TV for a moment. "Hoping Kansas City ties up the series tonight and takes it the full seven." He looked back at Scotland. "But other than that, I don't care. I'm a Braves fan."

"I never followed the game that close," Scotland lied.

Kinsey rolled his eyes and shook his head. In his day, he'd been a scrappy outfielder who could shag a fly ball hit just about anywhere and he had a decent arm—strong and accurate. But the one weakness he couldn't compensate for was his ineffectiveness at the plate. He never hit a homerun in his life, and no one expected as much. Coaches did expect him to bunt, which he'd done with a great deal of consistency when called for. All other times he had no patience at the plate, and didn't walk as often as anyone expected. If it wasn't a bunt situation, Kinsey would swing for the fences, hoping to connect and maybe benefit from a freak reaction of physics and land a shot out of the park. The result was usually grounders or pop flies. But if he'd been born with Scotland's eight-inch height difference and extra ninety pounds, perhaps Kinsey's life would have changed dramatically.

Scotland didn't wear a watch, but he checked the clock on Kinsey's credenza a number of times.

"You in a hurry to get some place, son?"

"I didn't come to watch the game," Scotland said. "I'm just here for the next job."

Kinsey pointed to the bar along the opposite wall. "Why don't you pour us a couple of drinks?"

Scotland shrugged, rose, and walked to the bar.

"If you want the next assignment," Kinsey said, walking over to retake his seat on the couch, "you've got to tell me what's troubling you."

"It's just some family shit," Scotland said, stopping at the bar, facing the opposite way. "What are you drinking?"

Without seeing Scotland's face, Kinsey had no way to interpret his reaction. "Dealer's choice, my boy. Whatever you're having."

"Easy enough."

"Now, I don't usually pry, but I can't have you going out to represent me, to protect my interests, if you're a loose cannon head case over whatever's troubling you."

"It's nothing like that," Scotland said, filling glasses with bourbon.

Kinsey let the moment go silent, waited to hear or see something he otherwise would have missed. As Scotland handed Kinsey his drink, Kinsey said, "Out with it."

"Not that it's any of your damn business," Scotland said as he sat, "but if you really gotta know, it's some shit with my sister."

Kinsey sat up and put his drink on the table. "Is that right?"

Scotland ran off at the mouth, and Kinsey let him. Kinsey had to suppress a number of smiles as he listened. Above everything, he took pride in the collateral damage from the fishing ban he'd orchestrated.

"This is good," Kinsey said. "It shows you're loyal. And I don't mind telling you one little bit that I like this development, son." His dry lips cracked as they held a smile. He turned his attention to the game and watched back-to-back foul balls. He tried to remember how long Scotland had been with him. He wasn't sure what month it was that Scotland had joined the team. He'd have to ask Ronald downstairs in the office tomorrow. Regardless, the boy had just passed a test Kinsey hadn't even given. "Yes, sir. Loyalty," Kinsey said. "That Pete Rose fellow there surely doesn't have any of that. He should have stayed with the Reds."

"Isn't he like the best player in the world?"

"They don't call you Charlie Hustle if you ain't getting the job done," Kinsey said, pointing at the television. "No, he's one hell of a ball player, I just don't trust him. And I'm a pretty good judge of character." Kinsey looked at the television again. There was a conference on the pitcher's mound. "Trust and loyalty go hand in hand, son. You're loyal, which means you're trustworthy." No matter how big Scotland was, Kinsey needed him to be trustworthy. Things would get increasingly dicey the closer time got to filing the paperwork with the elections office. A portion of that was in the hands of this young man—that is, if he proved himself.

The Phillies scored two runs in the third and the home crowd roared with hope and anticipation.

"Leave your sister's name and address on Ronald's desk downstairs on your way out. I'll take care of it going forward." With those words, Kinsey felt a sudden rush of adrenaline or power or whatever polite society called it these days. It was the only thing that got his pulse going, besides Maria. The thought that he'd be able to get that rush exponentially as Governor made his hands shake. He held them clasped in his lap and watched a foul ball, then another pitch in the dirt.

The crowd was calm in the stands and Joe Garagiola and Tom Seaver took pauses in the announcer's booth. The only sound in the room came from a hum in the air conditioning ductwork over head and through the little rattle from the register mounted on the wall above the door.

Scotland's eyes closed for a count of two, which signaled defeat to Kinsey.

"I'm not as dumb as you think," Scotland said.

Kinsey laughed despite the disagreement on Scotland's face.

"I've got some college," Scotland said. "But I don't have all the answers."

"Some college?" Kinsey said. "What? It didn't work out? Let me guess. They wouldn't let you major in shotgunning beers and banging chicks. Plus they expected you to wake up for eight o'clock classes on your own."

"Hardly."

"But you didn't finish?"

"No. I didn't." Scotland placed his empty glass on the coffee table.

"I suppose you failed out and they pulled your funding?"

Scotland looked up and blew out a long exhale before saying, "I was married then. I worked part time at Publix and carried a three point five GPA. We had a baby."

"So you quit school to provide for the family."

"No. We were doing just fine with my job and student loans to cover school."

Kinsey leaned forward and tugged on his beard. "The pressure got to you, then?"

"Our baby died."

DING.

Kinsey's alarm clock rang to signal it was time for his phone call to his wife and kids. He hated to dismiss Scotland just when he'd opened up like a weather-beaten coconut, but no matter how intrigued he was by Scotland's story, he couldn't delay the call. "I'm afraid I'm going to have to move on to other business," Kinsey said with as much a smile as he ever used. "I really must stay on schedule. But why don't you use some of the cash you're making to buy new clothes, a new pair of shoes. You look like shit. We need to remify that. And, here." Kinsey tossed him a set of keys on a gold ring.

Scotland caught the keys, apparently surprised and confused as to their purpose.

"It's the white Bonneville under the awning near the tennis courts."

Scotland combed his hair off his forehead with his fingers. "You're giving me a car?"

Kinsey laughed at the naiveté. "Don't mistake this as a gift, Scottish. It's a company car, one of the privileges and responsibilities that come with being in my employ. Do you understand me, son?"

Scotland, still looking at the keys, nodded, his mouth open as if unable to comprehend. "And don't abuse it. I'll have eyes on you everywhere you go. Do I make myself clear?"

Scotland looked up and held Kinsey's gaze. "Don't talk to me like a kid, Kinsey," Scotland said with a flat tone.

"Anyway," Kinsey said. "You'll be driving to the port on Friday. You'll need a dependable car."

Scotland retrieved his empty glass and tilted it back to wet his lips with any liquor that might have remained. "What's at the port?"

Kinsey stood. "Platinum will give you the details."

Scotland didn't reply and he didn't get up.

"What's the matter, boy? You seem to have a little hitch in your giddy up."

Scotland looked up. Kinsey liked being looked up to, though he didn't have the luxury of time in which to enjoy it.

"You want me to highjack a ship?"

"For heaven's sake, Scottish. The ship will already be in port. Are you soft in the head, son?"

"But you want me to steal the shipment."

"Not the whole fucking boat-load. Don't get your shorts in a twist, son. It's one pallet. Everything will fit in the trunk of this car. Maybe some in the back seat, but you'll have plenty of room and plenty of speed to get out of there quick if it comes to that."

As Kinsey picked up the phone on a side table, he motioned for Scotland to close the door on his way out.

By the time Scotland got outside, the space between his ears felt muddled. He heard what sounded like an Atlantic storm in his head, and anger shot his pulse rate up higher than it ever got in the gym. It might have been excitement, though. It might have been both. Maybe it was a lot of feelings he didn't truly understand. He'd never talked about the baby to anyone other than Dana.

He jogged toward the tennis courts. He took a shortcut between buildings two and four and doubled back toward the complex's entrance. Just like Kinsey had said, in the row of covered parking next to the tennis courts was a 1979 Pontiac Bonneville. The car was white with a white vinyl top. Chrome bumpers. Its white vinyl interior, mud flaps, and dual headlights seemed to glow. The back seat was bigger than his bed. It was the only Pontiac sedan he'd ever seen with mag wheels—chrome rims, black wall tires as wide as Scotland's ribcage. Looked as intimidating as he felt and as proud as he wanted to be. "This is too nice for me," Scotland said.

The keys dangled from a ring attached to a pressed plastic replica of the state. It read "Kinsey for Florida!" on one side with the man's name bold across the panhandle and "Florida for Kinsey!" on the other with his name stacked down the peninsula.

He looked over his shoulder as if someone would grab his hand if he tried to start it. The dash shined from the light on a pole in the parking lot. Scotland swiped a hand over the steering wheel. It started up on the first try.

The Bonneville had air conditioning, which he set to high, and power windows that he lowered with flicks of the switches as he pulled onto the main road outside the apartment complex.

For the first time in his life, Scotland had cash in his pocket and was driving a luxury car. He twisted the radio knob to the left and to the right, searching the dial for the loudest, hardest song he could find. He came upon The Allman Brother's "Ramblin' Man." Guitar chords vibrated in his ribcage. Scotland had known few moments of total enthusiasm, and he wanted to get the most from this opportunity. He pressed the pedal to the floor and belted out the song's chorus as loud as he could.

It was the smoothest ride he'd ever experienced. After a while, he felt his foot getting wet, but dismissed it as a phantom memory of driving his old Pinto. Three miles later, he felt water squishing between his toes and pulled over. He crammed himself down on the floorboard and felt the wet floor mat. He assumed it was the air conditioner condenser frozen up or something. He wasn't sure. His knowledge of cars was strictly limited to the outside, and he didn't have any tools or a flashlight so he got back in the driver seat, shut off the AC and drove with the windows down.

He wanted to show his buddies, but didn't want to explain. His friends from Sharky's, Mike, Barry, and Paul, were decent guys. Hard workers. And they all had names that no one ever questioned. He envied that. Thinking about them while driving a car like this made him feel guilty. Those guys were busting their asses, and he just broke a law or two and got this sweet ride. He had to stay away from them. They'd know something was up. One of them could get pissed off or jealous enough to punk him out to the cops or to Scotland's parole officer. He couldn't risk it.

Instead, he drove to the mall near the university and bought a new jean jacket, a half-dozen pullover shirts and a pair of ostrich skin boots. The salesman threw in a pair of socks, and Scotland left wearing everything but the new shirts, carrying those in a bag that he tossed into the back seat.

He spent the next couple hours driving. He wanted to drive all the way down to Miami and cruise US 1 up to Daytona. The real deal, extreme scenic route. Instead, he drove out to the beach and cruised up Gulf Boulevard. Drove back across the bay into Tampa, then back over the bridge toward Dana's house. He got a half mile away and made a U-turn. He wound up instead at a drive-in movie. He didn't know what was playing. Didn't care.

CHAPTER NINE

On Friday, Scotland spent half the day looking out the window at the car, his car, parked in front of his duplex. When it was time to go, he drove faster than legally allowed with the windows up and stereo off so he could hear the engine purr its way up to ninety when he had the room. He pulled into the Gulf Breeze parking lot and waited for Platinum by the car, not wanting to let it out of his sight for fear that somebody would take it away from him. Waiting there also gave him the opportunity to lean backward, rest his elbows on the front fender. The heat from the hood cooked his arms a little, but he didn't move. Someone could be watching him from a window in one of the buildings and he'd never had a better chance to look cooler.

The only action his efforts brought was two squirrels chasing each other around the fat trunk of an oak tree in his field of vision. The sun was half an hour away from setting and the yard glowed golden red. One squirrel stopped its running through the green grass and stood on its hind legs, exposing a white figure-eight patch of fur. The squirrel darted off to the pine tree twenty feet deeper into the light. The other squirrel poked around in the grass. Scotland figured it was looking for food, but he didn't know if squirrels ate worms or grass or if some sort of nut fell from the oak tree. He'd taken a survey course in college to satisfy his science requirement, but botany and zoology were not included. This was the type of question he'd get stuck in his mind and go look up in The Castle's library. He'd gotten familiar with the leather-bound encyclopedias there.

The squirrels chased each other up the oak tree again,

spiraling it like a barber's pole in brown and darker brown until they reached a low limb, where they ran out and jumped to a pine tree and then disappeared.

Maybe they were a couple. Maybe they were brother and sister. This made him think of him and Dana as kids, him always chasing his big sister around the yard, then on bikes when they got older.

Scotland crossed his ankles and looked as high up the tree as he could. The edge of the fender dug into his forearms a little. After a time, he dropped his head forward and rolled it around to loosen his neck. He tapped his foot on the crushed shell parking lot and hummed an old Ventures song in his head as he watched for the squirrels.

The air hung warm, near-eighty degrees. Halloween was a week away, yet it felt like June—warm, but with a hint of cool, like holes in the humidity. It was too warm for his new jean jacket, which lay folded on the backseat.

Once it got fully dark, Platinum rounded building number four with a pair of shotguns held over one shoulder. His other hand gripped a military ammunition box that looked too heavy to swing by his side. A pair of binoculars hung from his neck by a black strap. They bounced into his ribs with each step.

"You ready?" Scotland asked.

Platinum raised the ammo box. "You know how to handle a shotgun?"

"The canoe club gave me a ribbon for it."

"Aye, matey!" Platinum rested the ammo box on the hood of the car and threw a mock salute.

"I'm getting tired of that bullshit." Scotland popped open the box and shoved a handful of shells into his pocket. The posturing was familiar. The casual way in which he grabbed ammo was not. His fingers vibrated with each fistful, but he concealed that, best he could, by moving fast between the box and his pockets. Puffing himself up distracted his thoughts from what he was actually doing.

He didn't look up when he finished speaking. Instead, he examined the pink casing of a shotgun shell from the box. He couldn't believe that something pink could cause so much damage. There was no way to know if he was prepared to fire a shot if it came to it. If he had any luck left, he'd be happy to hold the shotgun mute and get away clean without having to find out.

Platinum placed the ammo box and his shotgun on the floor in the back seat. Scotland rested his across the denim jacket folded there.

For reasons Scotland didn't understand, he liked Platinum. He would have denied it if anyone asked, but the man was tough. Scotland had to respect that. Strong and fast like a rattlesnake, and just about as warm. Maybe Platinum had been raised that way, but the shit he saw in Vietnam had to harden him. Platinum never talked about his war-time experiences, but it didn't take a headshrinker to figure out that the roughest shit he could get into in Tampa was tame by comparison.

The engine turned over with its throaty purr. Scotland shifted into drive and took a left on Providence road.

This was the kind of bullshit job Platinum wouldn't miss when Kinsey was Governor. And he assumed this would be his last. Turn over this work to Scotland and the next new guy. Kinsey hadn't mentioned that to him, but this had to be a training opportunity for Scotland to take over this shit work. Platinum envisioned himself in a three-piece suit, walking up the steps of the capitol building in Tallahassee, being shown on television protecting Governor Kinsey from any credible threats.

Scotland drove down Highway 60 toward the Ybor district, as per Kinsey's instructions. Port Tampa dominated much of Hillsborough Bay, but for a thousand dollars a pop, an enterprising stevedore had given Kinsey all the leads that he heard. Told them right where to be and when.

A haze of phosphate dust hung in the air along the channel leading into Tampa Bay. They stored that shit in silos along the waterfront, tons of it waiting to be fed onto barges to fertilize the world's crops. If it had a smell, Platinum had long been immune to it. The pier where the boat was supposed to dock lined a stretch known as the banana docks, a flat expanse near tied-up boats and trucks parked in the distance. Even in the cloud of dust that looked like snow in the light breeze, they were exposed.

"Take a right at that warehouse on the corner," Platinum said. Palm trees lined the far side of the main pier. In the distance, a natural gas tank loomed ten stories tall. The banana docks were deserted except for the litter of discarded banana stalks with their multitude of machete wounds. "Pull up over there by the fence."

As soon as they got out of the car, a stray dog, some kind of retriever mix, bound up to Scotland, who took a knee and greeted the mutt like it was the family pet.

A wave of nausea swept through Platinum and he dry heaved. "That thing could have rabies," Platinum said. "Fleas. It looks like it's got mange."

Scotland rubbed the dog's head without looking up. "I think she's all right."

Platinum scanned the horizon, binoculars pressed to his eyes. It was dark, and the lights on the pier didn't illuminate much of the water. A boat horn crowed out on the channel, and for a moment filled the distance between him and the Tampa skyline. Even in October, the humidity here was high enough to make him want to jump into Ybor channel just to cool off.

The dog ran to check out one of the discarded banana

stalks lying on the pier. "Those banana stalks are loaded with spiders," Platinum said. "I saw one big as my hand one time when I was a kid. Scared the hell out of me."

Scotland jogged over and shoed the dog away from the banana stalk, as if that would have an impact on its life. But there was time to kill, so Platinum let him fuck around with the rabid port mutt.

Bay water lapped the pier and seawall. It smelled of diesel fumes and dead fish. Across the channel, oil storage tanks and towering grain and phosphate silos crowded the shore like linemen at a buffet. Platinum was familiar with the area from the summers he stayed with his grandparents. His grandfather had taken him there not for the bananas, but rather to get water from a pump on a well not far from there. The water was heavy with sulfur, but the old man drank it because he thought it contained medicinal properties. He'd fill three old milk jugs and carry two himself. Platinum would struggle with the weight of one. In the mornings, the old man would shake a jug and fill a juice glass with the copper-colored water. He lived to ninety-one.

Platinum watched the channel through the binoculars. The shipment they awaited was due to arrive on a broken down sightseeing boat converted to dry goods hauler.

"You done this before?" Scotland asked. He held a stick in his hand, which the dog jumped for.

Platinum set the binoculars on the hood of the Bonneville and looked at him. "I do what needs getting done."

Scotland threw the stick. "Why you up Kinsey's ass so much?" The dog took off and almost got the stick before it clanked twenty yards down the pier.

Platinum couldn't help but laugh. "I'm helping make him Governor."

"And you think he's going to set you up with a legitimate job in his administration?"

Platinum thought, *this guy has some balls.* He didn't resent this, but rather found it promising that the big guy's brain worked in a direction other than "eat, sleep, and lift weights." There was still the time to kill, so Platinum said, "Kinsey has made promises, sure. But even if he fucks me over, he's still going to be Governor."

Scotland bent to take the stick from the dog's mouth. "And that would matter even if he fucks you over?"

Platinum swallowed hard, but his saliva felt thick as sausage gravy in his throat. "You haven't known him long enough to know he's exactly what this state needs right now."

Scotland shrugged and threw the stick again, watched the dog disappear into a shadow. He turned his attention to the bay.

"He runs all of that, too," Platinum said. "The Gulf, I mean. That's how powerful he is." Right then Platinum realized he'd said too much. Kinsey would cut out his tongue if he slipped up and mentioned Eddie Joyner to the new guy. Platinum picked up his binoculars and pretended to look for the boat. "This is his *old* car, you know?" he said.

"Pretty damn cool, too."

Platinum leaned back onto the Bonneville. He hoped the comb in his back pocket scratched the paint. "He gave me my car, too. A Camaro Z/28. Beautiful. And fast as hell."

"I've seen it. Good for you. Now what exactly is the plan here?"

Platinum didn't detect any sarcasm. This surprised him and he was glad to turn the topic back to business. "Scoring some serious Benzos."

"What the hell is that? Italian mopeds or something?"

"Benzos? Benzodiazepines."

Scotland's face didn't register any recognition.

"Pills. Shit man where you been?"

Scotland picked up and threw the stick again. "Fucking pills?"

Platinum laughed, held the binoculars to his eyes and

lowered them before he got to see through them. "These things are good as gold."

"He's a fucking drug dealer?"

Platinum laughed. "No. Not personally." He didn't have any reservations about sharing this information. The new guy needed to know this stuff so he could take over the port business. "A buddy from his college days is a podiatrist, the skinny guy downstairs at the Gulf's office. You must have seen him. Anyway, he doesn't practice anymore, but he's still able to write prescriptions."

"Why would people get them from him when they could get them from a real doctor?

"That's the thing. Some of these people don't really need the pills, but they want that buzz. You know?"

Scotland took a moment as if he was processing the information. He looked away, then back to Platinum. "Is the money from that worth fucking around with drugs?"

Platinum checked the horizon through the binoculars as he said, "Think bigger, Scotty."

"Bigger than money?"

The binoculars didn't reveal any movement on the water. Platinum said, "I probably said too much already. Never mind."

"Fine with me," Scotland said. "How's this shit supposed to go down here tonight?"

Platinum had lost track of the port mutt. Didn't know if the mongrel was chasing Scotland's stick or if he was muzzle deep into a stalk full of spiders. "It's nothing, really. When the boat docks, three or four guys will bring out these bundles the size of bed pillows. I walk up with this shotgun pointed at their balls and you back this big-ass car right up to us, pop the trunk, and grab the other shotgun." Platinum pointed to the backseat.

Scotland looked out at the water. "Just for show, right? We fire warning shots if we have to?"

"Relax. These guys have wives and kids and none of them wants to die because of some bullshit pills. They'll load the car for us and then put their hands up. That's when we drive away."

"You just take it?"

"We just take it."

"You make it sound simple. How many of these have you done?"

"Easily a few dozen." There were only seven really, but that sounded too low. "I lost count."

"I find it hard to believe they wouldn't take precautions if you've ripped them off that many times."

"It's always a different boat, a different crew. We're good to go." He figured they'd be able to get in one or two more such robberies before word spread and the crews started to protect themselves.

"Who did the other jobs with you?"

Platinum looked at him, without speaking.

"Shit. Lighten up. Just trying to pass the time."

This was something Platinum felt was clear for discussion. He wanted to talk about it, to reveal all that he knew, to prove to Scotland that no matter his size or strength, he'd never be as ingrained with Kinsey. They had history and he couldn't help taking advantage of the bragging rights. "The first time was with the Kula brothers. Those guys are pros. The rest were with this guy everybody called Skillet on account of his greasy hair and flat face. He worked for Kinsey like a year. Never told me his real name."

"What happened to him?" As Scotland asked, the dog came back with the stick. "Nobody's saying. Just fell off the earth."

Scotland threw the stick and the dog took off after it. "You ever look for him?"

"I don't spend time hunting things I don't care to find."

"So you weren't buddies?"

Somehow this conversation felt like a breach of Kinsey's trust. "Look, man. I'm not in this for friendships. This isn't a fucking get to know you session. All right? My only loyalty is to Kinsey. You got that?"

"Whoa. Down-shift, there, pal. I'm here ain't I?" He petted the dog as it returned with the stick again. "We'll get the job done."

Platinum didn't like to think about Skillet or what became of him. Now that it was in his head, his whole mindset shifted. "I'm not worried about this fucking job. This'll be a piece of cake. I just don't need all this jibber jabber in my head right now."

"This dog is better company anyway," Scotland said, tugging at the stick clenched between the dog's teeth. "I'll wait for your signal to rip it in reverse."

After waiting silently for twenty minutes staring through the binoculars, Platinum saw the boat. It was white and had sheet metal covering the windows where tourists used to watch for dolphins and manatees in Tampa Bay. Its engines chugged under the bulk of the load it carried. The flag it flew had the familiar stars and stripes of the American flag, but there was only one white star on the blue field in the upper left. "Our country had only one state when that flag was made," Platinum said.

"That's not our flag, dip-shit," Scotland tugged on the skin and fur under the dog's ears.

"Then whose is it?"

"I'm not a hundred percent, but I know it's a foreign country."

As the boat pulled closer, a squat man with thick forearms climbed down a rope ladder from the main deck and hopped to the pier. Platinum lowered the binoculars but continued to watch.

A van pulled onto the pier and rolled to a stop near the boat.

Platinum reached back and picked up his shotgun. Scotland did the same. "The stuff we want is always the first thing they unload."

Voices from the boat called out to their guy in the van. Even in the distance, their language sounded harsh and precise.

Platinum focused on the activity around the boat. A panel where the tourist windows used to be slid open and four guys worked like ants, carrying loads on their backs. He waited until he saw the fourth guy lumber out, carrying the fourth sack of pills. "Okay," Platinum said with two open palm smacks on the Bonneville's door. He leaned into the open window. "Watch me in the rearview mirror. When I get within blasting range, you slam this bitch in reverse and back up to us."

Scotland nodded, holding the shotgun in his lap.

"Do not fuck this up." Platinum picked up the stick and threw it as far as he could into the water, hoping the fucking dog would jump in after it. He anchored his shotgun at his hip and walked forward.

The sound of a boat horn echoed in the bay. He walked at a steady pace, cautious, but confident despite the zip-tie feeling around his throat that he always felt when he got amped up like this.

"All right, gentlemen!" he said, holding his shotgun at the ready. The shotgun, along with the element of surprise, was enough to make the men drop their pill-filled sacks. They raised their arms. He'd had men this size and color at the end of his rifle a few times. He shook his head to bring clarity to his eyes. They were on a pier, not in a jungle. He'd fired shots often over there, never knowing who he hit. His experience at this range only came from the first heist like this where the Kula brothers did all the work. Platinum had just been a bystander with the same shotgun. Now though, he was in charge and his objective was not to shoot. The energy he got from those four deck hands was fear and anger and maybe even embarrassment as they were forced to surrender to his firepower. Platinum had always preferred the power and control of hand-to-hand combat.

Before he could speak again, Scotland roared the great white Bonneville backward and skidded to a stop half a yard from their knees.

Scotland didn't exit the car right away.

"Come on," Platinum yelled, holding the shotgun on the guys.

After a delay, Scotland emerged with his shotgun in one hand, the keys in another. He fumbled with the keys, dropping them onto the pier.

"Get your shit together, Ross," Platinum said.

Scotland got the trunk open, then swung his shotgun into position on his hip.

"Pills!" Platinum pointed the barrel of his shotgun toward one of the sacks. "Trunk!" He waved the shotgun toward the car. "Now!"

No one moved for a moment. Platinum wanted to pump the shotgun to punctuate his command, but doing so would eject a perfectly good round already chambered. He didn't know how many shots he might need. Instead, he soundlessly aimed the barrel at one man's face until they jumped to lift the sacks. The first sack nearly filled the trunk.

Platinum motioned to the sacks on the ground and then to the trunk. "Load us up and we'll part friends."

The second sack took up the rest of the room, which meant they couldn't close the trunk. A skinny guy in stained coveralls wrestled the third sack into the back seat. Before they could get the fourth in, there was a gunshot. The report was from a pistol, and came from the main deck of the boat. It echoed off the corrugated walls of the warehouses along the pier. The boat crew scattered, leaving the fourth sack to fall to the ground. It had been a decade since Platinum took live fire.

He fired a shotgun blast in the direction of the shot, but he was out of range. Scotland fired, and fired again. By the time Platinum yelled, "Drive!" he was reloading. "Drive!" Platinum yelled again, lunging for the passenger door.

Scotland ran back to the driver's seat, slammed the car into drive and spun out fast enough to throw the second sack from the open trunk. A shot hit the car with a loud ding and Scotland skidded the car, narrowly missing a dumpster. A second shot landed with a thump. "Faster!" Platinum yelled as he ducked.

A week later, Kinsey revved his Mercedes at every stoplight along US 41. The toe of his ostrich-skin boot mashed and released the accelerator as he wove between cars in the north-bound lane. He hadn't been to the Gulf Breeze in a couple nights and had gotten a later start than he planned. He could've been home in time to watch the Carter-Reagan debate in his pajamas with a bowl of ice cream on his chest, but he wanted to watch it in his office. Alone. He would feel a greater connection to it. He could study it.

He parked in front of his office. The lights were off downstairs, but upstairs Maria had a drink waiting for him. "Isn't this a nice surprise," he said, taking the glass from her waiting hands.

She wore leggings and a white linen shirt, belted at the waist. Her hair was up, held in place with a tortoise shell comb. She kissed him hard on the mouth and hugged his neck tight enough to make him spill his drink. "I put the ice cubes when I hear Mercedes in the parking lot."

"How'd you know I'd come tonight?" Kinsey pulled far enough away from her to down half his drink.

Her eyes gave nothing away. Instead, she said, "I miss you, Allan."

Hearing those words flooded his nervous system with

pleasure fast as an injection. "I'm here now," he said and pulled her to him with enough force to knock loose the tortoise shell comb. Dark hair tumbled. He smoothed some away from her face, tucked some behind her ear.

"It has been too long," she said, bending down to hug him with her ear on his shoulder. "Do you have much work tonight?"

"I do," he said. "And the debate is on in a few minutes." Kinsey walked to the television and switched it on. "I have to watch it."

He took a seat on the couch, crossed his left leg over his right and pried off a boot. He switched legs and pried off the other. He placed the boots parallel, pointing toward the door. Maria brought him a napkin from the bar for him to dry his shirt. He reached up and took it, then swatted Maria's ass the way he smacked horses that were in his way. "Yah!" he wanted to yell and get her to run to the opposite end of the acreage. She was not a ranch horse, though. She was a beautiful woman he wanted to keep close...just not right now.

Kinsey's blood coursed through him like firewater. He sat up, rested his elbows on his knees. The presidential debate happened once every four years. And, more importantly, the tips he could glean from a candidate as personable as Reagan might prove invaluable.

Maria took a seat on the couch next to him. She slid out of her pumps and pulled her feet up underneath her, the way cats do.

On television, a stern looking woman on the screen talked, but Kinsey stared at his woman's steely shins. The way her instep curved under her. If there were more time, he'd take her right there, but his attention was called back to the television when Howard K. Smith introduced Carter and Reagan.

As he introduced the panelists, Maria asked, "What is this Barbara Walter's thinking?"

"Please, Maria," he said. "I want to listen."

"That outfit and hair. It is terrible."

Kinsey hadn't noticed, but he *was* struck by how blue everything was on the debate set. The carpet. The giant curtain with the ominous rectangular opening. However, it was the space between the podiums that caught his eye the most—the distance between the men. It was as great a gulf as separated Kinsey from his own future opponent, Bob Graham. Kinsey thought for a moment about how he might be able to use that in his campaign. He grew hypnotized by the blue carpet and saw his face on Reagan's body, Graham's on Carter's.

Reagan was still answering the first question when Platinum walked in without knocking. He entered the room slow as a bride. "How you been, Mr. K?" He nodded toward Maria and walked up to the back of the loveseat opposite Kinsey's spot on the couch.

Kinsey didn't bother to turn his head away from the television. "I've been busier than a two dollar hooker at a Teamster's convention."

Platinum laughed more than necessary. "That's a good one."

Usually, Kinsey liked the way the guy thought. Liked the way he worked. His loyalty. Kinsey had lured the man into his employ by covering overdue jai alai bets at the fronton near Gandy Boulevard. Platinum earned out of his debt within six months. That was four years ago. Platinum rode out some lean times when Kinsey was overextended and there wasn't much coming in, but those days were long behind them both.

Kinsey tried to focus on the debate, but Platinum started in again. "Are you mad as all get out about the pill heist?"

Kinsey cursed under his breath for the timing of it all. The television's sound wasn't loud enough to cover Platinum's voice. This was the first opportunity they'd had to discuss the matter. The incident which had cost him a quarter of a million dollars. "I'm plenty disappointed," Kinsey said, facing the TV, but seeing almost nothing on the screen. The restraint was a slight of hand he'd learned from his father, who had learned it from his father before him. Over the years, Kinsey had heard analogies that included "silver tongues" and the benefits of using "honey instead of vinegar," but what really drove home the notion was when his father sat him down in his office at the farm. Kinsey, Allan as everyone called him in those days, was all of fourteen years old, sitting in his baseball uniform, the laces of his spikes knotted together with the shoes straddling his shoulder. His white pants and white socks orange from the clay on the diamond. Some action at second base had caused a jagged rip through his pants at the knee, which bled onto the torn edges. He'd been thrown out of the game for reacting to a questionable call. The umpire was wrong, and young Allan Kinsey, the scrappy little ball player who played like he was poor, yelled back, "Bullshit!" That got him tossed from the game.

"Never," his father had said, "let your emotions get the better of you. It makes a man look weak."

"But he was wrong, Father."

"That's beside the point. He's the umpire, the authority on the field. If you want supreme power over a baseball field you have to become an umpire. But while you're a player, you would be wise to respect the position, regardless if you agree or not." His father removed his glasses and polished them with his handkerchief. "Take this incident for example. This umpire," he said, waving his glasses in the air before him. "He made a bad call that went against you. You think he's wrong and you're angry."

"Who wouldn't be?"

"You have every right. I'm not implying otherwise." His father placed his glasses on his face by tugging the ear pieces into place then stood up, walked to the window overlooking the wrap lines on the production floor. "But what I am saying is that it's inexcusable to lose control and raise your voice directly opposing his authority." He turned to face his son and added, "How much better off do you suppose you'd be if you handled this completely opposite?"

"What do you mean, opposite?"

"Well, perhaps, when you're called out, you say, 'I believe I was safe. Perhaps you can make a close call go my way next time.'"

"That wouldn't change anything."

"The only thing yelling changed was getting you here in front of me."

"But even if I did what you say, there's no way to know if he would hold up his end of the bargain."

"Do you think yelling gives you leverage? That impugning his authority puts you in a better position? No. What you can count on is self-control. If you utilize it. If you do, like in this case with the umpire, he might have agreed it was a bad call and appreciated the calm way in which you disagreed with him. He might find you a reasonable young man and therefore be more inclined to agree to your proposition. Perhaps he'd be inclined to do so repeatedly."

Allan Kinsey had relied on that lesson ever since. But while his father had taught him self-control as a way to manipulate people, the man never, in his life, mentioned the advantages of retribution and revenge.

Platinum just stood there, hands resting on the back of the loveseat like Kinsey's own son awaiting punishment for getting crayon marks on the wall.

Kinsey had dismissed Platinum periodically in the past, but tonight, of all nights, this kid, this mutt he'd rescued and made his head of security, held his head cocked, eyes wide, top lip shaky.

"Yes, I'm disappointed we lost half the haul." Kinsey took a pull from his drink. "I'm not happy about the money left on the table, or on the ground, in this case. But shots were fired.

Neither of you were killed. That's the important thing. Come on, now. Have a seat."

Platinum quick stepped around the loveseat and plopped himself down. "It wasn't my fault," he said. "It wasn't Ross's fault either. Not entirely."

Kinsey looked toward the television. Sat back. Looked into Platinum's gray eyes, and said, "What are you implying?"

Platinum leaned his elbows on his knees. In a whisper he said, "Your boy, Scotland, was slow getting out of the car." He looked over his shoulder at the door and back. "And I can't help wonder if that would've made all the difference."

Kinsey stared at the blue carpet on the debate set. Instead of hearing what Jimmy Carter was saying, he turned Platinum's words over in his mind. He wondered if the big guy froze, or if he simply paused to better assess the situation. After a moment, Kinsey said, "I'm just glad neither you boys were hurt. And I mean that. From now on, we'll have some Cubans do that sort of thing for us. Gang style." Kinsey turned his attention back to the debate. Reagan bowed his head, cocked it to the side and came up with a smirk. He was schooling the President on how to win a debate and the President didn't even know it. That combination of head movement and facial expression was the thing Kinsey committed to memory.

Maria reached over, grabbed Kinsey's glass and said, "Let me refill you." She unfolded her legs and was up the moment her feet hit the floor.

"See if he'd like a drink," Kinsey said, pointing toward Platinum.

"I'll get it," Platinum said as he got up and followed Maria to the bar.

Kinsey watched Maria grab an ice cube with the little tongs she'd removed from the silver ice bucket. Platinum reached over her shoulder and picked up the vodka bottle. They moved in close proximity, like a young couple in the bathroom before work. It unnerved Kinsey to the point his right eye began to twitch. After Maria poured bourbon into the glass, she reached for a napkin and Platinum let her pass in front of him with the briefest touch of his hand across the small of her back, just below her belt. The touch lasted a second, at most, but Kinsey had seen it. So brief. So familiar. His eye stopped twitching and the room was cast in a red shadow—he wasn't sure a blood vessel hadn't burst in his brain. No mere friends or acquaintances could share such intimacy as that delicate touch.

Kinsey heard nothing coming from the television, nor could he hear their voices from the bar. His fingers tightened on the arm of the couch and his stomach rolled up into his throat like in waves of acid. He did as he'd trained himself to do. Held it all in. Didn't let the stress of it change his personality or facial expressions.

Maria walked up and handed Kinsey his drink. "I was up all night," she said. "If it's okay with you, I go to sleep now."

Kinsey took inventory of the muscles required to respond. Everything was in its relaxed state as he said, "That's quite all right, darlin'. I'm glad I got to see you today."

"Did I surprise you?"

"Oh, you surprised me," Kinsey said, trying to keep his voice calm. "Yes. Yes, yes."

"Good night, Papi," she said as she kissed Kinsey's forehead, then walked to the door, closing it softly behind her.

Kinsey looked at Platinum. "Where most politicians simply keep their noses planted firmly in the asses of the rich, I know the power to get things done is with the people. When you want the freshest cut of beef, you don't go talk to somebody wearing a tie in an office. No, sir. You go talk to the butcher, who'll show you the cow it's about to be carved from."

Platinum's face twisted up, his tan forehead creased near his blond hairline.

Kinsey turned his attention back to the television.

CHAPTER TEN

On Thursday afternoon, Scotland drove to meet Kinsey at Gulf Breeze. He wanted to go see Dana at the diner and make sure Kinsey was getting money to her, but Platinum had called to set up the meeting. He hoped the meeting wouldn't take long.

He hadn't seen Kinsey in the week since that cluster-fuck at the port. Scotland was still pissed, but couldn't help standing a little taller than usual. Tonight, he'd been instructed to wait in the parking lot. Platinum wouldn't tell him anything except where and when. Scotland could only assume Kinsey had heard about the gun shots and wanted to see the damage to his car personally.

Scotland waited in the car for ten minutes. He tapped the wheel and changed radio stations every other song. He didn't know how long Dana's shift at the diner would be, and he had to catch her there before she left.

Ten more minutes later, Kinsey exited the clubhouse with a cigar burning between his clenched teeth. He groaned at the site of Scotland and raised his arms as he barked a greeting Scotland couldn't understand as he walked toward him. He wore a tan suit without the vest and black shoes with a Cuban heel.

Scotland looked down at his jeans hanging loose around the shiny boots he'd bought only a few days before. The same boots that had gotten hung up under the brake pedal that night at the port and kept him from getting out of the car as quickly as he'd wanted. He had no trouble this time, and slammed the car door behind him as he called out, "Now before you go yelling about your car, Kinsey, I want you to know how bullshit it is I got shot at in the first place."

"Oh, yes. Yes," Kinsey said, flicking an inch of ash from his cigar. "I do apologize for that most unfortunate surprise. As you're beginning to see, none of this is an extinct science."

Kinsey puffed his cigar. The cloud of smoke obscured his face for a moment before billowing away in the sunlight above them.

Kinsey held out a bulging envelope. "Here you go, son. Your share from the other night."

Scotland took the envelope, squeezed it and said, "I thought my money was going to that address I gave you."

"That check went out days ago. This is extra." He puffed his cigar. "For you."

"What about the car?"

Kinsey went around to the passenger side and bent down to get a look at the bullet holes. He stuck his finger in one and then the other. "Bang. Bang," he said. "Acceptable damage. It's not enough to warrant a new car for yourself."

"It's not that," Scotland said. "I can fix it." He wanted to take the words back, but it was too late. He wasn't sure why he spoke them.

"How's that, son?"

Scotland had no reason to lie about it. "I worked auto body at The Castle. I can fix it."

Kinsey smiled around his cigar. "Absolutely not," he said. He pulled the cigar from his mouth. "I appreciate the offer, but you risked your life to complete the mission. That kind of loyalty is impressive."

Scotland shrugged.

"That's why you were rewarded, son."

Scotland liked the idea of getting the bonus, but he wondered if Kinsey was aware they'd come back with only half the load. He wasn't about to tell him. Not now. Not ever if he could help it. And still, he was positive this one job wasn't big enough to sway Kinsey like this, even if they had made it back with the full shipment.

"Come with me," Kinsey said, walking toward the stairs of building two.

Scotland had it in his mind that he'd go stake out Dana's diner and wait for her to get off work and head home. He could follow her for about a mile then get her to pull over and give her this new stack of money. He had no idea how much time this meeting with Kinsey would eat up.

Atop the second floor, Kinsey swung open the door to apartment number one. It had a covered balcony big enough to bowl on. The sliding glass doors were open and there was a breeze blowing an Oriental wind chime hanging from a hook above the railing. The perspective was the right angle to overlook both the pool and the tennis courts on the property. The periphery afforded a decent look onto a number of balconies in building one. One might even be able to see into the apartments at night if the blinds were open.

"Maria decorated the place. She's into earth tones. It's got as cozy a feel as you're ever going to get." The brown sink matched the equally brown oven, dishwasher, and refrigerator, which matched the toilet and tub. "Maria says the appliances represent trees in the forest. The orange shag carpet is symbolic of the fallen leaves up north this time of year."

If he didn't point them out, Scotland never would have noticed. Didn't care. He just wanted to get on the road to see Dana. "This is nice," he said, walking back toward the front door. "This where you stay?"

"No, son. This is where you're going to live."

"Me?" Scotland walked over and clapped Kinsey on the back hard enough to make him wobble. With a laugh, he said, "Yeah. I'm gonna live here."

"You're proving to be a real asset to me, Scottish. Would be good to have you close by."

"You must be confusing me with somebody else. I'm not going to pay rent on a place like this."

"I'm not going to charge you anything."

"You're just going to ding my account so that I'm never able to pay you off."

"Sometimes in life, son, there is no catch."

"Look," Scotland said. "A company car is one thing, but I'm not in for whatever funky bullshit you think you might get out of the situation." Scotland rested his hand on the brown hood of the brown stove and stared down into Kinsey's eyes.

"Relax," Kinsey said, meeting Scotland's stare. He said it dismissively, and his face was bunched up.

Scotland hated to be condescended to. It made him feel dumb. He turned to face the living room and said, "I go from the roach motel to the Ritz for free?"

"Starting today, if you'd like."

"Look, Kinsey. This is really cool of you to offer. It's the nicest place I've ever seen, but..." He walked around the counter and into the living room, stopped to look out the sliding glass doors at the tennis court. "But I don't plan on being around here long. As soon as we're square, I'm shoving off."

"Sure," Kinsey said as he made his way into the living room. "Sure. I take no offense to that. But in the meantime, why don't you live here, comfortably?"

Scotland smiled. "A reason doesn't come to mind."

Kinsey clapped his hands once and dropped them. "How long will it take you to pack out your place and get over here?"

"The packing'll take five minutes, if that."

"It's quiet around here this week. Take your time. Settle in whenever you're ready."

"Man," Scotland said. He stood by the couch facing a television as big as the one in Kinsey's office. "This really is just the nicest place I've ever seen." He lifted a pale green pillow off the cream-colored couch. "I've never had nice stuff like this. Comfortable stuff. It looks like a rich person's place."

"I'll pass along the compliment to Maria."

"She's very good at it."

Kinsey exhaled and kinked the right side of his lips into that creepy smile he had. "Yes. Well, I'll leave you to do what you must." He handed Scotland a key. "Enjoy your new home."

Scotland collapsed onto the couch. He propped his feet on the oak coffee table and stared at the empty tennis court.

CHAPTER ELEVEN

The Gulf Breeze parking lot sat quiet except for the cracked shells crunching beneath Scotland's boots. It was three in the morning. He couldn't sleep so he went out, not for a walk, but to look around—at the cars. There were Camaros and Pontiacs and one of those ridiculously small Honda rice burners. His Bonneville, even with the bullet holes, was the nicest car out there. He stood and looked, still unable to believe that it was his.

The air had dried out. Gotten a little cooler. After so many months of sweating it out in the tropical heat, he'd forgotten that temperatures leveled off this time of year. He wasn't cold, but, for a moment, he wished he'd worn a shirt. He kicked a few tires as he walked around, eventually finding himself next to the clubhouse. Kinsey's headquarters. The lights were out and the door was locked. He let the knob go, resigned to go back to his apartment to try and get some sleep. After a couple foot falls onto the crushed shells, he stopped at the Bonneville to retrieve the folding knife he'd transferred from his old Pinto and stashed beneath the seat. The clubhouse door was easy to pop.

Inside, the place was dark. He stood for a moment near the door to let his eyes adjust. Cool air floated over his shoulders, causing him to shiver. He wondered if they always left the AC so low. The first desk he got to was like his parole officer's desk. Dave was an organized guy, but not compulsive about it. Scotland never liked the idea of having a desk job, himself and was reminded why as he looked at the stacks of papers and phones on every desk.

Scotland found himself near the back of the room and

stood for a moment, as if trying to hear the echoes of what the hell happened in there during the day. He thumbed through a stack of papers on a metal desk to his left. He looked over his shoulder and clicked on the desk lamp. Scanned through land acquisition and real estate paperwork. His eyes glazed over the thick documents. He didn't have to spend the time reading them to know Kinsey benefitted from each one. And that reason was why he kept digging. Desk to desk. He shuffled papers, intent on finding anything remotely incriminating so he could have something to hang over Kinsey's head. He kept looking. In the top drawer of the desk in the corner by the windows was a leather-bound ledger with a thick rubber band holding it closed. He wondered if it listed all the hapless fuckers who'd gotten sucked into Kinsey's scam.

He took the ledger, clicked off the light and went to the bigger desk in the far corner, where he clicked on the desk lamp and pulled out the chair. The sturdy wood top was covered with a calendar blotter that featured scribbles in red and blue ink. Everything was written in the same hand. All print. The initials "E. J." appeared a couple times in the past month. The first was in red ink and read "Pay E. J." The next was on Tuesday in blue ink: "Call E. J."

Scotland flipped open the ledger. Numbers filled columns. He'd taken an accounting class in college and knew what he was looking at well enough to follow the credits and debits. The desk blotter had piqued his curiosity, so he searched the ledger's columns for dates corresponding with the notes on the blotter. The ledger was meticulously kept, and among the entries, there was the clear line item of "E. J.—$5,000." The flush of excitement never peaked because he didn't know what it meant. He thumbed through the pages. Saw no other such entry among the many other line items until he got to the same date on the previous month. Again, E. J. —$5,000. The same payment had been made every month back to the beginning of the ledger. These monthly payments to E. J. weren't the highest amounts listed, but they were the most regularly occurring.

CHAPTER TWELVE

On the Wednesday following Election Day, Kinsey opened the pool and had Piglette's Barbeque in West Tampa deliver a shitload of ribs, pulled pork, and all the sides. Gulf Breeze tenants filled the area. Booze flowed and dozens of women were in bikinis. Scotland didn't have much experience with parties and, like at Sharky's, he felt more comfortable on the perimeter. He hadn't been with a woman since he'd lost his job at Sharky's and the sight of all that flesh stood him up taller and made him like his chances of rectifying that. A tingle shot up Scotland's neck. At Sharky's, he'd had his pick of the single girls who always wanted to make it with a bouncer. He didn't have that leverage of power here.

Women outnumbered men three or four-to-one, each of them in bikinis, except for Maria who stood close to Kinsey, holding his arm. She had on a sundress and sandals. Big sunglasses and a floppy hat covered her in shade. Kinsey and Maria were glued to each other. Kinsey wore terry cloth swim shorts, his hairy chest exposed—more fit than he looked in a suit.

Scotland was still the new guy and didn't really know anyone. It wasn't hot enough for everyone to be in the pool, so he padded around the pool deck barefoot in cutoff jeans, a bottle of Michelob in his hand. He nodded to a girl with light brown hair who stood by the boombox. She wore a bikini top and little red gym shorts. Scotland had to talk to her.

The air was clear and cool, a perfect partner for the sun in the absence of humidity. Smells of smoked meat swirled around the air, combining with the smoke from Kools, weed, and oak logs burning in the barbeque.

The Kula brothers each had a paper plate piled high with pulled pork and coleslaw. They barely looked up as they forked in food as if there was a prize for the first to finish. They were the only people, besides Kinsey and Maria, he recognized. He would have liked to take this opportunity to break the ice with those big fuckers and see if they'd speak to him. If it wasn't for the girl in the bikini top and gym shorts, he might have.

Scotland dug his hand in his pocket. Instead of the comfort of his lighter, a jolt of panic surged through him. His pocket was empty. He checked his other pocket before remembering that he'd left it in his new apartment because the plan was to go swimming. He exhaled and laughed, relieved and disappointed. Without the lighter, he was left to hold his beer in one hand, his other pointlessly in his pocket.

He was about three steps away from her when they'd first made eye contact. The blue-green color of her eyes popped, framed as it was with her tan face and red hair. Scotland smiled. She smiled back and shifted her weight onto her right leg, seductive. That was all the invitation he needed.

From out of nowhere, Platinum grabbed Scotland's wrist. Scotland's breath caught from the surprise.

"Let's practice hold escapes," Platinum said.

Scotland shrugged out of the grip. He clenched his fist, ready to slug Platinum in the center of his chest. Instead, he held up his beer and said, "Not now, man. Let's eat, drink, and be merry!" He smiled back at the girl in the bikini top and gym shorts as he patted Platinum on the shoulder. "We'll do that another time."

This left Scotland near the boombox, inches from the girl in the bikini top and shorts. A Fleetwood Mac song played loud, but mellow. There was no mistaking Stevie Nicks. A group of three girls stood off to the side near the boombox and danced like cattails around a pond. Scotland didn't know what this girl's story was, and finding out was all that mattered to him.

Up close, Scotland could tell that she wasn't as young as he was, but it didn't matter if she was near thirty.

She danced where she stood. Scotland checked out another girl, but turned back to the one in front of him and watched her hips sway. "Hey," he said. "I'm Scotland."

"Amber," she said as she continued to dance. Sometimes when a chick didn't question his name it meant she wasn't interested. Amber's hips wiggled and her knees bent as she danced, while her feet and hands stayed where they were. She smiled at him. "I don't think I've seen you around here before."

"I just moved in last week. You work for Kinsey?"

She raised her hands over her head in her dance. "Don't we all?"

The sun warmed the back of Scotland's neck and shoulders. The roundness of Amber's cleavage in her bikini top warmed him everywhere else. Her face was tan and pretty, but she was no girl. She was a woman and Scotland couldn't look away.

"I'm thirty-two," she said.

"What?"

"You're staring. Most people stare when they're trying to figure out how old I am."

"I wasn't."

"You're a bad liar."

"You're a gorgeous thirty-two."

"That sounded honest."

Scotland didn't dance along, but he wanted to keep the conversation going. "What do you do for Kinsey?"

"I manage the personnel office at his property management company."

"That sounds like a pretty big deal."

"Not really." Amber stopped dancing. "I've just known

him a long time. He was nice enough to give me a job and I worked my way up."

"From what?"

"I met him when I was a dancer at the Tanga."

Scotland had seen a good number of strippers in his Navy days, but he'd never actually had a conversation in a different setting with one, current or former. She had the muscle tone of a girl who still stripped, on stage or elsewhere.

"So you and him..."

"Yeah. Sure. For a little while." She stood with her hands on her hips and shook hair away from her face. "We're just friends now. Plus, he's my boss." She looked across the pool. "You know, like everyone here."

Scotland didn't trust that. No matter how long ago Kinsey and Amber had their romance, there was no way Kinsey would be happy about Scotland being with her. Scotland turned around, shifted his attention from her to the other girls who were drinking and dancing and laughing. So many to choose from, but he was drawn to none of them the way he was to Amber.

Platinum walked up, ignored Amber and said to Scotland, "This party is lame. Let's spar or something."

Scotland waved. "Not now, man. Later."

"Come on," Platinum said. "You'll forget what I've taught you if you go all weekend without practicing."

There was nothing to be gained by tangling with Platinum there, but that sonofabitch didn't know when to quit. "Not now, man. This is a party. People have food and shit."

"Don't worry, Scottish. I won't make you look too bad in front of your lady friend."

Scotland looked toward Amber, and though she tried to hide the smile on her face, he could tell she wasn't interested in an exhibition bout. "It's not the time or place," he said.

"Come on, man."

"Why don't you talk to one of these pretty girls and see if

any of them will let you try out holds on them."

Platinum looked at Kinsey and Maria as they danced near the diving board. He stared in their direction for a long moment before looking back to Scotland. When he did, his face was clenched. The hoods of his eyes rolled forward like awnings that cast his nose and mouth in shadow. It was some sort of hurt or longing. And, in that instant, Scotland added the pieces together. It made sense that the boss's girl would cheat on him with his best looking employee. Scotland had no proof beyond gut instinct, but it didn't matter. It didn't involve him and he intended to keep it that way.

Platinum leaned forward and sat his beer bottle on the ground. As he came up, he said, "I'm telling you, you'll forget if you don't practice."

Scotland patted him on the shoulder. "Tomorrow, I promise." Scotland turned to face Amber.

"This is Kan-set-su," Platinum called out, and before Scotland could react, Platinum had Scotland's arm bent backward.

Red strobe lights filled Scotland's head as the pain in his arm surprised him.

"See how your joint is locked? Your arm is in the wrong position to muster any kind of strength. The arm is in danger of breaking at the elbow. You're in pain and fear is eating all your courage."

Scotland couldn't deny the pain, but the bit about the courage was wrong. He held up his beer to show respect for the beverage, but also to reach it toward Amber. "Hold this for me," he said, his voice thin in his throat more from the lean he had to make than from the pain in his outstretched arm.

Platinum held Scotland's arm in position. It was different than the hold he'd used on Scotland the night they busted into his place. The pain was similarly intense and sharp as if he'd had his elbow nailed to a board, and within seconds his right hand went numb, but his left hand was free and his feet weren't blocked from moving. He wanted to call a stop to this bullshit. This was a party, not a fucking gladiator ring. Getting out of this quietly wasn't an option though, because Platinum was an asshole and Amber was watching. He couldn't call it off, and he couldn't move his right arm. There was no pride in losing this way, so Scotland shot his legs out behind him. As he sprawled, he wrapped his left arm around Platinum's shin and yanked. Blood flowed in Scotland's mouth from where he'd bitten his tongue in the process.

Using his weight and his left hand, he maneuvered himself over Platinum. It was a high school wrestling move that came back to him as naturally as tying his shoes, even with the dead arm. The urge to bounce Platinum's head repeatedly onto the river rock pool deck faded as his right arm got some feeling back. A party like this wasn't the place for violence. Instead, Scotland tightened his grip on Platinum and sat back on his heels as he'd done on the mat in wrestling matches to watch the clock tick down the final seconds. The music had stopped and everyone stood around them, watching.

Kinsey applauded from atop the diving board. "That's enough," he hollered, and signaled to the Kula brothers with a snap of his fingers. The brothers put down their plates, walked over, pulled Scotland off Platinum and helped Platinum to his feet. Platinum's face was red and his hair was messed up for the first time Scotland had seen. He was breathing hard and his face was screwed up like he wanted to yell or cry. He paced around, looking at the crowd, and started to say something to Scotland. Maria walked up next to Kinsey. Platinum's demeanor changed. He exhaled and his face unclenched to where he looked like himself again, except for the messed up hair.

"Just a demonstration," Scotland said, his throat so raw he could barely get the words out with an even tone. "No problem. It's cool."

Platinum didn't say anything, just stood there as the Kula brothers walked back to the meat cooking on the grill. He walked off without looking back at Scotland, and made his way to the ice chest of beer.

The music started up again, but the party vibe didn't return with it. Perhaps the display scared them all or made them want to fight too. Scotland wasn't sure. He'd won the little contest, but it didn't feel like a victory.

He looked over to Amber. She offered his beer bottle, which he accepted back from her. "Thanks," he said.

"You're so fast. So strong." She ran her hand over Scotland's triceps and he realized for the first time how sore it was from where Platinum had his arm bent back.

He watched Platinum drink a beer by himself. If he'd been too drunk to talk to women before he was sober now, but maybe too shamed. "Wait here," he said to Amber. "I'll be right back with a couple fresh ones for us."

"Sounds good," she said.

He walked around the pool and clapped Platinum on the shoulder. "That was fun, man. It would have looked better if we weren't both so drunk." Scotland hadn't downed more than one beer so far. He didn't know how many Platinum had, but he was happy for the advantage. That wiry bastard had gone harder than necessary.

"That wasn't the escape move I taught you."

"Got to admit it was effective, though."

"If that was a real situation, I would have snapped your arm like a twig and you wouldn't have done anything but cry for your mama."

"Look," Scotland said. "I came over here to make sure you were okay. If you're going to be a dickhead, I'll just see you later." He grabbed two bottles of Michelob from the cooler.

Platinum blocked his way. "You may have won this round, but just wait."

"First of all, I told you I didn't want to fuck around with

that at this party, but you kept on. Second, I didn't win shit. We're on the same team, you fucking pud." His words stunned Platinum for a split second and Scotland slipped past. Before walking away, he said, "But speaking of waiting, you might want to leave Maria alone. Kinsey isn't stupid."

Platinum reared back with his fist only to drop it at his side. "Listen, new guy, I don't know what you're talking about. And neither do you." Platinum's volume drew attention. He quieted himself, spoke through clenched teeth. "You never want to say anything like that ever again."

There was no way to know what people had heard, but Scotland shut down the conversation. "Okay, man. Forget it." Scotland didn't put the odds too high that he'd guessed wrong. He was convinced Platinum had a thing with Maria. "And you might want to talk to some of these girls before they start leaving," he said. "If you don't, he'll probably have to assume you're either banging his woman or you're some kind of a homo."

Scotland walked back to Amber.

She hadn't moved from her spot, except to dance in place. "Let's go back to my place and get high," she said.

Scotland loved the sound of that, but he wasn't willing to risk getting hit with a piss test the next time he checked in with Dave. But if he said no, he'd lose her to some other guy who would be more than willing to go with her. Scotland smiled at her as the movement of a topless girl caught his eye as she opened the door to enter the ground floor office area. The open door reminded Scotland that, for once in his life, he had a nice place to bring a woman home to. "Instead," he said, "why don't we go to my place and get down?"

They were together every night for the next two weeks, staying at either's apartment. Hers was on the ground floor and she had a waterbed where they repeatedly exhausted each other.

Scotland used the quiet time of her sleeping to let himself into the Gulf Breeze office again with his folding knife, but this time, he didn't hesitate to go up the stairs to Kinsey's door. He didn't know if there was something incriminating up there, but he couldn't shake the curiosity.

No light shined from the gap at the bottom of the door, but he rested his ear on the surface in case there was something to hear on the other side. He checked the knob and found it unlocked. He folded the knife and stuck it in his back pocket.

As he swung the door open, Scotland tried to figure out why he was there instead of nestled up to Amber in bed.

Inside Kinsey's office, Scotland felt the sensation of cold air flowing down his neck. It spooked him for a minute until his brain registered the AC vent in the ceiling. He wished he had a flashlight because he couldn't risk turning on the overhead lights. Instead, he clicked on a lamp on the credenza behind Kinsey's desk. The beam of light illuminated the map on the wall—the green and blue pins in scattered clumps. As he walked around the desk, he remembered the first time he'd been there, the nerves he'd barely contained as he stepped up to the poker table that he hadn't seen since.

Scotland opened the wide desk drawer just below the desktop. He didn't know what to expect, but he didn't expect it to be empty. That struck him as odd. No notes on the desk, and nothing in the drawer. He checked the drawers to his left. All empty. He checked the small drawer to his right, but it also was empty. Scotland opened the deep and final drawer. This also held no secrets or incriminating evidence, but rather an elaborate shoeshine kit. The work of shining shoes was familiar to Scotland from his days in boot camp and in The Castle, but he couldn't imagine Kinsey spitting and rubbing and buffing and edge-dressing his own shoes.

Scotland got up and walked to the bar. Popped the top to the bourbon and took a healthy swallow right from the bottle. Kinsey didn't keep incriminating evidence in his desk. That was for the guys on salary downstairs. The number crunchers and schedule planners. At Tampa Beef & Bird, he must have a whole floor of his office building dedicated to accountants. Here he had that New Jersey transplant, Ronald, keeping track of everything.

Scotland checked beneath the couch cushions, then moved all the pictures on the walls looking for a hidden safe, but there was nothing. The place was clean. For all Scotland knew, Kinsey kept it that way so he could deny involvement in any illegal activity. If anything, he was even more interested to find out what or who E.J. was. Scotland replaced the cap on the bourbon bottle and took the stairs back down to the desk that held the leather-bound ledger.

He wasn't surprised to see a new entry in the same amount.

CHAPTER THIRTEEN

On Thanksgiving, Kinsey stretched out on the sofa in the living room of his family home. He'd been born in that room thirty-eight years earlier, and now his own son, nine-year-old Stevie, sat on the floor with his back against the sofa, his head as close to his father as possible.

The television showed the football game in color. The Bears and Lions. The Lions had beaten his Buccaneers the previous Sunday, and Kinsey resented that his team's season was already a bust. They had twice as many losses as wins. Technically, there'd been a tie, but Kinsey viewed a tie as a loss because it wasn't a win.

Stevie faced the television. He wore brown dress pants, a yellow oxford shirt, and his father's class ring on his thumb though it was still many sizes too big. When they were together, Stevie almost always asked to wear the ring. Kinsey couldn't resist.

The ring reminded him of being a sprinter on the track team. Of starting a band called Millionaire Sportcoat with fraternity brothers, in which the young Allan Kinsey played an adequate bass. His father had made him quit the band when he graduated and put him to work at the cattle ranch office. The reward for having shoveled shit every summer since he was old enough to avoid stepping in the manure was conscription into the front offices.

Kinsey looked at his son and ruffled the blond hair on his head. If he wanted to play in a band someday, he could do so without ever having to worry about cows or cow shit.

Stevie looked back at his father after each play. The ring spun on his thumb with every movement. Kinsey again ruffled the boy's hair.

Kinsey wasn't schooled in the art of relaxing, but he had one definition of feeling like a whole person and this was it. One of the rare moments Kinsey was off the clock, able to relax and enjoy the holiday with his family. His son was what all that other shit was about. Kinsey wanted to leave his son more than just a cow pasture and a meat plant. He wanted to offer his son everything he could ever dream of.

Kinsey crossed his legs at the ankles. The smells from the kitchen weaved into every Thanksgiving meal he'd eaten since childhood. The memories permeated the walls, the windows overlooking the formal gardens outside, the curtains, furniture, inch-thick area rugs, and the wide-plank oak floors. The woman doing the cooking had been his nanny from the time he could walk. She was his surrogate mother, and her own daughter was the housekeeper. Together they prepared a meal with plenty extra to take home to their own families at the end of the day.

Kinsey turned his attention to the television. The game interested him even though his Bucs weren't playing and despite not having money on the line. The score was tied.

"If nobody scores they tie, right?" Stevie said.

Kinsey looked at his son. Saw the innocence in his eyes. "You're forgetting about overtime. If no one scores, they'll go to overtime."

With his eyes still wide and his face in a grin, he said, "If nobody scores still, then it's a tie?"

Kinsey patted the boy's shoulder. "I suppose it would be. Yes. But I hope not."

"That's good if they tie," Stevie said. "No one loses."

Kinsey sat up and motioned for his son to join him on the couch.

The boy hopped onto the couch and scooted back until his legs were unable to touch the floor.

"Let's get something straight before you get another minute older." He situated the boy so they were facing each other. It took Kinsey a moment to distill it down to language a child would understand. "Now listen, Stevie, a tie is a loss because it isn't a win. Do you understand? If you don't win, you lose."

Stevie looked up at his father, all sweetness and optimism, but Kinsey was sure he saw the knowledge register in the boy's face.

Kinsey sat back and pulled Stevie along with him. He leaned his chin on the boy's head. His blond hair was overdue to be cut. His mother liked it long like that, but if it were up to Kinsey he'd take the boy to a proper barber. He wouldn't give the kid a flattop like the one he wore growing up, but he'd get it off the collar and over his ears at least.

The living room drapes were shut now, but a beam of light stabbed through to shine a sliver onto the couch and television.

He faced the mantel where his father had propped an elbow as he stood reading the evening paper every night after dinner. The old man believed that he sat enough in the course of a day and that he didn't need to do it in the hours before he went to bed.

Kinsey's wife, Christine, walked into the room, her high heels on the wood floor announcing her approach and arrival before they were silenced by thick Persian rugs. She was a thin and feminine figure, in an orange dress and pearls. Their fifteen years of marriage and the two children she'd carried had done nothing to diminish that in her. "Dinner will be served in half an hour," she said. "How does that sound, gentlemen footballers?"

"I'm hungry," Stevie said. He sat up quickly, a hungry child distracted from the life lessons his father shared by the food his mother promised.

"But the game's not over yet," Kinsey said.

"I know, Allan, and I'm sorry." She patted Stevie's head. "Bertie put the turkey in the oven an hour sooner than I planned. I just found out. I'm not at all pleased. She's apologized, but we'll have to eat an hour earlier than planned."

Kinsey reached for her hand, to pull her to him, but she stepped back.

"I cannot put dry turkey in my mouth or I will die," she said. "And if I can't have turkey on Thanksgiving Day, I'd just as soon be dead."

This was the first year her parents weren't making the trip from Gainesville. Kinsey wasn't sure why, exactly. The first excuse was that their dog wasn't doing well and they didn't want to leave him. The next thing he knew, Christine had reported they wouldn't make it because their car wasn't running so good and they wanted to have it looked at before they took a long drive. Both seemed reasonable to Kinsey, and he didn't give a shit if they were there or not anyway. His in-law's presence wouldn't alter his plans to watch football with Stevie, eat until he felt he would burst, then sleep it off for a while in front of more football or the news or whatever the networks ran.

"Go wash up and put your tie on," she said to Stevie.

Kinsey pulled his son to him with a tug on his shoulders. The boy was thin and light just as Kinsey had been. Just as they both would always remain. "I'll send him up as soon as there's a commercial," Kinsey said. "I don't want him to miss any of the action."

"Well, no one likes cold turkey and hot cranberry sauce. And the girls have worked hard on our meal. We don't want to seem ungrateful on such a day as this."

Stevie mumbled from the confines of his father's bear hug, "Yes, ma'am."

Kinsey loved these rare, unguarded moments. Time with his family had been so brief the past couple years. "Where's Caroline?" Kinsey asked his wife about their daughter, the older of his two children.

"She's on the telephone."

"Seventh grade girls plotting the future of mankind, no doubt."

The doorbell chimed with a series of bings and bongs like a town square clock tower. A few moments later, the house-keeper appeared in the living room doorway. "Pardon me, Mr. Kinsey, but there's a man to see you, sir."

Kinsey looked down at his son. "What could be more important than what I have in this room at this moment?" He reached out and touched his wife's cheek. "I'll not be receiving any visitors today, Alice. Have him call me at the office tomorrow."

"He said it was urgent, sir."

Kinsey looked at his wife. "Urgent? On a day such as this?"

"He looks real troubled, sir."

Christine asked, "Is he waiting in the foyer?"

"I asked him to wait outside, sir. I hope that's okay."

"It's fine," Kinsey said. "Did he mention his name?"

"Mr. Joyner, sir."

"Joyner?" Kinsey released his son and slid his feet into his house shoes.

"Who's that dear?"

Kinsey couldn't divulge that information to his wife, in front of his son, no less. He stood, hands on his hips. He had no lie at the ready. Instead, he said, "I'm not sure, dear. I'd better go remify this intrusion."

"Well, do be quick. Dinner will be served soon."

"I know."

"And would you bring a bottle of Beaujolais to the table on your way back?"

"It's a holiday, dear," he said on his way out of the living room. "I'll bring two."

Kinsey's front door stood roughly the same dimensions as an upturned pool table. There was a latch chest high and he swung open the door.

The air was crisp. Beyond the potted palms flanking the doorway, Eddie Joyner stood limp on the front porch. Kinsey didn't know for sure, but he assumed Eddie had just come back from the track, probably had a racing form tucked in his back pocket. Probably had a thousand dollars on the football game. That habit had cost this poor bastard everything. He had the downturned mouth of a man whose wife had packed up the kids and moved back with her mother in Ohio.

Eddie wore blue slacks and a pullover shirt with a limp collar and terrycloth stripes at the shoulders. To look at him, no one would guess that he hauled in a director's salary at a state agency. "I'm sorry to bother you at home, Allan, but this can't wait."

Kinsey wanted to rip a spindle out of the porch railing and swing at him like it was batting practice. In another place, he probably would've, but this was his home. He couldn't bring that shit here. Through a smile, Kinsey said, "I can't say that I'm pleased by this surprise, Eddie."

There was no way to know if neighbors were watching. The closest house was a hundred yards away, and no one would remember a friendly visit at his doorstep. And none of them would hear him if he kept his voice down. Kinsey clenched down on his molars and shook Eddie's hand.

"I wanted to tell you face-to-face, Allan."

Kinsey stopped shaking hands and said, "You're burning through the money I'm giving you too fast, Eddie."

Eddie exhaled with his shoulders rounding forward. "It's not the money. Jesus, Allan. It hasn't been about the money for a while now."

Kinsey pulled the door shut behind him. "Then why would you come to my home on a holiday?"

"I'm done, Allen."

"Done?" Kinsey walked Eddie away from the door to the other end of the porch. "Eddie, my friend, there's no reason to do anything hasty here now is there?" Kinsey guided Eddie toward the railing. "Last I heard, you were pleased with the increase."

"I was," Eddie said, leaning his palms on the rail, as if for support. "I think. I don't know. I'm all muddled in my noggin these days. But what I do know is that I can't do this anymore."

Kinsey could have Eddie hidden in the safe room at the Gulf Breeze if they'd met there. But they didn't. It happened here at his home. On Thanksgiving Day.

Eddie walked to the porch swing. He only caught the edge of the seat and the swing took him back as he sat.

A flash of excitement surged through Kinsey, a shot of hope that he'd fall, maybe hit his head. This was dashed as Eddie balanced himself and took a seat.

"That was close," he said.

Kinsey turned to the yard and noticed the summer tanagers, ruby-throated hummingbirds and eagles down from the cold air off the Chesapeake looking for warmer climates to build nests and start their families. A pair of eagles had begun a nest in a tall pine near his garage. This happened almost every fall. Some years no young were produced. This year, Kinsey couldn't help but hope to see a pair rise up out of the nest and add to the population. But more abundant and guaranteed were the return of red-shouldered hawks perched atop telephone poles watching the ground for witless lizards and snakes.

This was Kinsey's favorite weather—the kind he liked to run in. He could run in weather like this forever. He could ride a motorcycle in weather like this even longer. Kinsey leaned against the railing, crossed his ankles. "Are you taking heat from the Governor?"

"I did," Eddie said. "But I've handled that."

The landscaper had missed a clump of grass clippings near the apex of the circular driveway. Kinsey focused on that for a moment. The grass was once alive and purposeful, but now it was dead, useless, and unsightly. He would have Christine call them out to address this oversight.

Kinsey looked back toward the neighbor's house a hundred yards away, reminded himself that he was visible even here on his own property. Through clenched teeth, he said, "Then why couldn't this wait?"

Eddie tugged at the cushion fabric under his legs. "I haven't slept much lately. I feel like I've been run over and somebody poured battery acid in the wounds."

"You feel like it's eating you alive."

"Exactly. It keeps me up at night."

Eddie was one of the scholarship students who somehow made it into Kinsey's fraternity at the University of Florida. As with even the most tenuous connection, Kinsey had exploited that to get in close with Eddie and then get him indebted.

"You're in the wildlife business, Eddie. You must be familiar with the swamps down around these parts. Aren't you?"

"I grew up near the Everglades," Eddie said. "Wrote an article for *National Geographic* about the wetlands."

"You ever hear of the gator trappers who lost their arms to gators?"

"I've heard of many."

"The first of the ones I'm talking about bled to death while yelling at the gator for taking his arm. The second guy got the hell out of there and found a hospital as fast as he could. He's doing fine. Got a real nice prophylactic. You can't hardly tell." Kinsey reached out and took hold of Eddie's arm. It was thin and trembling. "Pretend this is a fake arm, Eddie. And be glad you're alive."

Eddie looked down at his arm, shook his head.

"And better than a fake arm, Eddie, you're getting cash. Good cash."

As soon as Kinsey said it, he regretted spoon-feeding him such a statement. There was only one way out of it. "And," he said, "I'll tell you what. Since you're doing such a tremensdous job, I'm going to increase your payment by an extra thousand a week. How does that sound?"

Eddie didn't take the bait. He kept his eyes downward.

"Come now, Eddie. That has to be more than you make in a week. And that's on top of your usual payment."

"No matter how much you give me, I'll just have to shell it out to support my ex-wife. It's the only way to keep her quiet."

Kinsey sat on the bench to the left of the door. "Eddie, Eddie, Eddie. You told your wife?"

"She overheard me talking to you back in the beginning, on the phone." He looked over his shoulder and lowered his voice. "She was upstairs and I never heard her pick up the extension."

Kinsey remembered the call. He should have had that conversation face-to-face, but he'd been anxious. Kinsey stood, walked over, and sat next to Eddie. "Now look, old pal," he said. "It always seems coldest before the dawn. There's no need to panic. She can't prove anything. Even if she could, she wouldn't cut her nose beside her face. It'll all work out. Just wait and see."

Eddie pulled at his shirt collar as if to take pressure off his throat. "I almost don't care if she goes to my boss or the cops. This has been eating at me for too long already. I'm going to burn in hell." He sobbed into his hands.

Kinsey elbowed Eddie in the chest. The solid contact was satisfying to Kinsey who wanted to roundly beat this bastard. "Get a hold of yourself!" he said through clenched teeth. "Goddamnit, man. Get yourself together."

Eddie sat back and rubbed his hand over his chin and cheeks. "My house was almost as nice as this."

"There's nothing to be ashamed of, Eddie. I think this is all just a misinterpretation of perspective."

"Don't try to polish a turd for me, Allan."

"Let me tell you something, Scooter," Kinsey said, breaking out the old college nickname in an attempt to make him feel the connection that went back a couple decades.

Eddie's face froze in time for a second or two.

Kinsey said, "You know way more about the reproduction process of fish than I do, but as we speak those fucking grouper are multiplying. When you lift the ban, the fishermen will be so busy hauling money hand over fist they'll forget all about this blip in history."

"If they find out, they'll lynch me."

"No one needs to know anything. Look, you've done a good job burying this thing with bureaucracy."

"But my name's on it. They'll know."

"And you're the expert, aren't you?"

"Somebody could do their own study and prove me wrong."

"Experts disagree all the time."

"But it's a lie."

"Well, now you're just being childish."

"I can't do it anymore, Allan." He sobbed quietly again. His face contorted until he couldn't keep the emotion bottled up and he let out a cry as if he were in real pain. Kinsey hadn't heard a grown man cry before and he wanted to run inside and slam the door.

"Stop it."

Eddie dried his face with his handkerchief and blew his nose.

As they sat there a moment, in silence, Kinsey's wife opened the door and her shocked face meant she didn't expect to see them out there. "I thought I heard voices out here," she said. "Allan, I thought you were getting the wine. I didn't realize we still had a guest."

"This is Eddie Joyner. He's an old college friend." Kinsey looked at the ring on Eddie's finger. It was identical to the one on Stevie's thumb at this moment.

Eddie used to be worthy of the ring. Now, Kinsey wanted to rip it off his finger.

Christine leaned a hip on one of the potted trees beside the door. "Shall I set another place at the table, Edward?"

"Unfortunately," Kinsey said, "Edward can't stay. He's on his way to a big spread at his in-law's place."

"That's too bad." To Kinsey, she said, "I'll get the wine. Will you be ready in ten minutes?"

"I'll be there in five."

"Excellent. Goodbye, Edward. It was nice meeting you."

Eddie spoke up. "Nice meeting you, ma'am."

Once Christine was back inside, the idea of having Eddie stay seemed worth considering. Eddie was too loose a cannon to be set free to do God knows what. The devastation was written all over him. He'd lost everything he'd worked to get: the wife, the kids, the house, the life. Now all he had was work and a dump in Apollo Beach. But still, Kinsey didn't feel bad for him. He brought on all that misfortune and drama himself. He was weak-willed. Given every advantage in life, but too self-absorbed to say no when he needed to most. The dumb bastard. Fuck him, and the horse he rode in on. Kinsey wanted to tell him exactly that, but he still needed Eddie to keep the fishing ban going.

Kinsey was reminded of the conversation with his father that day he was ejected from the baseball game for arguing with the umpire. The lesson about catching more flies with honey than vinegar.

Eddie Joyner was not completely unlike Kinsey. They stood even—height wise—and aside from Eddie's beer gut they weighed about the same. Kinsey liked to think he hadn't changed all that much since college, but Eddie had aged as if he'd been left out in the rain.

"Do you realize," Kinsey said, "that I haven't seen you since we made our little deal."

"You keep sending your pissants to deliver the money."

"Now, Eddie. I made it clear right up front it would be a good idea if we kept our distance."

"You were never really a good friend anyway."

"That hurts my feelings, Eddie." Kinsey held out his hand. Though it had been months since he'd seen him, and he didn't really care if he'd ever see him again, it was imperative that Kinsey kept Eddie close and placated for now. As they shook hands, Kinsey said, "But you're right. I've let myself get so busy I haven't taken any time to socialize with my friends. But you know what, Eddie? We're eating early. Why don't you join us?"

Eddie seemed stunned for a moment. He didn't speak right away and he stared up at Kinsey like a kid at the gate of an amusement park.

"Sure," Kinsey said. "That'll give us some time to catch up."

"It's not that simple, Allan."

"Nonsense," Kinsey said, opening the door and guiding Eddie through. "There's not a problem in the world that don't seem smaller when your belly's full."

Inside, Kinsey hollered, "Christine, Eddie will join us after all."

"Wonderful," she said as she stepped from the dining

room into the foyer. Nodded toward Eddie. "Any friend of Allan's..."

Eddie brightened when he saw the table decked out with casserole dishes of mashed potatoes, cornbread stuffing, green beans, and cranberry sauce. The kitchen help disappeared back into the kitchen to tend to the hot oven and dirty pans. Stevie sat with his elbows on the table, and Christine waved her hand in a gesture of sweeping the boy back to sit up straight. He complied.

"Well now," Eddie said, "this is quite a festive table. Everything smells delicious." He walked over to Christine and asked, "You're sure this isn't an imposition?"

"Oh, Lord no. We are happy to have you, Mr. Joyner."

"My friends call me Eddie."

"Please take a seat at Allan's right. You are our guest of honor."

Stone crab claw appetizers preceded dinner. Eddie was as Florida-bred as was Kinsey and he dunked his cold claw meat into the mayonnaise-mustard sauce.

During a struggle with a crab claw, Kinsey's ring flew off Stevie's finger as he plucked away. It landed silently on Eddie's lap.

"Allan, I presume one of these is yours." He'd slipped the wayward ring on his bare ring finger so he had a matched set.

"Oh," Christine said, "you fraternity boys."

Kinsey took the ring, and the cue to speak up and tell his side of the story to prevent Eddie from telling his. "S.A.E. The best years of our lives, right buddy?"

Eddie nodded. "The best."

The turkey sat on a silver tray the younger maid, Clara, delivered to the head of the table as ceremoniously as she could with that limp of hers. She walked slowly under the weight of the platter and the bird. She was a thin girl of twenty and Kinsey liked her well enough. She wore her blue uniform dress with a white apron tied around her waist. She bowed as she backed away from the table.

Kinsey wiped his fingers on the napkin on his lap and picked up a knife. The practical and prudent course of action was to treat Eddie as a welcomed guest, but he'd just as soon carve up Eddie as the bird. "Eddie," Kinsey said, "Stevie is in for one drumstick. Would you like the other?"

Eddie held a wine glass to his lips and said, "I'll leave that for you fine people to decide."

Kinsey carved the bird with precision passed down from his father. It was a skill he looked forward to teaching Stevie in a couple years. He should be beside his father now, watching him carve, but the kids had been trained to behave properly when they had company. Kinsey wouldn't undermine the years of training. His distraction over the issue caused Kinsey to cut an uneven slice of turkey and embarrassment flushed through him. All eyes were on him. "I'll take this damaged slice." He put it on his plate and focused himself to slice more accurately.

The knife and fork in his hands had come from the breakfront behind him. They'd been handmade and polished by a blacksmith in Desoto County at the turn of the century and were longer and sharper than store-bought versions. They'd been passed down to him, and he would pass them on to Stevie someday. Kinsey would gladly pass along all the old stuff to his son. He looked at his son, who had been watching him carve. There'd be no limits to what the child could become with the head start Kinsey was burning both ends of his candle to provide.

Kinsey tucked away his anger at and resentment of Eddie. He hated the sour taste brought on by bottling up his reactions, but he winked at Stevie, who waved back with a lifting of his huge drumstick.

As a way to inject a new energy into the air, Kinsey said, "Hey, Stevie, why did they let the turkey join the band?"

"Why?"

Kinsey put down his fork and leaned in. "Because he had the drum sticks."

Eddie seemed to laugh harder than Stevie, but that was fine with Kinsey. The tension had been lifted and Kinsey sat back and noticed smiles all around the table.

The dinner was cooked to perfection, but despite his best acting performance, every bite tasted like paste in Kinsey's mouth. His job wasn't to enjoy his meal, and he was no longer just the loving father and husband he wanted to spend the holiday being. Instead, he took his bites while staring into the face of a degenerate like Eddie Joyner, who didn't even have the decency to keep his mouth shut when he chewed. He didn't belong at that table. Eddie Joyner was a man who was supposed to take orders from Kinsey, not break holiday bread with the Kinsey family.

While taking a forkful of turkey, Kinsey seriously doubted his ability to keep the nice act going. A few moments later, Clara said, "It's my pleasure," in response to Eddie's loud, "Thank you!" after being served a second helping of green bean casserole. She'd smiled as she said it, but Kinsey didn't believe for a minute that she felt that way. At best it was acceptance or possibly indifference, but it couldn't have been pleasure. Regardless, Eddie Joyner smiled big. He was simple in Kinsey's eyes. He didn't have to thank her at all. She was doing her job. And Clara could have been less enthusiastic in reply, but everybody fared better when they smiled. This was a reminder to Kinsey. He understood that campaigning would require a gift of patience equal to or greater than Clara's.

"This is without a doubt the best cornbread stuffing I've ever had," he said, showing a mouthful.

"Why, thank you, Eddie." Christine smiled as if she were genuinely pleased. "It's an old Kinsey family recipe."

After dinner, Eddie raised the remainder of his wine and proposed a toast.

"I'd like to thank the incomparable Christine Kinsey for

welcoming me into your home and sharing this holiday with me. And I'd like to say, Godspeed, Allan.

Kinsey shrugged and nodded toward his glass as a way of telling everyone to drink.

After the dinner dishes were cleared, Eddie ate a slice each of pumpkin and apple pie, both a la mode, and drank three cups of coffee. After that he insisted on personally thanking the girls in the kitchen with praise and hugs. He returned from the kitchen to compliment Christine on the fine presentation any man would be proud to call home and ruffled Stevie's hair, who recoiled but said nothing.

Kinsey led him to the study.

Inside, a mini-bar sat on the waist-high shelf of a book case that ran the length of the wall and included first editions by Faulkner, Fitzgerald, and Hemingway. Kinsey poured two highballs then flipped open the lid on a sturdy cedar humidor. "Cubans," Kinsey said. "Help yourself."

Eddie held his drink and picked a robusto out of the humidor. "Like we're best friends all of a sudden?"

Kinsey snipped the end of his cigar with cigar scissors. "We've always been friends, Eddie." He handed the scissors to him.

"We don't see each other socially." Eddie waved off the scissors and bit the cigar cap with his incisors.

Kinsey held a wooden match to his cigar, puffed and rotated. Between puffs, he said, "Mmmm. I do believe these cigars are rolled on the thighs of virgins."

"You never really talked to me in college, either."

"Fast flying hawks pass each other in the sky." Kinsey handed Eddie the matches. "You know that's true. And hawks like us aren't the kind to laze about on wires and the like. But that's behind us. We're here now and you've just celebrated a national holiday in our home. That brings us close. Makes us family."

Eddie had his cigar lit, a billow of smoke like a cloud over his head. A flame burned on the end of his cigar. He blew it out and waved at the smoke. "Part of the reason I agreed to falsify that information was to get in business with you somehow. I thought it would bring us closer together."

"You're smoking a Cuban cigar in my study, Eddie. I'd say your plan worked."

Eddie sat on a leather club chair and puffed his cigar.

Kinsey walked to the far side of the room and pulled open the door to a closet. From a chest-high shelf he pulled down a red Igloo cooler which he walked over and set on the desk.

Eddie didn't move.

Kinsey opened the lid. Instead of a six-pack and some ice, the entire compartment was filled with stacks of cash.

"What's that?" Eddie said.

"This is forty-two thousand dollars that I've been saving." Kinsey's voice didn't quiver and his heart rate didn't accelerate. He had an identical cooler, filled in the same way, under a blue tarp in the garage. "Consider this early payment for the month of December, and your bonus. You'll be getting the regular amount next month, as well."

Eddie exhaled. "I told you, I don't want any more money. I'm done."

Kinsey closed the lid and pushed the cooler to within arm's length in Eddie's direction. Kinsey didn't speak. He had the hook in Eddie's mouth.

Eddie shook his head and held his hands up. "It's just so wrong, you know?"

Kinsey opened the lid to flash the cash at Eddie "Take tomorrow off and go to the track instead. Play the matinee. Enjoy the long weekend."

Kinsey stared at Eddie, whose nose was red from all the wine they'd drunk.

"Let me off the hook here, Allan," he said. "Will you?"

Kinsey didn't reply right away and the air grew thick with Eddie's desperation. The joy Kinsey took from watching

Eddie fight the urge made up for the pleasure he lost during the meal. He kept quiet for a moment longer. Finally, they both smiled. A hurt look in Eddie's eyes made Kinsey realize Eddie didn't have the balls to turn himself in.

"It's too late," Eddie said. "I'm giving up that life."

"Okay. Sure. But I'll tell you what." Kinsey shoved the cooler closer to him. "Why don't you just hold onto this? If you decide to not treat yourself a little and tap into it over the weekend, just bring it back to me on Monday at my office and we'll get some lunch. Deal?"

CHAPTER FOURTEEN

On Tuesday morning, Scotland drove downtown. Like most December days in Tampa, there wasn't a cloud stuck in the sky to block the saturated kind of blue you find on old hatchbacks. The sun was still low in the East and the bank signs lining the street unanimously flashed: Temperature—70 degrees. But he was sweating. He slapped the steering wheel before wiping his forehead with the back of his hand. It was stupid to have let Amber talk him into taking a snootful of the primo shit she carried in a compact in her black leather purse.

Things had been going well. He lived in a place with three sizes of towels and no stains on the carpets and no burn marks on the countertops. He drove a car with power windows and air conditioning and a stereo loud enough to shake the windows. Getting laid every day was a huge bonus to this comfortable life, as was enjoying Amber's cocaine. It was in no way serious, the relationship nor the drug usage. It was all fine for the fun stuff, but she was not girlfriend material. Today, though, he wished he hadn't taken that bump.

He parked on Platt Street and walked past a bakery and a bar decorated for Christmas with evergreen garlands and wreaths outside and aerosol snow sprayed into the corners of the windows in a sad attempt to replicate some idyllic winter image.

There was enough clear glass in the windows for Scotland to catch his reflection. He wore one of the shirts Amber had bought him. It was a scratchy cotton-poly blend with long sleeves half an inch too short. Short enough for the fish tail to poke out at his wrist. He noticed for the first time how loose his clothes were on him. He hadn't been eating regularly, choosing, instead to party with Amber. And he hadn't been in spitting distance of a weight room for a couple months, though it seemed more like years.

Inside the county building, air conditioning chilled the back of Scotland's sweaty shirt. It stuck to his skin as he lurched toward Dave's office, as he'd done every Tuesday for the past eleven months. He tried to walk as slowly and casually as he always did, but he couldn't be sure if he pulled it off. When he got to Dave's office, he tried to slow his heart rate by taking deep breaths.

Dave didn't move when Scotland opened the door. He was slumped over his desk, his face on his arm like a pillow, his bulbous head still. The first thing that shot through Scotland's mind was that the poor bastard was suffering a nasty hangover. Scotland relaxed a little and the pressure in his chest unclenched to a medium grip. If Dave was hungover he'd be too wrapped up in his own after-effects to notice Scotland was in the middle of his burn. He wanted to move fast, get in and out before anyone suspected anything. He cleared his throat, but still Dave didn't move. "You okay, man?"

Scotland wondered if he might just be plain worn out from assembling the brand new girl's bicycle that rested on its kickstand in front of his desk. The bike had a sparkly banana seat in pink to match the frame, the hand grips and the streamers.

"What's the matter, buttercup?" Scotland said. "Are you upset Santa brought you this instead of a blue bicycle?"

Without moving, Dave said, "It's for my daughter."

"No shit. I was just fucking with you."

"Don't fuck with me today." Dave's voice was muffled as he spoke into his desktop. "Of all days."

"Why?" Scotland said, reaching over to pour himself a cup of coffee. "Who died?"

Without lifting his head, Dave pulled out that old copy of *Trouser Press* magazine with John Lennon on the cover. He pushed himself up, his head and chest rising off the desk. His eyes focused on the magazine. "Don't be so fucking crass." His suit was wrinkled, like he'd slept in it, but his face didn't look like he'd slept at all. He had dark circles under both eyes and his nose was red and puffy. And his hair was out of place. The look in his eye wasn't jovial like usual.

"What'd I say?" Scotland shrugged his shoulders. "I was just being a smartass. What's going on?"

"You haven't heard?"

"Heard what?"

Dave set the magazine down on the desk. He leaned in and rested his elbows on his knees. "You really don't know?"

"Know what, goddamn it?" Scotland sipped his coffee. "What's the big secret?"

"Where were you last night that you didn't hear the news?"

"I worked late and went straight home to bed." The truth was he'd been honeymooning with Amber and didn't bother to turn on the television all weekend. Monday had found him so exhausted that he fell asleep at four in the afternoon and slept through the night.

Dave slapped the top of his desk. "Well, he's dead. He's dead and you missed it."

At first, Scotland thought Dave was talking about Kinsey. But just as quickly, he pushed the thought away. Scotland's mind reeled through all the names he could think of, but none of them knew Dave. He tried to scroll through the names Dave had ever mentioned. He talked about his boss, but never by name. Any other chit-chat usually involved his family and they were all females. Finally, Scotland asked, "Who are we talking about here?"

"John Lennon!"

"John Lennon?" Almost every day of his life, Scotland had

heard that man's music in some form or another. Even the Armed Forces radio played his songs. Scotland had never been a fan, but he was surprised to hear about his death like this.

"He was one of a fucking kind," Dave said. "You wouldn't get it. There are no leaders in your generation."

Scotland didn't get it. Lennon's transformation from lad from Liverpool to world weary hippie just didn't impress him.

"Some bastard shot him. Last night." Dave wasn't in tears, but his face was red and clenched and his eyes were gooey like he had been crying at some point.

"I'm sorry," Scotland said. "I didn't know he meant so much to you."

"You have no idea."

Scotland didn't. He'd never even gotten this broken up about the loss of people he knew. He supposed he'd be pretty torn up if something happened to Dana or his nieces, but a stranger?

"He was the voice, man. He said everything we always wanted to say. You know? And he lived the life we all wanted to live. And he was gunned down by a freak with a fucking gun."

Scotland wanted to step back and disappear down the hall, but he couldn't be sure Dave would remember to log him in and make his check-in official.

"How could you not know? Don't you have a television in your apartment or a radio in your car?"

"I play records at home. Eight-tracks in the car."

"Any John Lennon songs?"

"I wish I could say yes here, Dave. I really do."

"You don't know what you're missing." Dave punched his desk. "I found out from Howard Cosell last night."

"They announced it during the football game?"

Dave held out his arms inviting, more like begging, Scotland for a hug.

Scotland took a step back. A flush of discomfort began in

his toes, evaporated through the pores on his scalp and left a taste like bus exhaust in his mouth. "Jeez, man." He held up his hands. "I'm not your fucking wet nurse."

Dave froze—didn't even blink. "You're right," he said. He dropped his arms by his side. "This is my work. I must do my job."

"I didn't mean to sound like a dick or nothing," Scotland said. "I'm just in a bit of a hurry today."

"Why?"

"Why am I in a hurry?" Scotland tried to buy some time. He didn't have anywhere to get to, he just wanted to get the hell out of there. He couldn't use work as an excuse because he'd told Dave he worked nights so he wouldn't be expected to answer the phone in the evenings while he was out doing jobs for Kinsey...or having drinks in a club with Platinum or Amber. He'd waited too long to answer. It felt like five minutes passed. "I got a brunch date," he said.

"Is that right? Maybe that accounts for the new boots, the fancy shirt. Where did you get that gold chain around your neck?"

The necklace, like the shirt, had been a gift from Amber. Well, not a gift so much as an encouraged purchase. She took him to the mall and told him what he should buy. Scotland had bought the stuff to impress her, but he liked some of it himself. He didn't hesitate to buy her a pair of jeans here or a new purse there. He didn't dare tell Dave that he was seeing a former stripper, or whatever she was, but he could be honest enough to shut him up and move this along. "This girl I've been seeing bought it for me."

"She did, did she?" Dave coughed out two muted laughs and his face relaxed from the force. "How long have you been seeing her?"

Scotland had never done the math, hadn't given it any consideration at all. "A month or two, I guess."

"Where did you meet?"

"What difference does it make," Scotland said. He rubbed his nose with the back of his hand.

"I'm just curious."

"We met at the pool of that new apartment complex I moved into. She was in a bikini and she's hot. Okay? I'm guilty."

Dave shrugged and said, "If she's buying *you* jewelry, you must be doing something right."

Scotland didn't want to get into it. Even mentioning the apartment complex to Dave felt wrong. He didn't want to give up any more information about that private part of his life and he didn't want to spend more time in front of Dave than he had to because his nose itched and it felt like it might be bleeding again. "But talking about jewelry on such a sad day seems too crass," he said, using Dave's word against him.

"Ahhhhh. Don't remind me. I enjoyed forgetting for a minute." Dave bridged his knees with his forearms and rested his head there. "Oh, damn. Damn. Damn."

With the focus shifted, Scotland felt his ribs relax a little and he got a deeper breath. The downside was that Dave wasn't taking care of business so Scotland could get on with his. Scotland said, "The only way to face adversity is to suck it up and soldier on."

"I work with criminals every day of my life." Dave sat back to a slumped position in his chair. "I just can't believe I live in a world where a guy like that can be gunned down in the street."

The amazement in Dave's eyes is what struck Scotland the most. It was a viscous stare, at once disbelieving and mesmerized. His chin wavered and his lips curled to stifle a whimper. Scotland looked toward the file cabinet to give Dave what privacy he could.

"You're lucky you weren't into him. You'll never know this pain."

Scotland turned back in time to see Dave's face buckle. He

sobbed openly for a moment before pulling out his handkerchief. He swiped his face, blew his nose. "Ahh, goddammit," he said. "Enough." He pulled himself upright and tightened the knot on is tie. "Get yourself together, Dave," he said.

Scotland just wanted to get his pay stub logged so he could make this visit official. He wasn't sure Dave, if left unattended, was up to the task. He unfolded his pay stub from Tampa Beef and Bird.

Part of Dave's job was to photocopy the paystub and type up a form in triplicate to make this visit official. The way he sat in his chair today, all dejected like he'd just lost a cross country foot race, told Scotland the man was incapable of doing anything quickly, if at all, that day.

"Where's the Xerox machine? I'll go make the copies."

"Not necessary." Dave looked up. "This is my job. I'll get it together. You can go now."

Scotland wiped his nose, just in case there was residue left there. "You sure?"

"If it was anyone else," he said, "I might be embarrassed."

Scotland shrugged. "You mean him or me?"

"Him, you knucklehead."

The week before Christmas, Scotland found himself in Kinsey's office standing beside Platinum for a meeting. Rumor had it that Kinsey would dish out new assignments and Scotland was up for a little excitement.

Kinsey threw darts at a dartboard mounted on the wall beside his desk. Scotland didn't recall seeing it there before and assumed it was new. "On Wednesday night," Kinsey said, "I want you boys to go pay our friend a visit." The toe of Kinsey's right shoe rested just behind the duct tape line on the floor. He hit two single twenties and a triple.

"Which friend?" Scotland asked.

Platinum spoke up like the nerdy kid in the front of the class. "Eddie Joyner. Our guy at the Fish Commission."

"All right," Kinsey hollered. "That's all the talking that needs to be done about *who*. Now let's discuss *how*."

Scotland thought back, recalled Platinum mentioning a name at the port. Tried to recall. Either way, the name matched the initials in the ledger. There's only one reason Kinsey would pay that much money to a man in that position. It took everything in Scotland's power to keep still. To keep quiet. Pressure seemed to build through his neck and into the top of his head. There'd be time enough to deal with Kinsey. First he needed to talk to this Eddie Joyner, get his side of it. But still, Scotland wanted to bash Kinsey's skull. He wanted to bash in Eddie Joyner's skull, too.

"I want it simple," Kinsey said. "Clear and concise. You scare him. That's all. You understand?"

"I know how bad we need him, Mr. K," Platinum said. "We'll take care of it."

CHAPTER FIFTEEN

The parched tarmac of Davis Island Air Field vibrated beneath Kinsey's cowboy boots. His helicopter—he called it his "bird"—had its blades spinning and ready to take him wherever he wanted to go. The rapid-fire, chopping sound filled the air between him and Maria as she remained seated in Kinsey's Mercedes, parked fifty yards off to the side of the helicopter

This was the bigger helicopter of the two he owned through his business, but he thought little more of them than he did his electric toothbrush or any other tool that made tasks more convenient. These birds were responsible for patrolling the cattle farms of Tampa Beef and Bird. In his father's day, a team of men made the same rounds on horseback. There was no radio communication in those days, so anything out of the ordinary was not known until they reported to the office upon the gritty hours of their return ride. These days, Kinsey's office paid someone to maintain constant radio contact with the pilots. Kinsey wasn't bothered with reports unless something was seriously wrong. And now he had the newer and bigger bird standing by to fly him and his mistress from downtown Tampa to the northeastern reaches of Hillsborough County where it touched lines with Pasco and Polk.

Maria sat in the Mercedes, looking sexy in her green dress with her legs crossed and her fuck-me pumps. Kinsey tugged at his tie to loosen it an inch or so and unbuttoned the collar of the white shirt he wore beneath a tan cardigan his wife Christine had knitted him. He adjusted his aviator sunglasses and exhaled as he tugged the bill of his Purina Feed & Grain ball cap. The moment he let go, a gust of wind off the bay brushed over him, blowing his hat off his head.

Kinsey turned as his hat flew over the car and past Maria as she got out. He lowered his sunglasses on his nose and looked at the helicopter. The Kinsey family business logo—TB&B—was stenciled in blue on a white background. His blood surged through his sternum to his thumbs. He employed hundreds of people and yet had no one now to chase his hat as it tumbled twice in the blowing wind. "Fuck it," he said, and turned to face the helicopter.

The pilot signaled something with his hands inside the cockpit. Kinsey didn't understand the signal and looked at the tinted window to see if the hand movements would repeat. When they did, Kinsey looked to the car and yelled, "Let's go."

Maria's heels clacked on the faded tarmac as toned legs carried her from the car to the open helicopter door. Kinsey positioned himself in front of the opened door to help Maria. He showed her the handle to grab on the fuselage, and where to step on the skid to give her an advantage of leverage. He'd learned this from necessity and without the heels, Maria was the exact same height. He held her free hand as she took a large step up. The angle of her legs made her dress ride up her thighs as she pulled herself into the cabin and Kinsey got a glimpse of tanned ass and the lace around the leg holes of her underwear. He knew her body well and would never forget the things she did with it. He tried to focus and erase that from his thoughts.

Kinsey always looked forward to field trips such as this where he flew and walked around his development sites. The birds-eye view and just touching the soil there made him part of the process. He wore boots to make hazarding the sandy walk easier. On his first such project he'd shown up in a suit which got stained by mud and wingtips that never fit right again. This particular trip would bring a much bigger payday, but this was a ride he didn't look forward to.

Once aboard and buckled in, the ascent in the helicopter failed to give Kinsey that feeling of excitement it usually did of going up to see the land he owned and the land he wanted to obtain. Today, though, he had a bitter taste in his mouth and he didn't want to be near Maria.

The headphones almost blocked out the high-hertz hum of the engine and thwacking of the blade rotating overhead, a noise perceptible most vividly in his ribs. The sound and the sensations were like driving over the reflectors embedded in the lines that divide road lanes. Through the windshield and windows along the side door, Tampa unfolded beneath him. It was impossible to focus on any single thing for long. They flew over the community college, across Dale Mabry Highway, and passed right over the Buccaneers' stadium which looked small from up there, but still bigger than everything else. He recognized other buildings and neighborhoods, knew who owned which stretches of land beneath the green treetops, and could identify every road running through the flesh of his state like tributaries to the Hillsborough River.

Maria sat beside him, squeezing his leg. Kinsey adjusted his glasses over his eyes, and the headphones he wore over his ears to communicate back and forth with the pilot.

The eastward ride was bumpy in unpredictable patterns. Some bumps jostled them as if he were driving his Mercedes in a cypress swamp. Others dropped his stomach as if someone toggled the gravity switch. There were moments where he looked over at Maria, who breathed shallow as if whispering a disco song, her head pressed to the headrest.

The pilot apologized over his microphone. Said the air should smooth out when they got east of the city.

Maria's color faded from tan to pale to green. Kinsey

hated her. Could barely stand to look at her. He raised his voice into the microphone built into his headset, "My petite flower is wilting back here. Maybe we should do this some other time." He sat back as a surge of contentment flooded his torso. Relief followed the decision.

"It's your call, Mr. Kinsey," the pilot said. "But I can't guarantee when the air currents will be any better in the next week."

"I need to see Loughton Groves before then," Kinsey said to Maria. "They need a decision in three days."

"This may be your best bet," the pilot said.

Kinsey looked to Maria. He wanted to spite her, but she smiled until her green cheeks dimpled and nodded. Their hands squeezed each other's.

Kinsey nodded and gave him a thumbs-up.

The air got even choppier. The helicopter bounced around and Kinsey tightened his seatbelt across his lap to prevent gaps that would jar him in this turbulence. He looked at Maria. Sweat visible on her forehead, gone was the Maria-ness that made her beautiful.

"How long will that take?" she asked, her head hung low, her eyes upward and expectant.

The pilot looked at his watch, "I can have us over there in eleven minutes if you don't mind a few more bumps."

Kinsey looked to Maria again. He wanted to cradle her in his arms. "Fine," Kinsey said. "But find smoother air, will you?" He patted Maria's knee. "Hold on. This will be quick." If she heard him, she didn't acknowledge.

Kinsey felt a surge of blood to his temples that radiated heat across his brow and over his ears as he thought about his security chief, the man he called Platinum, leaving Maria's apartment one anguished morning; the audiotape recordings of his phone conversations with Maria; photos of them in bed. Evidence that would hold up in any courtroom.

He didn't want to think about that now. The land they

were going to see was deep into the unincorporated county, completely undeveloped. It had the potential of being his biggest residential development project to date.

As they approached the property, vast areas of green and brown land without an inch of concrete opened up before him. Unspoiled land. The land as he imagined it was in the time of his childhood, thirty years ago when he was a third grader shooting rabbits in the woods with the .22 rifle his father had given him. As pristine as it had been in the days of the Seminoles and the dinosaurs before them. The land where wild hogs chased him and his friends up trees until their gunshots chased them away.

The air smoothed out. The ride was calm. The pilot let out a loud sigh.

Kinsey seethed inside, yet he couldn't help admiring the green space he would spoil so he could one day protect and preserve other parcels from overdevelopment so his grandchildren could thrive in the same environment he grew up in.

Maria glanced up and swallowed hard, seemingly grateful for the smoother air. She picked at a chipped fingernail long enough to glance out the window. She smoothed her finger over the jagged paint on her nail as if embarrassed by the imperfection, clearly attempting to disguise her airsickness.

Kinsey leaned over. He felt the seatbelt cut into his lap, but struggled against it and slid open the crew door on Maria's side. Wind rushed into the cabin and blew Maria's hair into his face.

The pilot contorted in his seat and hollered, "What the hell? Close that door!"

His sunglasses were identical to Kinsey's. Kinsey held the door open with one hand and squinted against the wind blowing into his face. The altitude seemed higher suddenly and wind made him conscious of the helicopter's speed. So high. So fast. He fought to hold the door open with one hand. With his other hand, he grabbed Maria's head and pushed it into the opening. She struggled against him, but he bore down with his left hand and summoned the strength necessary to push her head, neck, and shoulders through the opening.

His skin chilled from the cool December air, made cooler by the altitude. He pushed harder on her head. Yelled, "You broke my heart, you fucking whore." The rotor wash and the headphones kept the sound of his voice from reaching his own ears, but he felt the words strain his throat. He had no way to know if she heard him. "Fuck!" he yelled.

Her seatbelt wasn't tight and she'd come off her seat a little. Her hair whipped at him now and strands caught in Kinsey's mouth. The idea of closing her head in the door long enough to unbuckle her seatbelt and shove her all the way out surged through him like whiskey.

"Shut that door immediately!" the pilot yelled. The helicopter ascended as the pilot fidgeted his attention between Kinsey and the air on the other side of the windshield.

The guy had worked for Kinsey for more than ten years, but Kinsey had no confidence the pilot would keep his mouth shut. Kinsey's arms struggled to hold Maria and the door, but anger raged through him instead of muscle fatigue. He looked away from the pilot and at Maria's flailing arms as they slapped at the bulkhead in an attempt to gain purchase and push herself back into the cabin. Kinsey grunted from the frustration. He changed his grip from her neck to her shoulder and pulled her back in. Fastened the door closed. His ears popped with the pressure of altitude.

Maria yelled in Spanish. Screamed, at Kinsey. A solitary string of words that she rattled off like automatic gunfire.

Kinsey leaned toward the pilot. Yanked the seatback. "Don't you ever question me again. You understand? I thought she was going to vomit." Kinsey sat all the way back into his own seat. "I really did," he said more to the pilot than to Maria. After a few minutes, he tapped her knee. "We're almost there," he said.

Maria didn't speak for the rest of the flight. Kinsey knew it was killing her to keep her mouth shut. That wasn't her style. She was vocal, mouthy. Unable to hold her tongue or keep her temper from flaring. Hers was a head full of opinions. Enthusiasm. Kinsey usually loved when she argued with him. He kind of wished she would now. But it was too late for arguments. Reconciliation. Makeup sex.

The helicopter pitched forward. "Mr. K, I'll have us down in a minute."

Kinsey turned his attention to the window and marveled at the stretches of land beneath him. Pins on a map were never as impressive as seeing his land from the highest possible vantage point.

They descended into a clearing of pines and palmetto scrub near a pond on the undeveloped Loughton family property that Kinsey was interested in buying. This parcel was fifty thousand acres tucked away in the northeastern part of Hillsborough County, a couple miles from the nearest paved road. The pond beside their landing spot was black and weeded over with tall grasses and cattails.

On the ground, Maria flicked her seatbelt buckle and opened the door beside her even faster than Kinsey had done mid-flight. She took no time or caution in jumping to the ground, where she landed with her high heels stabbing into the sandy earth like tent stakes. With the door open, the cool December air filled the cabin. With a hint of struggle, Maria kicked each foot free and stormed off toward the edge of the palmetto scrub.

Kinsey sat back. Felt the overhead rotor blade slowing to a gradual stop. There was no way to know if the pilot bought the airsickness excuse. As he took off his headphones, he saw the microphone and assumed the pilot knew the truth. If she hadn't been buckled in, she surely would have flown over-board.

"Sorry, Mr. K," the pilot said. "I thought…"

"You thought what?"

"I didn't realize you were trying to help her. I couldn't tell from up there."

Kinsey smiled at that and watched Maria. It took many steps with those high heels to traverse the clearing. She walked toward the edge of the scrub—palmetto and pines sprawled out in every direction, all the way to the horizon. She stood cast in full sunlight. Pine needles provided little shade. She was yelling. Probably in Spanish though Kinsey couldn't tell.

"Look at her," Kinsey said. "She's more out of place than a pearl in a pig pen."

"She is striking, sir." As he reached the edge, the pilot added, "She shouldn't stray so far. The wild hogs out here are ruthless."

"What's striking is the potential of this fucking land."

The pilot didn't respond.

"You don't think it has potential?"

The pilot turned sideways to face Kinsey. His matching sunglasses staring into Kinsey's. "I understand development and progress and all, but it's still a shame that stretches of nature like this are disappearing."

Kinsey pointed out at the scrub land around them. "Progress makes the wetlands go away. DDT makes the mosquitoes go away. Air conditioning makes the heat go away. But I make homes for the complainers to live in. Guys like us are the last generation that really wants nature. You know what I mean, son?"

"I know. It's just a shame, is all."

"Do you know who we're building these houses for?"

The pilot looked out at the land before him. "People with money?"

153

"We're building houses for people looking for a better life. And where better than the Sunshine State to start that better life? What's not to like? It's year round golfing with beaches nearby. Like being on vacation every day for the rest of your life. People have been blazing a trail down I-95 for the past thirty years. Well guess what? Miami is crowded. And expensive, to boot. And don't get me started on what the boatlift did to the area. No, sir. What these good people want is a nice, clean place that's affordable. A place for working stiffs to raise their families. No projects. No traffic. No snow. They'll be so happy to be away from the morass of the great North, because these aren't just houses, they're trophies to these people. We're making trophies here, son. This parcel happens to be for much bigger trophies, granted, but it's all the same. And we're presenting them to the fine people flocking to our fair peninsula. And every one of them is a voter. They'll remember the man who gave them trophies. They'll help me be the next Governor. And then I'll protect and preserve even bigger parcels of land."

"You know, you've got my vote."

Kinsey didn't care if this guy voted or not, but he said, "Thank you, son. Be sure to tell your friends. And in the meantime, just remember that everything we do for them here will feed your family. Your family likes to eat, don't they?"

"More than you can imagine."

"So keep that in mind the next time you question bullshit details like the size and shape of some fucking swamp land. Or what your boss is doing in his own fucking helicopter."

"Point taken."

"Sometimes you have to chop off toes to save the foot, and then chop off the foot to save the leg." Kinsey sat back. It was the first time he'd ever said that out loud. He'd have to trust people to get where he's going which was as much a leap of faith as flying in a contraption like this. He laughed as he scratched his head where his hat had left a ring around his hair.

The pilot checked his watch. "The weather is only going to get rougher the longer we stay here, Mr. Kinsey."

"Yes." Kinsey slapped the back of the pilot's seat. "Right. Okay then. Take off."

"We'll have to wait for your lady friend."

"No we won't."

"Sir?"

"I want you to get this bird in the air now."

"You can't just leave her out here?"

"She's lucky it's not August."

"It's four miles to the nearest road."

"That's her problem." To hell with her, Kinsey thought. But he wasn't prepared for Maria to sprint the distance back to the helicopter once the rotor blade got spinning again. She banged on the door, but Kinsey held the handle.

"Don't be a child, Allan," Maria yelled as she tugged on the door handle.

Kinsey held firm and shook his head.

Maria pounded on the door, ducking as the propeller reached maximum revolutions above her head. She pounded and seemed to be pleading or even begging. Kinsey didn't know if she begged for forgiveness or simply not to be left out there.

Maria pounded on the window. Her strong fists thudded like distant gunfire, but the anguish on her face was all too close. Tears puddled in her eyes. Kinsey read that as panic more than regret for what she had done and that meant little to him. She continued to pound and cry harder. "Up," he shouted into his microphone.

"Sir, are you sure you want to do this?"

Kinsey leaned forward and grabbed the pilot by the throat, pulling him across his seat until his torso and head were in the backseat area. He heard gurgling in his headphones. Kinsey said, "If you question me again, I will have your eyes poked out and the only thing you'll ever fly again is a fucking kite you won't even be able to see. Is that perfectly clear?"

"All right. Jesus." The pilot said. "Don't get all excited. I'm on your side, remember?"

Kinsey let him go and reached over, opened the door for Maria.

Anger beamed from her eyes, and she was still crying, soft whimpers now. She climbed to her seat and hugged her knees, rocked a little.

"Now," Kinsey said. "Let's go." Kinsey sat back and listened to the thrush of the propeller increase.

The pilot worked his levers and lifted them off the ground. Maria didn't fasten her seatbelt. Instead, she sobbed through a cold stare at Kinsey as they ascended.

With his hands in his lap, Kinsey watched the ground shrink beneath them and thought about all the good times he'd had with Maria over the past year and a half. She was so lovely to look at. So sweet to spend time with. Sexy in lurid ways that left him exhausted.

Then he thought about the pictures of her with Platinum.

Kinsey leaned across her and slid open the door. Maria slapped at Kinsey's arm, but he focused on holding the door open and used his other hand to shove her sideways in her seat. She gripped onto the doorframe. He pounded her splayed fingers with his fist. She hollered curses in Spanish again until he reared back and placed his foot in her mid-section. "I was always good to you," he said as he straightened his leg and forced her out of the helicopter.

Her decent as the helicopter climbed to cruising altitude seemed in slow motion. She grew smaller like a doll falling to the ground, and then small as an ant, and finally out of view as the pilot took them southwest.

The ordeal sent a clot of emotion to his throat.

He swallowed it down and pulled closed the helicopter door.

He imagined his life was simpler in this one way, but it was exponentially more complicated as sadness would overrun him like new residents flocking to his state.

CHAPTER SIXTEEN

A Skynyrd guitar riff licked the back of Platinum's neck as Tampa shrank in the rearview mirror. They began the thirty-minute drive to Apollo Beach with the radio off, but he couldn't take it. Scotland sat beside him in the passenger seat, his knees as high as the dash, head touching the roof. His arms crossed over his chest were as big around as Platinum's thighs. *Dumb muscle*, he thought. There was no animosity between them for the moment, but they didn't shoot the shit, either. They drove past strip malls and motor courts and hit more red lights than Platinum ever had before. Stopped at one, he'd reached over and turned on the stereo. The tape in the deck was his favorite. Music roared from the Alpine speakers mounted in his rear dash. The guitar chords climbed the back of his neck and into his ears like freezing flames. It made him drive faster, and he liked that, too. They drove like this, through Riverview and Gibsonton.

He lowered the music when they reached Big Bend Road. They were getting close. He slowed down as they drove through a neighborhood of cinder block houses. Platinum felt more oxygen in his lungs suddenly. The prospect of doing a job well for Kinsey excited him, and he couldn't wait to pressure this Eddie Joyner guy into keeping the fishing ban going. Platinum preferred more sophisticated jobs that utilized stealth and swiftness, but he was comfortable playing the heavy—especially with a big guy like Scotland with him. More important, however, was getting Kinsey the results he wanted. He was confident in this job. Platinum had had contact with Eddie Joyner before and they got along well

158

enough. Now he would just have to convince the man his participation was no longer subject to negotiation.

Scotland held a bat across his knees. "What you got for a weapon?" he asked.

Platinum held his palms on the wheel, fingers tucked together like knife blades. "My hands are my weapons," he said.

"Whatever works for you," Scotland said, and looked out the window.

The truth was, Platinum had taken Kinsey's advice and had tucked an untraceable .38 into the waistband of his jeans. "This'll be nothing like the port. It's just a squirrely guy and we're just talking," Platinum said.

"I don't understand why we can't just knock on his door. Like normal people."

"He may run."

"We know where he works. Where he lives."

"For fuck's sake, you questioning bastard." Platinum punched the car's ceiling. He took a deep breath and hoped he hadn't left knuckle indentations on the outside. "We can't take chances. And I can't explain to you how big a deal it is to get this job done right, man. And that's no shit." While Kinsey never ordered the sneak attack method, Platinum wasn't going to risk spooking the guy and complicating Kinsey's life. "We'll do it my way and we'll do it right. Got it?"

"Yeah. Shit, whatever."

Colored lights hung along roofs, and some houses had wreaths on their front doors. Green grass and palm trees never looked right to Platinum. All the houses were single-story cement block, the better of which were covered with stucco. A couple houses had plastic snowmen in the front yards. Platinum couldn't get used to the lack of snow on the ground or even a chill in the air.

After a few slow minutes driving down old asphalt,

Platinum said, "Where is this guy's house, anyway?" He rubbed his ear.

"Right fucking there." Scotland pointed to a cinder block house with a flat roof. "Now we're sure he lives alone? I don't want to bust in on a bunch of kids or an old lady in a wheelchair or something."

Platinum was surprised that Kinsey's dumb muscle was prepared enough to ask such a question. "All the financial paperwork Kinsey dug up says he's divorced. Sends checks every month to his ex and his kids in Ohio or Iowa." He couldn't remember which. It didn't matter. "He lives alone. We're good to go."

They parked on the street just past the house and walked up the driveway behind Eddie Joyner's baby-shit-brown pickup truck. Scotland left the bat on the front seat and Platinum didn't ask why, because he knew.

The grass hadn't been cut in weeks. Plants and shrubs wove together as they competed for moisture and sunlight. An old bicycle made orange by exposure to the weather leaned against a mound of dirt near a tin gas can and a chipped plastic kiddie pool. Two metal garbage cans with rusted-out bottoms sat on their sides between the front door and the garage as if Joyner hadn't had the energy to go all the way.

"You believe this bum?" Platinum said.

Scotland flicked on the flashlight and led the way through tall grass around the house.

They chose the back door for less visibility from the road. Platinum reached for the screen door and pulled slowly to minimize the croaking hinges. He signaled Scotland to hold it open so he could get to the lock on the entry door.

It was the same type of cheap doorknob he'd sliced open on Scotland's shitty duplex door not so long ago. But this time, there was a deadbolt. Platinum pulled his kit from his back pocket and unrolled it to select from the jewelers screwdrivers and dental tools he'd modified for lock picking.

As quietly as possible, he worked the dental tool into the key slot and scratched around until he felt the tumblers. Scotland could have knocked or kicked the door down, but Platinum wanted the full advantage of surprise. "Okay." Platinum gave Scotland the thumbs-up sign. "Ready?"

Scotland nodded and turned off the flashlight.

Platinum eased the door open, silently, and held his finger to his lips.

Inside the kitchen, his eyes burned from ammonia in the air mixed with the smell of bacon grease. It was like he'd put his head into a urinal at a truck stop. A cat weaved its way through Platinum's legs. He stiff legged over the cat and aimed his pistol two feet from its head.

"I thought your hands were your weapons," Scotland whispered.

"I fucking hate these rodents," Platinum said low and breathy.

Another cat jumped from the refrigerator onto the countertop which made Platinum swing his gun in that direction.

"Put that thing away," Scotland whispered through clenched teeth. "We're just here to talk. Remember?"

Platinum hated to admit the dumb muscle was right, but he had to let it go and focus on the job at hand. But still. "They should all be shot," Platinum whispered, tucking his pistol into his lower back. "Fucking rats."

Scotland stalked over to check the darkened hall off the kitchen. Platinum followed the light from the room in front of them and found Eddie Joyner sitting on the couch in the living room. His face was lit by a seashell lamp with a dim bulb and no shade. Shadows framed fear in his eyes. His shirtless torso was pale. His neck and arms were tan. Next to him sat a red pillow embroidered with a picture of a cat. On top of that was a shiny pistol. Easily within reach. A nickel-plated .45.

Platinum didn't move. Reaching for his weapon meant Eddie would reach for his.

Instead, Eddie shook a Salem from the pack on the end table and said, "Howdy, boys," as if he'd invited them. "Come on in and make yourselves comfortable." He gestured to a threadbare wingback with a dress shirt draped over the tall side nearest the couch. The pocket was monogrammed in blue with the initials E. J.

Eddie fumbled with a match book, striking about a dozen times in succession until he threw the useless match toward the ash tray on the floor beside a picture in a frame with broken glass. In the picture, Eddie wore a suit and smiled. Next to him were two kids and a woman pretty enough to be in movies. His hands shook as he tugged at another match. He could mix paint with nerves like that. He struggled and dropped the second match. Scotland reached over with the blue and yellow flame of a lighter. Eddie lit his cigarette and exhaled heavily into the air. "Thank you."

Without noise from a television or radio, the rushing of a slight breeze through the heavy vegetation outside was the only sound in the room. It came in through the same crack in the curtains as the glow of the neighbor's red and green Christmas lights. Eddie's nervous puffing filled the room with the noxious smells of smoke.

"Now, Eddie, my man," Platinum said. "This is a hell of a place you got here."

"Lost my real house in the divorce. You should have seen it. It was every bit as nice as Kinsey's. Not that it's any of your business. I bought this place back when I still had partial custody of the kids. It was nice. Not new, but decent. The kids felt like they were camping when they were here." He crushed out his cigarette with the heel of his loafer and reached for the gun.

Before Platinum could grab his, Scotland plowed into Eddie like an offensive lineman pushing until Eddie was halfway up the wall and the pistol fell to the floor. Scotland pressed a forearm into Eddie Joyner's throat. Any more pressure and he would have dented the wall with the guy's brainstem.

"Enough," Platinum said, kicking the pistol back toward the kitchen. His voice was a bark that sounded distant in his ears. The only other sound was the gurgling coming from Eddie's throat. "Enough," Platinum said again. He grabbed Scotland's elbow. "Easy there, Killer."

Scotland stepped backward.

"We don't want to hurt you." Platinum took hold of Eddie's sweaty arm and pulled him back onto the couch. "So let's just calm down here and talk this out."

Scotland huddled over with his hands on his knees. He didn't look winded, but rather relaxed, as if he'd enjoyed that.

The room got quiet again, and this time the breeze through the plants outside sounded like applause.

Eddie twitched and tugged on the cat pillow pulling it in every direction—spastic yanking so the fringe draped the front of the couch cushions.

"The only reason we're here," Platinum said, "is that Mr. Kinsey would like to encourage you to 'keep up the good work' as he put it. So no need for guns or craziness."

Eddie shoved his hand between the couch cushions and came up with another pistol. It was also nickel plated, but a small caliber Platinum didn't recognize. Before Platinum or Scotland could react, Eddie put it to his temple.

Platinum's entire body clenched. "Don't do anything stupid, Eddie. Think of your kids." He slowly reached for the pistol tucked into his jeans.

"I became an agent," Eddie said, "so I could uphold the ideals of Teddy Roosevelt. And that bastard, Kinsey, he's no Teddy Roosevelt. He's ruining the entire Tampa Bay area for his own political gain. You tell Kinsey I'll see him in hell!"

Platinum heard the metallic click of a pistol's hammer being cocked.

Scotland lunged toward Eddie's arm and hollered, "No!"

Eddie swung the gun barrel from his temple to under his chin and painted the wall with his brains.

The report from the gunshot smacked Platinum's head and deafened him. He couldn't hear, and he couldn't look away from the gore flowing in trails down the wall. "Fuck!" Platinum shouted.

It was the third suicide he'd witnessed. Death had never shocked him, and suicides weren't really deaths to him anyway...they were quitting. If the deceased didn't care enough to conceal the act, Platinum didn't see a reason to care about their departure from the land of the living. But this one was a big deal because it would displease Kinsey.

After staring for some time, Platinum said, "This is bad. This is really fucking bad."

Scotland looked from the dripping wall to Platinum's face. "Fuck!" Scotland hollered and kicked over the wingback chair. The shirt hung in midair a second before floating to the floor.

"Well, he's got eternity to think about it now," Platinum said. He turned to leave and Scotland grabbed his arm.

"Where are you going?"

"We're out of here."

Scotland pointed. "What about him?"

"What about him?" Platinum fired back.

"We just leave him?" Scotland walked toward Eddie's slumped corpse.

Platinum ran up and crossed in front of Scotland. "What are you going to do?"

Scotland tried to side-step, but Platinum anticipated it. "I'm going to lay him down and cover his face."

"Why not just leave the police a greeting card signed, 'Love, Scotland Ross,' with your home address? Why would you risk involving yourself?"

"We are involved," Scotland said.

Platinum shoved Scotland toward the door.

As they walked, Scotland called back, "No one deserves to be sprawled and uncovered like that."

A light rain was falling as they exited Eddie's house. Scotland stood in the driveway and looked up, filling his mouth with water. It was a clear, cool spray he wished could wash off everything he'd just witnessed. Without warning, a wave of heat and pressure rolled through his gut and he bent over the azaleas growing wild in the side yard and vomited hard.

Platinum stomped past him, saying, "Shit. Shit. Shit," all the way to the car, where he placed his hands on the roof and began rocking it sideways. "Shit. This is so shit." He looked over his shoulders at the rain slick streets and slipped into the driver's seat, hardly opening the door.

Scotland stood and let the rain wash his face as he drank what he could catch in his mouth. There was not enough water to quiet the acid in his throat. He wiped his hands over his face and slicked back his hair, but felt no cleaner having done so.

Platinum started the car, but kept the lights off. He reached across and shoved open the passenger door. "Let's go, goddammit," he said with a barked sort of whisper.

Most of the houses in the neighborhood were dark, their Christmas lights off. It was Christmas Eve, and Eddie Joyner was dead. If anyone had heard the gunshot, they'd probably dismissed it as a car's backfire, especially in the absence of a second shot.

Scotland got in the car.

Platinum drove, focused on the road. "Kinsey is not going to like this."

Scotland watched Platinum's hands gripping the steering wheel as if it were a towel he was trying to wring dry.

"He's not going to like this one fucking bit. We are fucked. This is so fucking fucked!"

Scotland was still shaking off the visions of Eddie's head exploding and the spray of its contents onto the wall. Just thinking about it made his throat constrict. Air came and went at a reduced pace and volume. Swallowing his spit was difficult. The air in the car smelled of loose change and cigarette butts and felt warm on Scotland's neck. All the conditions were present to make him vomit again, but his throat was too tight for the chaos in his stomach to climb. He wasn't sentimental, and he'd never met Eddie Joyner before, but he had to sit back and force himself to breathe deeper.

Platinum continued to wring the steering wheel and repeat, "This is so fucking fucked."

"Relax," Scotland said. "I thought you've seen hundreds of dead bodies."

Platinum looked over at Scotland, ignored the road as he said, "I fucking have, man. But none of them were important to Kinsey, man." He turned his attention to the windshield, wrung the wheel some more and added, "He's going to flip out. This isn't good. Especially today. This is no fucking good at all."

"Look," Scotland said, swallowing the acid in his throat. "It's Christmas Eve. No one will look for him this weekend. We've got until Monday at least."

"You're suggesting we keep this from him?" Platinum's eyes got wider and he tilted his head forward as if those were fighting words.

Scotland didn't even try to hide his surprise that Platinum bought that far into Kinsey's bullshit. He shook that off and focused on the situation, because he certainly didn't need any shit with Kinsey.

He thought for a moment and said, "Why ruin his Christmas? Besides, he doesn't need to know we were there when the crazy fucker pulled the trigger."

"What's wrong with truth? We didn't do anything."

"That's the problem. We didn't prevent this. See? He's going to want somebody's head for this. You're his fucking Security Chief. I'm the low man on the totem pole. I don't want to get axed right now. You know? Plus it's not a lie. You saw that bastard's eyes. He was dead long before he ever pulled that trigger."

Platinum shook his head. "We can't wait. He's got to know now."

Scotland leaned his head out the open window and let the breeze cool his throat. After a moment, he leaned back into the car. "Call him on Monday."

Platinum squeezed the wheel, back and forth. "It can't wait. I'm his Security Chief, and his security is threatened."

"Eddie Joyner's dead, numb-nuts."

"Look," Platinum said. "It's not real complicated. Sooner or later the cops are going to find Eddie Joyner stinking up the neighborhood."

"It was suicide."

"The cops will figure that out, but they'll still be curious who the guy was. Where he worked and what he did. If you know what I mean."

"You think they'd connect him to Kinsey? To us?"

"We don't know what kind of records Eddie Joyner kept. That's the wild card in this whole fucking thing."

"Damn," Scotland said. "You got more on the ball than I thought."

* * *

Kinsey skidded the Mercedes to a halt just inches from the front of the clubhouse building. It was the first time in a week that he'd been to the Gulf Breeze. If he had his way, he'd have kept away until Monday, but Platinum's call sounded urgent and he'd give no details over the phone.

Kinsey didn't want to be there. Hated the drive over. He was supposed to be home playing Santa by arranging the kids' gifts under the tree. Driving to the Gulf Breeze on such a night was made more painful by the hole in his gut caused from missing Maria so damn much.

He slammed the car door behind him and walked the three steps to the entry porch. He paused and pulled a quarter from his pocket and got a Coke from the machine by the door. He popped the top and felt the carbonation tickle its way down before he entered the offices on the ground floor. He found Platinum and Scotland waiting on the stairs leading to his office. They were seated and speaking conspiratorially when Kinsey entered.

"Now what in tarnation is so urgent as to take me away from my family? Is something wrong with Eddie Joyner? What did he say?"

Neither man spoke up.

After some time in Kinsey's office listening to Platinum beat around the bush, and to Kinsey complaining about being pulled away from his family's holiday, as if Christmas was solely his, Scotland said, "Look, Mr. K. The deal is Eddie Joyner's dead."

Kinsey smacked the wall beside the dartboard. "What did you do?" Before anyone could answer, Kinsey lunged for Platinum. He grabbed him by the throat and yelled, "You blood-thirsty fucking psycho. What did you do?" Kinsey was shorter than Platinum by a few inches or so, but he had a grip on Platinum's collar and didn't appear willing to let go until he got some answers.

Scotland thought about watching this unfold, but he couldn't stand by and see matters worsen. He walked over, as non-threatening as possible, as if he were still a bouncer and this was two dudes pissed off in a dispute over quarters lined up on the pool table. "All right, boys," Scotland said, like he always did. Rookie bouncers always grabbed the aggressor since he was the one causing damage at the moment. Often that resulted in the hostile guy redirecting his anger to the one trying to break up the fight. More often than not, it was better to simply reach for the guy getting beat so he could save some face, in the process making the other guy realize he'd won. Sometimes neither one wanted interference from anyone. If he grabbed Platinum, Kinsey might take advantage of the easy target. If Scotland pulled on Kinsey, he might redirect his rage toward him. Scotland sort of inserted himself into the mix by wedging his hip between them. There were no punches being thrown, but there was momentum alternating back and forth. The only danger Scotland felt was that of tripping. Kinsey kept his hands firmly on Platinum's collar, at arm's length. Platinum didn't retaliate much more than refusing to be pushed backward. Perhaps he gained an inch every time, but he never made a sudden move.

"None of this is going to change things," Scotland said, his shoulders separating them. "We need to talk this through."

"He killed him, didn't he?" Kinsey said to Scotland. "He fucks everything up."

Scotland straightened a little. This was the first rift he'd witnessed between the two and he wondered what it was really about. Kinsey's right hand came away from Platinum's collar.

"Eddie Joyner's dead," Scotland said, "but he killed himself."

"Bullshit!"

"Serious shit!"

"How?"

"With a pistol."

Kinsey released Platinum completely and took a step back. "That ungrateful motherfucker," he said. "And you found him like that?"

"Yes!" Platinum said. "He was dead when we got there."

Kinsey's expression went smooth.

Scotland figured Platinum's lie was the stronger play and said, "Yeah. It was a huge mess."

Platinum flattened his collar and rubbed the back of his neck. "The stench of his bowels was pretty bad, Mr. K, but he couldn't have done it long before we got there because there wasn't that reek of decay yet."

On any other day Kinsey would have told them to fuck off, but he wasn't thinking clearly. His head had a tornado in it. He opened his desk drawer and slammed it hard enough to rattle a picture of the Sanibel lighthouse off the wall. It crashed to the floor with the distinct sound of glass shattering. He reached his arms and swiped everything off his desk. Paperwork, books, his "World's Greatest Dad" coffee mug, the trophy, and an assortment of office supplies clattered to the floor. "Goddammit!" he yelled.

He stood, brushed his hair with his hand and exhaled in an effort to regain some semblance of composure.

It was one thing to have the fishing ban scam effectively shut down—the loss of revenue would be significant—but Eddie Joyner was dead. The thought of it made everything beneath his ribs feel heavy, sodden. Suicide on Christmas Eve. Kinsey couldn't let himself dwell on the demise of an old friend and father, whose kids would never think about Christmas the same way again. Because of him. There'd be time for that later. He compartmentalized his emotions and stood there for what seemed like twenty minutes trying to sort his thoughts. His efforts were unsuccessful. His ass burned beyond control from the mere presence of that fucking rat bastard, Platinum. The slimy bastard stood beside Scotland. Kinsey never wanted to be seen in moments of uncontrolled anger, but they were there and he had to deal with them. "Well?"

Platinum took this as his cue to speak up. He rattled on with some bullshit assurances that they might've prevented it if they'd gotten there sooner.

Kinsey didn't have any interest in what this idiot was rambling about. He couldn't stand to have Platinum in the same room, let alone listening to him speaking.

Kinsey cut him off. "That's quite enough. I'm done talking about this for now. Just get the fuck out of here."

Scotland turned to leave and Kinsey called out, "Not you, Scottish. You stay."

Platinum slapped Scotland on the shoulder and said, "Nice knowing you," as he turned to leave.

Shit, Scotland thought. This was it. He was about to be fired. He stood with his hand in his pocket spinning the Zippo in continuous revolutions, end over end. He stopped it. Flipped open the lid. Lit it. Snapped the lid shut. He pictured himself packing up and moving out of the apartment and having to give back the car. His Pinto had been parked out by the tennis courts since he'd moved in. The tires needed air. Probably a new battery, too. Worse than the thought of returning to his life of poverty was that he'd no longer be able to help Dana and her family.

Kinsey stood by his desk. His hands on his hips and he was breathing in and exhaling as if he'd just swam from Cuba.

Before Kinsey spoke, Scotland squared himself to face Kinsey. He released his grip on the Zippo and removed his hand from his pocket, spread his feet shoulder width apart and bent his knees to better absorb the blow.

Two things were absolutely true for Platinum. One: he couldn't do anything about Kinsey's reaction to the problem. Two: he couldn't shake the excitement of the evening. He didn't realize it at the time, but watching Eddie Joyner's brain explode up the wall had brought a flood of nerve endings to the surface. He needed to put all that sensation to positive use. He needed Maria for that.

He sneaked around to the back of her building and climbed up the magnolia tree and onto her balcony. When he entered through the sliding glass door, she wasn't visible in the living room.

The kitchen light was on which was enough to light the entire apartment. A half-decorated plastic Christmas tree stood near the lanai doors. The couch was still there, but gone was Maria's little dog, Rafael. There was no sign of either of the dog or Maria. And in place of her desk there was an actual dining room table. No sketches or receipts covered it.

He walked to the bedroom where he found her closet empty, as was the bathroom medicine chest and counter.

Platinum didn't know what to think. He ran scenarios about why she might have left, but all of them involved a plan to return. This didn't look like Maria was coming back. But even if she wanted to leave without saying goodbye, she couldn't have done it that quickly. She just didn't operate like that.

He sat on the couch and rested his chin on his fist. His mind clicked like a pinball machine as he worked over the angles of the situation. After a moment, he stood quickly and moved to the sliding glass door, which he closed silently behind him. He climbed over the railing and shimmied to the ground, which he hit running all the way to his own apartment.

Kinsey surprised Scotland by pouring two drinks and handing him one. They sat on the couches facing each other at ninety degrees. The television was off, but neither spoke. They both sat grim-faced, and shaking their heads. In that solemn moment, Scotland looked as if they were paying their respects to Eddie Joyner, but Kinsey offered no toast to his memory so neither did Scotland.

"This is real nice and all," Scotland said after a few moments, "but if you're going to fire me, I'd rather you just do it and let me get on my way."

Kinsey's head shot up. Mourning replaced on his face by surprise. "Fire you? Why would I do that?" He laughed. "No, son, I'm not firing you."

Scotland took a drink. His eyes cast down at his new boots.

"Is something wrong, Scottish?"

Scotland wanted to shout, "I just saw a man kill himself." The urge overcame him with a rush of fluid in his throat and behind his eyes. He locked himself down. Made his body water-tight. As much energy as that took, he still had adrenaline coursing through him and he couldn't get past the image of brain matter splattering the wall.

Gruesome as it was, what made it worse for Scotland was the image of the only other dead body he'd seen before. This wasn't anything like his son's death—he didn't actually watch his son die—and maybe it was the memories tugging at his heart, but he couldn't keep sadness away in that moment.

"Look," Kinsey said. "You're basically a good-hearted kid. That's fine for everyday life, but in certain circles it's something you'd be better off doing without."

Scotland knew what he was saying, but asked, "What's that supposed to mean?"

"I'm just saying that in my employ things are often out of our control...or in our control. Bottom line is that death is final. No sense dwelling on it."

"You don't think a man's life has value?"

"Is that what you're hung up on? I thought you were worried I was going to fire you."

"I am. I was. Shit, I don't know what the fuck I think." He took another drink. "I just watched a man die tonight."

Kinsey watched Scotland's shoulders sink and round forward. The guy had just basically confessed that Platinum had lied about getting there too late. It didn't matter in the big picture. It did, however, make him hate that bastard even more. "This thing really got to you."

Scotland looked up. "I puked."

"Inside or out?"

"Outside. In some bushes."

Kinsey sat back and took a sip of his drink. "That's fine."

"They called it Sudden Infant Death Syndrome," Scotland said.

Kinsey's jaw locked up. He remembered their earlier conversation well, but didn't connect Eddie Joyner's brains splattered on a wall with the lifeless body of an infant. The thought of losing one of his own children was something he couldn't mentally process, and he forced himself to shake off the image. He took a pull from the bourbon. "That's rough."

"Ain't nothing worse in the world than seeing your baby balled up and blue."

"Jesus."

"It changed me. Made me think that no God existed. To see someone so innocent taken so coldly stripped me of all faith." Scotland talked more about his wife's subsequent

174

meltdown and abandonment, which left him with nothing. Kinsey wondered if Scotland was going to bust through the levee and fall into a crying jag as he talked about the ambulance driver carrying out the baby wrapped in his blue blanket. "They assured us that we weren't to blame, but my wife never got over it. She left me. Went back home to her parents in Detroit. I didn't have anything keeping me there, nothing to work for, so I left. Joined the Navy. I wanted to see the world through a porthole. You know? That was my plan."

"Shit don't always work out, does it?"

"Pity is a complete waste of fucking time."

"Aren't you the stoic soul?"

Scotland pointed with his glass. "See? That's your problem, Kinsey. You've only been on one side of the pity equation. You and people like you think that dishing out pity makes you special. But it doesn't. What makes a person special is deserving pity but rejecting it."

This pleased Kinsey somehow. The honesty, perhaps. "That's quite the inspiring soliloquy, Scottish. To be quite honest, I'm surprised to discover your depth on the topic. But rest assured. I've only been faking pity all these years. Truth is, I've never actually given a shit."

They both laughed. It was a hearty laugh that broke the ice as far as Kinsey was concerned.

"That's why you need to surround yourself with good people," Kinsey said. "Solid workers and loyal motherfuckers. You know? Not so straight that they can't break a few rules now and again, but not so lawless that they fuck you over. You know what I mean, son?"

"Sure I do." Scotland nodded and stared at his boots.

"Well," Kinsey said, "I suppose we have to wait until they appoint a replacement then try to convince him to keep the ban going."

"Maybe," Scotland said, "the new guy'll just keep it going without looking at it."

"That's quite unlikely. The higher-ups were pressuring our dearly departed Eddie Joyner. I'm willing to bet acreage that ending the ban will be the first item on new guy's agenda when he accepts the position."

"He hasn't even been dead a few hours and we're talking about his replacement."

"Speaking of replacements…" Kinsey said and stood. He picked up their glasses and took them to the bar. "This might cheer you up."

"Liquor rarely cheers up anyone."

"Not the liquor, a promotion."

"What are you talking about?"

Kinsey walked back and handed Scotland a rocks glass filled with Jim Beam and looked him in the eye as he asked, "How would you like to be my Security Chief?"

Scotland took his glass. "You've already got one of those."

"What if I didn't?"

"What are you talking about?"

"I'm asking you if you'd like to be my Security Chief. It's a yes or no question."

Scotland took a pull of his drink, but didn't give away any other details. He was harder to read than he'd been at the card table the first time their paths crossed. Kinsey studied Scotland's face. Knew the hard sell might drive him away. "I'm serious. I've been impressed with your work, tonight's activities notwithstanding."

"I'm listening," Scotland said.

After a moment, Kinsey said, "The pay for the job is double what you've been getting."

"You're firing Platinum?"

"Not exactly."

Scotland looked up at the ceiling for a moment, then lowered his eyes to stare into Kinsey's. "You're not saying…?"

Kinsey pointed without lifting his arm. "Never had you pegged for a Boy Scout, Scottish."

"Of all the people I've wanted to kill," Scotland said, "I ain't starting with him."

"But he's doing wrong by you. Don't you get it?"

"I don't."

"This guy is threatening you."

"Maybe in the way a lapdog threatens to bite your finger or your ankles."

"He's threatening you, just the same. Threatening the whole operation which could bring us all down." Kinsey's hands squeezed his glass as he spoke. He wished it was Platinum's throat, but the big guy next to him was his best hope of that. "If I take a hit, we're all taken down."

Scotland shook his head in long, slow passes. "I'll do some shit because I need the money, but I ain't murdering anyone for it."

Kinsey sipped his drink. "You better get your mind right, boy."

"Why me?"

"Why not you? Don't you think you're able to do the job?"

"I'm plenty able, but why don't you send the Kula brothers?"

"Their mother has met Platinum. For some reason, she's taken a shine to him. I wouldn't ask her sons to kill somebody she likes."

"But you'll ask me."

"You're not her son."

"Platinum will still be dead though."

"That's the spirit, big boy."

"Why do you want him dead?"

"The 'why' is for me. The 'how' is for you."

Scotland walked toward the door. "I'm not doing it. No way. He's a dick, but I'm not doing it."

Kinsey exhaled. "You must. And you will. Enough belly aching now. Let's talk turkey. It's got to look like an accident. Cut his brake lines, I suppose. Or kill him however you like and make his corpse vanish. Completely."

Scotland set down his drink with the hard knock of glass on the bar. "I watched a man die tonight, and you want me to kill another? Don't you have any fucking respect for human life besides your own?"

"You best mind your manners when you're talking to me, son. Never forget your place."

"Manners have no place in a murder discussion."

"I'm trusting you with this."

"You shouldn't."

"Oh, but I should."

"You don't know me very well."

"But I know people. Surely that pale-haired weirdo has gotten under your skin. I saw you at the pool last month. You know you want to strangle the life out of him."

"I've seen enough death for now."

"That's all right, my boy," Kinsey said as he leaned over and patted the arm of the couch. "I understand you're tired and shook up from all the excitement. You just go on up to your apartment and get some rest. Sleep on it. If you decide you're not ready to advance to the next level, I'll understand."

"Well, I expect you're going to shoot me in the back on the way out, but you do what you got to do. I'll do what I got to do.

"Look, Scotland, I don't like this anymore than you do," Kinsey said.

Scotland looked like he'd just licked the business end of a nine-volt battery and he shook his head once as if to clear the shock of hearing Kinsey use his real name for the first time.

Kinsey swiped imaginary lint from the arm of the couch, tried to look sad about the state of affairs. "But I'm in this, son. I've got something going here. Just do this one bad thing for me and then we can do some good."

"You've said that to me before. Jesus. Everything you're saying is bullshit. This is never going to stop. There's always one more dirty job, and this is way over the line. I'm not killing anyone for you. I don't care how much it pays."

"Come on, Scottish, my boy. Why fight it? You don't want to stop making this kind of money. Besides, you're good at this line of work. A natural, just like me. And you're smart, too. You know people. Hell, you knew Platinum was no good so you kept your distance when a dumber man might have tried to brown-nose a guy in his position. Strong and smart goes a long way in my world. You'll be glad you stayed."

Scotland said, "The only one I'd like to kill right now is you, you smug sonofabitch. Playing God with land and politics is one thing, but a man's life is another." He shouted, "I'm paid up with you." He stepped closer toward the door. "I'm out of here."

Kinsey sat back and rubbed the back of his neck and hollered, "Guys like you always come back."

Scotland threw the door open hard enough for it to rebound off the wall and slam shut behind him.

CHAPTER SEVENTEEN

Scotland had kept his seabag mostly packed. At the ready. Standing by. Packing the rest of his belongings involved zipping his shower kit and shoving it in with socks and underwear from the top drawer opposite the bed. He noticed the new jean jacket he'd bought himself and the Jordache jeans and silk shirts Amber had bought. He took his jean jacket off the hanger and stuffed it into his seabag, but left the new shit hanging there in the closet like flags of a fallen country.

He shoved the seabag into the back seat of the Bonneville and fired up the engine.

He kept the lights off to attract as little attention as possible. He shifted to reverse and the transmission changed silently. The tires crunched the cracked shell parking lot. When the car faced away from the apartments, he pulled the switch and lit the road before him. He wanted to press the gas pedal to the floor and sling shell fragments into the eyes of anyone watching, but he went easy down the driveway, rolled by the tennis courts. The old Pinto needed air in three tires. Fixing that would require jacking up both sides of the car, pulling off the tires, driving to a gas station and pumping air, then doubling back to put the tires back on the car. The battery had to be dead and it probably needed oil, too. Instead of dealing with it, he drove on.

Out where the driveway met the road, Scotland slowed to a crawl. He steered slowly over and parked on the grass, next to the big, oak Gulf Breeze sign. The engine vibrated the hood of the car, but he couldn't hear it. He opened his door and heard the engine's throaty rumble as it idled. He got out, opened the back door and pulled out his seabag, hoisting its heft over his shoulder. The weight of it caught him in the back of his ribs, disrupted his balance. The air hung still all around him. No movement, no moisture. It seemed like air that didn't belong to Florida it was so foreign. With both doors open, the lights on, and the engine running, Scotland walked away from the car with a series of backward steps. He then turned and headed left, up the road, on foot.

He walked a mile without seeing a single car. "Merry Christmas," he said to no one.

The air turned colder and he stopped, set down his seabag and pulled out his denim jacket. It was his, but it wasn't. He'd bought it with Kinsey's money. Scotland held the jacket with his arms extended. He could drape it over the road and walk away like he did with that beautiful fucking car. Instead, he put on the jacket. It was his. He earned the money he paid for that jacket. He was cold and he wore his own jacket.

He hefted the seabag and looped the strap over his right arm, felt it dig into his shoulder. He walked another mile before he saw headlights shine up the road toward him. Scotland turned and walked backward, slowly, and with his thumb held out.

A semi rolled slowly past Scotland and pulled over with a hiss of hydraulic brakes. Scotland ran through diesel fumes and the red glow of brake lights. The trailer was emblazoned in bold script "Tampa Beef & Bird."

"You've got to be shitting me."

As he approached, the truck's passenger door jutted open. Scotland climbed onto the running board and swung it wide. The cab of the truck smelled like stale piss and wintergreen snuff. The driver wore overalls and sang "Silent Night" out of tune as he leaned upright, back into his own seat.

The seabag weighed down Scotland's shoulder and he strained to maintain balance.

The driver looked decent enough, wore an unbuttoned flannel shirt and the same mesh ball cap Kinsey always wore. "Where ya headed, partner?"

"Daytona," Scotland said.

"Well, hop on in then. I'm taking the 400 all the way to Jacksonville, but I'll get you close."

Scotland hefted his seabag onto the floorboard as he climbed into the passenger seat.

The guy said, "Won't have time for a stop in Disney World, but we'll pass it." He ground the gears enough to rattle the truck cab as he found first and began to roll forward. "And, shit, to be honest with you, Daytona's more the kind of amusement park gentlemen like us prefer. Ain't that right, partner?"

The thick, brown shag carpet lining the walls and ceiling of the truck cab made Scotland feel like a marsupial. He sat back and stretched his neck. "That's something I plan to find out as soon as possible."

After a few minutes, the driver said, "They call me Meat Man."

"Meat Man?" Scotland said. "Because you deliver meat."

Meat Man shook his head and grinned. "Nah. I had that name long before I took this job."

Scotland didn't know what to say to that.

Before he could think of something, Meat Man swatted at Scotland's shoulder and said, "I'm just messin' with you."

Scotland said, "Do you have any idea what kind of psycho your boss is?" He didn't know why he said it. He needed the ride and no good could come from spooking the guy. And even if he believed him, there wasn't shit a truck driver could do to bring down Kinsey. Trying to would only get him fired. Scotland couldn't be responsible for that.

"Why would you say that about Bob Wheldon?"

"Who's Bob Wheldon?"

"My boss."

"Not him. Your main boss. Kinsey."

"You work at the plant?"

Scotland grinned as the image of handing Dave his phony pay stubs flashed through his mind. "Yeah. You could say that."

"Well, I can't help it if you're bitter, partner. But Mr. Kinsey is good to the rest of us. Not as visible as his father was, but he treats us well nonetheless."

"You go to Daytona often?" Scotland asked, hoping he'd take the bait and change the subject.

"Three times a week. My wife and kids are in Jacksonville." The guy sang the line, "I'll be home for Christmas," and smiled at Scotland.

"Is Daytona nice?"

"Sure it's nice. They got beaches you can drive on. Cars drive up and back all day long like a never-ending parade. I've seen Mustangs and GTOs, shiny convertibles with the tops down and chicks in bikinis waving like crazy. And everybody's drunk. You know? Everybody's got a beer can or a booze-filed Big Gulp cup in their hands."

"The girls are good looking?"

"Shit. They're all great looking when you're drunk and half naked in the sun and they're drunk and half naked in the sun. If you know what I mean." He laughed and poked his elbow toward Scotland a couple times, but didn't quite reach.

"I had a girl, back in Tampa," Scotland said, Amber on his mind. "She'll be hard to top."

"Shit. Three drinks in the sand will make you forget all about her. Trust me."

Once they were past Lakeland, Meat Man ran out of songs. He picked up his CB radio microphone. "Breaker, breaker," he said. "This here is Meat Man, and I'd like to introduce you boys to a passenger I picked up outside of Tampa. He's a love-sick, muscle guy. Like some sort of gladiator or something. He's looking to start over in Daytona.

Any ya'll know some way to help, uh..." he paused, looked at Scotland, then said, "Spartacus, here?"

A series of disembodied voices separated by static and clicks greeted Spartacus and welcomed him to the confines of their own truck cabs. Scotland felt his face redden as he looked out at the black night through the windshield.

Meat Man handed Scotland the mic and said, "Say hello, Spartacus."

Scotland took the mic. "Just press this button?"

Meat Man nodded. "That's all there is to it."

"What the hell." No one knew his real name so it wasn't really him. He was playing a role. He pressed the button and said, "Ten-four, good buddy. This here's Spartacus riding shotgun with Meat Man and we're eastbound to Day-toe-na Beach. I hear there's some fun to be had there. Over."

The rest of the ride consisted of a chorus of voices offering welcome, as well as things to do in Daytona. If he'd had a pen and paper, he would have written down the names of the bars and the parts of the beach to check out. A slight argument crackled through the CB as four different voices disagreed on the best place to get fried shrimp. Scotland committed some of the recommendations to memory. The biggest help was the name of a motel with weekly efficiencies on the cheap. "Tell 'em the Gambler sent you. They'll give you a deal."

The truck rolled to a stop along the shoulder of the A1A with a deep cough of compressed air. "I'll drop you here, partner," Meat Man said. "It's just a couple blocks from where you need to go."

Scotland shook Meat Man's hand.

"Merry Christmas, partner," Meat Man said.

Scotland hopped down from the truck cab and pulled his seabag onto his shoulder. He shut the door and walked in the direction he'd been given.

The sound of waves echoed off the buildings along the beach. The air felt lighter and cooler with a breeze that made flags on poles flutter. Scotland tugged up the jacket's collar and walked directly to the place the Gambler recommended. The Sand Dollar sign stood thirty feet in the air. It had the required faded depiction of a sand dollar on it, but this was in pink neon. The bottom portion read "Vacancies" in green neon.

A low cinder block wall surrounded the parking lot, a beige Chrysler Cordoba on blocks in the corner. There were no new cars in the parking lot like at the Gulf Breeze. There was no tennis court or swimming pool, no three-story buildings with covered balconies. This motel had four concrete buildings with low roofs and ocean views.

In front of the center building, three guys sat in lounge chairs drinking beer on the walkway outside their rooms. They were close enough to converse without having to yell. One guy said, "And that was the most white bikinis I ever saw at one time."

Scotland pushed open the office door.

A lady wearing a robe and a Santa hat dozed at the desk, the test pattern glowing on her muted TV. "What do you want?" she said when Scotland entered.

Scotland stood tall, confident, as if he had the password to comfort and safety. "The Gambler told me about your place here and said you'd treat me right."

"Gambler?" the lady said. "You a friend of his?"

"Sure. I just talked to him on the CB a few minutes ago."

"And I'm supposed to set you up?"

"He said if I mentioned his name you'd give me a deal." Scotland stood with his seabag at his feet and his hand in his pocket, spinning the lighter. This place wasn't the Gulf Breeze, but that was a fair trade-off to get away from that crazy fucking Kinsey and to finally be in Daytona.

"Well, hell. Why not?" The woman's facial folds levitated into a happiness he'd never anticipated. "Did the Gambler say when he'd be coming this way?"

"No, ma'am."

"All right," she said, sort of blushing and tugging at the lapels of her robe. "Efficiencies run ten dollars a night, forty-five for the week or one thirty-five for the month, paid up front." She looked at Scotland.

In that moment, Scotland wondered how old the woman was.

"I suppose you'll be wanting to see the room before you pay," she said.

Scotland pulled out cash. "That won't be necessary."

He paid for the week—long enough to bag the price reduction, but short enough to keep his options open.

Scotland slept in the next day. By noon, he'd showered and washed his clothes in the sink. His pants and T-shirt hung to dry over the edge of the tub. It was the first time in months that he felt clean. His skin felt different. Still stretched across his bones, but lighter. Smoother. Cleaner. His boots leaned against one another beside the nightstand. He was barefoot, wearing his only pair of cutoff jean shorts from his seabag. He grabbed a white towel off the hook in the bathroom and headed out to sit in the sun.

On the beach side of the motel, the three guys from in front of the building the previous night had made their way to the sand with their chairs in a similar arrangement facing the water. Each man held a beer can.

Scotland nodded in their direction before bending to spread his towel on the sand a ways down from them. He sat with his weight on his arms, his ankles crossed, and stared at the water. The view of the water was not unlike that on the deck of his ship. The first time he sat on deck staring at the water with no land in sight, he realized how small he was. How vulnerable. That kind of adventure, along with the honest work, was what he missed the most. He loved that it made him forget everything else. Back before it was taken from him.

This moment on the beach would have been relaxing if not for his heart racing. The sand and the water wasn't soothing enough to shake Kinsey and all that bullshit back in Tampa. Being on the opposite side of the state had to be far enough away from Kinsey's reach.

It was Christmas. The air was seventy or seventy-five degrees. The sun was warm, but not hot enough to make him sweat.

After an hour of the sunshine, Scotland went back to his room to make a phone call. He dove across the bed, his sandy feet dangling over one end while he reached over the other to pick up the phone on the nightstand beside his boots. He cradled the handset between his shoulder and his chin as he dialed.

"Dana, it's me," he said when she picked up.

"Scotland, my God. Merry Christmas."

"Yeah. Merry Christmas." For the first time, he thought it might actually be.

Dana said, "Thanks to you, the girls had presents to open. They're thrilled."

"Yeah, well, that's the reason I'm calling."

"What's wrong, Scotland?"

He didn't want to disappoint her. Didn't want to seem like he was giving up on them or was a failure for losing another job. "The bad news is that I can't send any more money." Before she had time to reply, he added, "But the good news is that Mark will be going back to work soon."

"You...what are you talking about?"

Scotland swung his legs over the bed and sat up. His sandy feet splayed on the carpet beneath them. He cleared his throat so he would be heard loud and clear. "The fishing ban is about to be lifted and Mark can go back to work."

Dana didn't reply right away. Scotland heard her breathe in and out a couple times and he could have sworn he heard relief in each exhale. After a moment, she said, "And just how do you know this valuable information?" She spoke with the same tone as she'd done when he was a kid.

Scotland wanted to tell her, wanted to spill everything he'd been keeping from her those past many months. "No good could come from you knowing."

"But you're sure?"

"I don't have it in writing, but I'm pretty fucking sure."

"Mark'll be so pleased!"

"Will you guys be okay?"

"I would assume so. Are you okay? What the fuck, Scotland. Where are you?"

"Daytona."

"You finally made it there?"

"I had to get out of Tampa for a while."

"You've been trying to get out of here ever since you got here."

He didn't want to get into it with her. He said, "Just tell Mark to get the boat ready. And tell the girls I said, 'Merry Christmas.'"

Later that afternoon, Scotland walked through the parking lot and down the sidewalk, past the Holiday Inn on the corner. The sign stood on stilts and cast a green shadow the size of a school bus. The place was new and clean and he could have stayed there, but he didn't want to spend the extra money.

Near the corner of A1A and Seaspray Street, he saw a sign that read "Rooms for Rent." The buildings were concrete block without the decency of stucco or any kind of siding, but the complex was right across the street from the beach. It wasn't fancy like the Gulf Breeze, and it certainly wasn't like that magical house in the ad he had tacked up on his refrigerator, but it had a partial view of the Atlantic from the parking lot, which meant there'd be at least partial water views from some of the rooms. He wondered how much one of those went for.

He kept walking. He liked being on foot. He'd rather get to know a small area well than speed through a dozen towns in a car.

There was no way to find his dream cottage. The picture pinned to his old refrigerator had been taken from back of the house so there was no way to know the address. There was no mention of the street that cottage was on, but he knew the address of the realtor's office, though he was sure the cottage from the ad had been rented by now. He didn't know his way around. A convenience store sat up ahead. He hoped they sold maps.

As he stood in the 7-Eleven and unfolded an area map a girl with wet hair fanned across her bare back like a palm frond caught his eyes. Her skin had the shine of baby oil that had cooked in the sun. Tan skin showed beneath the bikini straps all the way to the Budweiser towel she had wrapped around her waist. Mirrored sunglasses hid her eyes, but he'd bet a hundred dollars they were blue. She had a volleyball tucked under one arm and a Michener novel sticking out of her canvas tote bag. She paid for a pack of Winstons and a carton of orange juice with exact change and placed them in her tote. Scotland assumed she lived close enough to walk there and back barefoot. She was the kind of girl he'd like to see behind his white picket fence someday.

He followed her out. In the sun, she looked no older than Scotland, maybe a year or two younger. That could be perfect. It was too early to approach her, though. He didn't live there yet and wasn't set up properly. He couldn't bring her to the motel. He must wait until he had the cottage.

He stopped by the next day, at the same time, and bought two quarts of beer. He did so again the next day, and the day after that.

On Monday morning, Platinum went to Kinsey's office, knocking before entering. His shave was clean and his shirt was pressed—he didn't want to give Kinsey any reason to be cross with him today. They hadn't seen each other since Christmas Eve and the bad news about Eddie Joyner.

Kinsey sat on the couch with a shoeshine box between his feet. The box was made of oak and instead of a handle, it had a foot-shaped perch for a shoe to rest on, angled down. Kinsey held his cowboy boot over one hand and worked brown polish into it with a wood-handled brush. Platinum was surprised to see him shine them himself, and recalled evenings in boot camp when he and his fellow Marines shined their boots. He didn't figure rich guys did that sort of thing themselves.

The Kula brothers stood along the back wall like Secret Service protecting the President. Instead of suits and sunglasses, they wore silk shirts and polyester pants from the Big and Tall department at Sears.

Kinsey didn't speak. He paid full attention to the boot.

The room was quiet enough to hear the Kula brothers' mouth-breathing. Their inhalations and exhalations matched the rhythm of Kinsey's brush swishing across the boot. Platinum knew in times like these it was best not to speak unless spoken to.

Kinsey spit on his boot and worked it in with the wood-handled brush. Once he was satisfied, he held the top of the boot as if to see his reflection. "There seems to be a problem with your buddy, the meat head." He smiled—not at Platinum, but rather at his reflection in his boot.

"I've been wondering," Platinum said. It was the truth.

The bulk of his free time had been spent wondering where Maria had gone and why. In his weaker moments, he feared that she and Scotland had run off together. If the car hadn't been found at the edge of the property, he might have gotten carried away with that thought.

Platinum had no idea where Maria might be and Kinsey didn't mention her name. He wanted to ask, but had been unable to figure a way to pull off appearing concerned, but not interested. Or maybe it was supposed to be the other way. That's why he didn't ask. And not knowing kept him from sleeping at night. He feared Kinsey had found out about them. He didn't know for sure, but he couldn't find any other explanation for her disappearance. And Kinsey looked at Platinum differently now. Not so much different as less often. He used to look Platinum in the eye when he spoke, but now, he acted more interested in his boot.

"I need you to find him and bring him in," Kinsey said.

Platinum nodded. Couldn't stop nodding. He was relieved that he was being assigned such a task. It reaffirmed his status as Security Chief. "It's been five days. He might have gotten pretty far."

Kinsey threw the brush. It hit Platinum in the shoulder before he could get out of the way. "That's not my concern," Kinsey said. "Just find him and bring him to me."

The glancing blow of the brush surprised him more than it hurt. He'd never seen Kinsey so torqued. "I'm on it, Mr. K."

Kinsey opened the shine box, took out another brush, and began the process on his other boot. "I don't have to remind you that he might try to resist."

"I would imagine," Platinum said. "But his size means nothing to me."

"Don't underestimate him. He's clever enough to make us all think he's just a happy sort of Joe working for beer money. Don't be fooled. He'll try to manipulate you. He'll say things that aren't true to get you on his side."

"I'll shut him up if I have to."

"Good," Kinsey said. "But he better be alive when he gets here. That's all I'm going to say about that."

One of the Kula brothers stepped forward and said. "You want us to go with him, Mr. K?"

Kinsey lowered his shoe brush. "If I wanted you to go I would have told you to go." He waved the brush. "Now wouldn't I?"

"Yes, sir," the Kula brother said as he stepped back to the wall beside his brother.

"Besides," Kinsey picked up his boot and brushed across the leather, "Platinum will be much less conspicuous. I'm hoping to avoid a scuffle. This job requires Platinum's stealth and cunning."

"I won't let you down, Mr. Kinsey."

"You better not, son. You better not."

Sunlight stabbed through the kinks in the aluminum blinds covering the windows in Scotland's motel room, but what woke him was the ache of dehydration in his head and in the back of his throat. He would have tried to sleep through the pain, but it was Tuesday morning, or afternoon, and he had to pull himself together and call Dave if he had any prayer of getting credit for his weekly parole requirement. The sooner, the better.

His vision was foggy and his tongue felt like dry feathers in his mouth. He licked his lips a couple times, but the action provided no moisture. He turned to reach the phone on the nightstand only to discover a woman in his way. Scotland propped himself up on an elbow and tried to clear the sleep from his eyes and cobwebs from his mind.

The woman was also naked, the top sheet kicked down to her ankles. It was a fine body—he got a good view of side boob like half a grapefruit, her hip, ass, and legs—no fat or scars. Judging by how pale she was, she hadn't been in Florida long. Wild brown hair covered her face. He wasn't sure who she was.

It had been the kind of night where he'd poured shots of whiskey and cans of beer down his throat with no sense of the tank getting full. Same as the past few nights.

He reached for the woman's shoulder and rolled her over onto her back. Her wild hair followed, or stuck to drool and he still couldn't see her face. He reached to swipe the hair aside, but her hand caught his wrist in mid-air. "I'm sleeping," she said. "We'll fuck again later."

He recognized her voice. She was the one he'd lost a game of eight-ball to at the Reef toward the end of the night. She'd been the one who'd said, "You lost the battle, but you won the girl."

He climbed over her to pick up the phone, felt his piss hard-on jab into her ribs. The urge to piss increased, but he had to hurry. He crimped the phone between his ear and shoulder and dialed Dave's number from memory.

"You're where?" Dave said.

"I'm in Daytona."

"Daytona? You're supposed to be here today."

"That's why I'm calling you. Am I on time?"

"You better get your ass back here for your appointment."

"I'm phoning it in this time, Dave. Cool right, man?"

"It most certainly is NOT cool." Dave wasn't one to raise his voice, but there was a ton of hostility behind his words when he wasn't happy about something. "How did you get the time off of work to traipse over to Daytona?"

Scotland's brain double-clutched and the gears ground into one another. He should have anticipated the question. More silence passed than Scotland wanted, but he couldn't think of anything to say. The naked woman moaned and rolled over.

"The question isn't rhetorical, Scotland. What about your new job?"

Scotland's stomach knotted. The girl looked comfortable—exactly the opposite of him in that moment. He reared his head backward, partially to stretch, but also to allow in more air before he said, "I sort of had to quit."

"Goddammit, Ross."

"It's not like that, Dave. Really. Next week, I'm heading down to Miami."

"Oh, you are?"

"Yeah. I met up with a boat captain the other day. He's delivering a cabin cruiser from Newport to South Beach. He drives rich people's boats south in the winter and north in the summer. He invited me to join his crew. It isn't a lot of money, but it would be a fresh start. And on the water of all places, where I've always wanted to be. Daytona is nice, too." He looked at his seabag and thought about the cottage he still hadn't found. "This'll be my homeport, Dave."

"That's quite a fantasy life you've created there, young Mr. Ross. But are you forgetting you have a number of months of parole to serve out?"

"Come on, Dave. I'm better off finding this new job in a new city. There are a ton of clubs here. I'm sure I could line up bouncer gigs between boat deliveries."

"Absolutely not." Dave's fist rattled his metal desk. "You're assigned to my district and you will report to me. If you want to relocate and establish charge in another district, there's request paperwork to fill out and procedures to follow. In the meantime, you're appointment is here, not over the phone."

"You've got to let this slide. Just this once, right?"

"Do you have any idea the paperwork generated to keep accurate records? There are reams of shit that get boiled down to a folder for the director so he can make himself comfortable on the toilet and see at a glance who showed up on time, who does or doesn't have a job, and who didn't make it to their appointed check-in. Guess which one lands you back in jail."

Scotland stretched the phone cord across the woman and sat cross-legged on the bed. "It's just one check-in. And I'm just on the other side of the state."

"You're asking me to falsify county records? I'm not losing my job for an ex-con on a bender."

This paper jockey thing wasn't like him. "I'll come back and do the paperwork before going to Miami. Just don't make me come all the way back right now."

"It's just three hours away."

"Not on a bus it's not."

"That's your problem," Dave said through gritted teeth. "And let me tell you another thing, mister. I've seen my share of scumbags in my time and you ain't one of them. You're almost done. You've kept your dick out of the dirt for the better part of a year. Don't fuck it all up for yourself now. So, with that said, I have to warn you that you better get your ass in here before the close of business today or I'll be forced to file a report and kick it upstairs."

He forced the words to his lips. "Don't do that, Dave. I'll get there as soon as I can."

Scotland let the receiver fall and watched it land next to the woman's ass as he got up and walked to the bathroom.

When he came out, he found his jeans wadded up on the opposite side of the bed and got dressed quietly. Not quietly enough, because the girl rolled over.

"You going somewhere?"

"Yeah." Scotland picked up his seabag, slid the strap over his shoulder. "Stay if you like. The room's paid for until Friday."

Where would Scotland go with no car and a five-day head start? Platinum didn't know, but he assumed hitchhiking was involved. He also figured the airport and bus station were natural choices to check first.

He wanted to get started right away, but instead of his car, Platinum went to his apartment.

His bedroom held a bed and a small desk with the book *Art of the Renaissance* lying open. Next to the desk chair stood an easel with an eighteen-by-twenty-four inch drawing of the Mona Lisa. Platinum tossed it to the floor and replaced it with a clean sheet of nine-by-twelve paper. He picked up a pencil and sketched a box, then filled it with quickly drawn shapes all in the same light stroke. He stayed with it for an hour—another hour—constantly filling in the contours of a face taking shape. He worked fast, but was precise with his line definition. There were no lights or shadows in his mind, but rather the fine detail of each facial feature lodged in his memory, the wave and movement of the hair. He worked better with a live model in front of him or from a photo, but his mind was clear and the image was sharp. He knew the shade of each eye, the ridge of brow line, the shape of the nose, lips, and chin, and he recreated it all on the page in an exacting portrait.

He threw down his pencil when he was satisfied that the likeness was complete. He picked up another pencil and shaded in the background with a heavy hand, darkening all the negative space, which made the face pop lifelike with dimension on the page.

He grabbed a mostly-empty, purple velvet bag with Crown Royal written in gold script and ran out of there without locking his door.

Three planes were lined up on the tarmac outside the terminal at Tampa International. Two had rolling staircases at their doors. The terminal smelled of bleach and floor wax. Only a handful of people sat in the rows of seats. Platinum assumed the bulk of the traveling had been done on Saturday and Sunday as people returned to colder climates after a Christmas visit to the tropics or came back from a trip home for the holidays. He hadn't been on an airplane since the long trek back from Laos.

The ticket counters were unmanned, except for the Pan Am counter on the far side of the terminal.

Platinum jogged over, the ticket agent watching him approach. She was a middle-aged gal with a uniform a size too small for her, and not in a good way. Her hair was in a bun on the top of her head and she seemed happy to see Platinum. "And where are we headed today."

"I'm not going anywhere. I just want to ask you some questions."

"Are you a policeman?"

"No, ma'am. But I'm looking for somebody. A man. A big guy. Like a bodybuilder. Traveling alone. You see anybody like that in the last few days?"

The woman leaned her hands on either side of her keyboard and said, "I'd sure remember somebody like that."

Platinum pulled out the rolled piece of paper from his back pocket and spooled it open to show her Scotland's likeness. "This is the guy. Look at his face. He might have come through here on Christmas Day. Did you have flights on Christmas Day?"

"I worked a double that day and every day since, and I'm telling you I haven't seen him."

"Damn," Platinum said.

"That don't mean he wasn't here. Hell, you should've seen this place on Thursday. It was nuts."

Platinum didn't have time for chit-chat. He jogged back out to his car.

* * *

Platinum drove the ten miles from the Tampa airport to the Tampa bus station with a heavy foot and reflexes like a pilot. As he drove, his heart raced in time with the Chevy engine. "Let me get lucky, one time," he said.

The bus station held more activity than the airport, but it wasn't crowded. A couple with a newborn waited on a bench in the center aisle. A couple of teenagers leaned against the lockers and smoked cigarettes, probably stolen from their mothers' purses.

Platinum stopped the first porter he saw inside the station. The guy leaned on his dolly. He had a pack of Lucky Strikes in his shirt pocket and wrinkled, brown skin like a crumpled grocery sack. Platinum unspooled his drawing to show the porter.

"Hey, old timer, you by any chance see this fella in the past few days?"

The porter looked at the picture then up at Platinum. He looked down again and pulled a pair of glasses from behind the pack of Lucky's in his front pocket. He put them on slowly, leaned in to get a closer look. "Nah, sir." The porter backed up and took off his glasses. "I don't know if you're looking to help or hurt that fella, but either way, I ain't never seen him before."

Platinum thanked the porter for his time, but wanted to yell at him for taking so long to be worthless. Platinum let himself be agitated. It gave him adrenaline and he moved quickly. Holding open the portrait of Scotland, he waved it in anybody's face he could find. "Have you seen this man?" he'd say each time. He worked his way through the ticket agents at each end of the station, as well as three porters and four passengers. The next porter he asked was younger, not much past Platinum's own age. He sat backwards on a chair near the corner of the station, in blue coveralls with the sleeves cut off. He looked like he'd be more comfortable around airboats than buses, but he might have seen something.

Platinum walked over to the guy, who just sat there working a toothpick in his mouth. Hard to believe this guy was expected to help women and children with their luggage. Platinum held open the drawing. "You haven't seen this guy in the last couple days, have you?"

"Yeah. I seen that guy."

"You sure?"

"I wouldn't have noticed him, but he was in a real hurry, running through here like O.J. Simpson in that Hertz commercial. Yep. That's him."

"Which train was he heading out on?"

"What's it worth to you?"

Platinum handed the guy a five dollar bill. "Now tell me what train he was heading out on."

"Man, you don't know shit. I should charge you another five bucks. He wasn't going. He was coming in."

"Coming in?" The idea felt insane to Platinum. "You're sure he was coming in."

"Yeah." The porter tapped the picture with his index finger. "This guy. I watched him get off a bus from Daytona and run through here at about a hundred miles per hour. Hit the doors leading to the street and I don't know where he went, but he sure was in a hurry."

"What day was that?"

"What day? Man, you really don't know shit." The guy laughed and crossed his sleeveless arms.

Platinum shoved another five bucks in the porter's hand.

"It was not more than ten minutes ago. You just missed him."

Platinum took off through the same double doors Scotland had so recently exited.

Scotland exited the parole building and squinted at the sunlight. He was tired and hungover and unconvinced he'd successfully faked his way through his meeting with Dave. But his check-in was official and he'd gotten there in time. Outside, he was not as tuned in to his surroundings as he might normally have been. He'd slept in fits on the bus, but woke feeling more hungover than earlier that day. His head felt like it was made out of a rock that was burning from the inside out. His eyes were dry from the heat in his head, and his legs felt rubbery. He had to lock his joints to remain upright. The weight of the seabag over his shoulder made every step dangerous.

He stood on the sidewalk along Cass Street. If there were any cabs in the city of Tampa, none of them were on Cass Street. There had to be cabs near the bus station, so he headed back that way. As he crossed the street, he heard a voice call out, "Hey, Scotty. Where you been?"

Scotland turned to see Platinum jogging toward him. He wore black work boots, jeans, a dark blue silk shirt, and a black leather jacket even though the weather wasn't cold enough to warrant it. His white-blonde hair bounced as he ran.

Scotland kept walking and Platinum matched his pace. "You disappearing got everybody nervous."

Scotland looked around for the Kula brothers. A part of him just knew those big bastards would round a corner and drag him off by the arms.

"What's wrong with you, Scotty?"

"I'm not fond of surprises on a good day."

"Is this a bad day?"

Scotland switched shoulders with the seabag and said, "It is now."

"That some kind of crack?"

"Fuck you," Scotland said, without breaking stride.

"The time away hasn't put you in a better mood, I see."

"Got nothing to do with my mood. Unless you count suspicious as a mood."

"Suspicious of me?"

"Imagine that."

"I understand. And that's cool. I imagine I would be too if the situation was reversed."

Scotland had to look down to conceal a grin. If Platinum only knew how close he was to being shot by the revolver Scotland carried in the seabag over his shoulder, the man would shit. Scotland considered telling him the scenario, but held it back.

"But think about it," Platinum said. "If I wanted you dead *and* I knew where you were going to be, do you think I'd jump out in broad daylight and say hello first?" He walked backward, his hands held out at his sides.

The logic added up in Scotland's brain, but it didn't earn a lot of trust.

"Besides," Platinum continued, "if Kinsey wanted you dead, he'd have sent the Kula brothers."

Scotland couldn't give that argument any weight, because he knew differently.

"Seriously, man. The last time I saw you was the day Eddie Joyner gave himself the ultimate headache."

Scotland had been able to put that out of his mind for the past few days, though because of the drinking required in forgetting his brain still swam in the brackish low tide of vodka and bourbon.

"I just want to make sure that's the reason you took off. Because if it is, it'll pass. You get over those things quick. Don't blow an opportunity of a lifetime over it. You know?"

"I thought you'd be pissed."

"What? About you disappearing?"

"What did Kinsey tell you?"

"He said you quit, but I guessed that when I saw your Bonneville abandoned near the Gulf Breeze sign."

"Did he tell you why?"

"Of course he did. But that doesn't matter."

Scotland didn't believe for a minute that Kinsey told Platinum the truth. Scotland didn't believe Kinsey capable of being truthful. "You think it's because of Eddie Joyner's brains spraying the wall?"

"It's pretty fucking coincidental, now isn't it, Scotty boy?"

Scotland tried to hold in his facial expression, and Platinum also played it cool. He didn't smile or blink. The marks of someone bluffing didn't usually stand out to Scotland like this. It made no sense for Kinsey to tell him the reason, and Kinsey wasn't the kind to make up a lie about it. Scotland was convinced that Kinsey hadn't told Platinum a thing, and now this sonofabitch was bluffing.

"If I'd've known you missed me, I would've called. You been looking for me long?"

"Nah. I haven't been looking for you at all." Platinum tugged at the waistband of his jeans. "I just figured I'd catch up with you here."

"How'd you know where to find me?"

"It's Tuesday, dumbass," he said, pointing toward the parole building. "I might not have had as much college as you, but I know how to read a fucking calendar." Platinum slapped Scotland on the shoulder. "You look like you could use a drink."

Under the weight of the seabag, his rubbery legs threatening to give out, Scotland straightened himself. The sun reflected off the pavement and right into the backs of his dry eyes. He didn't want to spend any more time with Platinum. That was a part of his life he wanted to leave behind. "I've got some place to be."

"Just one beer. It'll take five minutes."

Scotland looked around again for any trace of the Kula brothers—or anyone else in a window with a rifle pointed at his chest. Perhaps on another day Scotland would have let his suspicions take him in a different direction. As it was though, there didn't appear to be any immediate threat. Even Platinum seemed calm and for lack of a better word, sincere. The air felt light and clean on Cass Street and the hair on the back of Scotland's neck rested flat along his skin. He saw no reason to postpone his first drink of the day any longer. "What the hell," he said. "A little hair of the dog might do the trick today."

"Exactly what the doctor ordered," Platinum said. "I'm parked right around the corner."

They drove west into a sun that hung low enough to blast through the windshield with glare that bent around the sun visors in their down positions. The Seven Seas Lounge was a windowless building almost directly on Kennedy Boulevard, barely a sliver of curb. You could just about simultaneously touch the front door and passing cars. Only two cars were in the parking lot on the side, the happy hour crowd an hour or so away.

Inside, the only bright light was a shaft of sunshine coming in through the door they'd just entered. Three guys sat in chairs along the stage where a big-titted blonde chick danced naked except for the tassels on her nipples. She spun them clockwise and counter-clockwise, but had difficulty getting them to oppose one another. A poor showing, even for the day shift.

At the bar, Scotland rolled his sleeves down. He hated the shirt he was wearing. Amber had bought it for him. He didn't remember putting it his seabag, but it was the first thing he'd grabbed on his way out of his motel room in Daytona that morning. He ordered a shot of Jack and a beer back from a soured bartender with a Joe DiMaggio nose. Platinum simply said, "Same."

Before the drinks came, Scotland realized he had only three dollars in his pocket. He'd spent seventeen dollars on the one-way bus ticket from Daytona and the rest of his money was stashed in his seabag. "Is your car locked?"

"No. Why?"

"I've got to get something out of my seabag."

Platinum shrugged with a smile on his face. "Be my guest," he said.

Scotland squinted into the sun again as he made his way out to the car. The passenger door opened smoothly and the new-car smell made him miss the Bonneville he'd never be able to drive again. For that brief moment, he had a foot back in the good life where money and comfort was everywhere. He found the sock stuffed with the remains of his bankroll and peeled off two tens and a five. He didn't owe Platinum anything more than not taking his life, but he aimed to buy the man a parting drink and say his good-byes.

As he clasped shut his seabag, he took another whiff of the new-car smell and thought about pulling out the revolver. Instead, he left the bag shut and slammed the door behind him.

Back inside the Seven Seas, a new girl had taken the stage and was still mostly dressed as a nurse with stiletto heels. Scotland kept an eye on her as he walked past and slapped a ten on the bar. He hopped onto his stool and said to Platinum, "Your money's no good here."

"I'll get the next round."

"No," Scotland said, reaching for his shot of whiskey. "Just one round. It's on me. Then, I've got to find a place to crash for the night."

"I might have an idea for you."

"Forget it. I'm not going back to the Gulf fucking Breeze."

They clinked shot glasses and downed the whiskey.

"It's like we're getting a head start on New Year's," Platinum said.

Scotland laughed. "It's been New Year's Eve for the past four days."

Neither reached for his beer right away. Scotland felt the warmth course down his throat and into his fingers and toes. The last place to feel the alcohol was his head, but once it hit, the fuzziness in the room cleared and his legs firmed up.

Platinum picked up his beer. "Cheers."

They clinked glasses again and the crispness of the beer coated the inside of Scotland's dry mouth.

While the nurse stripped down to her garters and those heels, Linda Ronstadt sang on the stereo. Scotland didn't know the song, but he'd recognize her voice anywhere.

He drank more of his beer. As he neared the bottom of his glass, he said, "Well, this has been fun, but I think I'll grab my bag and head out."

"Where the hell are you going to go?"

"I don't know."

"Come with me, back to the Gulf."

"That's not happening." Scotland's ribcage sank to his hips. His shoulders rolled forward and he leaned heavy on the bar. The booze went straight to his head, made him heavy.

"I'm willing to bet it is," Platinum said.

"You're out of your mind," Scotland said with a hand on Platinum's shoulder. "You're not strong enough to make me do what I don't want to do."

Platinum held up a purple Crown Royal bag and poured its contents onto the bar. An assortment of empty gelatin capsules rained out.

"What the hell is that?"

Platinum crumpled the bag into his palm and slipped it into his pocket. "You know way more than Kinsey feels comfortable about."

"Is that...?" Scotland pointed at the empty capsules.

"Ten of the pills we stole in the port heist? Why, yes, it is. And the contents were all in your beer."

Scotland dismounted his bar stool and ran for the men's room. It was dingy space with a shitter stall and an overflowing urinal. He pushed open the stall door and bent over the commode. Before he could get his finger down his throat, Platinum pushed in behind him and grabbed his wrist. Scotland pulled back, but he didn't break Platinum's grip.

"Don't fight, Scotty. Your strength has been neutralized by a million milligrams of muscle relaxers."

Scotland swung a punch at Platinum's head, but he ducked out of the way easily. "This is how you're going to get me back? You don't even have the balls for a fair fight?"

"That's the difference between us, Scotty. I'm not a knuckle-dragger like you. I'm smart enough to avoid that kind of shit whenever possible."

"You're a fucking puppet."

Platinum took off his belt, wrapped it around his hand. He mouthed the words "fucking puppet" and swung at Scotland.

Scotland saw it coming and turned as much as the stall allowed. The punch grazed his temple. His ear took the worst of it, but at least it wasn't a direct hit. Before he could turn around again, Platinum landed a knee in Scotland's gut and doubled him over. All his air was taken out with the blow. As he raised his hands to defend himself, the belted fist came down again. Scotland reached out, caught it in a wavering grip. He tried to wrestle Platinum back with this hold, but instead of being pushed back he was pulled out of the stall. With all his momentum, Platinum landed another knee to the ribs. Another. Scotland still couldn't breathe and his torso felt on fire when he tried to take in air. The back of his head smacked into the tiled wall beside the towel roller. The impact knocked his chin into his chest and the recoil made him nauseous. Scotland slid down the wall in slow motion, sat slumped. "You're going to die."

Platinum smacked his belted fist into his palm. "That's tough talk coming from someone on his ass."

"Not me, you dumbass."

"Who? Kinsey? Ha. He said you'd tell me some crazy shit.

Talk crazy all you want. You'll be asleep inside of ten minutes, if I had to guess."

"He wanted me to do it. That's why I left."

"You're out of your mind from the pills, and fear, maybe. He wouldn't kill me. He needs me too much. You, he'd kill. I'm surprised I wasn't given the order."

Scotland felt a pinch at the base of his skull and everything went dark.

Platinum removed a coil of wire from the pocket of his leather jacket. He bit the free end and clasped Scotland's comatose hands in front of him as he unspooled it with his free hand. He wound the wire in a figure eight pattern, over, under, around, and through until they stayed that way. The big guy's size and strength didn't impress or intimidate Platinum, but he sure as hell wasn't going to ignore it. If Scotland tried to free himself, the wire would cut through his wrists like cheese.

Once he was convinced the wire wrap was unbreakable, Platinum yanked up and down on Scotland's bound wrists. "Who's the fucking puppet now, Scotty boy?"

Platinum punched Scotland in the head once again for good measure for all the shit he'd been talking. There was no way for Platinum to get around the fact Scotland could have been telling the truth about Kinsey. He sat down on his heels and stared at the tile by his feet. Kinsey must have banished Maria when he found out about her and Platinum. He *could* have given Scotland the order to take him out. But if Kinsey wanted him dead, he would have been dead already. "No," Platinum said as he stood. "No." He poked the toe of his work boot into Scotland's ribs. "My job is to bring you back to him and that's what I'm going to do."

Platinum removed his leather jacket and draped it over Scotland's clasped hands and reached to pick him up. He was heavy as a church. Platinum had to abandon the first attempt and reposition himself to get a better grip and more leverage. The second attempt got him upright, but the weight was off balance and he had to let Scotland drop to the floor again. He slapped Scotland in the face—hard—with an open right hand. "Wake up." Scotland stirred, but didn't come fully to life. That was fine. Platinum didn't need him fully animated. Would prefer that he not be. All he needed was the big guy's mind semi-conscious. Muscle memory would do the rest for him. And on the third attempt, all systems were go. He got Scotland up and positioned so that walking was possible.

They got plenty of looks on the way out, but nobody seemed to question a drunk's ability to hold onto his coat while another human being was required to provide the propulsion necessary to get the drunk guy out of the bar.

CHAPTER EIGHTEEN

Kinsey stomped across the Gulf Breeze parking lot to building 2, crushed shells crunching beneath his cowboy boots. He wore brown Sansabelt pants with his Smith & Wesson .41 tucked into the waistband, the handle against his hipbone for quick access.

Apartments 2A and 2B were separate units that had an adjoining door. No one lived in either unit. Kinsey used them as his storage facility for merchandise pinched by the men he employed.

The Kula brothers waited for him outside the door marked 2B. The straining, thin fabric of their matching shirts accentuated their size.

Kinsey reached up and clapped each of them on a shoulder. "He's really in there?"

"He sure is," Mo said. "Platinum's still in there, too."

This news pleased Kinsey enough to double-clap Mo's shoulder.

Kinsey was one of a few people who could tell the Kula brothers apart. They were identical, except Mo's nose was a little different. It was just as wide as Bo's, but it connected to his face differently—not as snug a fit. Kinsey couldn't believe other people didn't pick up on that.

He looked up at the Kula brothers. "Excellent. Excellent. But can you believe that bastard?"

"I can't believe either one of them," Bo said.

After a shared laugh, Mo opened the door and Kinsey went in first; the Kula brothers followed behind.

The living room was made larger by having no kitchen. Rows of commercial-grade shelves filled the space where the couches and coffee table would go. Along the walls was an assortment of cellophane wrapped works of art. Paintings mostly, framed and leaning against a wall where a table and chairs would go. A couple sculptures were bubble-wrapped heavily enough to blur the subjects. A tag had been taped to each item, cataloging it all with numbers that corresponded to a ledger in a drawer in the downstairs office.

Near the far wall, four aluminum garbage cans sat with lids shut tight. These cans contained the lion's share of the pills Scotland and Platinum had lifted from the port.

The bedroom area of 2B had been converted into a sound-proof cell with padded walls and a metal door that locked from the outside.

Kinsey walked into the cell as the Kula brothers took their positions flanking the doorway.

The padded cell always made Kinsey feel safe. He'd had it designed with double drywall, acoustic tiles behind the padding on the walls, and doubled up on the ceiling. If the Russians were ever to drop the bomb, it was the place he'd go.

Light from the double row of fluorescent bulbs overhead lit the place like daylight though there were no windows to reveal the darkness outside. A folding table and four folding chairs were the only furniture in the room except for a stainless steel cutting-table from his meat processing plant near the door. The table served as a tool bench of sorts. A canvas bag of tools sat ready for use on the tabletop beside a first aid kit. A chainsaw rested on the lower shelf beside a length of chain coiled there.

Platinum stood as Kinsey entered. He grinned like an idiot and motioned with his hand, as if Kinsey wouldn't have noticed Scotland slumped in a chair, unconscious, the bulk of his torso folded over his legs.

"I got him, Mr. K." Platinum's knees dipped a time or two as he spoke. "It wasn't easy, but here he is."

Kinsey walked over to Scotland. He bent down to assess the cut above his eye and the contusions on his cheekbones and forehead. "And you don't have a mark on you, Platinum," he said without looking back at him.

"This should prove once and for all how good I am at my job, Mr. K." He was bouncing by this point.

"Yes. Good work." Kinsey stood and placed a hand on Platinum's shoulder to steady the excited fucker. "I knew you'd find a way to bring him back alive. You perform all the tasks I assign you in a manner that far exceed my expectations, son."

Platinum's smile carved into his face severely enough to show almost every one of his capped teeth. He bounced on his toes again. "Thank you, Mr. K. That's good of you to say."

Kinsey put his hands on his hips, faced the Kula brothers, and nodded toward Scotland. "Wake him up."

Platinum grabbed a handful of hair draped in Scotland's face. He yanked it back with one hand and reared back with the other, rotating at the hips and shoulder to whirl around and smack Scotland with an open hand.

The slap roused Scotland, but didn't bring him to.

Platinum switched hands and reared back to deliver another smack, to the other side of Scotland's face.

That one brought him around. He moaned, said something unintelligible—a couple of words, not a full sentence. He moaned again.

Kinsey snapped his fingers and pointed. Platinum sat down in his chair, quickly and without a word.

Scotland moaned once more. The muscles in his arms tensed as he tried to spread his hands, but his wrists were still bound. He struggled to free his hands. After a silent minute, he gave up and sat back.

"You are bound, son," Kinsey said, "because this is the way you were brought to me."

Scotland remained silent, but he looked up at Kinsey as if

he couldn't quite make out the facial features before him. "Kinsey?"

"That's right, Scottish. We're reunited." Kinsey picked up Scotland's head and shook it. Scotland's neck was like string. Kinsey craned it sideways where Platinum sat slumped in the chair directly to his right. "Our friend, Platinum here, has taken it upon himself to restrain you." He let go of Scotland's head.

Scotland didn't speak, but he held his stare in Platinum's direction.

"You can't run from me, Scottish," Kinsey said through clenched teeth. "You should have known better than that, son."

"I walked away." Scotland kept his eyes on Platinum. "I never ran."

Kinsey raised his hands and raked through his hair. "I don't have time for semi-circles."

Scotland said, "Semi-circles? Do you mean semantics? Jesus. You really need to get a grip on common expressions."

"Be that as it may, the fact is you disappeared. Now, I don't care where you went or what you did, but I do need to know who you spoke with and what you might've said."

Scotland sat back and shook hair from his face. "I understand your paranoia, Kinsey, but I haven't said shit."

"What about your parole officer?" Platinum said, rising from his chair.

Kinsey pointed. Platinum sank back down into his seat.

"He'd be the last person I'd tell about any of this."

Kinsey folded his arms across his chest and rubbed his beard with the backs of his fingers. His caught himself with his head jutted forward, anxious for that to be true. "You expect me to believe you haven't spoken a word about our conversations?" He waved a hand behind him to indicate his office, the map on the wall, the Gulf Breeze itself, and all the stuff that couldn't be seen in that cell or anywhere else. "You expect me to believe you haven't said anything about any of this since last I saw you?"

Scotland licked his lips and said, "I'd give you my word, but I don't suppose it would do any good."

Kinsey kicked Scotland's chair hard enough to turn him sideways. The kick hurt Kinsey's toe, but the shot of pain energized him. "You're damn right it'll do no good. Your *word* means shit to me." Kinsey paced back and forth across the room to walk off the damage to his foot. He pulled out his revolver. "Loyalty is based on trust." He walked closer to Scotland. "I'll spare you the entomology of the word, but my daddy used to say, 'Loyalty is as important to the world as the sky is to Heaven.' Do you know what that means? It means trust isn't something I give out like cars or apartments. And when I trust somebody, I expect them to be there to represent my best interests just as I would represent theirs." Kinsey waved the revolver over his head as if to add an exclamation point. "It's a low motherfucker who's capable of treating friends so disrespectfully. A disloyal man is a man capable of nothing good." Kinsey felt winded when he finished. After a series of shallow breaths, he raised the revolver and fired one shot into the center of Platinum's chest.

The report of the .41 Magnum imploded Kinsey's ears. He thought he heard the bullet pierce Platinum's skin, breaking bones, driving shrapnel into his heart.

Platinum looked down at his chest, astonished. He covered the hole with his hand and looked up.

Kinsey raised the revolver and aimed at Platinum's head—but held fire. Platinum's eyes closed, but Kinsey smacked him across the cheek with the gun barrel. Even if for an instant, he wanted Platinum to look into his eyes and see the revenge swirling in his soul. Wanted him to see the unspoken words in his head, "*I know what you did!*"

Kinsey lowered the revolver for a moment so there'd be no distraction from the information behind his eyes, then re-aimed at Platinum's head.

The shot would go in clean, dead center of the forehead, but it would exit with a mess behind him, all of which was unnecessary and might disturb the surprise frozen on his face.

Kinsey stood and admired his marksmanship, his ears were filled with both percussion and the airy feeling of relief.

He handed the revolver to Mo.

Scotland said, "You're a twisted motherfucker."

It took a moment for the words to penetrate Kinsey's ears and register in his mind. He'd almost forgotten about Scotland Ross. He turned and walked to Scotland's chair. Kinsey leaned forward. "Have I ever claimed to be anything to the contrary, son?" Kinsey held out his hand and Mo brought the revolver back to him. Kinsey gripped the revolver, held it pointed at the ceiling. He still had the power of revenge coursing through him. Shooting Scottish would add to it, but he hesitated. In his mind, the reality of the operation losing two men in one night was huge. Kinsey considered how morale among his staff might suffer. He didn't need anyone else getting the idea to betray him. Kinsey raised the revolver in his hand and smashed it down with all his strength into Scotland's jaw.

Scotland thudded on the floor in a heap of unconscious muscle.

"All right, boys," Kinsey said. "This is a gift from me to you." He holstered his revolver in his waistband and declared, "I'm not going to kill him."

"You're going to let him live?" Mo said.

"You two have at him. But I suggest you let him live long enough so he can dig his own grave." Kinsey kicked Scotland's unconscious torso. He stepped to his right and kicked Platinum's lifeless body. "Take them to the island and bury them." He stepped back and kicked Scotland again.

"Make him dig both holes before you kill him. How do you boys like that idea?"

"It'll be our pleasure, Mr. K."

They each scooped up a body.

CHAPTER NINETEEN

Scotland came to with a sore jaw and his teeth jammed together. It was full daylight and he was forced to squint. He shielded his eyes with his bound hands as he lay on his back absorbing the pitch and roll of the floor beneath him. It was the unmistakable feeling of being on a boat. The smell of salt water registered in his brain the same instant he heard it slapping the hull beneath him. He groaned and reached out his hands for purchase on anything he could use to pull himself upright.

"Scotty's coming around," one of the Kula brothers said. He held a revolver two feet from Scotland's heart while his brother drove the boat. "You want me to shoot him?"

"Don't be a dumbass," the Kula behind the wheel said. "If you hit the boat, we're fucked. Besides, we're almost there. Cut his hands free so he can climb out and dig the holes."

The Kula with the pistol nodded.

The wire wrap job Platinum pulled on him earlier dug into Scotland's wrists. Now, on his back with two big guys standing over him reminded him of the Casta boys when he was twelve. Scotland's head rang with pain and his body was stiff. He seethed over this turn of events, but he was also energized by the memories of that fateful day outside the convenience store when he defied the odds and surprised himself.

As best Scotland could tell, the boat was a Wellcraft, about nineteen feet. They were taking some rough swells, whitecaps all around them. Mo or Bo or whichever one had the gun lifted a seat cushion and pulled out a pair of angled pliers. He handed the gun to his brother behind the wheel and set about cutting through the wire. Scotland couldn't believe they would actually free his hands. If the shit were reversed, he'd wait until the last possible moment, just in case. The best move he could think of now was to keep his mouth shut. From his position seated on the boat's deck, Scotland held his arms up to facilitate the wire cutting. The hull slapped every other wave and it was like the water had turned into cement. The impact jolted Scotland's spine every time the twin outboard Evinrudes launched the boat and gravity brought it down. The pointed tips of the pliers poked dangerously close to Scotland's eyes a couple times. While he wasn't going to complain about having his hands free, he wasn't big on the idea of losing an eye in the process.

Once the wire was cut, Scotland stretched his arms wide, arched his back. His sternum cracked like knuckles. He uncoiled the rest of the wire from his wrists and tossed it overboard. Blood and salty air ran into the cut and raw skin where the wire had been.

He pulled himself to his feet. His knees were loose as he struggled to recall his sea legs. Whatever ability he'd developed in his short time aboard a warship was now rusty. This was the first time he'd been on the water since those Navy days.

The Kula brother with the revolver braced himself on the railing with a straight arm. He stood stiff in the knees and the only thing that moved was his anvil jaw as he worked a piece of gum. Platinum lay rolled up in vinyl flooring and banged around the boat's stern.

Before long, they were in a stretch of the Gulf of Mexico deep enough to shine bluer than the green areas near the coast. Too far out for such a small scarab. There were no other boats in the water—because of high seas, probably; but also because of the fishing ban that had the commercial fleet handcuffed to the docks.

The boat headed west. In the sun's glare, the Kula brothers looked more alike than ever with their slicked-back hair and sleeveless T-shirts. They were both barefoot, their pants rolled up around their ankles like Huck Finn, their pointy dress shoes secured in the bench-well beneath the driver's cushion. They clearly knew what they were doing, but seemed as unprepared for a boat ride as Scotland was, like they'd been caught off guard, had other plans.

The wind whipped as the boat sped farther out. The windscreen was closed, and Scotland had to assume it was to protect the pomade in their hair. Gulls called overhead, so they couldn't be *that* far out yet.

"Are we going to Knob Island?" Scotland said.

"What do you know about it?" said the Kula holding the gun. He was easily two of Scotland.

Engine noise was surprisingly quiet considering the horsepower of the twin motors mounted a couple feet behind them. "Just some shit I heard."

"About Kinsey?"

"I don't reckon you guys can be talked out of this."

"Shut the fuck up."

Scotland held onto the rail with one hand. As he did, the tail of his tattoo peeked out of a sleeve not quite long enough to reach his wrist. His other hand was in his pocket, spinning his Zippo between fingers that played over the corners of the lighter as if it were a Rosary. Scotland didn't know any prayers to whisper, so instead he said, "Any chance I can *buy* my way out of this?"

"With what, you stupid prick?" the Kula with the gun said. "Owing money is what got you into this whole kettle of fish."

The driving Kula hollered back, "Do I got to drive this boat *and* keep that broke-dick motherfucker quiet?"

The gun swung back to Scotland, but lower this time, the barrel aimed toward his groin.

"I'm done talking for a while," Scotland said.

Judging by the sun, Scotland guessed it was about three

o'clock. He stretched his neck, trying to touch each shoulder with an ear and leaned his head back to feel the salt air wash over his face. The grit coated his lips and he licked them clean and enjoyed the crunch between his teeth. He was meant to be out on the water. Deep water. Sailing the Pacific and the Atlantic. The Indian Ocean. This boat was not a ship, but because he was going to be shot and buried on a tiny island in the middle of the Gulf, it was as close as he'd ever get again.

The water got choppier the farther they got out to sea. The engines whined as the propellers hopped above the surface, revving hard and loud. The noise was like someone playing with the throttle on a chainsaw, which he figured these guys had stashed somewhere on the boat.

Scotland had known the risks when he took off last week, knew something would happen if Kinsey caught him. But this was way more than the ass-whupping a reasonable man might expect.

Hand in his pocket, Scotland spun the Zippo and rolled his shoulders. His shirt was tight and cut off circulation in the armpits. The shirt's print was too small to be plaid, but too large to be checks. He hated the idea of dying in a shirt like that.

The island came into view slowly. First just a dot followed by an outline on the horizon all of a sudden it was a looming black mass off the boat's starboard bow. Scotland's lips tasted of salt and he couldn't stop licking them. The Kula with the revolver was checking out the island and Scotland considered his options, the first of which was over powering him, taking his gun away and shooting him and the driver. But even if he could wrestle the gun away, he didn't figure he could get off a second shot in time. His second option was to jump overboard and swim like a bastard. But, again, the guns posed a problem. Even without the guns, he was sure the cold-hearted Kula's would love to run him over and watch the propellers make chum of his flesh and bones.

The third, and worst, option was for Scotland to make them shoot him now so at least they got the inconvenience of having to cart his corpse off the boat and dig the graves themselves.

The boat slowed and the water softened as they neared the leeward side of the island. Scotland fingered the Zippo faster and faster in his pocket. He flipped it open, flicked the wheel. Felt the heat. The guy with the gun still peeked over his shoulder toward the island and the gun waved from Scotland's groin to his face. He flinched a little. He didn't want either of them thinking he actually flinched, so he played it off, pretended to look at something at the back of the boat. And for the first time, he noticed the red gas tanks in the well there just behind Platinum's corpse. He never realized he was that close to the tanks while he was lighting up his pocket.

A fourth option flashed in his mind. The idea raked through him like a piss shiver.

And without hesitation, the muscles in his lower back flexed as he lunged for the gas tank. It was a one-shot opportunity that happened in slow motion.

He reached out and grabbed the fuel line between his index finger and thumb. The rubber hose gave way with less resistance than anticipated. With it pulled free, gasoline flowed over his hand and onto the deck. The smell overwhelmed him, but he flipped open the Zippo and ran the flint wheel down the leg of his jeans. It lit. Scotland didn't know if they would fire their guns or duck for cover. He didn't wait to find out and he didn't look back.

The WHUMP sound of ignition behind him was immediately followed by heat from the flames that lit his shirt afire mid-jump. His flesh burned and he cracked his shin on the gunnel as he dove over the side.

The Gulf of Mexico extinguished him, but landing face-first forced water into his lungs. He needed a clean breath of air, but instead he kicked his legs and pawed at the water, forcing himself deeper and deeper so as to avoid any shots they might get off. Before he hit bottom, he felt the concussion of the flames detonating the fumes of the partially empty fuel tank. Pressure filled his ears and everything was silent. If the goons on the boat screamed like girls, he never heard it. It was quiet in that moment. Quiet brought safety, so he made his way back to the surface, where he coughed and spit up saltwater.

The boat was nothing but fragments set aflame from stem to stern. Patches of oil burned on the water's surface like stage lights. Black smoke rose into the dusking sky. Scotland floated as silently as possible, waiting to hear movement near the largest section of boat still afloat. But the only sound was the licking of the flames and the curling and charring of molten fiberglass, like marshmallows in a campfire.

He swam for the island, his shoes weighing him down, his pants creating drag in the water. Instinct told him to take them off, but he'd need them when he got to the island and it wasn't that far. He swam a few strokes before slowing to a dog paddle. He took another look at the island. It didn't appear any closer. He swam another few strokes and stopped again to check his distance. The next round of swimming was faster and for longer, and by the time he checked the distance again the water was shallow enough for him to stand. He took in a series of rapid breaths, then inhaled deeply and exhaled with a primal yell that came with the realization the island was the first place Kinsey would look for them, for him.

Scotland took a few more deep breaths, sunk into the water and backstroked away.

His boots were full of water and weighed him down. He tugged to remove one. His foot slipped. He kicked his leg up again and got a better grip on the heel and pulled. The effort made him tumble under water. He dropped the boot and contorted beneath the water, yanking off the other boot and letting it fall to the sandy bottom. Being lighter helped him kick upward. He broke the water's surface fast and with as big a gulp of air as he could get.

He swam back toward the area of debris, but it seemed farther now and he was getting tired. In boot camp, he'd been taught to take off his pants, tie the legs in knots and trap air through the waistband to make a flotation device. But that was in the safety of an Olympic-size swimming pool. He didn't want to reach down and unbuckle his belt. Didn't want to be naked in the water.

He felt around the wreckage and found an orange lifejacket. Half of it was gone, but he struggled himself into the straps. The ability to float without effort allowed him to relax. Even if he lost consciousness, his head might remain above the water…unless the waves flipped him over.

Even as the sun melted into the horizon the water didn't feel cold, but he'd learned in his Navy training that the body loses heat twenty-five times faster in water. By his rusty calculations, he had less than an hour until he lost dexterity in his fingers and hands. If he let his core temperature drop even a few degrees, his organs would work overtime trying to heat themselves up and this would exhaust him. He'd face disorientation and unconsciousness which meant he could drown.

He wasted no more time and swam through the debris. He pushed aside chunks of synthetic seat foam and plastic and through a widening patch of burning water. With the life jacket on, it was hard to paddle properly but he kicked through to the far side of the flotsam and pulled a section of the hull toward him. The piece was longer than he was tall and as wide as his shoulders. He hugged it to himself and curled one leg over the top. The jagged section where he laid his head had the scars of melted fiberglass. There was no smell to it except for the oily saltwater splashing into his nose and mouth as he kicked to put as much water between him and the island as possible. The sky was almost black now, and there was no moon to light his way.

Just him and the water now. It was every bad dream he'd had in his brief time aboard ship, the bad dream sailors have had since the first galleon set sail. He kept as much of his body atop the plank as he could and held on, hoping the sun would rise soon. He floated for hours blinded by dark. No lights from shore or sky pocked the darkness. His legs were numb and he was unable to breathe deeply. His throat was dry and thirst pulled at his tongue from his guts. Drinking mouthfuls of the saltwater he floated in was tempting, but it would be suicide. Waves smashed salt onto his lips and the sodium seeped into his body, dehydrating him further. He held onto the plank and tried to convince his mind that he was in front of a fireplace in a living room somewhere. He wanted to be covered in flannel and wearing boots and feeling the heat of small oak-burning flames licking over his hands. He wondered if that would ever be possible. He wondered if the sun would ever rise again.

It was impossible to know if he was headed toward the coast or farther out to sea. There were no gulls and the sky was too dark to be of any use.

He heard a crack, like somebody hitting a clean break in a game of eight-ball. It was impossible to know where it came from, but he awaited another. It didn't come. He waited longer. Hoped that it would come. The sound could have been a tension wire snapping aboard a passing ship. It could have been the fiberglass he was floating on. It could have been his mind. And he was so thirsty.

Cold worked through his body enough to make him shiver. It took all his strength to keep the chunk of hull he floated on in position beneath him. If it were larger, he could have crawled up there and curled into the fetal position. He could have conserved some body heat that way. He was pretty sure his feet were numb, but he couldn't hold them still long enough to know for sure. As best he could tell, there was no pain and he couldn't feel the weight of the water on his kicking feet. The meaty part of his legs and arms and all along his ribcage took the cold most severely. He slept atop the flotsam, hugging it to him, a leg thrown over in case his grip slipped.

Waves spilled into his mouth. Their spray stung his eyes. His ear was pickled. He wished he'd never met Donny Benes. He wanted to kill that asshole for getting him mixed up with a psycho like Kinsey.

In the morning, the sun scorched off the Gulf's surface. Scotland wished he had his sunglasses. His stomach was an angry knot leaning closer to his spine with each passing minute. Thirst was a chokehold that made it hard to breath.

He had never fished a day in his life, but he'd seen people along riverbanks and on bridges with lines cast out into the water. He knew what a bobber was and he felt like one now bobbing on the surface, the rest of him submerged.

The water looked calm near the horizon—that smooth seam between water and sky—but swells broke white with foam and everything was salty. He'd kill for a cup of coffee and to be dry. Clean. Comfortable.

The sun wore on him. He submerged so his head was just high enough out of the water for him to breathe, but the relentless sun cooked his face. He removed his singed shirt and tied it on his head and let the tail trail down his neck for more protection, like one of the oil sheiks in the desert. He passed the day holding on. Hoping.

Hope made him think of Dana and the girls. He wondered if he'd ever see them again. If they'd be okay. If Mark would go back to fishing and mistakenly catch Scotland's corpse some day in the near future.

This made him recall the night the problems between Scotland and Mark began—a day when Scotland visited on leave. He'd been in the Navy just under two years and it was his first stretch of time off since graduating boot camp. He'd flown in uniform and strangers kept buying him drinks. He got more liquored up on the plane than he planned. By the time he landed in Tampa, he caught himself slurring a word or two every other sentence. Before he could sober up, Mark picked him up from the airport in his pickup, an open bottle of Jim Beam between his legs. Scotland threw his seabag in the truck bed and took a swig before he closed his door.

Mark drove a straight line despite being as drunk as Scotland. He asked, "Is it as big a party in San Diego as I've heard it is?"

It was Scotland's first time in Tampa. The air was thick with wet heat that made his arms sticky. "San Diego is great," Scotland said. "But the real party doesn't start until we get overseas."

Mark pressed Scotland for all the dirt on the Green Light district in Korea, the Bar Girls in the Philippines, sex clubs in Hong Kong.

"It's like playing baseball in the international league and batting one point oh," Scotland said.

"Oh, man." Mark pounded the steering wheel with the heel of his hand. "That has got to be the best fucking thing in the world."

"It's all right," Scotland said, purposely underplaying things. But deep down, the women and the booze, and the travel and the rapid climb up the military ranks was all shit he'd trade in a cricket's heartbeat to go back to the way it was when he had a wife at home with a sleeping baby. The adventure stories Scotland told weren't so much bragging as they were a form of confession. The real sin though was that Mark didn't know how lucky he was.

The heat of November surprised Scotland that day on leave. He thought about removing his dress blue jumper, but instead, took another swig. As he handed the bottle back to Mark, he said, "We should stop for a real drink. I'm buying."

Mark doubled back and drove to the causeway, where they stopped at the Tanga Lounge.

Scotland was all for a titty show before being holed up for the long weekend with his sister and nieces.

Inside, the air was thick with cigarette smoke and old beer. Naked girls gyrated on stage and grinded on guys paying cash to have them do it, just like in every strip club in the world. Scotland felt comfortable in places like the Tanga. Had spent much of his time ashore in such clubs from San Diego to Korea. Mark didn't look uncomfortable, either.

As Scotland did a shot of tequila and chased it with a sip of Schlitz, Mark ordered a gin and tonic for a blonde woman wearing a red negligee. Scotland wasn't sure if Mark knew how much that would cost and didn't really care, until Mark started to paw the woman's red hemline. She demurely swatted his hands away, but Mark wouldn't stop.

"No touching," the bartender shouted. "Keep your hands to yourself or we'll have a problem."

Mark held up his hands like a bank robber caught in the act and said, "Just looking for a return on my investment."

On the way out an hour later, Mark said to Scotland, "Don't tell your sister we were here, okay?"

The ride to Mark and Dana's house passed with silence as Scotland pretended to sleep.

Mark and Dana lived in the house Mark had grown up in, on a side street off Gulf Boulevard in Madeira Beach. It wasn't a big house, but there were bedrooms for the girls and a pullout couch in the Florida room Mark had added onto the back. The girls were asleep when Mark and Scotland came in.

Scotland was tired from the long flight and all the drinking, and after hanging out in the kitchen with Dana briefly, he slipped off to that pullout in the other room.

Later that night, he heard Mark hollering and Dana sort of dishing it back, but more than not, she said, "Okay. Okay. Okay."

The first slap sounded like a tree branch snapping in winter. The second sat him up. There was no way to ignore it. He walked into the hall from the Florida room and heard Dana trying to be silent but not succeeding. The girls stayed asleep.

He pushed open the door and saw Dana's hands up over her head, in self-defense. A bedside lamp lit them both. Mark's right hand was reared back with his belt buckle in his fist. Scotland hated the fear on his sister's face. He lunged for Mark to get the belt away from him. He planned to settle everyone down and find out if this sort of thing happened often, but Mark spoiled that plan by slipping out of Scotland's grasp and landing a solid kidney shot.

Scotland went down on one knee and leaned back until the immediate pain subsided.

"You go mind your own fucking business, sailor boy."

Dana hollered, "Stop fighting," but she didn't move.

Scotland turned to face Mark.

"You spoiled prick, you," Mark said. "You think you're so damn important."

"When did I say I was important?"

"Your sister does all your talking for you. You're going

here or there and you're fixing this or that, like you deserve a parade. I'm fucking sick of it. It's not even your boat. You're just doing one fucking thing while somebody else navigates the open water. There's not even a war on anymore. All you're doing is wasting fuel."

Scotland felt like he should go, but he wasn't about to overlook the fact he'd busted Mark whipping his sister. "You think of me any way you like, Mark. That's your business. But you never, fucking ever, raise a hand to my sister again. You understand me?" He looked to Dana. He didn't figure Mark would answer the question. Scotland was more interested in how his sister looked. He couldn't tell if this kind of thing happened often or not.

Dana came out of her corner and said, "It's okay, Scotland. He's drunk. He don't mean nothing by it."

"Don't speak for me, woman." Mark reached out and backhanded Dana.

Dana took the blow by turning away and shielding her cheek.

Scotland railed a haymaker into the side of Mark's head. Before his knuckles even registered the impact, Mark slid to a heap on the floor. Scotland straddled him and rained down half a dozen rights to Mark's head before he straightened and landed three or four kicks to his ribs. It was mid-kick that Dana pulled him off. Scotland pushed down the rage. It boiled in his gut. He pointed to the motionless Mark on the floor and said, "That motherfucker hits you again, I'll fucking kill him."

The damage was a broken jaw, three chipped teeth, a concussion, and broken ribs that almost collapsed a lung. Mark pressed charges. The Uniform Code of Military Justice did the rest, despite Dana's emotional testimony to save her brother.

After serving his time in the United States Disciplinary Barracks in Leavenworth, Kansas, Scotland had moved to

Tampa prepared to have a strained relationship with Mark, but he never thought his brother-in-law would cut him off from his sister and his nieces.

Kinsey sat at the counter of a diner, sipping watery coffee. Hunger wasn't the reason he was there. The waitress behind the counter with the bad wig and the nametag that read "Dana" was his reason for being there. Her bare legs disappeared beneath her waitress skirt. She wasn't as tall as Maria, but these legs were the perfect length, and lean enough to reveal the muscle definition that Kinsey had always liked.

This was his last act through the Gulf Breeze operation. His crew was assembling his election campaign office and would be ready within a week, but he had this one last outstanding piece of business to wrap up.

He'd had one of his guys find out all he could about Scotland's sister. He learned about this place and that her husband was a grouper fisherman and that was all he needed to know.

He didn't reveal himself. He was just another motorist stopping off between Tampa and Sarasota. Dana was slow, but efficient. For tips, she smiled big and winked a good bit or did a slow bend for an ass shot or one forward for a face-full of cleavage. Kinsey had a laugh at that behind his coffee cup.

As she refilled his cup, Kinsey said, "You must surely need to relax after a day of this nonsense."

"You got that right, sugar."

Kinsey left two pills on top of a five-dollar tip.

By nightfall out in the Gulf, Scotland couldn't keep his eyes open. He hadn't yet slept for longer than a few minutes at a time.

In one of those unconscious moments on his second or

third day adrift in the Gulf, he stood in white sand beneath palm trees bent crooked enough for a guy like him to climb. He had a ring on his finger. It was tight, but comfortable. The blonde woman he'd seen in the convenience store in Daytona offered him beer in a bottle from the porch of his beach cottage. She encouraged him with words he couldn't hear to come drink with her by the pool. Her beer-tilting pantomimes blended into blowing kisses and signaling "come here" with her index finger, her hips, and her lips. Daytona. He loved this place and he never wanted to leave.

The hallucination ended when it started to rain.

Scotland made a bowl with his shirt and captured as much rainwater as he could. He drank a small sip as if not trusting the water as real. The fresh wetness coated his lips and the inside of his mouth and made him feel alive. He drank all there was and refilled his shirt bowl and drank again until his abdomen distended tight and full and for a moment he was happy. Immediately after, he fell asleep again. In the morning he wondered if that too hadn't been a dream because it had done nothing to ease his pain or slake his deeper thirst.

Kinsey made a point to go back to Dana's diner two days later. If something were said about the pills, he'd act relieved she'd found his missing medication. She said nothing, but gave him a longer look when he came in. Kinsey wasn't sure how to take it. There wasn't anger in her expression, but there wasn't overt joy either. He didn't want to make it awkward so he just stepped up to a stool and turned over the coffee cup in front of him. Dana said, "Hello, again," cheerful as could be and filled his cup.

Kinsey nodded with a smile. "Busy as ever, I see."

He sipped the same watery coffee and watched Dana dance through the same ballet of putting down plates, picking up empties, writing in her little pad, and flirting with old guys for an extra quarter here and there.

He left another five-dollar tip, and three pills this time.

His third and last planned trip to the diner was on Friday. It was a carbon copy of the previous two. Watery coffee. Cordial smiles. But Dana still didn't say anything. When he finished his coffee, Kinsey took out not a five-dollar bill but a business card. It had only a phone number embossed across the front.

"If you ever want more of those pills," he said, "call me."

Dana looked at the card, front and back. "It's just a number. I don't know your name. Who should I ask for?"

"Just say, it's Dana. I'll know it's you."

CHAPTER TWENTY

In between exhaustion and unconsciousness, through more days and nights adrift at sea, Scotland thought of the survivors of the whale ship Essex. He'd heard the story told by a grizzled chief on the bridge of their Navy ship one rough night. The chief was lean and salty. Had gravel in his windpipe and told of the sinking Essex and the eight men who survived. Scotland felt like one amongst them now, adrift in the sea for so long. But they hadn't been alone—companionship and cannibalism weren't options for him.

His only option for the meat necessary to sustain him was to catch a fish. Scotland knew nothing of sea creatures and had no means of catching one or a weapon with which to club a fish as it swam by. His only hope was to literally catch one in his bare hands.

On a cloudless morning, Scotland saw schools of fish darting beneath him. He unhooked his life preserver, released his flotsam, and dove.

He sunk down deep enough into the center of a school that he felt fish against his legs and grasping hands. The first effort produced nothing more than the belief that it was impossible.

The second attempt found him empty handed and exhausted from the effort. He was happy to find his flotation when he surfaced, but he knew if he didn't eat soon he would die.

He released the boat's broken chunk of hull and sank down again, thrusting his hands all the way together until he felt the resistance of a fish between his palms. Underwater, it was more like a pulse, but he knew it was a fish and he shot to the surface. He spotted his flotsam and kicked to it, his hands held high out of the water. He wanted the fish to get as much air as possible. It was the same to that fish as it would be for Scotland to run a marathon and then put a plastic bag over his head. The sooner the fish died, the sooner Scotland could eat.

He rested his elbows on the plank and held his hands skyward, as if the sun would cook the fish for him. Scotland looked up. The fish's tail pointed at him, flicked side to side and almost made contact with the tail tattooed into Scotland's flesh.

The Navy had taught him nothing about fish, and he found no humor in not knowing how long it would take for this fish to die. By the time the fish stilled, Scotland was too hungry to care if the fish was poisonous or not. Death would be a welcomed end to the hunger he'd felt these past days and nights.

The fish wasn't any bigger than Scotland's hand, smaller than the tattoo on his forearm. He bit into the side. His teeth gnashed through the scales, but not deeply enough to find sweet white meat. He pulled the fish away and looked at the damage he'd done. He spit loose scales into the air and bit in deeper until he was sure he crunched bone. The scales cut the insides of his cheeks and the roof of his mouth worse than a handful of Fritos. He chewed and strained the liquefied fish down his throat. What he didn't think he could swallow, he spit into the water. In this slow and methodical way, he devoured the body, then bit off the head and sucked on it, eyes and all.

This nourishment lessened the pain in his stomach, and pessimism gave way to new hope that he would survive.

As a way to keep himself company, he recited the Navy Hymn the best he could remember.

Eternal Father, Strong to save,
Whose arm hath bound the restless wave,
Who bid'st the mighty Ocean deep
Its own appointed limits keep;
O hear us when we cry to thee,
for those in peril on the sea.

It was just the first part, all he could remember. This verse became a song that he repeated over and over again as long as there was moisture in his vocal cords or until he fell asleep. When he awoke, he'd begin the song again, ad-libbing lines begging to be saved. "I don't want to go out like this, Lord. Please." Other times, in those most pessimistic moments, he'd try to bargain with God. "If you have to take me this way, please look after Dana and her girls. You owe us that much."

At one point, it rained for two days straight. The fresh water clung to the beard that now grew as bristly as blades of St. Augustine sod. Scotland sucked water from the hair on his upper lip. Played it over his tongue. The rain also calmed the sunburn on his face and seemed to wash his skin clean. He used his shirt to catch water, which he drank until his stomach sloshed against the current of each passing wave.

The water kept him cool during the day, but his skin was developing a rash from being wet so long. His pickled fingers developed white squares in the centers of their nails. As he removed his shirt from his head he found hair stuck to it. He didn't think anything about it, hadn't felt a pull, so he shrugged it off. The next time he went to rewet his shirt and put it back atop his head, there was more hair. Not just a few strands this time, but a clump like might have rolled down the cape in a barber's chair. His tongue was swollen, and raw from his inability to quit gnawing on it.

* * *

One day, he saw a ship in the distance. It could have been a mile away, but it was big enough for him to see. He waved his free arm with all the energy he could muster and yelled as loud as his scratchy voice allowed. He knew at that distance he must be a dot on the water to them. If he still had his lighter, he might've been able to reflect sunlight and attract the ship, but he had nothing.

He pulled himself onto the plank, gathered himself into a pushup position and then tucked his knees into his chest, like a surfer. But, even with the adrenaline, he only managed to bring them to his stomach. He was tired and weak, and engaging all his stabilization muscles was hard for him. Somehow, he balanced with the help of his arms, and rose to stand, shaky. He hollered out as guttural a noise as he'd ever heard and waved both arms wildly over his head twice before he fell and struck his chin on the board on his way back into the Gulf, where he got a lung full.

He surfaced slowly, coughing out saltwater, one hand on his jaw while the other grasped frantically for the flotsam that had just assaulted him. With both arms slung over the plank, he thought about letting go and swimming to catch the ship, thought about letting go and filling his lungs with salt water and sinking to the bottom and being done with it. Waves crested up and pushed him around for a minute and subsided.

A blowing horn jolted him awake and he fell off the board, but held onto enough that he didn't go completely under.

Fifty yards in front of him, the ship cast a shadow. Crewmembers crowded the rails and Scotland heard voices. It was the happiest he'd ever been in his life, yet he couldn't even hold his head up to look at them.

Aboard the ship, he was asked his name, in Spanish, by a mousey little man who had relayed the question from the captain, who spoke a language Scotland didn't understand.

Scotland sat on the ship's deck and was covered in a series of blankets. Relief had burned up the very last of the adrenaline that had been coursing through his veins. He couldn't keep his eyes open. He tried to yawn, but his mouth was too dry to allow the full motion.

The ship's captain said something that the mousey translator bent down on one knee to repeat to Scotland, in English. "The captain welcomes you aboard and is very concerned for your safety. We will do everything in our power to get you proper medical attention. Now what is your name?"

Scotland sat with his eyes closed, convinced he could speak, but didn't dare do so. He played mute from the shock and hoped they'd buy it long enough for him to come up with something. An alias. A cover. No matter how far away or how long it had been, no one in Tampa needed to know he had survived.

A corpsman arrived with a kit and a pitcher of water. He was a heavyset guy with soft facial features that Scotland saw through his hazy, heavy-lidded perspective.

They brought him to one of the berthing areas and the corpsman helped him in the shower. Scotland slumped on a chair and the corpsman had to hold him with one hand and angle him with the other to get the soap out of his hair. It was like being rained on again, and for an instant, Scotland hated it. He was too weak to do anything about it, but a moment later he realized the water was clean and soft and it was going to help him.

After the shower, the medic applied balm to his skin and dressed the worst of the sores on the backs of his legs, as well as the burns on his neck and back.

He was outfitted in dry underwear and two guys helped him into a middle bunk. The corpsman took his pulse while another man held a spoon of broth to his lips.

Scotland opened his mouth and allowed the soup to pour in. His lips were chapped and still salty from the Gulf, but he held the soup in his mouth before he swallowed. Once he did, he felt the cells in his torso awaken. He opened his mouth for more and another spoonful fell in. With more flavor in his mouth, more cells came alive. This pattern went on a dozen times or so, and he didn't realize he'd had too much until he wretched up and vomited over the side of the bunk.

The sailors in the narrow aisle laughed.

"Start slow," the corpsman said. "We are three days from land. You will survive to get proper treatment."

CHAPTER TWENTY-ONE

Scotland was draped in blankets from the ship. The corpsman rejected the crew's offers of clothes and shoes which might hinder the healing of Scotland's saltwater sores. The Port Master drove him in personally and honked the horn as he rolled up in front of Lee Memorial Hospital. He didn't know where he was until an orderly helped him onto a gurney and covered him with one of the hospital's blankets. Scotland caught on as he was wheeled down a white hallway while a doctor with glasses and a stethoscope leaned over Scotland, folded back the blanket and poked and prodded around his neck, ribs, and abdomen. "What is your name?" the doctor asked as they wheeled him into a room surrounded by curtains.

Scotland didn't reply. The interpreter on the freighter had asked that question and Scotland gave this doctor the same non-answer.

"Can you tell me what the date is?"

Scotland thought for a moment but had no guess. He shivered. There was all manner of voices in the emergency room, some yelling, some whispering among themselves, but only these two talking directly to Scotland. He shook his head.

"It's January third, dear-heart," a nurse said. "1981."

The doctor continued probing. "How long were you in the water?"

This was the first time Scotland contemplated how many days and nights he'd spent adrift. He'd lost count. He answered honestly this time, his voice scratchy in his throat. "I don't know."

He was moved from the gurney to a bed and the nurse plugged an IV into his arm. The bag's liquid dripped into his vein from a hook on a pole next to his right shoulder. The nurse walked around the bed and inserted another IV.

Everything hurt, a consistent ache through his arms and legs. He could move them freely beneath the blanket draped over him, but whenever he tried, his organs felt like they would burst. In that prone position, his throat felt like it was stuffed with a couch cushion and it was hard to swallow around the dryness. More than anything, he was hungry. The broth they'd fed him on the ship was salty and harsh and couldn't fill him.

He was a John Doe patient now, and he answered questions with "I don't remember" as a way to buy time. He couldn't risk word getting back to Kinsey.

They examined him. His skin was no longer shriveled from the water, but it was still tender. "He's dehydrated and malnourished," the doctor said, "with signs of lingering hypothermia."

The doctor bandaged Scotland's feet carefully and said, "How does that feel?"

"I'm all taped up and ready to wrestle," Scotland said.

The doctor laughed. He slapped his hand on his knee and used the momentum to propel himself up. "You get some rest," he said. "Your memory will come back once the shock wears off."

Scotland let them believe he was in shock. He was just happy to be alive, in a bed, beneath a blanket. He also took comfort in the fact that he was being taken care of and would get his strength back while resting there.

"Sweetie? The police sure are gonna want to talk to you," the nurse said. "When you're up to it, you let me know, okay, hon?"

Scotland lifted his head, looked for an exit sign. The nurse pushed his head back down.

His hand rubbed along his right thigh. His breath caught high in his throat, not because he was pantless beneath a pile of blankets, but because he realized he didn't have his lighter. His hand came out above the blanket empty and he didn't know what to do. He left his hand on top of the blanket. It felt dumb and useless to him. He missed the lighter, but was grateful it had been there for him when he needed it most.

The nurse patted his hair. "Rest easy, big fella. You're going to be okay." She looked at the doctor and said, "Still in shock. Poor baby."

The minute the doctor and nurse left him to rest, Scotland ripped the IVs out of his arms. He pushed the tape down to stop any bleeding and slung his legs over the bed. He slid down and tested his footing with as little weight as possible. His feet felt fine enough from the pills they'd been giving him, and with the cushion of the bandages. He placed more weight on them before standing. He wore nothing but the borrowed briefs, but he had to get out of there before the cops showed up asking questions. Behind the curtain, the patient in the next bed was asleep. He looked stable, but unconscious, and about Scotland's size. In Scotland's mind, the guy was a construction worker who had fallen. Perhaps they had to wait to do the x-rays for some reason. His clothes were folded on a shelf beside his bed. Scotland grabbed the jeans and flannel shirt. The work boots were big enough to fit over his bandaged feet. He left the guy's socks and slipped out as smoothly as his tender feet allowed.

His shoulders rocked as he limped, though the more steps he took, the less it bothered him. He turned the corner and went down a hallway.

He walked casually and no one chased him or even looked at him twice. He passed a payphone. He didn't know when he'd get another opportunity, so he stopped and picked up the handset while covering his face.

When the operator got a hold of Dave, he said, "Yes, operator," accepting the charges. After she gave the go-ahead, Dave said, "What the fuck are you doing in Ft. Myers? I thought we agreed you'd stay in town. You missed check-in again!"

Scotland whispered into the phone, "I'm in the hospital."

"Hospital?" Dave said "Are you okay?"

"Fine enough." Scotland shifted his weight from foot to foot. "It's a long story, but I can't stay here."

"No, you stay there. I'll see if I can get somebody to pick your ass up."

"Don't. No. I've got to get out of here. I don't have time to explain, but I'll call when I can."

"What the hell are you doing?"

"No idea. Can't explain now. I gotta go." Scotland placed the handset in the cradle and walked away from the payphone like he was anybody else. He tugged the collar of the construction worker's flannel shirt up around his face and walked into the lobby and up to the doors by the parking lot.

He didn't know how to hotwire a car, and he couldn't get far enough away fast enough on foot.

He walked out to the parking lot, where the air temperature matched the air-conditioned air inside. The sunlight of noontime heated up his resentment at having been trapped beneath it day in and day out while adrift. Now, with mobility and clothing, he ignored it and searched the parked cars for one with the keys in the ignition or on the seat.

As he peered through the rolled-down window of a Buick Skylark, a cop in a crisp uniform peeked in at him from the opposite side. "You looking for something, boy?"

Scotland stood. Denial would be an admission of guilt to this guy. If the situation was reversed and Scotland came upon a guy with shaggy hair and a beard stalking around parked cars, he'd be suspicious himself. Scotland reached into his pocket as was his reflex, but these were not his pants, and his lighter was now at the bottom of the Gulf. He didn't have enough time to be elaborate, but a good lie need not be. He looked through the rolled-down window. A pack of Winstons lay on the dashboard.

As the cop came around the car, Scotland studied his badge as he pointed to the pack of cigarettes. "I was going to grab my smokes, but I won't need them. I'm on my way in to see a buddy."

Within a few steps, Scotland could read "Hospital Security" on the badge pinned over the guy's heart.

The security guard smiled for a moment like he was relieved, too. He flashed a set of chompers that looked welded together with candy canes and bacon grease. He dropped his smile and said with a solemn voice, "I hope it's nothing serious with your friend."

"Me too," Scotland said, trying to hold back the resentment over having no choice but to abandon the parking lot.

Scotland walked back to the hospital, returned through the double doors and faced the lobby. A family with a kid whose hand was wrapped in a dishtowel sat huddled in the far corner; a blue-haired woman sat in the center by herself, knitting; a young couple with panic on their faces shook in the seats nearest the doors; and a woman, standing alone, leaned against the counter. She had feathered hair and wore cutoff jeans, a turquoise halter top, and black combat boots. She faced Scotland as he approached. Her eyes were outlined heavily, like she'd used a Magic Marker for mascara.

"Hey," he said.

"Hello." She folded her arms across her bare midsection.

"Are you here for medical attention?"

"Not personally," she said. "But it looks like you should be."

"Was. I'm good to go. What are you doing here?"

"I'm kind of waiting for someone."

"Your boyfriend?"

"Hell no," she said. "I just met the guy today. What happened to your hair?"

Scotland smoothed his hair back, conscious for the first time how thin it felt. "Look," he said, "I need to get out of here."

"So, go."

He reached into his pocket again, rediscovered that his lighter was gone forever. "I don't know where I'm going," he said.

"Where you trying to get to?"

He looked at her Magic Marker eyes. "I've got to get the hell out of here. Can you give me a ride?"

"I can't bail on the guy."

"But he's not your boyfriend?"

"I told you, I just met him today."

Scotland's mouth was still dry. He needed moisture, but all he wanted right then was to drag this woman by the arm and force her to drive him away from there, but that would only bring the cops running faster. He chose instead a more subtle approach. "Look, you don't know that guy any more than you know me and he's all the way in there." Scotland pointed behind the doors he'd escaped only moments earlier. "But you're willing to break my heart in person?"

"Break your heart? What are you talking about?"

"I've really got to get going, but I don't want to stop talking to you. If you drive me, we can get to know each other better."

She sighed, smiled big, and leaned on the counter again. "I can't believe it. Are you really trying to pick me up in an emergency room?"

Scotland caught the movements of two uniformed police officers in the hallway near a nurses' station. He ducked his head down and put his hand on her elbow. "There are a hundred songs I could quote you right now, but you know the answer to that question."

She rocked back on her heels and her lips parted just enough to register pleasure.

"So," he said, "if we're going, let's go."

She licked her lips and walked off with him, unable to match his strides. "I was really trying to give you my poker face, too."

"Please," Scotland said, "don't ever mention poker to me again."

CHAPTER TWENTY-TWO

After working the lunch shift, Dana pulled out the little card with the phone number from her apron pocket. The card was so white, the number so clear. Nothing bad could come from something that pristine. She dialed from the payphone outside the bathrooms.

"Who is this?" a man's voice said instead of "hello."

She cupped her hand over her mouth. "This is Dana, from the diner."

Dana heard the man on the other end suck in air from excitement. "Right. Yes," he said. "So good of you to call. And how is everything down at that fine establishment?"

"Cut the cutesy stuff," Dana said. "I need to talk to you about a steady stream of your tips. If you know what I mean."

"Yes. Yes, indeed, I do. And that would be my pleasure." Kinsey gave her directions to the Gulf Breeze and she wrote down every street and turn on her little pad, because she didn't want to miss out on this opportunity for the true relief those pills gave her. She tore off the sheet with the directions and folded it into her bra.

The drive up to Brandon was uneventful. She hadn't driven into town lately and there were new construction projects along her way. She took her time. She was anxious to score some pills, but she didn't have to be in a hurry. With the fishing ban finally and gloriously lifted, Mark was able to return to the water and get back at work fishing. He wouldn't be home until late. That, in itself, was something to celebrate. No matter how much love she had for her husband, a little time apart was healthy. It kept her sane.

With Mark home, Dana had been able to take off for a day at a time. Even when Scotland was sending checks, she'd timed these benders, these disappearances to her days off so she wouldn't miss out on money. She knew the checks would stop coming, eventually, and didn't want to miss a beat when that day came.

She drove a '72 Chevy pickup, the windows down and the AM radio turned up loud. Blondie sang "The Tide is High." Dana didn't understand all the words of the song, but it made her think of Mark. He was hauling in record catches and was happy to be back on the water. This made her need for pills greater, as she was expected to play wife and mother after a full day serving and cleaning up after strangers. She couldn't help resenting having to go home to do the same for her family. The pills made it bearable. She was happy to have received them as a tip the past few times the man had stopped in. She didn't want to stop feeling the way the pills made her feel.

The gas tank read half-full and there was plenty of sun in the sky for her to get there and back before the girls came home from school. With their father working again, it had been easy to have the girls full-time again, as opposed to spending weekends with Mark's parents. The pills took care of the rest.

She pulled into the Gulf Breeze parking lot. The clubhouse was fancy, with its wide porch and fancy Coke machine. She was glad she took the time to put on jeans and a sweater. The air was turning cooler, but more importantly because this place looked higher-end than she was accustomed to. The kind of upper scale that meant the pills might cost more than she could afford. If she'd shown up in her waitress uniform, people would think she was one of the maids or something.

She walked into what must have recently been office space. There were empty desks pushed up against a wall leaving a wide-open space in the middle.

"I'm upstairs," a voice called down.

Dana walked up the stairs to a room that was also all but emptied. There was a desk with a map on the wall above it, but nothing else to speak of.

The man from the diner stood up from behind his desk. He was dressed in the same kind of polyester pants and shirt he'd worn in the diner, but now he looked more relaxed. "You'll have to pardon the décor, or the lack thereof."

"Are you moving in or out?" she asked.

"Out, but that's a long story," he said. "I'm in the process of relocating, you see."

"It looks like something's up."

"Yes. Yes, it is. But instead of standing here missing the leather couches that used to occupy this space right around here, we should go downstairs to the pool. There are some nice lounge chairs there and we can chat."

"I'm not really here for conversation," she said.

"Well, you must be thirsty. Can I offer you a drink?"

"I wouldn't say no to some vodka."

"Well, the drink cart is down by the pool. Come along and we'll get ourselves fixed right up."

Kyla Brooks drove a mint-green Datsun 280Z with seats so close she grazed Scotland's knee every time she shifted gears. "So, where are we going?" she asked as she drove out of the hospital parking lot.

Scotland shrugged. "Just drive."

"You hungry?"

"Starved."

"How do you feel about barbeque?"

"I could eat a whole hog right now."

"I know just the place. Outdoor smoker as big as a steam engine and about twenty beers on tap."

Scotland looked over his shoulder out the back window.

247

His breath was warm on her neck as he exhaled. "Tell me this perfect place is at least ten miles away from here."

"Relax," she said as she crossed the bridge spanning the Caloosahatchee River. "After you eat, I'll show you the best bars in town."

Scotland leaned over again. Kyla thought it was so he could look out the back window again, but instead he reached into his back pocket, pulled out his wallet and thumbed through the bills there.

"Um," he grunted. "You might want to make it the *worst* bars in town. There's only thirty-seven dollars in here."

Kyla laughed. "If you tell me what you're running from, the drinks'll be on me."

Scotland nodded and stared out the windshield.

The place wasn't fancy by any standards, just ten plywood tables and a counter with a register on it. The grills in the kitchen were used to cook burgers and heat the meat smoked out back. The taps along the wall to the right of the counter were quiet now, but would likely be drained by a rowdy crowd that would dance and party to a band set up on the foot-high stage in the corner. The far wall was home to a mounted boar's head with a red placard beneath it that read "Pappy" in white letters. The entire place smelled like bacon.

They were alone except for Junior, the owner's son. He was a potbellied kid she'd gone to high school with. His eyes stayed glued to her every time she came in.

Junior stared at Kyla now as he wrote down their order and poured their beers. He ignored the guy with her, and Kyla ignored Junior, as she always did, and led Scotland to one of the tables and sat down.

Scotland had barely sat before he asked, "Is there a payphone in here?" He scooted his chair sideways, as if expecting to follow the direction she'd point.

"There's a phone booth at the far end of the parking lot."

Scotland sat back and stared in the direction of Pappy hanging on the wall. "I'll do it on the way out. I'm starving."

Kyla turned sideways in her own chair and kicked her feet up on the empty one next to her. Her boots were scuffed and she liked them that way. "So what was that all about back there?" she said.

Scotland picked at a knot in the pine tabletop with his thumbnail and held onto his beer with his other hand. He squeezed the mug's handle and sipped as if each swallow was magic. His nails were long and overdue to be cut, because he didn't impress her as the type to wear them like that.

"You're really nice," he said. "I shouldn't have involved you. It's just, I had to get out of there. I'll be fine now." He held up his mug. "This beer is fucking amazing." He sipped again. "After I eat, I'll get out of your hair."

"You're not in my hair. I'm just curious who you're hiding from."

He worked the knot on the table again and looked away. The surprise on his face was obvious, but Kyla also saw something else written there.

"What makes you think I'm hiding?"

She dropped her hands onto the tabletop and licked her lips. "Save yourself the trouble of bullshitting me. I'm not stupid."

"Okay," he said, looking at her. "You've been really cool to me, so I'll be straight with you." Scotland told her about leaving Tampa because of his last boss, though he didn't get into specifics, didn't even mention his name. Instead he told her simply: "He's a bad guy. I want him to think I've disappeared."

For a big guy, Scotland seemed not just paranoid, but defeated, like an abused German Shepherd. Kyla patted his hand as it paused over the tabletop knot. "There's more than a hundred miles between here and Tampa. I'm sure you're fine."

"So who was the guy you ditched at the hospital?"

"I didn't ditch anyone. I just drove someone there out of the goodness of my heart. I left with you out of the same organ's badness. The way I see it, the world is better balanced by my actions."

"So who was the guy?"

"Oh, he was just some guy I met down at the beach.

"What happened to him?"

"He climbed this light pole outside the Dairy Queen to impress me. Somehow he slipped and fell to the ground. I'm pretty sure he busted his arm. I figured the least I could do was drive him to get it fixed."

"That's pretty nice of you. But you're supposed to take monkeys to a veterinarian."

Kyla laughed as Junior arrived with a tray of food and two more beers. She nodded to Junior as he held his empty tray along his leg and stared at her. No one spoke, even after Junior walked back behind the counter.

While she picked at the skin and meat on her half chicken, he ate a plate of pulled pork, coleslaw, and two pieces of cornbread, and downed three glasses of Stroh's finest beer. Three sips into his fourth, his eyes got glassy. He sat back, then, as if that were a bad idea, leaned forward with his forearms resting on the edge of the table like he was trying to catch his breath.

"Are you okay?"

He looked dazed. Surely a guy his size could handle more than three beers. It couldn't be drunkenness that made him put his head on the table.

"Just great!" Kyla said. She picked up the check on the table and walked to the cash register. As she paid, she asked Junior if he'd help her get her friend to the car.

* * *

The back stairs of Kinsey's office led onto a pool area as big as the one at Dana's old high school. Probably big enough for Mark's boat.

A cast iron drink cart with glass shelves sat next to some lounge chairs and a couple of low tables with ashtrays on them. It was as fancy an arrangement as she'd seen. A place waiting for a party. She allowed herself to sink back on a lounge chair, letting the padding cradle her.

"All I've got is aged bourbon," Kinsey said.

"That'll do."

"Yes," Kinsey said. "Yes."

After some time enjoying their first highball, Kinsey pulled two pills from his pocket and held them up. "Would you like one of these?"

Dana sat up straight, too excited to conceal it. "Sure." She scaled herself back. Tried to look only mildly interested. "I should go pick up my kids," she said. Then her eyes locked with Kinsey's. "Another night won't kill them. I think we deserve to feel better, right about now."

He handed her a pill and she gulped it down with the bourbon.

Kinsey pulled a cigar from his shirt pocket and bit the end, then lit it with a long wooden match from the drink cart and sat back down.

"This is a hell of a pool," Dana said.

Kinsey blew a smoke ring. "Do you like to swim?"

"I haven't been in a pool since I was a little girl."

"We should plan a day sometime."

Dana watched the smoke ring widen and break apart, suddenly disappear. She put her drink on the low table next to her. "I want to go swimming right now."

"In the middle of winter?"

"I'll bet you the water temperature is at like seventy-five

degrees. Besides, those pills will make us too numb to notice if it isn't."

She felt his eyes on her as she removed her sweater and pulled her tube top down around her waist and removed it with her jeans. She'd gone without underwear that morning and let him have a view of her rear as she removed her wig as if it were a helmet. She bent at the knees to set the wig atop her wadded clothes. Her hair was cut short as a boy's. She cut it herself every couple weeks. Now, she smoothed it down with her fingers. At the edge of the pool—she didn't pause to test the water—she sprung into a little hop and jumped in feet first.

The plunge exhilarated her, but she wasn't cold. Water clung to her lashes as she surfaced. She swiped it away and wiped her nose on the back of her hand.

Kinsey said, "Your figure and manner of dress demand attention. You walk and talk like you're unaware of this fact. That lack of awareness makes you even more attractive."

"You talk like you're reading a book."

He blew another smoke ring. "But did you hear my words?"

"I heard, but who're you kidding? I must look a fright. My makeup's smeared and my hair's a mess."

"Your face would clean up quick enough, and I could buy you a new wig, dozens of them."

Dana liked the sound of that.

Kinsey stripped down, the cigar still clenched between his teeth. He draped his pants and shirt over a lounge chair. If he had modesty in him, he didn't act like it now. He stood there on full display for a minute. He was circumcised, and not much bigger than a junior high school boy. "I think we'll need these," he said as he picked up their drinks and delivered them to the edge of the pool.

Dana got a closer look at him looming over her. He was thin, but soft. Not wiry like Mark. His manhood was bigger than she'd first given credit, but hidden in a wad of curly hair. He bent down and vaulted himself into the water with no splash at all.

Dana sipped her drink. "I sure like the way this bourbon heats my gullet."

"You don't usually drink?" He puffed his cigar, blew another smoke ring.

"I promised my daughters that I'd give it up."

Kinsey flicked his ash off the cigar and studied her. "When's the last time you had a drink?"

"Six days. Beginning the day you gave me those pills."

"How long was that after you promised your daughters?"

"Week and a half. Tops."

"You could continue to hide the booze from them."

"Social drinking is all well and good. Hell, this country is founded on it. But being drunk just isn't ladylike."

"We all have our crosses to bear."

"They woke me up on a Thursday morning in front of the TV. I'd puked on the floor and wet the couch in the middle of the night and they saw it before I even knew I did it. I had to say something to make things better. Since I talked the talk, I've got to walk the walk."

"But you still need something to get you through, to smooth the rough patches."

She pushed off and breaststroked across the pool toward the deep end. Swimming felt effortless, as if she were a paper boat on a windy day. "I just love the way I feel."

"And you want to continue feeling that way, don't you?"

Dana kicked over to the edge and grabbed hold. She spit out a mouthful of water. "I probably can't afford as many pills as I'd like to have."

"We may be able to come to some kind of arrangement."

Dana released the coping and backstroked toward Kinsey. The sky above her was all but cloudless and that suited her. She had no need for clouds when she was riding so high.

"This is like bath water."

"Heated. I left it on today. Planned to take one last dip."

"That's right. Where you moving to?"

"Not just moving. I'm switching my office to headquarters."

She treaded water. "You a military man?"

Kinsey sipped his drink. "Not exactly. I'm talking about my campaign headquarters. You're looking at the next Governor of this great state."

She stopped treading long enough to splash at him. "Governor?" she said as she lunged up with a push of her arms and a kick of her legs. "Yeah, right."

"Well, they're not going to just give it to me. I still have to earn it, but that shouldn't be a problem if all goes according to plan. Yes, ma'am. And I'd like to know I'll have your vote come election time."

"When is that?"

"Well, that's not until next year. Almost two years. But it's never too soon to start."

She swam back to the edge near Kinsey. "Good luck to you." She lifted her glass.

Kinsey smiled. Held up his glass and took a drink. "So," he said. "About these pills?"

Instead of answering, she set down her drink and swam closer to him. The water between them was warm and soft and she said, "What kind of arrangement are we going to work out?"

Kinsey reached for her hand and placed it on his cock. The pubic hair had relaxed and given way beneath the water and she felt him grow in her hand as she looked him in the eye. He rested his cigar on the edge of the pool and guided her to the steps in the shallow end, where he bent her over. Her elbows rested on the top step and water sloshed between her breasts and into her chin as he jack-rabbit-fucked her from behind. The taste of chlorine reminded her of the summer days all the neighborhood kids went down to the public pool. She'd worn her first bikini there. Gotten her first kiss atop the high dive. And now this.

Dana felt the pounding and a pressure inside as Kinsey did his thing, but she was too numb from the pill and the drink to find any pleasure, or pain, in the act.

Afterward, Kinsey retrieved their drinks and his cigar. He reclined on the steps and said, "I keep an apartment in that building." He pointed with his glass. "I keep the pills there and we can get comfortable."

She seemed to perk up when he mentioned the pills. She leaned over and tussled her short hair with her hands to beat out the pool water. "Maybe for a minute or two. I should get home."

"You don't have to go home."

Dana tugged on her wig. "I'm a married woman, Allan."

"If you change your mind," Kinsey held out his hands, "you're welcome to stay in one of the apartments. It's fully furnished and you will have complete privacy."

Kinsey walked with his hand on her ass as they crossed the parking lot and up to the door marked 2A.

CHAPTER TWENTY-THREE

Kyla's Datsun was a sixteenth birthday gift from her grandmother. More than a dozen guys had sat in the passenger seat in the four years she'd had the car, but none had been totally unconscious. And they all lacked the magnetic pull this guy had. She couldn't pin it down to any one thing, but she was sure it wasn't just his needing help at the moment.

As she drove, she wondered where she should go. She'd already driven and ditched one guy at the emergency room, but maybe this guy needed to go back. She couldn't believe she'd have to do the same thing again.

The hospital was on the way and not far once they crossed the river. She drove while keeping one eye on his unconscious form in the passenger seat. It was impossible not to think of his warm breath on her neck, the sweetness in his eyes when he'd apologized for involving her. With the belief that she could help him, she passed the hospital without slowing down and headed to her house.

Pulling into her driveway, she stopped beneath the shade of a twenty-foot magnolia tree. She got out and ran around to open the passenger door. Scotland was still out cold. Shaking his shoulder lightly got no effect, so she shook harder until his head lolled side to side. She held her ear over his mouth to make sure he was breathing. Relieved that he was, she stepped back and straightened. She reached down and slapped her fingertips into his left cheek with three quick smacks. "Hey," she said. "I can't carry you in."

It was around three in the afternoon, and none of her neighbor's cars were in their driveways yet as everyone was still at work.

She closed Scotland's door and walked a couple houses down to Mr. Tangello's house. She had to knock three times before Mr. Tangello opened the door. He wore tan slacks with a white belt and a plain white T-shirt that had gone gray. "You?" he said and took off his glasses. "What do you want?"

"Hey there, handsome." Kyla tried to smile big.

"Don't tease an old man."

"You're not old. You're young and strong and I need a favor."

After Kyla explained, Mr. Tangello closed the door halfway. "No, thank you. No way. I'm not helping you get mixed up with any of your hooligans. I still have a trench in my grass from your man friend with the motorcycle."

Kyla shifted her weight onto her right leg. "They're nice guys, Mr. Tangello. They just get a little nuts when they drink."

"Well, you might want to marry an Osmond or something. You need to change your ways, hussy," he said as he closed the door.

Kyla walked back to her car. She couldn't just leave Scotland there. She turned to look at her front door, then spun back around to the empty driveways of her neighbors. It was about seventy degrees and the car was in the shade. She walked to the car, bent down and pulled the lever to recline Scotland's seat. He'd be fine, but she wanted to be there when he woke. After shutting his door, she walked around and got behind the wheel. Her seat reclined easily and she closed her eyes.

***

Kinsey unlocked the door and guided Dana inside 2A. The blinds were all drawn and before he could steer her around, she found the light switch and flicked it on herself.

She held the door for balance. "Wow. Your apartment is messier than your office."

The room held the same inventory that had been there for the past month or so, and would continue to until it was all fenced. He would have left this stuff to the discretion of the Kula brothers...if they had come back.

"The bedroom is immaculate, however." He guided her over to the door, where he stopped and kissed her as a distraction so he could turn a key in the padlock. It was their first kiss and it was subtle at the beginning, but grew more aggressive. Kinsey held the side of her face in one hand as their tongues probed each other's mouths. He smoothed his other hand over her shoulders and down her arms and lowered his kiss to her neck as he worked his way around to her back. He grasped her by the wrists, yanking her hands together and upward.

She moaned. "You like a little rough play, do you?"

Kinsey held her wrists with one hand and pulled open the door with the other. As the door opened, he shoved her inside the cell and held her near the butcher table, where he picked up a roll of duct tape. She was dazed from the abruptness, and it was easy for him to tape her wrists together. Once he was done, he pushed her over to the chair where he had killed Platinum.

She sat there, breathing heavily as he pulled his shiny chrome revolver from a canvas bag on the table. He walked slowly toward her as he tucked the revolver into his pants.

He stared at her a minute, then shoved two fingers into her mouth and clamped her jaw with his other hand so she couldn't bite down. It was like giving medicine to a calf. "Right now it is my fingers violating your mouth, but it could easily be the barrel of this revolver if you don't tell me where your brother is hiding." Kinsey pulled out his fingers and released her jaw.

"What are you talking about?"

Kinsey backhanded Dana across the face, heard the clink of his wedding band on her teeth. Dana struggled at her restraints, tried to wipe blood from her lips. Instead, she spat a red stream at Kinsey who side-stepped it easily. "Never again. Do you understand me? Never again answer my question with a question. Now where is Scotland?"

Dana licked at the split in her lip and looked up at Kinsey. "Scotland," she said, "is the northern part of Great Britain."

Kinsey smacked her with an open palm forehand. "You smartmouthed bitch!" The contact felt solid on the side of her head where his fingers had clapped her ear. Her wig flew off and she rocked sideways. "You can't possibly be stupid enough to think you can stall me."

"Who the fuck are you?" she said. "And what do you want with my brother?"

Kinsey grabbed her short hair and yanked her head back so her face looked up at him. The split in her lip bled and her right eye began to swell. "I told you my name hours ago. Your brother works for me. And he has disappeared and I'd like to talk to him."

"I haven't heard from him in weeks. And that's the blunt truth."

Kinsey took another cigar out of his shirt pocket. He bit the end and lit it, blew smoke. After a few more mighty tokes, Kinsey flicked the ash and blew on the burning orange ember. He ripped open her sweater and yanked her tube top down, pausing the lit end of the cigar an inch from her tit. "Where is Scotland Ross?"

She squirmed and tried to push her chair backwards. "I don't know. I swear!"

Kinsey pressed the lit ember into the milky-white flesh just above her nipple.

Dana screamed and flailed her legs. Kinsey stood back, toked on his cigar and blew a few more smoke rings until she settled down.

She whimpered, but didn't outwardly cry. Instead, she breathed through her clenched teeth with wet inhalations and openmouthed exhalations.

Kinsey held his ground. "I'm going to ask you again. Where is Scotland Ross?"

"Honest. I haven't heard from him since Christmas. If I knew where he was I'd tell you. Shit. I don't want to be tortured. I honestly don't know where he is."

Kinsey paced around the room, cigar clenched between his teeth. He walked around her chair and yanked back her head. With the cigar inches from her throat, Kinsey said, "The next burn will hurt more than the last. Now tell me where he is."

Dana's top rested around her waist, her burned breast exposed. Kinsey moved the cigar closer to her throat. There was tension in her neck muscles and her chin quivered in fear, but she did not speak.

Kinsey stood upright and placed the cigar back in his mouth, released Dana's hair. She let out a giant exhale as he walked over to the butcher table near the door. From the canvas tool bag, Kinsey pulled out a knife in a sheath. It was the knife he wore on his belt while hunting boar and deer in the woods. He held the knife so it glinted the overhead light into her eyes. She was breathing heavily and in obvious pain, her eyes more fearful than they'd been with the threat of the cigar. Kinsey traced the tip of the knife up her legs and came to rest at her abdomen. He leaned just enough weight into the handle that the point indented the flesh without breaking the skin. "If you're not going to help me," he said. "I might as well kill you."

"I swear I don't know nothing." Her eyes were closed tight as if wishing away this whole business.

"I believe you." Kinsey lifted the blade away and walked

around the back of her chair. "Since you can't lead me to him, I'll just wait and see if you lead him to me." Kinsey cut the tape binding her hands and wrists.

Dana fell forward, off of the chair, and hugged herself, cradling her burned breast.

Kinsey walked past the butcher table and out the door, leaving it open. He walked out to the main space of the apartment and found a silver service set. He took the tall pitcher to the bathroom and tried to fill it in the sink. The pitcher was too tall, so he turned and filled it with water from the tub's faucet. On the way back, he grabbed a bag of pills from the can where they were stored.

Inside the cell, Dana was still hugging herself on the floor. He tapped her head with the toe of his boot. "I'll leave these on the table. Take them as needed for your pain. See? I'm not a bad guy, but nothing good comes without a fee."

Before he closed the door, he called back, "I'll let you know if he comes looking for you."

CHAPTER TWENTY-FOUR

Scotland dreamed he was underwater. He kicked once, then again to propel himself to the surface. On the third kick, he saw Kinsey behind him. He had two rows of shark's teeth and was sailing through the water like a torpedo. Scotland stretched out and swam as fast as he could, waking himself with the solid thud of hitting something hard. He gasped as he came awake, out of breath from holding it underwater for so long in his dream. He was dry and in a car, and his heart felt like it would pound through his sternum.

"It's okay," a female voice said as someone pulled his hands down and away from the roof and passenger door. "You're safe."

Scotland cut his eyes over at her, unable to move his head. "What?"

"You're safe here. It'll be okay. Can you walk?"

"I would hope so."

She guided him out of the car as if he were a hundred years old. "I'm not crippled," he said, despite feeling weak and frail, as if his bones were brittle.

With her help, he lumbered ten or so steps from her car into a house with an American flag flying near the door. She let him in and helped him to the couch where he collapsed.

"I'm sorry," he said. "I'm usually much more energetic." He breathed heavy and the room spun a little.

Kyla laughed and leaned against a side table, onto which she tossed her rabbit's foot key chain which landed with the rattling of keys. She swiped her forehead with the back of her hand. "That was close. If you'd fallen on the floor, I wouldn't have been able to get you up."

"I'm fine here. But I need another favor."

She didn't appear winded, but she didn't answer right away.

"Do you have a phone that will reach in here?"

"The cord in the kitchen stretches to the front door."

"Can you dial a number for me and bring me the phone?"

Kyla picked up a pencil from the table where she'd tossed her keys and slid open the drawer to pull out a little pad of paper. The pad was a thin rectangle in white, with "Edison" printed in blue at the top. "Ready."

"The number is 813-555-3903."

Kyla tore off the sheet of paper and headed for the kitchen. Scotland propped his head on the arm of the couch as he watched her pick up the receiver from the wall-mounted phone. She read the number off the piece of paper she'd set on the counter and dialed. Her smeared eye makeup made it look like caves were hiding her eyes. She trailed the cord behind her on her way back to the couch and handed the handset to him. Up close, her eyes were chocolate brown and softer than they'd been in the emergency room.

"Thanks," he said.

A voice was already talking on the other end of the line by the time he put the receiver to his ear.

"Dave, it's me."

"Me? Who the fuck is me? I know a hundred and fifty-seven Me's."

Scotland looked at Kyla. She was looking right at him and almost close enough to touch if he'd had the strength to reach out his hand. He cupped his hand over the phone and prepared himself to ask for privacy, but abandoned the notion.

"It's Scotland Ross, Dave. Listen, I'm in a tight damn spot and I'm going to need about all the understanding you can muster."

"I've about had it with this," Dave said. "Why are you being a dumbass all of a sudden?"

"Dave, listen to me," Scotland said with a glance in Kyla's direction. He couldn't look at her as he spoke, so he stared at the receiver. "They tried to kill me."

"Bullshit. Who?"

"I don't want to name names."

"You can't expect me to blindly buy some horseshit story, Ross. Give me a name or I'll write this up as a probation violation and deliver it to my supervisor before the ink dries."

"Man, I don't know if saying it out loud will open a can of misery on you. I'd hate to do that."

"You've got no choice. Either you give me something I can believe or you'll be one of America's Most Wanted."

Scotland gathered enough strength to drive an elbow into the couch cushion. "Fine. Shit. His name is Kinsey. He's a cattleman gangster out in Brandon."

"How'd he try to kill you?"

"It's a long story."

"How you know a guy like that?"

"I worked for him. That was my job."

"The short-lived janitor job at Tampa Beef and Bird?"

"That's the guy."

"You got fired, and now you want to start trouble for the boss man to get even."

"Not exactly." Scotland shifted to get more room for his shoulder against the cushions. "Look, I'm not admitting to breaking any laws, but he's a bad guy getting away with a lot of shit."

"You're suggesting this cattle farmer tried to kill you?"

"It's straight up, Dave. I wouldn't mess up my record if I had a choice. I barely escaped with my life. I wouldn't make up shit like this."

"If this is bogus, you're going to do real time."

"It's not bogus. Have your boys check him out. Not at the

meat plant. He keeps that separate. He operates the shady side of his empire from the Gulf Breeze."

"From a boat?"

"No, the Gulf Breeze apartment complex in Brandon."

"I'll have it checked out and I'll run interference for you here. But this is the last limb I'm going out on for you."

"Just promise me you'll keep my name out of it. Even if you get the bastard."

"Get real, Ross. Neither one of us is in a position to promise shit." Dave slammed the phone down before Scotland replied.

Scotland's ear took the full brunt of the noise. He couldn't move the phone away. He was breathing hard and felt like he'd just run a marathon. After a moment, he got his breathing under control, but he couldn't help feeling exposed now that word was out. The phone fell to his lap as he forced himself to sit up enough to peel back the blinds over the window. Light from the setting sun forced him to look away, and as his vision returned to normal, he found Kyla staring at him. He turned his head just enough to face her and held out the phone.

She took it from him by getting close enough for his hand to touch her thigh, high up by the hip bone. "That didn't sound good." Her assessment of the phone call made him smile, which brought a smile to her face in return. She said, "At least I finally know your name."

She hung up the phone, then walked back and sat on the edge of the couch by Scotland's feet. Her torso was long and angular. She turned and reached to tug off his boot, but Scotland tucked his knees. "No. That's okay. I'd like to leave them on."

"Make yourself comfortable," she said. "You're going to be here awhile."

Scotland watched her. There'd been no surprise on her face when he'd moved his feet. There was no judgment either.

Instead, there was kindness in the centers of her dark eyes. "Why are you doing this for me?"

"Are you kidding? This is the most excitement I've had in weeks. Besides, you said you wanted to keep talking to me. Remember?"

It hurt when Scotland laughed. He held his hand over his ribs. He was still full from the barbecue, and the fullness stretched his shrunken stomach. "I still mean it, too. I just can't believe you're being this cool."

"Is someone really trying to kill you?"

Scotland lifted his head again and looked at her. He held out his hands. "Take off my boots if you don't believe me."

Kyla wanted nothing more than to spend time with Scotland, but he was out cold again. Whatever ordeal he'd survived, it'd zapped all his strength and he slept for eighteen hours straight. During that time, Kyla placed his boots under the coffee table and propped his bandaged feet up on a pillow with "Home Sweet Home" embroidered on the front. It was noon the next day and she was free except for a couple hours of practice ahead of her. She had a gig lined up for Wednesday night, but with this new development, she wished she didn't. She covered Scotland with a quilt her grandmother had made from the same fabric as the pillow.

She didn't know what to do with herself.

Hours passed with her sitting on the floor of in front of the television, the sound turned down low. It was a console model about as big as her car and the screen gave a movie-theater experience sitting that close and low.

She'd cleaned the kitchen and refolded all the clothes in her closet and drawers as a way to fill time quietly, but finally she could no longer avoid that she had to get in her practice time.

At eight p.m. she figured she could get in a couple hours practice before having to stop at ten. She never practiced later than ten because no matter how late and loud her partying might get, one thing the neighbors could never complain about was her practicing too late.

With her weeks' worth of housekeeping done, Kyla opened the door to the spare bedroom she used as a practice room, then shut it quietly behind her. Her Ludwig drum kit was set up in the corner. The shells were green starburst and she had it set up exactly like John Bonham.

She put the headphones over her ears and cued up the song she had to learn on her reel-to-reel. With a pair of hickory drum sticks in her hand, she hit play and raised her arms ready to go. She hesitated. Raised her arms again, prepared to jump in on the next bar, but hesitated again. In as long as she could remember, there hadn't been a time that she didn't want to be behind a drum kit. Now, all she wanted was to be out in the living room, watching Scotland sleep.

Finally, without banging a single beat, she holstered her sticks in the open maw of an up-turned cowbell mounted near the snare drum and shut the light off on her way out of the room.

Scotland didn't wake the next morning. Kyla checked for the rise and fall of his chest to make sure he was still breathing, but otherwise didn't disturb him. He was out, but not in a peaceful sleep. The quilt bunched up at his throat and draped to the floor. Tension in his face made her think he was in pain, maybe still shook up over things she didn't yet know. She wanted to know, but unless he could suddenly project the images from his head, he'd have to be awake to tell her these things.

She wondered how much longer he could sleep. She had the gig to practice for, but still didn't want to.

Kyla stared at the phone while eating a bowl of Corn Flakes. She took a bite with a loud slurp of flakes and sugared milk. Curiosity gnawed at her. She looked down toward the slip of paper on the counter. An urge to pick up the receiver and dial the number there made her cough milk into her sinus cavity.

Instead, she set down her bowl, picked up the receiver and cradled it between her chin and shoulder while dialing a number from memory instead.

After eight long rings, the clunking of the receiver being lifted relieved her.

"Who the hell calls me this time of day?" an angry voice yelled on the other end. It was a rough and masculine voice, but smooth as his singing voice.

"Tilly, don't be mad."

"Kyla?"

Kyla wasn't surprised Tilly recognized her voice right away. He was the lead singer and bandleader, but also a guy she'd dated off and on a couple months ago. They never had anything serious, and he acted cool with that, but he was both good in bed and a steady source of pick-up gigs—both traits were important. Kyla's life was incomplete when she wasn't playing to a live audience at least a few times a month.

"Tilly, I don't think I can make it tonight and I wanted to give you as much notice as possible." She spoke fast to get out all the words before Tilly cut her off.

"Are you ill, baby girl?" he asked, to Kyla's surprise.

"No, but a friend of mine is."

"I don't care about your fucking friends, Ky. Have your ass there on time and you better know that new song."

"Really, Tilly. I'll call around and find a replacement drummer."

"There's no time to get somebody else familiar with the set list." The sleep was gone from his voice now. "Besides, your picture is on the flyers. People are expecting you. And if you blow me off tonight, you'll never get a gig anywhere closer than Key Largo. You hear what I'm saying, baby girl?"

Of all the threats in his response, the one thing that got to her was the bit about the audience expecting her. She loved the way people cheered during her solos and how they erupted at the ends of them. Kyla switched sides with the phone, and with her free hand played absently across the edges of the notepaper with Scotland's mysterious Tampa phone number written on it.

She hung up with Tilly and poured herself a cup from her grandmother's old Mr. Coffee Maker, which she took outside to the screened lanai. A wicker table with four chairs dominated the space. She took a seat and pulled a Salem from the pack next to the ashtray. After lighting it, she tossed the match into the ashtray and watched it burn to its end, then peeked in through the sliding glass doors at Scotland on the couch.

A few hours later, Kyla held her hickory drum sticks in one hand, the other on the reel-to-reel rewind button. This time she didn't hesitate. She pushed the button and played along to the Fleetwood Mac song she'd have to play in Tilly's cover band later that night. She struggled with a fill in the song and rewound the tape to play it over and over. Her headphones made her ears sweat, but she listened to the drum fill and rewound it again. Hit play and tapped it out with the sticks on her thigh. She rewound again a little farther and turned to the kit and played it note for note. She played out the song and finished with a crash of cymbals.

As she removed her headphones and shook out her hair, she saw Scotland at the door.

"If you did all that to wake me up, you succeeded."

"Are you kidding? If I wanted that, I would've played all day yesterday."

"Yesterday? What day is it?"

"Wednesday."

"What day did we meet?"

"Man, you're a mess." She stuck her drumsticks in the cowbell. "That was Monday."

"Seriously?" Scotland tucked his hair behind his ears. "Wow."

"I'm done here, so I can hang out until my gig tonight."

"Yeah. Cool." Scotland leaned on the doorframe, a hand shoved in his pocket.

Hair fell in his face again and she walked over and smoothed it away. "You slept for, like, forever, not counting the time in the car. Are you feeling better?"

"I drank some water from the sink, but I'm pretty hungry again."

Kyla fed him cereal and coffee and he took his time with both. As he ate, he hunched over the bowl, as if he didn't have the strength to hold himself up. It was silent in the house, only the faint sound of a lawnmower outside somewhere. "I inherited this place from my grandmother. She wanted me to get settled and start a family. In the meantime, I guess I stay to be close to her. You know?"

Scotland nodded. He didn't talk much and she was happy just to watch him eat. She didn't get the chance to take care of her grandmother in her remaining days, but she enjoyed looking after Scotland as he slept, and now that he was awake, even more so.

She set him up in the bathroom with a bar of soap, shampoo for his long hair and beard, and also with a new tooth brush she always kept in her purse, just in case.

He exited the bathroom, his hair slicked back and a towel around his waist. He was a muscular guy, but lean. His ribs looked like they were stretched over with paper. Without the sleeves of a shirt, Kyla noticed the tattoo on his forearm. It took her a few moments of not-so-subtle staring to make out what it was. It struck her as odd. He didn't seem like a Bible-thumper though with his hair long and wet down his neck and the beard, he could be a stand in for Jesus, himself.

"Your clothes are in the washing machine. It's a small load so it'll be quick. Do you want a robe or something while you wait?"

Scotland stood, a little confused maybe, and didn't answer her.

"You know what? I've got a pair of sweatpants that'll fit you. Let me see if I have a T-shirt that'll work."

"Thank you."

Kinsey killed time in his office at the Gulf Breeze on Wednesday while he waited for Donny Benes to show up. He liked Donny well enough. But more importantly, he was the last guy Kinsey could trust with the illicit affairs remaining on his agenda. Donny was loyal and hard-working, he just lacked that killer instinct.

Almost everything had been packed out of the office already. The map still hung on the wall, but the pushpins were of no great value to him anymore. His revolver sat on the desktop. He wheeled his desk chair over to the window overlooking the parking lot. He sipped bourbon from his highball glass while he waited for Donny's red T-bird to pull into the driveway.

The entire complex was quiet and still. He'd had all the tenants vacate their apartments. Paid for the trucks to take their shit anywhere they wanted to go. He was going to sell the place when he was finished, and an empty place would show better than a complex full of non-paying tenants.

Kinsey was finishing his third drink when a pair of headlights grew larger in the driveway, finally coming close enough for him to confirm they were attached to Donny's T-bird.

Kinsey scooted his chair backwards until he was behind his desk again. Yesterday's newspaper sat on the desk next to his revolver, and it made for adequate reading while Kinsey listened to Donny's footfalls climbing the stairs.

"You're late," Kinsey said.

"What's with this town?" Donny wore bellbottom pants and a plain, white T-shirt stretched over a belly shaped like a cannon ball. He was over six feet tall and had curly mutton chop sideburns. "I pulled into a gas station and got all turned around. There's no signs for shit on the streets out here." He held up two full McDonald's bags. "And I couldn't find the fucking burger place so I had to circle around three times out there on Highway 60." Donny walked over to Kinsey's desk.

"Well, you're here now. That's what matters."

Donny went to set down the food on Kinsey's desk but Kinsey stood.

"Don't put that there."

"Where we going to eat?"

"That isn't for us."

"What's going on? What's happened to your office?"

"You have your shotgun in your car?"

"Am I going to need it?"

"I hope so. But in the meantime, I need you to run those bags of grease on over to 2A."

As Kinsey poured his fourth drink of the day, Donny stomped back up the steps. He was white as the McDonald's bags he still had in his hands. "She's dead."

Kinsey looked at Donny for a sign of a joke in his words, but there was none. Kinsey sat back down and scooted across the room to the window overlooking the parking lot.

"You're sure?"

"Couldn't find a pulse. She's on the floor. Has a bag of pills spilled out in her lap. Looks like she ate them one at a time until she went to sleep for the last time."

Kinsey threw his highball glass and it crashed against the

272

map behind his desk. Fragments sprayed onto the desktop and bourbon stained the wall in little rivers flowing south. He rose from his chair and slapped Donny with the back of his hand. "Goddammit," he yelled.

Donny took the blow and responded with a cock of his head, like a stunned hound. He didn't go down and he didn't lose his grip on the McDonald's bags.

"Look, Mr. K." Donny shifted both bags to one hand. "I'm sorry that girl's dead, but you don't got to take it out on me."

Kinsey kicked the McDonald's bags as if punting from his own ten yard line. French fries flew in all directions, along with chunks of bun and greasy burger meat. "Goddammit," he yelled again.

"Take it easy, Mr. K." Donny stepped backward, burgers and fries squashing beneath his shoes.

Kinsey ran his hands over the sides of his face as if warming his cheeks. He stopped and crossed his arms over his chest, felt his heart beating beneath his right wrist. He dropped his arms and walked back to his desk, where he shook broken glass from the seat and sat down hard in his desk chair. He leaned his elbows on the desk and spun the revolver in a loose circle as he tried to think things through.

"Should we do something with the body?" Donny asked. He stood amid the mine field of fast food and shot a worried sort of peek out the window overlooking the parking lot. "Call the police or something?"

"No," Kinsey barked. "Don't even touch her. I want that sonofabitch brother of hers to see her dead before I kill him."

"How do you know he'll show?"

"He'll show."

"I heard he might be dead already."

"He's still alive. I feel it. I don't know how he dispatched the Kulas, but I just know he's still alive. That means he'll be back. If we don't have him by Monday morning, I'll assume

I'm wrong about that. Then all we'll have to do is get rid of
the woman and get on with our lives."

"Campaigning!" Donny raised his fist.

Kinsey ignored him.

CHAPTER TWENTY-FIVE

At eight that evening, Kyla put on jean cutoffs and the Led Zeppelin T-shirt she'd gotten at a concert in New York. She drew in her eye makeup heavier than normal, and after she laced up her combat boots she filled a leather TWA bag with drumsticks from the closet in her practice room. Before leaving, she stopped at the couch in the living room.

Scotland was awake, but lay sprawled with his feet on the armrest, torso slumped sideways, and a thick arm hanging over the side, hand resting on the carpet. In that moment, he was a version of every boyfriend she'd ever had and she wanted to chase him out with a broom. But she was into him, especially with his health issue and the mystery around him. She had to keep him around to see how things would play out for him and between them. For now, however, she had other issues to attend to. "Will you be okay for a couple hours?"

Scotland lifted his hand from the floor and used the momentum to propel his torso upward from the couch while swinging his feet down.

"No, stay there. It's cool. Rest. I'll be back as soon as I can."

"I'll help you load your drums."

She walked over and placed a hand on his shoulder. The skin and muscle there was tight.

"That's a Bonham replica kit," she said. "May he rest in peace. It doesn't travel. Besides, I drive a Datsun. Where would I put it?"

"I thought musicians played their own instruments."

"I can make any drum kit sound good. I'll play a bucket and a washboard if I have to, but that kit," she hooked a thumb to the practice room, "stays here."

"Is there anything else I can do to, you know, be helpful in some way?"

Among all the men, boys, really, that she'd been around, so few were the type to offer their help even when it would have been nice to have a man around. She laughed as a way to control her surprise. "Nothing," she said. "You just concentrate on feeling better."

"I'm going to look for a job, first thing in the morning."

Kyla didn't hear that from the men in her life. "Again," she said. "Let's just get you well before you worry about any of that."

The crowd at the Gator Lanes Lounge was adequate for a Wednesday night, and appreciative of the bands set list. A few of the regulars danced. Most people there weren't bowlers, but half a dozen guys at the bar wore matching shirts and drank pitchers of beer. The tip jug came back mostly empty every time it went around, but the scattered applause was almost enough for Kyla. Each song was like a step up a mountain she couldn't wait to reach the summit of and run down the other side.

She didn't have to break down the drum kit at the end of the night because Tilly had one of the guys do it for her when they were dating. She let him do it this time as well, but she didn't hang around for a drink. Instead, she raced out of the Gator Lanes' parking lot.

She was anxious to get back, but hungry too. She hadn't eaten since that morning. The 7-Eleven on the corner near her house was her only option that time of night, so she went in and bought two frozen burritos and a six-pack of beer. She'd split it with Scotland if he was still awake.

He wasn't.

* * *

At six a.m. on Thursday, Kinsey drank coffee inside apartment 2C. He wore only the pair of pants he'd worn the day before, his revolver shoved down the waistband. His hair was wild from the pillow. He peered through the blinds between sips just in case Scotland showed up looking for his sister. Donny Benes had two more hours on his shift watching out for any signs of trouble, but Kinsey couldn't sleep. It had been a restless night, with him jolting awake with every dry twig and branch that snapped or creaked outside his window.

He sipped his coffee and pushed on the revolver's handle to make sure it was secure.

He didn't see Donny, and figured he was roving, patrolling the property, his shotgun at the ready in case Scotland Ross tried to ambush the place in the dark.

After another cup of coffee, and still no sign of Donny, Kinsey grew more curious about where Donny might be. A chill coursed from his shins to his ears. If Scotland had disposed of the Kula brothers, he'd be more than able to mow through Donny Benes in less than thirty seconds.

Kinsey didn't take the time to put on his socks before stepping into his boots. He pulled the revolver from his pants and walked out the door, gun first. He didn't see anything moving. He walked on the balls of his feet in an effort to be quiet on the sidewalk as he made his way two doors down to 2A.

He let himself in and exhaled a sigh when he flipped on the light and saw that the lock on the cell door was still closed. Donny's red Thunderbird sat in the parking lot parked next to Kinsey's Mercedes, both unmoved from when they'd arrived. Kinsey wanted to call out to him to make sure he was okay. He raised his gun, his finger on the trigger, stepped slowly to muffle the conspicuous crunch of shells as he crossed the parking lot. He walked between buildings, through the grass, to see if Donny had gone around back.

He wasn't there.

Kinsey walked to the pool area, his emotions surging with curiosity and fear. He passed through the clubhouse, pivoting side to side, pointing the revolver, and made his way up to his office.

Without needing to turn on a light, Donny was in full view, reclined in Kinsey's desk chair, his feet on the desk, snoring like a bulldog. He'd taken off his shirt and had draped it over his torso like a blanket.

Kinsey raised a foot to the chair and shoved it, sending Donny crashing into the wall.

Donny stirred from the impact. "What the fuck?"

"Wake up!"

Donny stood awkwardly and put his shirt on. "What?"

"You're supposed to be on lookout."

"You expected me to stay awake all night?"

"Use your goddamn head." Kinsey had his fists balled. He swallowed down the hostility. There was no choice. "You're smarter than that."

CHAPTER TWENTY-SIX

Around noon on Thursday, Scotland sat in Kyla's kitchen on a metal stool with a cushion covered in red Naugahyde.

"Just the hair," he said. "This beard is good. Kinsey hasn't seen me with a beard before."

Kyla had offered to cut his hair after watching him struggle to do it himself in the bathroom. If he'd had clippers, he would have been done before she got up.

She held the scissors over her heart now. "He doesn't know you're here, does he?"

Scotland pulled back the blinds over the kitchen window and peeked out to the back yard. "Maybe. Why risk it?"

"How short do you want to go?"

"Don't take it down to the scalp or nothing, but pretty short." Scotland wanted to make himself as unrecognizable as he could. He'd keep the beard for the same reason.

Kyla seemed to know what she was doing. At one point her shirt-covered tit brushed right across his lips. Without all the Magic Marker around her eyes she was pretty, and he was well enough to be enticed.

She stood in front of him, clipping away at the top of his hair. She was barefoot, wearing tight nylon shorts and a white tanktop that hugged her torso. Up close, her skin wasn't ice white, but smooth and milky, unburdened by the sun. He followed the faint pattern of veins beneath the surface; in a different situation, he'd take a chance and reach out and hold her waist in his hands. He wouldn't allow himself that now because he didn't need any delays in putting more distance between himself and Kinsey.

His plan was to buy a bus ticket to get him as close to

Daytona as possible with the money he'd found in the wallet
he'd lifted along with the clothes from the guy at the hospital.
He'd set aside enough money for postage to return the wallet
to the address listed on Thomas Jablowski's driver's license.
He would put a note where the bills had been. Perhaps the
note would be an IOU, but in any event he'd include a few
words of thanks and apology.

As soon as she was done, he planned to towel off and hit
the road.

"You ever been in jail?"

He wasn't shocked by the question. "Military prison.
You?"

"Really? Me? No." She laughed and swatted at his arm
with the comb. After a moment, her face lost its upward turn
and got serious. "Why military prison?"

"I was in the Navy. And truth be told, I beat a guy to
within an inch of his life."

"This was over a woman, I assume."

"Yeah, but not like you think. I was trying to help her. Her
husband got a little handsy and shit and I couldn't have that. I
just stepped up. It went downhill from there."

"You wanted the woman for yourself?"

"Trust me, it wasn't like that." He didn't want to get into
his family dysfunction.

"That's so fucking cool. You're like a superhero or
something."

"Hardly."

She took this opportunity to talk about herself. Scotland
was a captive audience, so he listened. The hair she clipped
fell to his lap as she told him about her grandmother and her
fond memories of spending summers in that house and how
strange it was to sleep in her room and how she still cried
every time a piece of mail came with her grandmother's name
on it. That last part touched the same spot Scotland had felt
for Dana the day she showed up asking for his help. He

couldn't help wondering if Dana would cry if something should happen to him.

"That's really cool of you," he said.

Kyla pulled the comb out of her mouth. "What do you mean?"

"The crying. That's cool."

"You mean sweet?"

"Okay. Yeah. That."

Her whole face softened. The tension holding her facial muscles sort of fell, as if a chord had been pulled. Her eyes were glassy and he wasn't sure, but he couldn't risk having her sobbing all over him. "We better change the subject," he said.

Kyla looked away for a few seconds then back to Scotland. "Doesn't matter. We're done." She placed the scissors on the table she'd served him an omelet at only an hour earlier and put the comb between her teeth. With her hands free, she rustled Scotland's hair to shake out any clippings. She used the comb to part on the left side and patted the top with each stroke of the comb. "There," she said, lifting his chin to get a better look. "With that hair and that beard, you look like a country and western superstar."

"Is that good?"

"It's very good," she said as she walked around him swatting away clumps of hair from his shoulders, which turned into her rubbing her hands over his exposed chest.

Scotland reacted reflexively below the belt. He wanted to give in, but he didn't need a delay or a complication like that. He stood and shook off the sheet he'd been draped in. But before he could verbalize his decision, they were locked together at their lips.

They kissed with passion. He had a hunger in him that she was prepared to fill. She buried her nose in his neck as he lifted her and carried her to the bed in her room. His strength ran out and they collapsed onto the bed. "You're not well enough, maybe," she said.

Scotland pushed himself up and looked at her. He didn't speak, just looked at her.

She tore at the draw string on his sweatpants and said, "You'll be fine."

They stripped each other. There was no fat on his body and his muscles were broad, above and below the belt. His beard was rough on her face as they kissed and rough on her shoulder as he positioned himself on top of her. He was gentle when he entered her and they found a rhythm immediately. It made her hips shake, and everything else in the world went away.

Within a few minutes, Scotland's body tensed. She thought he'd overexerted or otherwise hurt himself at first. His face was contorted, but as he throbbed between her legs she knew it was the opposite of pain that he was in.

When he finished, Scotland lay back and said, "Just give me a few minutes for my battery to recharge and we'll keep the party going."

Kyla would hold him to his promise.

CHAPTER TWENTY-SEVEN

Scotland woke on Friday morning to the smell of coffee. It was the second week in January, yet the open windows allowed in air incapable of chilling his skin. The coffee aroma reminded him of the coffee he used to drink in better days. That thought didn't sadden him this time though. There was no pull at the pit of his stomach or water pooling behind his eyes. Instead, he was motivated by the smell. He slid out from between black silk sheets, put his tender feet on the floor, and rose with less effort than he would have thought. He felt stable where he stood. Not one hundred percent yet, but strong.

At the sink in the bathroom, he splashed water on his face and ran his wet fingers through his hair. It hadn't been that short since his Navy days. His beard was growing in dark, and he wanted it to grow fully to hide more of his face.

He put on the elephant-gray sweatpants and the green 7UP T-shirt Kyla had been letting him wear. The shirt was tight and dug into his armpits near his chest. He rolled his arms backward in a few circles, like a drunken buzzard coming in for a landing. The effort to loosen the shirt's fit was futile and he gave up. He chose instead the activity of peeking through the blinds on all the windows to make sure nothing was out of the ordinary, that he wasn't being watched. He didn't know the neighborhood well enough to know what was ordinary, so he dismissed anything that didn't look overtly sinister—as if someone coming to kill him would drive a black van with a skull and crossbones painted across its side. Perhaps Kyla was right. Perhaps all those miles between there and Tampa were enough to keep him safe from Kinsey.

Maybe it would be okay to hang out there for a while and get to know Kyla better. She wasn't serious girlfriend material, but she always smelled good and he didn't want her to feel used.

Kyla sat on the couch, eating a bowl of cereal and watching *The Price Is Right*.

"Hey," she said. "Did I wake you?"

"It was the smell of coffee. Fucking amazing smell."

She set the bowl down on the coffee table next to the box of corn flakes. "I'd get up and pour a cup for you, but you've proven yourself strong enough to help yourself."

The veins in Scotland's neck dilated and he felt his head flush from the way she smiled at him. He walked to the kitchen and poured coffee into the mug Kyla had waiting for him on the counter. He cupped the blue mug with both hands and sipped tentatively, anticipating the heat. Both hands still on the mug, he carried it to the couch and sat next to Kyla.

"You need to eat," she said.

"I could eat."

She scooted to the edge of her seat and filled the bowl with cereal. She poured milk from a jug she had under the coffee table and slid the bowl in front of him. "Last night was amazing," she said. "But I have a gig tonight to practice for."

"I understand." Scotland sipped his coffee. "Do your thing."

"Are you up to coming with me tonight?"

Scotland looked down at his 7UP shirt. "I can wear the clothes you found me in."

"No. We can stop at a cool store I know and get you some new jeans and a nice shirt."

"You better make it a Woolworth's," Scotland said, thinking about how little money he had in that wallet.

"My treat. Think of it as an early birthday present. When's your birthday?"

Scotland had to think for a moment before he realized that

he'd missed it while he'd been floating in the Gulf of Mexico. "It's a long way off," he said.

"No problem. Call it an early Valentine's gift." She leaned over and kissed him on the forehead. "Now let me go practice and we'll go out this afternoon."

"No matter whose money gets spent," he said, "I'm picking out my own shirt."

"I'm cool with that," she said as she walked down the hall.

Scotland picked up the cereal bowl and watched a housewife on television applaud herself for guessing the price of floor wax.

By his third bite of cereal, Kyla had started to bang away at her drums. A series of slow syncopated beats that repeated over and over, slowly at first, but built in tempo until the sound was continuous. She sustained this all through a commercial break. Scotland didn't care to hear the television. The drumming paused at the same time a retiree with a pot belly was trying to win a car. As he guessed the second digit in the price, Kyla began banging again, but this time the music sounded more evenly timed, part of a song. Scotland chewed to the rhythm of the backbeat to a song he couldn't name.

Before the retiree found out if he'd won the car, the local news station interrupted the broadcast. Bob Barker and the game show had been replaced by graphics filling the screen by proclaiming "Newsflash." In the moments between Kyla's songs, Scotland heard trumpets coming from the television and he assumed the sounds of frantic typing were mixed with the trumpets. In the time he'd lived in Florida, Scotland had gotten used to the local stations' habit of doing newsflashes in advance of tropical storms during the summer and fall, but he couldn't imagine what could be so important this time of year.

Scotland raised the cereal bowl to his mouth, but kept his attention on the television. He took a large spoonful and watched as he chewed.

A newscaster in a tan suit with white shirt and brown tie stood in front of a police station. The camera stayed close on him as he spoke words Scotland couldn't hear over Kyla's drumming.

Scotland continued to eat and stare at the screen and as the camera panned back a little, he recognized the Sherriff's office. It was in Tampa. "Of all the places." Scotland scooted closer to the coffee table and took another bite of cereal as the camera panned back farther. He stopped mid-chew and milk leaked out his mouth and into his beard. On the screen, next to the man in the suit, stood his brother-in-law, Mark. He had panic on his face. The words at the bottom of the screen said "Tampa Woman Missing."

Scotland dropped the bowl, which spilled onto the table and floor. He hollered toward Kyla's closed door. "Stop playing. Stop playing." He got up, lunged at the television and cranked the volume, but still couldn't hear. He held his ear to the speaker for a futile moment before running to Kyla's closed door. He swung it open. "Stop playing," he yelled again.

Kyla jumped when she saw him. She took off her headphones. "What's wrong?"

"TV," he said. "News." He ran back to the living room and now the volume was loud enough to hear before he even got in front of it.

The television screen was filled with a photo of Dana in her wedding dress, before she started wearing a wig. The bottom of the screen still read "Missing Tampa Woman."

The image impacted him like a two-by-four to the back of the head and he felt like his stomach was being yanked out of his throat. As the newsman spoke, Scotland sank to one knee. As he knelt, his ribcage filled with panic. "Oh, holy shit."

Mark stood inside the television. He wore green coveralls and his hair was rumpled. He nervously tugged at the hat in his hands. He had tears in his eyes and a microphone in his face. "Please," he said, "I just want my wife to come home. If you've seen her, please bring her back to me. We got kids."

As the newscaster recapped the details of his sister, Scotland stood. His stomach was still in his throat, but he had an idea where Dana might be and he *would* find her.

"What's happening?" Kyla asked, standing behind Scotland.

Scotland pointed to the living room window. "You know how I'm always looking out the windows, making sure they haven't caught up to me?"

"It breaks my heart a little every time I see you do that."

"Well, they're not looking for me. They haven't been. Because they're waiting for me to come to them. That's my sister."

"Oh. Oh, my God." Kyla sat down on the couch and stared at her feet for a minute.

Scotland stormed into the kitchen and picked up the phone. He was so shaken up he couldn't remember the number. He banged the receiver against his forehead and in doing so he'd looked down. Saw the slip of paper with "Edison" embossed across the top that Kyla had written the number on the other day. He dialed each digit, waiting for each spin around.

"Dave. Have you seen the news?"

"Who is this?"

"Scotland Ross, Dave. Have you seen the news?"

"I work for a living, Ross. I don't get to sit around and watch television all day."

"Find a set and turn it on. My sister is missing."

"Missing?"

"It's Kinsey. Kinsey's got her."

"So the guy who tried to kill you has now kidnapped your sister."

"Yes."

"Look, Ross. So far the guy checks out. I had a deputy

look into it. He's clean. Hasn't even had a speeding ticket since 1972."

"You're not going to help me with this?"

"There's nothing I can do. And, while we're on the subject, your file has officially been sent upstairs."

Scotland dropped the phone and it clanked when it hit the linoleum. He ran into the living room where Kyla was glued to the continuing news coverage. He grabbed her by the shoulders. "Do you have a gun, by any chance?"

"A gun?"

This wasn't the first time he'd wished he had his long lost seabag. "Forget it." He let go of her shoulders and turned. "Can I at least borrow your car for a while?"

"You're not going. It's crazy."

"If you let me borrow your car, I can be there in less than three hours."

"This sounds like a trap."

"You're probably right. But when the bait's your only sister, what else can you do?"

"Let the police handle this, Scotland."

"No time for that," he said as he took her keys off the end table.

She walked over, placed her hand on his chest. "Don't do this alone. Wait for the cops."

"That's my sister." He pushed her to arm's length. "I've got to do something."

"It's too dangerous."

"That's why I've got this," he said, holding up the dangling rabbit's foot on her keychain. "I'll be back as soon as I can." He stepped into the work boots and, without tying them, stormed out the door fast for a guy in his condition.

"Well, fucking great!" Kyla slammed the door behind Scotland. Instead of watching him drive off in her car, she kicked the table beside the couch. The car was insured. If he totaled it or never brought it back, she'd get a new car out of the deal. She'd been unable to stop him and though she admired that in him, she was worried. But he would come back. She convinced herself. He'll be fine and he'll come back. Her more pressing issues should have been getting a ride to the gig later that night and practicing for it.

In the face of few options, after cleaning up the spilled milk, it seemed practical to sit down at her drum kit and put the headphones over her ears. She didn't hit play on the reel-to-reel, nor did she pick up her sticks. Instead, she thought of him storming out of the house in those sweatpants and that tight T-shirt. She was surprised he hadn't tripped over the untied boot laces on his way to the car. She shook the image of him from her mind and focused on the drums.

The set list for that night's gig was taped to the wall beside her. She ran down the list to find where she'd left off before she'd been interrupted. The song was a Tilly original that she'd learned the first time she'd heard it. She decided to pick up there and work through the set list as originally planned. She picked up her sticks, Ludwig 2B's just like John Bonham used to use. She twirled the right stick as she checked that her door was shut. It was open. She stuck her sticks into the upturned cowbell and walked to the end table in the living room. She took out the pad from the drawer, but the page was blank. She tried to remember where she'd last seen the paper with the number on it. She remembered a couple of the digits she'd dialed for him, but wasn't sure of their order. She checked the coffee table. Moved aside the cereal box, looked under the bowl. The paper wasn't there. She couldn't call Directory Assistance, because she didn't know Dave's last name or where he worked. She checked the table in the kitchen, but there was nothing there besides her scissors and comb. She walked to the phone, prepared to ask an operator to connect her with Dave in Tampa just to see what would happen.

As she picked up the receiver, she saw the slip of paper on the countertop. She took a deep breath and dialed the number.

Wind through the open window washed over Scotland as he sped north on US 41. He hid a fifth of Southern Comfort between his legs. A Molly Hatchet song blared on the stereo, and Kyla's rabbit's foot brushed over his knee when he mashed the gas pedal. He drank not to get drunk, but rather to steel his nerves.

The shocks buckled over every pothole and the brakes grated on worn out pads. He had the seat pushed back as far as it would go, but his legs were still cramped. There was no air conditioning in the car, but he didn't take the time to lean over and roll down the passenger side window. A glancing blow of air was better than none. The sun was right above him and would soon begin baking his left arm as he drove. The gas gauge read just past half, but he didn't plan on stopping again unless he had to. That was as far as his planning went. The rest was just urgency. And rage. And, though he forced himself to squash it down, he had some fear in him, too. He took a long pull from the Southern Comfort. He couldn't help being mindful of the possibility of ending up like Platinum. Despite that, he sped on.

CHAPTER TWENTY-EIGHT

Kinsey sat in his office with Donny Benes, lecturing him on the finer points of going strictly legit. "I'm telling you, Donny, my boy. As soon as we clear up this matter with your boy Scotland Ross, we'll relocate to the shiny office on Franklin Street and we'll glad-hand it with the public every day. No more of this dark shadow stuff for me, son. No, sir. I'm ready to be seen."

"You'll have to cut off that beard then, won't you?"

"Yes," Kinsey laughed as he pulled at his chin hairs.

"You'll look younger without it."

Kinsey scratched the underside of his chin. "Don't try that perverse psychology on me, Donny. Looking young is why I grew the fucking thing."

Sometime around two in the afternoon, Kinsey heard a car pull up. He walked to the front windows overlooking the parking lot expecting to see a familiar face. He was surprised to see a squad car. The lights and siren were off, which pleased him. He said to Donny, "This complicates things."

Donny stood next to Kinsey at the window. "What are they doing here?"

"I don't know, but don't panic. Just sneak your ass down the back stairs and go around the building. The sliding door to 2A is open. Hide in the cell."

"With the corpse?"

"Just fucking do it, Donny."

As Donny crept down the back stairs, Kinsey walked back to the desk. He slid the revolver into the waistband at the small of his back and pulled out his shirt to conceal it. He raked his fingers through his hair again then walked down the front stairs.

"Good afternoon, Deputy," Kinsey said as he stepped out into the daylight and leaned against the Coke machine. "What can I do for you?"

The deputy was a head taller than Kinsey and wide in the middle. His gun belt hung low. "Well, sir, it's kind of a funny thing." He swung his shoulders to face the other deputy behind him.

Kinsey said, "You boys interested in renting luxury apartments?"

The deputies laughed. Kinsey scanned their faces and was disappointed that he didn't recognize either of them.

"Nothing that funny, sir." The heavyset deputy crossed his arms over his chest so that the badge was pointed in Kinsey's direction. It looked like a practiced move, and Kinsey thought about him in front of a mirror, crossing and uncrossing his arms a hundred times.

"Well, surely," Kinsey said, "the Sheriff must have been spooked enough about something to send you boys out my way. Is everything okay?"

"From what I can tell," the deputy said, "everything is copacetic, sir. Our orders are just to observe and report."

Kinsey looked up at him. "Observe and report what, exactly?"

"Don't rightly know, sir. I guess we'll find out." The deputy leaned against the hood of his car and crossed his legs at the ankles. The other deputy stood where he was and crossed his arms.

"You fellas should have been here back in November when we had a pool party. That would have been something upon which to observe and report. There were two dozen girls in bikinis running around, splashing each other. Chicken fighting in the shallow end. I saw a top or two ripped clean off."

The deputies rumbled their approval first, followed by their disappointment they'd missed it.

Kinsey didn't know what might be going on, but he took comfort knowing he had his revolver with him instead of having left it in his desk drawer.

"Well, now, that's quite all right, boys. I'm glad you're all here," Kinsey said in his podium voice. "Feel free to look around all you like. Let me know if you'd like to get into any of the apartments. I've got master keys upstairs. Always happy to help. And when you're done, I'd like to tell you how I'll help law enforcement officers, such as yourselves, when I'm Governor of this great state."

Kinsey walked to his car and hefted a box off the passenger seat—a box from which he distributed Kinsey for Governor key chains and bumper stickers, as well as his promise of higher wages for law enforcement.

Scotland killed the engine and coasted the Datsun to a halt just inside the Gulf Breeze driveway. He thought better of driving all the way up, remembered the way Kinsey liked to stare out the front window of his office. It was too good a sniper's spot, and Scotland wanted to go unseen. He pulled the car behind the Gulf Breeze sign and set the emergency brake with a metallic clank, and set out on foot without taking the time to lace up his work boots.

He passed the old playground area on his way to the outer stretches of the property. Sunlight filtered through the canopies of oaks and pines, but wasn't bright enough to illuminate his steps. He walked slowly to ensure solid and soundless footing. His feet were sore. The noise of a bulldozer's engine roaring and pay loader banging the ground stopped him for a moment until he determined it far off in the distance. Perhaps land such as this was being scraped clear, maybe even for one of Kinsey's housing developments.

Scotland crept through the scrubland to the deeper woods on the adjoining property. The air smelled of pine needles and lime wedges and the ground was dry enough to crack beneath his footfalls. The brush was thick and fallen pine branches snagged him and he stepped right out of his boot. He hopped back, retrieved it, and took the time to lace and tie the boots. As he was bent over, he heard voices. They were too far off to make out the words. Scotland walked slowly, each step intentional. As he approached the back of building three, the voices grew louder. He peered around the building and got a view of a squad car and a red T-bird near Kinsey's office.

Kinsey was holding court with a couple of deputies. Had them laughing. Kinsey clapped the deputies on their shoulders and they laughed some more. For a moment, Scotland's mind refused to believe what he saw.

He thought about walking right up among them and turning himself in just so he could have them find Dana and clear his name with Dave. But he didn't do that because he didn't trust Kinsey. Kinsey might have called these guys to protect him from Scotland, might have filled their heads with all sorts of notions. He couldn't be sure how far up the department Dave had sent his file. Those cops might have a warrant for his arrest. What would become of Dana? He couldn't risk it.

The longer he stared at Kinsey the more he wanted to kill the motherfucker. Scotland wiggled his toes in his boots and tugged on his beard as he tried to figure out his next move.

Within moments, the cops shook hands with Kinsey, who walked them to their car and waved at them as they drove off.

Scotland ducked back between apartment buildings. He couldn't get to Kinsey, but he had a pretty good idea where Dana might be. Scotland walked behind the buildings and stepped onto the concrete slab that formed the patio of apartment 2A. He cupped his hands over the sliding glass door, but duct tape and garbage bags had been placed over the doors. There was no choice. He'd come this far, he had to keep going. Scotland held his breath and tested the handle. The door slid open. He was surprised it was unlocked. He pulled the door shut behind him. Stepping inside was like driving down the highway at night with your lights off. He could smack into anything.

Inside, he felt the walls for a light switch. With the center light on, not much had changed. There were the familiar rows of shelves and merchandise spread about, and no one had waited to ambush him. Scotland made his way to Kinsey's secret room. The padlock on the cell door was unlocked and resting on the loop of the open hasp. This didn't sit right with Scotland. It was too easy. Maybe it was a trap that the cops outside were in on. Kinsey had cops on the payroll. Why not those deputies who just left? Scotland's neck hairs stood on end because he'd taken a beating in that room and gotten tossed into the Gulf immediately after.

He had no weapons, but he had to know what was on the other side of that door—if she was in there, and if she was okay.

After a moment, Scotland reached out and eased the door open.

Donny Benes lifted his head off the table when Scotland walked in. He sat with his chair at a slight angle and looked as if he might have been sleeping. "Jesus, Scotland. You're alive."

Dana was slumped against the far wall. Her eyes were open, but she didn't move.

Scotland looked at Donny, then turned back to look at her. "Is she dead?"

"Yeah," Donny Benes said without moving. "She was like that when I came in, I swear." He pointed toward the plastic bag that had spilled off her lap. "Looks like she kept eating pills until she, well, you know."

Scotland sank to his knees and crawled toward Dana. The concrete beneath her was stained from her waste and the smell was strong, but he hugged her to him and roared out a string of sobs severe enough to run his throat dry. Snot streamed from his nose as he rocked her and he let it drip onto his arms. It was not just Dana's lifeless body he cried for, but for his long-lost son, as well. Each death compounded the other. He was consumed by sadness and the missed opportunities to take care of Dana and tell her he loved her. To say goodbye.

With a jagged inhale Scotland regained a little composure. He wiped at his nose with the back of his hand and got to one knee. He reset Dana's wig to a proper angle and stood.

Scotland lunged across the small room and landed a blow to Donny's head. The impact felt like hitting a cinder block and the punch recoiled in Scotland's shoulder.

Donny stood and held out his hands as defense, but Scotland charged and worked the body, bashing ribs and gut in as rapid a succession as he could muster. Donny slid down the wall with his forearms blocking his face.

"This is all your fault!" Scotland stepped back, grabbed the folding chair Donny had been sitting on, and smacked it down on top of him. The effort of lifting and swinging the chair taxed Scotland. His chest felt tight around his lungs.

Donny stayed on the floor where he went down. He held up a hand and said, "It wasn't me. It's Kinsey, man. That guy is nuts. I never wanted this to happen. I'm not even part of his gangster bullshit. I got kids, man. I just needed him for the money from his land development. That's it, I swear. I didn't kill her, man. I swear."

Scotland lifted the chair again, but held it on the backswing. "Are those cops outside in on this?"

"No. They just showed up. Kinsey's freaked out about them."

Scotland raised the chair higher to initiate another blow.

Donny pushed at the air between them. "I swear. I swear on my kids' lives."

Scotland lowered the chair. Spun it around and straddled it backward. He took a moment to catch his breath and noticed a double-barreled shotgun leaning against the workbench near the door. He walked over and picked it up. Both chambers held shells. He aimed it at Donny. "You got two options."

Scotland marched Donny out of 2A to stand on the sidewalk in front of the building with the shotgun barrel pressed into his spine.

Being January, there was no humidity in the air. The sun hung high, but it was cool. The 7UP T-shirt's sleeves barely covered Scotland's shoulders and despite, or maybe because of, the adrenaline coursing through him, his arms were cold. Scotland wasn't sure if time slowed down or if his brain sped up, but he was able to contemplate the outcome of the scenario playing in his head. He was holding his breath. Every muscle in his body tensed in that instant. That gave Scotland some kind of power for at least a moment. Perhaps long enough to march these bastards into the office, call the police and hold them there until the deputies returned.

Scotland raised the gun barrel and pulled one of the triggers. Fired a shot into the sky. Birds took off from the canopies of the pines and oaks, flapping and chirping as they fled the danger beneath them.

Kinsey walked out onto the clubhouse porch, slow and cocky. He wore his usual white shirt and brown slacks, the handle of a pistol sticking out of the waistband.

Donny held his hands high, his elbows flared. "He doesn't want to shoot me, Mr. K," Donny said, "but I'm afraid he will if you don't do what he says."

"Ross?" Kinsey said as he leaned against the red and white Coke machine. His shoulder hit about halfway up the red metal siding. He looked over the roof of his car and squinted. "Is that you, son?"

"Yeah," Scotland said from behind the double-barrels.

Kinsey crossed one ankle over the other. "We've been worried sick about you, Scottish."

"I bet you have."

"I like your haircut, but that nine-o'clock shadow makes you look like a lowlife, son."

"Shut the fuck up, Kinsey." Scotland thought about water in that moment. Being adrift for days. Tired. Starving. Not knowing if he'd live. He rested the shotgun barrel over Donny's shoulder, used it as a mount to take aim at Kinsey. This also made Donny a shield. "Drop your pistol, Kinsey, or I'll make Donny deaf and drop you at the same time.

"Do what he says, Mr. K," Donny shouted with a shaky voice. "Think of my kids."

Kinsey pulled out the revolver and rested it by his side. "Relax, Donny. I'm not going to shoot you. And Scottish isn't going to shoot me. He can't kill anyone. Don't you know that?"

"It's buckshot, Kinsey. I'll just aim at your crotch. I got no problem taking out your lower half."

"You're not going to shoot anyone, son. We all know you're too smart for that. And that's good. That's very good. You want a better life. That's why I want you around, Scottish. I want to give you a better life."

"Like the life you gave my sister?"

"Well, that was unfortunate, Scottish. I sure hated to hear about that."

"*You* fucking killed her!"

"Let's not jump to conclusions, son. Now drop your weapon," Kinsey said, from the clubhouse porch.

"Way I figure it," Scotland said, "even if you aim real good, at this distance I'd say you'd be more likely to hit Donny than me. The buckshot I got loaded would surely ruin your day before you get off another shot. So why don't you just drop the pistol and kick it over this way."

Kinsey looked over his shoulder, cocked an ear toward the trees with the sounds of birds and frogs, and then did as he was told.

The pistol landed ten feet away, but still on the porch deck.

Scotland wanted to shoot Kinsey, had his finger on the trigger. But as he looked down, that fucking fish stared up from its sightless perch on his forearm. Scotland lowered the gun. Chucked it to the ground. "That's my sister in there!" he yelled as he sprinted up the clubhouse steps and lunged for Kinsey.

Donnie fell away to crouch between the cars.

Kinsey tripped as he backed away from the Coke machine. Scotland was on him before he got fully upright and spun Kinsey with a round house punch. As Kinsey fell backward, Scotland grabbed him in a headlock, one arm squeezed into Kinsey's throat and the other at the back of his head. He pushed with equal force. It was Scotland's opportunity to say anything he wanted, as he was sure he had Kinsey's undivided attention.

Small gurgling sounds emitted from Kinsey.

Donny sagged quietly by Kinsey's parked car. Hunched over, his hand on the trunk, as if still trying to catch his breath.

Breath wasn't so free to Kinsey. He struggled to get each one. He flailed weakly in Scotland's grip, but he never made contact and it wasn't enough to wriggle free.

Scotland's energy surged. He'd never felt this strong.

Kinsey's life balanced in the crook of his arm. He decided there was nothing to say.

Scotland strengthened his grip, repositioned his forearm to cut deeper in to Kinsey's throat. A voice in his head told him to let go, to get the police involved and let them prosecute this scumbag. That thought lasted all of a second and a half before Scotland realized Kinsey's lawyers would have him out by morning. Judges wouldn't care about a down and out woman overdosing, and Kinsey would buy off any judge and jury that did.

No. The obligation was Scotland's. He owed his sister that much.

He checked his arm position. His left forearm pressed into the back of Kinsey's head. It was the same chokehold Platinum had used on Scotland way back when Platinum and Kinsey had broken into Scotland's place in the middle of that fucked up night.

The only thing Scotland saw now was rage behind his eyes. He contracted his arm muscles. As the tension in his shoulders wound tighter, Kinsey's throat crimped a little more. He applied more pressure into Kinsey's throat and the back of his head. He heard the gurgling and knew all it would take was one final contraction of muscles to snap Kinsey's neck. The arrangement of his forearms prevented him from seeing the Jesus fish, but the thought of it was enough. At the last second before Kinsey's neck snapped, Scotland rammed Kinsey's head into the side of the Coke machine and let go.

Kinsey sank to the porch floor and flop-kicked himself backward a couple feet.

"You're going to spend the rest of your sorry life in jail, motherfucker." As Kinsey sprawled on the ground, Scotland kicked him in the ass with the flat of his boot. "Let your lawyers get rich off you."

Kinsey slumped face up, legs twisted, hands out to his sides gasping for air.

Scotland turned to see Donny hunkered down by the car. When he turned back, Scotland caught sight of Kinsey scrambling to get to the revolver which he fired wildly as Scotland dove behind the opposite side of the Coke machine for cover.

The shot rang out. Filled the air around him. Hit Donny.

Donny groaned and held his shoulder. Kinsey scrambled his boot heels in an effort to gain traction enough to stand. Scotland was unarmed and incapable of outrunning bullets. The sound of Kinsey's heels continued to scrape on the porch floor.

The world blurred around Scotland. The back of his throat burned with the fear of being shot in the face. He crouched and spread his feet wide, slammed his shoulder into the Coke machine's sheet metal side like an offensive linemen blocking a linebacker. As the Coke machine leaned, Scotland thought of Dana. He reached down, grabbed the bottom lip of red metal and hoisted it over with all the strength and velocity he had left in him.

The crash of cans inside failed to drown out the thump of the machine landing on Kinsey's legs and torso. Kinsey's pistol landed a few inches past a hand that would never reach it. He gurgled, dark blood trailing from the corner of his mouth.

As Scotland stared at him, a wail of sirens got louder and flashing lights refracted off the tree line along the main road outside the Gulf Breeze property.

CHAPTER TWENTY-NINE

The next morning, Saturday, January 10th, Scotland woke to a poking in his ribs. He turned on the bunk in his cell and rubbed his eyes. He squinted up at the silhouette of a deputy holding a golf club over his shoulder. "Let's go, Ross," he said. "You made bail."

"Bail?" Scotland swung his legs and put his feet on the floor. He'd kept his shoes on and grabbed his T-shirt, which lay draped over the foot of the bunk. He looked through the bars near the deputy as he slipped his head through the neck hole. "Who?"

"Fuck if I know," the deputy said. "The desk sergeant don't make a habit of boring us with shit we don't care about. Let's go."

Scotland relieved himself in the sink-mounted toilet. When he finished, he took the time to tuck in his shirt, as if for inspection aboard ship or at The Castle. He washed his hands in the sink and rinsed his mouth with water. A shiny square of metal served as the mirror above the sink. His hair was scruffy. It was all too familiar. He smoothed a cowlick with water from the tap.

The deputy slid open the cage door, which rattled in its track. The sound gratified Scotland as he stepped out the cell and into the freedom on the other side. "Straight ahead," the deputy said, pointing with the golf club—a sand wedge from the looks of the angle of the face.

As Scotland walked, his borrowed boots slipped beneath his bandaged feet. He glanced into each cell he passed. A pair of eyes in every one watched him pass. He almost expected to see Kinsey staring back. He felt numb. Relieved. He would never have to worry about Kinsey again. Scotland had seen him die, and saw it again in his sleep. The dream didn't wake him or disturb him, but rather comforted him. Confirmed that the man was gone. The dream that did wake him in the middle of the night was not that horror of time gone by, but a new horror. This was a dream of Dana. She wasn't in a casket, but prone on the floor in an apartment converted to a prison cell, a bag of pills spilled on her lap. He wanted to remember her at sixteen, wearing a yellow sundress and running, barefoot, through the backyard of a place they lived with one of their mother's boyfriends. There'd been so much life in her eyes then, a shine to her long hair. His sister was dead and he had no one else in the world.

After Scotland cleared discharge, a slovenly desk sergeant handed over the only items they'd taken off Scotland when they locked him up—his bootlaces. He didn't take the time to lace them up, instead walked out with them slung over his shoulder as they rang the buzzer to open a metal door on the other end of the hall. Scotland was happy to walk out. He wanted to inhale a breath of free air, but was stopped cold by the sight of Dave waiting on the other side.

"What the hell are you doing here?"

Dave walked up and grasped Scotland on the shoulder as the door closed behind him. They shook hands, but Scotland was too surprised to squeeze his hand.

Dave said, "First thing, I'm sorry for your loss. But you should know that Dana's kids are safe with Mark, and will live with his parents when he's out to sea. So you don't have to worry about that."

Pressure released in Scotland's chest. He hadn't thought of the girls, and Dave's words were consolation he hadn't known he needed. He exhaled. Felt lighter. Nodded to signal that he understood. "Good," he said. "That's good.

Dave gestured toward the door Scotland had just exited. "I sprung you as quick as I could."

Scotland clapped Dave on the back and looked him in the eye. "Thanks."

Dave led Scotland down the corridor to the elevators.

"What happens now?" Scotland asked.

Dave pushed the down button. "There'll be a trial. You'll get full immunity if you're willing to testify."

"How do you take a dead man to court?"

"Dead man?" Dave pulled out a notebook from his shirt pocket. Flipped it open and read. "Donny Benes, superficial gunshot wound. He was treated and released. Allan Kinsey, in a coma at Tampa General. He lost a lot of blood and they had to amputate both legs at the hip, but recovery is likely."

Scotland pulled the bootlaces from his shoulder. Twisted them in his hand. Coiled them in his palm, and squeezed. Of all the people who'd died, it should have been Kinsey.

"The trial could be a long time coming."

"I don't suppose it would hurt to delay my move to Daytona further. It doesn't really matter anymore. I don't care." He had no pockets for his hands. No lighter to comfort him.

"If the prosecution can prove a fraction of what you told me, you'll be good."

The elevator doors opened with a ding, but the ride down began in silence. Despite the good news, Scotland couldn't shake the grip around his throat. Tightness from the knowledge he would have to face the world alone now. He didn't want to think yet about death. Or about funerals. He elbowed Dave in the ribs. "I thought you weren't going to help me."

Dave smiled. "Yeah, well, on Christmas Day, there was a suicide out in Apollo Beach. Nobody suspected foul play, but the widow, a real looker named Doris Joyner, came forward and implicated your man, Kinsey. Do you know anything about that?"

"I know a thing or two." Scotland looked at the floor numbers just above Dave's head. "That was a straight-up suicide. I do know that."

"We'll talk about this another day. The real kicker was that the department got a positive ID on a couple chunks of a boat that washed up on Ft. Desoto Beach and…"

Scotland lost interest in the explanation. He knew the boat. Wondered if any of the found remains was his plank.

"Hey," he said. "Hey, how did your daughter like her bike?"

"What? Oh. Shit. Yeah. She loved it." It wasn't like him to speak in fragments like that, but then he opened up a little. "Her legs aren't strong enough yet, but I put training wheels on and guide her along."

"That's great," Scotland said.

When the doors opened, a woman in a green dress got on the elevator as Scotland and Dave exited. She was about the same age as Dana had been. The past tense left a bad taste in his mouth. Made him look down at the floor, at his boots. Dana was gone. He still had blood connections in the nieces he'd probably never get to see, but he no longer had someone who knew him. A void made by death, made worse by leaving him utterly alone. He uncoiled the bootlaces in his hand. Flipped them over his shoulder.

Dave kept talking as they walked toward the glass doors leading out to sunshine and the rest of Scotland's lonely life. Dave clapped Scotland behind the neck in an affectionate way and shook him. He let out a laugh and said, "I also got a very persuasive phone call from her." Dave pointed outside, where Kyla was waiting with the Datsun and a smile.

ACKNOWLEDGMENTS

Tremendous debts of gratitude are owed to many people who helped or at least humored me during the writing of this book. Instrumental in this process were (and continue to be) Tracy Crow and James R. Duncan, who have been deeply patient, helpful, and inspirational. To Mark Fleeting, Pinckney Benedict, and Fred Leebron, who praise and chide and are never wrong. To Matt Flaherty, Mike Kobre, Tim Wright, Carol Dee Turner, and everyone in the DD-214 Writers' Workshop, the Queens University MFA program, as well as many of the journal and magazine editors who've published my stories, essays, and articles, particularly: Jonathan Sturak and Eddie Vega at *Noir Nation*; Anthony Neil Smith at *Plots with Guns*; Steve Weddle at *Needle: A Magazine of Noir*; Nicholle M. Cormier at *The MacGuffin*; Jerri Bell and Ron Capps at *O-Dark-Thirty*; Jon Chopan, Tracy Crow, and Cliff Garstang at *Prime Number*; Mary Akers at *r.kv.r.y.*; Ralph Pennel at *Midway Journal*; and for including early versions of Scotland and Kinsey in their publications, special thanks to Eric Beetner for including me in the *Unloaded* anthology and Ron Earl Phillips for putting Scotland in the spotlight for the very first time in *Shotgun Honey*. (It's my sincere hope that everyone reads all these fine publications.)

I'm immensely thankful to Eric Campbell (and everyone at Down & Out Books). I don't know what the odds are that we'd live in the same town, but that makes this even more special to me. I'm also thankful to Eric Beetner for a kickass cover, and to Elizabeth White for some mighty-fine guidance, as well as to Emily Bell, Dan Wickett, Donald Maas, and

Lorin Oberweger for their insights along the way. Also to the assorted crime writers and readers with whom I've connected in various capacities online and in person.

I'd also like to thank those whose presence influenced me in the early years of this adventure: James O'Neil; Willie Reader; my third-grade teacher, Mrs. Dickerson; Ronald "Bo" Walston; the Wilsons of Mobile, Alabama; Mark Amen; Mark August; Lyn Biliteri; H. Kermit Jackson; Ty Jones; Denny Sawyer; my Navy buddies, Joe Paul, Curt Jarrett, John Louthan, Perry Chastain, James "Bubba" Smith, Scott Dickerson, and all the San Jacinto Plank Owners; and my lifelong friends who are like brothers to me, Jeff Prince, Chris Hartnett, Anthony Acitelli, William Barnes, David (Hezy) Hemed, Paul Drew, and Kurt Hopson.

And I'm forever thankful for my entire family, but especially my parents, Carol and Jack, who showed me the way and kept me on the path.

The biggest thanks of all goes to my beautiful and infinitely-understanding wife, Lauren, who got on this rollercoaster with me when I thought it would be easy and loved me even after finding out that it never is. I wouldn't trade you for anything in the world!

Born in New York and raised on Florida's Gulf coast, Jeffery Hess served six years aboard the Navy's oldest and newest ships and has held writing positions at a daily newspaper, a Fortune 500 company, and a university-based research center. He is the editor of the award-winning anthologies *Home of the Brave: Stories in Uniform* and *Home of the Brave: Somewhere in the Sand* (Press 53). He holds an MFA in creative writing from Queens University of Charlotte and his writing has appeared widely in print and online. He lives in Florida, where he leads the DD-214 Writers' Workshop for military veterans.

OTHER TITLES FROM DOWN AND OUT BOOKS

See www.DownAndOutBooks.com for complete list

By Anonymous-9
Bite Hard

By J.L. Abramo
Catching Water in a Net
Clutching at Straws
Counting to Infinity
Gravesend
Chasing Charlie Chan
Circling the Runway
Brooklyn Justice

By Trey R. Barker
2,000 Miles to Open Road
Road Gig: A Novella
Exit Blood
Death is Not Forever
No Harder Prison

By Richard Barre
The Innocents
Bearing Secrets
Christmas Stories
The Ghosts of Morning
Blackheart Highway
Burning Moon
Echo Bay
Lost

By Eric Beetner and
JB Kohl
Over Their Heads

By Eric Beetner and
Frank Scalise
The Backlist
The Shortlist (*)

By G.J. Brown
Falling (*)

By Rob Brunet
Stinking Rich

By Dana Cameron (editor)
Murder at the Beach: Bouchercon Anthology 2014

By Mark Coggins
No Hard Feelings

By Tom Crowley
Vipers Tail
Murder in the Slaughterhouse

By Frank De Blase
Pine Box for a Pin-Up
Busted Valentines and Other Dark Delights
A Cougar's Kiss (*)

By Les Edgerton
The Genuine, Imitation, Plastic Kidnapping

By A.C. Frieden
Tranquility Denied
The Serpent's Game
The Pyongyang Option (*)

By Jack Getze
Big Numbers
Big Money
Big Mojo
Big Shoes

(*)—Coming Soon

OTHER TITLES FROM DOWN AND OUT BOOKS

See www.DownAndOutBooks.com for complete list

By Richard Godwin
Wrong Crowd
Buffalo and Sour Mash (*)

By William Hastings (editor)
Stray Dogs: Writing from the Other America (*)

By Jeffery Hess
Beachhead (*)

By Matt Hilton
No Going Back
Rules of Honor
The Lawless Kind
The Devil's Anvil (*)

By David Housewright
Finders Keepers
Full House

By Jerry Kennealy
Screen Test (*)

By S.W. Lauden
Crosswise (*)

By Terrence McCauley
The Devil Dogs of Belleau Wood (*)

By Bill Moody
Czechmate
The Man in Red Square
Solo Hand
The Death of a Tenor Man
The Sound of the Trumpet
Bird Lives!

By Gary Phillips
The Perpetrators
Scoundrels (Editor)
Treacherous
3 the Hard Way

By Tom Pitts
Hustle (*)

By Robert J. Randisi
Upon My Soul
Souls of the Dead
Envy the Dead (*)

By Ryan Sayles
The Subtle Art of Brutality
Warpath
Swansongs Always Begin as Love Songs (*)

By John Shepphird
The Shill
Kill the Shill
Beware the Shill (*)

By Ian Thurman
Grand Trunk and Shearer (*)

By Lono Waiwaiole
Wiley's Lament
Wiley's Shuffle
Wiley's Refrain
Dark Paradise

By Vincent Zandri
Moonlight Weeps

(*)—Coming Soon

Made in the USA
Columbia, SC
28 April 2018